TO DIE IN
CALIFORNIA

NEWTON THORNBURG

TO DIE IN CALIFORNIA

LITTLE, BROWN AND COMPANY — BOSTON — TORONTO

Published simultaneously in Canada
by Little, Brown & Company (Canada) Limited

PRINTED IN THE UNITED STATES OF AMERICA

To Mark and Douglas,
My Sons

TO DIE IN CALIFORNIA

1

Though he was looking down through gusting snow at a box holding the body of his firstborn son, David Hook's eyes were dry. His heart was dry. He might have been some stranger who had absently wandered in upon this gathering among the gravestones and now found himself standing in the very center of it, and with eyes not only dry but cold too, a reporter's eyes. He missed nothing, not even the simple antique beauty of the scene, its evocation of an America all but dead and buried itself now: these neighbors of his, these countryfolk in their shiny Sunday best, the hard vital weathered men and their drab women and cool longhaired young, who had gone to school with his son and made hay with him and maybe even loved him too, for there was weeping among their ranks, tears falling from some eyes anyway if not from his own.

As much as it was possible to love a cemetery, Hook loved this one, mostly for its rows of small ancient stones and the messages they bore, their litany of pioneer hardship and loss and courage. But he also liked the remoteness of the place, its quiet hilltop serenity and its shabby grounds from which one could see for miles, an experience all too rare in the flat farmland of southwestern Illinois. Now, though, in mid-December, that same view made for poor shelter against the wind, which blew Reverend Hodson's words at him in gusts, like the snow:

"I shall not want. He leadeth me beside the still waters. He maketh me to lie down in green pastures. He restoreth my soul."

1

The Reverend's squat figure facing him across the coffin obscured Hook's view of his wife's grave, but he was able to see the first Hook family marker in the cemetery, that of his great-grandfather James Hook. The modest stone was no less laconic than the man himself was reputed to have been, giving only his name and dates, 1855–1904. When Hook was a boy the place still had been known as the "old Baptist graveyard," having been the burial ground of a country church that had burned down on this same hill around the turn of the century. But in recent years, in fact ever since the Second World War, people generally had called it Hook's cemetery, possibly because his farm had grown to surround it on three sides or maybe because they knew that it was he who kept it up after a fashion, swinging in with a tractor and sicklebar a few times each summer to mow down its everflourishing crop of weeds.

So in effect this day Hook was burying his son in ground that touched his own and bore his name as well. Yet as he stared at it now, at the sandlike snow whipping under the coffin into the black pit beneath, he felt as if he were placing his son not in some familiar ground of home but in an alien, almost lunar soil. He had his arm around his two surviving children, sixteen-year-old Bobby on the outside and the year-younger Jennifer in between, both hugging each other, trembling and crying in the desperate grip of his arm. He himself would not cry, *could* not cry. He knew that if he allowed himself that luxury for even a moment he would end up falling on the casket like some poor sobbing peasant mother and that it would take men, it would take farmers like himself, to pull him free. So he held on to all he had in the world now, his two children and his rage—for there was still that, of course, and it had become his spine now, his blood and breath, his tomorrow and the next day and the day after that. As long as he had it, this treasure of rage, he could go on.

The Reverend Hodson's voice gusted at him again, puffed and preening now, for these were the man's own words and not his deity's. "And O, our dear heavenly Father, our blessed Jesus, we pray that Thou wilt grant eternal peace and life everlasting to the soul of this young man, whom, as we all here today can testify, truly lived his life according to the golden rule . . ."

Hook, who despised bad grammar in anyone pretending to eloquence, did not hear the rest of the man's prayer. The solecism, like a thrown rail switch, sent the train of his attention wandering off into the trees, the cemetery's graceful old maples and dead-leaved oaks, and he observed that the wind was shifting, was southerly now. If it held, the temperature would rise in the next few days. The thin snow would melt. Christmas would not be white after all, not that it would matter to him, for where he was going it would be green.

On his left his Aunt Marian suddenly cried out and Hook, feeling Uncle Arnie struggling to hold her, realized that it was all over, the ceremony finished. The Reverend was coming around the coffin toward him, his stocky figure properly bent and condoling, though Hook thought he could see in the man's doughy face a look of muted triumph. See? it said. You finally needed me. In the end you all need me.

Nodding, Hook thanked him but barely touched his proffered hand, for Jenny had collapsed against him and was holding onto his arm with all her strength—to keep him there, he knew, hold them both there, for to move away would be to acknowledge the finality of the thing, that their Chris, their shining splendid loved and loving Chris, was actually dead, actually lying there in that box about to be covered over with earth. To leave would be to accept that it was all not some fantastically detailed nightmare from which they would soon wake. Nevertheless Hook gently forced her away from the grave, moving slowly, holding her up, with Bobby on the other side of her—Bobby, who if anything had to feel even more bereft than they, for they at least had known where their lives had ended and Chris's had begun. They had not all their days played with him and gone to school with him and worked with him; they had not fought for their lives with him or lain together in the warm summer nights giggling at what scatological humor Hook could only guess at, smile at, from his room across the hall. Yet Bobby helped him with Jenny as they headed toward the gate and the cars lined up outside it, along the blacktop road.

On the way, friends kept stopping them, not so much to talk as to touch them with their hands, pat them, give them their twisted smiles of sympathy, which were genuine, Hook knew, for it was Chris in the coffin and not himself. Mrs. Corman, a neighbor and high-school English teacher as Hook himself once had been, tried to speak but had to give it up. He would have taken her hand and tried to comfort her but Jenny was still holding onto him, pressing her face against his shoulder. Even old Emil Strickler, whose last hundred acres Hook had bought at a fair price, and earned the man's undying resentment in the bargain—even Emil came up and put his hand on Hook's arm, squeezed him.

Others walked along with them. A weeping George Anderson cursed out loud. "It don't make no goddamn sense, Dave! Why *him*, huh? Why him? Why not us? Why not me?" Two winters before, when George had broken his ankle hopping down from a tractor, Hook and Chris had seen to it that the man's thirty-cow dairy herd went on producing through all the months of his mending.

They came to the cars and got in, Hook and his children into the rear of the first car, his aunt and uncle into the second. And it seemed ridiculous to Hook. They could have walked. A quarter-mile down the road, down the hill, was the gate to his farm; another quarter-mile back was his house. Yet he knew that they had to drive, that they had no choice, just as they had no choice but to suffer the presence of most of the mourners at his house for the next few hours, and for that matter just as he had had to suffer the absurdity of the whole ceremony, the rite of Christian burial. They lived here. They would go on living here. A man had to bend now and then. For himself, Hook would have preferred just the five of them, his family, bringing Chris's body here and lowering it into the ground next to his mother's with no more ceremony than the silence of their grief. And with this thought, as the mortician Rohmer discreetly closed the door of his prized Cadillac behind him, Hook felt the thing coming at him anew, and all out of control now. It was like being in a skiff on a fogged sea and out of nowhere there was suddenly this great dark shape slipping silently toward him through the mist, a ship's prow, a shape of death, of loss. And then abruptly it was gone, was past him, moving just as silently on. Someday it would not miss him, he knew. But now was not the time for it, not the time for grief. Now was the time for control.

Hook looked at Jennifer sitting between him and Bobby. Meeting his eyes, she put her hands to her face and Hook looked away from her, only to see his son whipping his head furiously back and forth. The boy's mouth was open; he was trying to speak.

"Some of them looked like they wondered," he got out finally. "Like they believed maybe he really did kill himself."

"We know better," Hook said.

"Why'd they have to lie out there? Why'd they—" But the boy could not go on. He began to pound his fist against his knee, slowly, but with brutal force.

Hook seized his wrist. "I don't know why. But we'll find out, son. We'll change it." The words felt good to him, good on his lips, like the cubed bread of a childhood communion, like the recitation that accompanied the bread's ingestion, a statement of faith and fact, solid, unarguable.

In the front, Rohmer started the car and they began to move down the narrow road toward the creek bridge and just beyond it the entrance to his farm. Along the creek bottomland stretching to their right about fifty head of Hook's Black Angus herd were placidly moving among the brokendown corn stalks, scavenging for any grain the picker might have missed six weeks before. It was a hobby for them, not a necessity; they got all the hay and silage they needed.

"I want to go with you," Bobby said.

Hook did not answer him. He would go alone, of course. The boy knew that. It was not a matter for discussion.

Except for the stretch of cleared ground along the creek, the rest of his land bordering the road was rough and wooded, virgin white oak and hickory with a sprinkling of maple and ash, and for Hook it was never anything but beautiful, the muted grays and blues of winter now, the black electricity of its barren limbs, just as important to him as the bright glory of its springtimes and autumns. And as always, he found it strange that such beauty was held against him, was somehow part of his neighbors' brief against him, along with his college degree and his unbelief and just his character in general, his cold unblinking inability to be or even pretend to be "just plain folks." That he, a farmer, a businessman the same as they, would leave this land along the road in a wild state instead of clearing it off and seeding it, making it work and produce—this, Hook knew, was one further heresy as far as they were concerned, further proof that he was not one of them. But as the Cadillac swung into his gravel drive now, leading the cortege over the cattle gate and up the long hill through the woods, Hook did not doubt the rightness of his decision. This strip of woodland was the stone wall of his castle. It was the moat between his world and that other, larger one outside, the one that had just cost him the life of his son.

As they reached the top of the hill the woods ended abruptly and the main part of Hook's farm stretched out before them, some three hundred acres of rolling pasture and hayfields, with his house and farm buildings lying among an island of trees almost in the center of the cleared expanse. Back on the other side of the blacktop, beyond the kindred strip of woods there, he owned a similar piece of ground, only twice as large. And two miles east, toward the town of Banner Hill, was the hundred acres he had bought from Strickler, flat rich land he planted to corn to fatten whatever cattle he did not sell to other feeders around the state. It was a large operation, one of the few big farms in the area, and it was almost wholly his own creation. When he had taken it over from his grandfather fifteen years before, there had been just the old one-hundred-sixty-acre nucleus, the house and barn and a small herd of pampered unproductive Jersey cows the old man kept because the high butterfat content of their milk consistently won him prizes at the county fair, if not much of a living. The new buildings, the added land, the three-hundred-head beef herd were all his own doing, with the help of Uncle Arnie and Bobby and especially Chris, who daily after school and each summer had worked like a man, or even better, like a man who cared. So there was no part of the farm, no fence or field or animal or building or piece of equipment, nothing the limousine drove past on the gravel road to the farmhouse now that did not carry with it, in Hook's mind, the image of his son.

They entered the island of trees and came to a stop at the house. There were already a few cars parked alongside the drive,

transportation for the ladies of the Bethel Baptist Church Philathea Class, friends of his Aunt Marian here to "help the family," which meant serve the mourners all the cakes and casseroles
and sandwiches and salads the ladies had brought with them
in the first place. Yet Hook was not ungrateful for their effort. Nor
did it bother him that some of the women would be in an almost
festive mood, that as far as they were concerned one church function was pretty much like another, a social gathering, a time for
fun and gossip. He could accept this, did not expect humanity to
suspend its grossness for even this one special day. But he wanted
desperately to be by himself now, just him and the children, or
ideally just him alone, if Bobby and Jennifer felt anything as he
did, aching for privacy, wanting to put his suffering beyond the
reach of another's eyes.

As Rohmer opened the car door and they got out, Hook gently
herded the children and Aunt Marian and Arnie into the house
ahead of him. Inside, a half-dozen Philathea ladies were standing about the food-burdened dining room table like sentries at
attention, and in uniform too, all with the same tightly curled
blue-rinsed gray hair and the same soft stout bodies stuffed into
rigid girdles and Sunday dresses off the half-size rack in Sears.
Aunt Marian went straight to them, crooning over the food,
accepting their embraces, returning them with a vengeance. But
all Hook could do was nod to the ladies as he and the children
moved through the dining room into the new part of the house,
which contained their bedrooms and the family room. Jenny
pushed ahead, running to her room and falling onto her bed. Following her in, Hook sat down next to her and put his hand on
her head, on her long blond hair. Bobby, coming in too, stood
inside the door looking down at the two of them.

"Well, it's over," Hook said. "This part is over."

Bobby nodded. "It's over."

Jenny turned her head away from Hook's hand. "I don't believe any of this," she said. "I don't believe this is happening."

From the doorway Aunt Marian intoned: "The Lord moves in
mysterious ways, His wonders to perform."

Hook looked at his aunt, his father's sister, rangy like most
of the Hooks, but heavy now after all her years in the kitchen,

7

nibbling, testing, cleaning up leftovers, a good kind proper Christian lady on the outside, yet all saddle-leather toughness underneath, tough enough to have kept her Arnie working all this time against all his better instincts, and tough enough to have stepped in and saved them all seven years before, when Hook's Kate had lost her life in the head-on crash near Alton and Hook for almost a year afterwards had spent his days like a man wandering in a battlefield searching for a death of his own. This same morning he had watched Marian salt her coffee and place the sugar in the refrigerator, and later he had seen her standing in the pantry shaking with grief, yet here she was now, so quick and easy with the mindless platitude. She was not a simple woman.

"I'm not going in the living room," Jenny said now. "I'm staying right here."

Her eyes filling, Marian looked at Hook. "Tell her, David. Tell her she can't. She has to come out."

Hook got up and put his arm around his aunt, patted her beefy shoulder. "You cover for us for a while, okay? You and Arnie."

"You're not coming out either? But you have to, David. You just have to. For a while anyway. A few minutes."

"Maybe later."

Uncle Arnie had come to the door now too. "Let 'em do what they want," he told his wife. "Me and you can handle it. All it takes is sittin'." Small and light for a Swede, Arnie Bergman at sixty was considerably outweighed by his wife, and usually out-maneuvered and out-opinioned too, but every now and then, when he cared, he would prevail. He prevailed now.

Aunt Marian moved toward the door. "All right. It's up to you, David. But try to come out, will you? They'll expect you to."

Hook would not commit himself. "For now, I'm going to stay back here with the kids, Marian."

But Jenny did not want that either. "Dad, I just want to be alone now. I just want to lie here alone. I'll be okay."

Hook touched her head again, patted her. Why could he not keep his hands off them? he wondered. They were here. They were right here, living. He could see them. "Sure, honey," he said. "Of course."

He turned to Bobby. "You want to go out? Walk a while?"

The boy nodded.

More out of habit than any compulsive fastidiousness, they put on boots before going outside, and it was a good thing they did, for the dung-rich soil of the farmyard had none of the frozen crust of the cemetery. Going past the barn, Hook saw that Coley Jonas, a neighbor's son he hired to help out occasionally, was already back for afternoon chores, in body anyway if not in spirit, for the youth was lying back on some sacks of protein supplement stacked near the feed mill, and he was smoking. Any other day and Hook would either have given him a roasting or fired him on the spot, since the hairline profit margin in cattle-raising did not allow such luxuries as insuring one's buildings at their replacement value. But this afternoon Hook simply walked on past the open door. The cattle in the feedlot, yearlings mostly, and accustomed to men on foot, barely bothered to glance up as Hook and Bobby moved through them and out the gate into the main pasture, a rolling dun carpet of brome and lespedeza and clover stretching out ahead of them all the way to a fence row of elm shade trees over a half-mile distant, and barren now, but still a favored haunt of the cattle, which Hook could see lying in clusters along the row, like scattered raisins.

Though Hook was taller than his son, and longer-legged, he had to step quickly to keep up with him. Where Chris had been built along his father's lines, slim and bony, Bobby had the good fortune to favor his mother, and the same subtle force that had kept her body firm of breast and belly and buttock till her death at thirty-eight was evident in the boy, in the solid wedge of his torso and in his athlete's rump and sturdy legs. A trackman like Chris, he had been the faster of the two, beating his older brother regularly in their wind sprints up and down the farm drive each morning before chores and breakfast. Yet Hook knew that the boy had counted these victories as less important than the fact that as the distance lengthened, as it stretched out to a mile and beyond, Chris had left him far behind, just as he had everyone else on the school track team and in fact almost every miler in the conference.

"I don't understand death," the boy said now. "I can't figure it."

"I know, son. Neither can I."

9

"One moment you're alive. And the next you're dead. It doesn't make any sense. Why live in the first place?"

Hook wished he had something to give the boy, but there was nothing. "I don't know," he said. "I can't say I know."

"If we believed—I mean, you know, if we were like the others around here, and I believed he was in heaven and that we'd all be together again someday—that I could see him again—him and Mom—" He was strangling on the words. "It would be easier."

"Yes. It would."

"All I wish is he'd never gone out there," Bobby got out.

They walked on. The distant elms were still distant, still miniature. The sky was overcast, and the air—Hook could not feel the air at all. He was not sure whether it was warm or cold.

"How are we so sure there's no afterlife?" Bobby asked.

"We're not."

"But we *are*. I know you are. I remember how you were after Mom."

Hook had no answer.

"If I could only see him," Bobby said. "Just once more."

Suddenly Hook's eyes were not dry. And for some reason Bobby chose that moment to look at him. Through his tears Hook saw the boy react, saw his first look of shock, as if he had been struck in the face, and then the whole surface seemed to give way, crumpling from the force of the blow, and he took off running. Hook followed, trying desperately to catch him and hold him, keep him from doing whatever it was he felt he had to do. But it was no contest. The boy flew across the snow-dusted turf, effortlessly increasing the distance between them. Yet Hook would not let himself quit, and kept puffing along after him, running as fast as he could in his heavy coat and boots over the slippery ground. And even when it felt as if his heart was about to chop through his chest he kept on, until finally he saw Bobby slip and fall up ahead, not far from the row of elms. Trying to get up, the boy slipped again, and Hook drove himself even harder, sprinting the last few yards till he had his hands on him finally, holding him, dragging him down into the snow. For a few moments the boy fought him, and fought the earth too, rain-ing his fists on both in a rage of impotence. Then Hook got his arms around him.

"Let it out, son," he told him. "It's all right. Let it out."

And Bobby did. "I loved him, Dad!" he sobbed. "I loved him! I loved him so much!"

"Me too," was all Hook could say. "I loved him too, son."

Hook sat there on the ground holding the boy for a while, hugging his quaking body, and in time the cattle began leaving the fence row one by one and came toward them, gathering a safe distance away to observe this curious ceremony in the snow.

At two in the morning, after lying awake for three hours, Hook dressed and went outside. He would just walk down the farm road and back, he told himself. He would smoke a cigarette, and he would try not to think about it all, Chris and the funeral and California.

As he closed the door behind him and started across the lawn toward the gravel drive, the dogs heard him and came barking from their post in the implement building. Hook silenced them with a word and then they began jumping at each other, nipping and wriggling and talking in celebration of this rare event, a moonlight walk with the chief himself. There were two of them: Mickey, a spayed boxer-collie cross, all sweetness and femininity, and a huge black German shepherd male Bobby had named King six years before, only to have Uncle Arnie and the times rename him Martin Luther, which in turn the years had shortened to Marty. Like most shepherds, Marty was a one-man dog. And Hook was that man.

Now the two animals sped down the gravel road ahead of him, all the way to the woods, then stopped and came whipping back. While he walked the half-mile to the blacktop and back, they would cover ten times that distance. Hook lit a cigarette. The sky had cleared and the mid-month moon was just a paring short of fullness. Reflecting off the snow, it made the night almost dusklike in its brightness. Under his shoes the snow squeaked wetly, melting. With the morning sun it would disappear. As he passed the feedlot some of the cattle came snorting to their feet, frightened at seeing a man on foot at so late an hour.

11

He came to the end of the cleared land and started down the road through the trees. Six months before, the woods would have been raucous with insect sound, but this night there were only his footsteps on the snow-covered gravel to break the silence. Yet he knew there was life out there watching him, night creatures crouched and silent, waiting for the great predator to pass on. And especially he knew the owl was out there, a great horned owl that for years had patrolled this strip of woodland dividing his farm, and which Hook saw every now and then in daylight, like a wolf sitting in a tree, its lemon Life Saver eyes glowing furiously at him for one long timeless second before the huge body would abruptly sprout wings and glide off through the trees to some other perch to wait for darkness and a renewal of the hunt.

Hook had reached the blacktop now, but instead of turning back he headed west along the road toward the hill on which the cemetery rested. To him, this strip of blacktop was like the nave of a cathedral, a path running between the great pillars and buttresses of the trees crowding the hills on either side, and indeed there were times in early morning and at sundown when the light filtering through the leaves and branches there created a rage of color not unlike that of a cathedral's stained-glass windows. Yet now, at night, Hook knew the small valley for what it was, a cathedral of death if anything, a kingdom in which the owl reigned and the only ritual, the only chorus, was the shriek and squeal and rustle of his victims. Hook felt no pity for them. Men were no better off. As far back as he could remember, he had had no illusions about the vulnerability of his kind. He had learned it the first time at the age of four or five, on a tricycle pedaling furiously to catch up with a neighbor boy on another trike, and had been right behind him when an automobile, braking, tires screaming, hit the boy broadside and sent him tumbling down the street like a football. That had been in Wauwatosa, one of the many Midwest suburbs where Hook had lived as his father kept moving from one job to another. Later, as an eighteen-year-old sailor during the last year of the Second World War, Hook had learned about death again, but in a different way and on a different scale. Waiting at Long Beach for his ship, a destroyer, to be refitted, he had been temporarily assigned to shore duty in a warehouse, and for a month had spent ten hours a day seeing to the handling and the storage and the shipment home of dead Marines. He had been a warehouseman of death.

But of course, you forgot. The years passed and you spent them with the living, and you even created new life yourself, and there was not much reason to think about death. You were like a rabbit in the spring sunshine feasting on soybean sprouts, and then suddenly it was night and the owl was on you and you never even heard his approach.

"Dad, where's Mom?"

"Alton. At the dentist's."

"Still?"

"Still."

"It's almost six. I'm starved."

"So make supper."

"She should've been back by now."

"She'll be here."

"When?"

"Soon."

But he had been wrong.

Hook caught himself now and consciously tried to put all that out of his mind. The dogs, finally tired of roaming the countryside, had fallen in beside him, Marty at his heel and Mickey wisely on the outside. The snow had melted off the blacktop, so Hook had no trouble walking up the steep hill to the cemetery. He did not know he was going to enter it until he had already done so, carefully pulling the old wrought-iron gate closed behind him in order that none of his neighbors driving past might see it open and conclude that he was there. It was one of the things he liked least about himself, that he valued the respect of men he in turn respected hardly at all. He did not care whether they liked him or not, but he would not let himself give them reason to think him careless or lazy or weak, even by their own standards. Whether grief or the show of it would constitute weakness in their eyes, he was not sure. He only knew that he did not want to be seen here in the cemetery at two-thirty in the morning.

The moon, shining through the trees, was so bright he could have read the legends on the gravemarkers. But he already knew

13

most of them by heart, and anyway his eyes had filled with tears again as he approached his son's grave, a mound of wreaths and sprays, a junkheap of rotting hothouse flowers festooned with gauzy messages of send-off and acceptance, death as simply a part of life, a transition between states of Christian felicity, here today and gone to be with Jesus tomorrow. But not his Chris. No, Chris was lying under all that garbage with his neck broken and his body carved like a holiday turkey in the name of truth, so that he might yield the secret of how he had died.

And suddenly Hook found himself attacking the grave, kicking at the mounded flowers, exploding them up into the air in a rain of wreaths and sprays and plastic buckets that sent the dogs scampering out of the cemetery to safety. Exhausted finally, he sank to his knees and begged himself to let it go now, weep, sob, moan, admit his loss, begin to live with it.

But he could not. All he could do was look ahead to California and his search for the truth of what had happened.

He would have given all he had to go back, even five days, to that other age before Chief Janson had come driving up to the farm in Banner Hill's one and only police car.

2

Hook and Arnie were in the implement shed tuning the new four-wheel-drive John Deere when Chief Janson drove up and parked. Though a personal call by the chief was a rare occurrence, Hook did not sense that something might be wrong, not even when he saw how the man got out of the car, so laboriously, carrying his badged cap and looking everywhere except at Hook and Arnie in the building. Janson was a caricature of the small-town cop, a crude pot-bellied extrovert who wore his holstered thirty-eight special like a loincloth and divided his time almost equally between polishing the squad car and drinking free beer at Harry's Tap and Billiards. As such, he was an easy target for the town's many humorists, including Uncle Arnie, who at the moment was busily forgetting to hand Hook a Phillips screwdriver as Janson moved hesitantly toward them around his car.

"Well, what do you know?" Arnie mused. "J. Edgar way out here in the sticks. What you been up to, David?"

Hook did not answer. He was wondering why the chief had stopped near the fence and was not coming on into the building.

"Look at him," Arnie said. "That gun ever goes off he's gonna be shorter by a full inch."

Hook barely heard him. The chief looked stricken, ill. Hook got up and walked out to meet him.

"Morning, Chief," he said.

But Janson did not respond. He just stood there leaning against the fence, still not looking directly at Hook.

"What's wrong?" Hook asked. "What's happened?"

The chief's eyes flickered at him and then slid away. "There's been a accident, Dave."

Hook had the feeling he was standing in front of a firing squad and though there was no sound yet, no report, the bullets were already on the way.

"Who? Where?"

The chief swallowed, shook his head. "In California. Santa Barbara."

"Chris?"

Janson nodded.

"Go on."

"He had a fall, Dave."

"And—"

"They called just a while ago."

Hook waited for a moment, but the chief did not go on. Somehow Hook got the words out. *"Is he alive?"*

Eyes streaming, Janson shook his head. "I am so sorry, Dave. Jesus, I am so sorry."

So the volley was in Hook now, exploding in his body, gutting him.

"A fall?" he said. It sounded so silly.

"And the bastards—" the chief got out. "They said he done it hisself, Dave. They said it was suicide."

The word was a reprieve. It was a command calling back the bullets, canceling his execution. *Suicide.* Then it could not be Chris. They had made a mistake.

The chief was crying openly. "I told this sergeant he was full of shit, Dave. I told him they just didn't know Chris. Chris wouldn't ever do that. Never in a million years, I told him."

Hook was hanging onto the fence, trying to stand on legs made of plastic hose. "It's a mistake," he said. "It is not Chris."

The rest of that morning passed like time during a drunk, a daze of activity that Hook would recall later only in bits and pieces. He remembered driving to Banner Hill to cash a check and to get Bobby and Jennifer out of school, and he remembered telling them about the accident later, when he had them safely back at the farm. He remembered Aunt Marian packing a bag for him, clumsily, with one hand, while holding the other in a fist pressed tightly to her mouth. And he remembered having to raise his voice to Bobby to make the boy understand that he could not go with him, that he had to stay behind with the others. But Hook had almost no recollection of the drive with Uncle Arnie to Lambert Field in St. Louis, or buying his plane ticket when he got there, or boarding the TWA jet he found himself on by one that afternoon. Throughout these hours, though, he was constantly aware that he was not doing the one thing that the Santa Barbara sheriff's police had expected him to do, and that was phone them. Chief Janson had given him a number to call and the name of the officer to ask for, a Sergeant Rider. But Hook had not been able to force himself to the phone, out of fear that by learning more about the accident he might put to death the one frail hope he still had, and without which he doubted that he would even be able to make it to Santa Barbara. As it was, he felt a sharp recurring pain in his chest and shoulder; his body was rigid with tension; he had diarrhea; he could not eat. He could drink, however, and the stewardess in First Class, where he found himself seated, was dedicated to seeing that he did.

"A drink, sir? Do you want a drink?" Her tone implied that it was not the first time she had asked him.

He nodded. "Yes. I guess so."

"What kind, sir? Martini? Manhattan?"

"Martini will be all right."

As she moved on, Hook wondered about the way she had looked at him, with distaste and even fear, and he could not understand it. He knew he probably appeared distraught, but that alone did not seem enough to explain her look. Then he happened to glance down at his hands and he saw what had caused her reaction: without knowing it he had pulled a copy of *Life* magazine out of its binder and, rolling it up, had twisted it almost in two. His hands, locked on the torn cylinder, were purple, the knuckles white. His veins stood out like nightcrawlers. Quickly, he stuffed the mutilated magazine into the pocket in the seat in front of him, a window seat like his own. There was no one next to him, and the young couple across the aisle had not noticed, were seemingly absorbed in the John Wayne western playing on the screen up in front. Only the stewardess had seen him, and she probably had ascribed the thing to fear of flying. So he felt safe. Then he caught himself. What did it matter anyway? Was he fool enough to believe that if others thought all was right with him, then that was how it would be? Yes, he decided. He was fool enough. He was frightened enough.

When the stewardess brought his drink, he forced himself to meet her eyes. She smiled uneasily and hurried on to serve the other passengers. Hook downed half the martini in two quick swallows, hoping the alcohol would help somehow. Out the window the sky was cloudless and crystalline. The sun shone fiercely on the jet's wings. Miles below, the earth looked cold and serene, a patchwork of tan and white and gray without a sign of life.

Coming in over Los Angeles, Hook was surprised at how clear it looked from above, and then he remembered that the winter desert winds had that effect upon the city, blowing the smog out to sea. He was not prepared for the size of the place either, its sheer sprawling immensity, beginning way out in the Mojave Desert and stretching to the ocean and as far down the coast as he could see from the jet, which circled wide out over the water in a holding pattern for ten or fifteen minutes before finally getting clearance to land.

On the ground, checking his watch, Hook realized that it was only two-thirty Pacific time, which meant he had an hour-and-a-half layover before the United flight departed for Santa Barbara. He decided to kill the time in an airport bar, and ducked into the first one he came to, a crowded T-shaped affair with a floor-to-ceiling window running the length of the room, and faced by a long low counter at which a score of travelers sat drinking and talking as they watched the jets coming in and taking off. The decor was sleazy modern, small plastic-topped tables with plastic bucket chairs on tubular legs. Hook found a corner table and ordered another martini, his third that afternoon. He did not particularly like the drink, but since that was what he had started with on the jet he wanted to stay with them now; his stomach felt queasy enough without his mixing drinks. Smoking, trying not to think, he finished the martini, still feeling nothing except the leaden weight of his fear. Near him, at the counter table, a gaudy old married couple on their way home from Hawaii were hurriedly sharing their lives' secrets with a young couple with a baby. In the time it took for Hook's fourth martini to be served he learned that the old woman hated Los Angeles and hippies, loved San Diego, had been married three times, urinated almost constantly in flight, and had had her left breast removed two years before, which made "this old bastard next to me here" love the remaining one twice as much. In return, the young couple revealed that in six years of marriage they had lived in five different cities in four states, that the husband was thinking of leaving his present job in Denver, and that they had almost ten thousand dollars in the bank.

Hook continued drinking, trying not to overhear any more of their conversation. Instead, he invited in the thought, the line of speculation, that had been circling around his mind like a hawk ever since the chief first brought him the news: What exactly were his chances? What was the likelihood that the body the Santa Barbara sheriff's police had was not Chris's but that of some other youth who had found or stolen his wallet? The last letter Hook had received from the boy had come from Taos, where Chris had spent a few days in some sort of commune, at the invitation of a friend of a friend who knew somebody—something like that. And he had been hitchhiking the whole time, all the way from Illinois over a month ago, so of course he had to have run into a lot of hippies by now, a lot of oddballs and bums and just plain thieves. One of them could have stolen his wallet. It was not beyond the realm of possibility. And perhaps the victim in this "fall" reported by Chief Janson, had been so crushed or mangled that he was unrecognizable, and the police might have had nothing to go on *but* Chris's wallet and identification papers. So, yes, there was a chance the boy was still alive—the slenderest of chances.

Once again he tried consciously to think about something else. A young mother with two well-dressed preschool children, a boy and a girl, had taken the table next to his own. While the mother ordered a whiskey sour for herself and Cokes for them, the two children stood there between the tables staring at Hook.

He thought of blowing smoke on them but settled for turning away, fixing his attention on a Japan Air Lines 747 jet loading on the ramp outside. The craft was unbelievably immense, a silver robot Gulliver being swarmed over by a Lilliputian ground crew, all busily tending to its vast needs and appetites. There was that to think about, to ponder in awe. But instead Hook found himself contemplating the black irony of the whole tragedy, that it should have happened in Santa Barbara of all places, for the town had figured crucially in his own youth, and in fact was one of the few places besides his farm where he had been truly and consciously happy.

Just after the Armistice in 1945 he had gotten a ten-day leave from Long Beach, enough time to have flown back to Chicago to spend a week with his parents in their newly rented house in Evanston, but it had seemed like so far to go for so little. His father, who had fled home and farm at seventeen, operated under the apparent conviction that he had been sent to earth by God to infiltrate the marketing departments of various consumer goods manufacturers and find out which of their top executives and ass-licking underlings were not performing their jobs properly—that is, as he would have performed them—so that he might bring this failing to their attention before being asked to move on to other mission fields, as he invariably was. And like all prophets, his father suffered for his beliefs, but he was not at all loath to share that suffering with others, especially Hook's mother, who over the years had been so consistently exposed to his attitude of aggrieved bitterness that in time it had become her life-style too. Together, they were like Victorian Methodist missionaries sweltering among the Hottentots, and consistently outraged that their charges wore so little clothing. So Hook had not bothered to tell them about his leave, and instead had taken the train up to Santa Barbara to swim and lie in the sand and be alone. He was nineteen and still a virgin, having failed to make it with, first, a whore, then with a gross ever-grinning Mexican girl his Navy buddies had fixed him up with in the hope of saving him from such an ignoble state of purity. But after that second failure they were no longer buddies so much as quiet mates who treated him with quiet scorn. So he went to Santa Barbara, alone.

He met her his first night there, while drinking beer in a tourist bar on the beach. Or rather he was picked up by her, was delivered by silver tray a card with the name Mrs. John R. Cunningham, Atlanta, Georgia, beautifully printed on it but almost obscured by the scrawled imperative: *Join me*. Though she was almost twice his age, she was still trim and attractive in a quiet moneyed sort of way, and it developed that he spent the rest of his leave with her, at the plush Biltmore Hotel on the beach, in a suite of rooms that was never without ice and booze and almost instantaneous service. She introduced him, first to a world of elegance, fine restaurants and exotic food and drink, mostly seafood and wine, which gave him the stamina to handle the second and far more dazzling world she also presented him with, that of sex. In nine nights and days he learned more from her, he was confident, than a squad of sailors could have learned in a year of weekend passes spent with the whores of Long Beach and Tijuana. He also learned to love the lady, though that was something she did not want to hear about, she said, because she was old enough to be his mother, and in fact had children of her own, plus a husband, back in Atlanta. Nevertheless her eyes had filled when they said goodbye at the railroad station.

"What's the matter?"

He had never seen or heard from her since, nor had he ever tried to contact her. She would have been in her sixties now, an old woman.

"What's the matter, mister?" It was the girl, standing almost at the edge of his table. And Hook realized it was not the first time she had asked him the question.

Her mother reached over and pulled her back, scolding the child, asking her where her manners were.

Hook finished his drink, paid up, and left.

The flight to Santa Barbara was actually not much more than a takeoff and a landing, since the ninety-mile distance barely gave the United jet time to reach cruising altitude before it had to start coming down again. As they came over the city Hook checked his watch: the time was four-forty. Through the window across the aisle he could see the sun already flattening as it dropped toward the Pacific out beyond Point Conception, bathing the Channel Islands and, out his window, the sea cliffs and the Santa Ynez Mountains behind the city in a scarlet glaze. The city itself lay mostly in shadow, its pervasive orange tile roofs and pastel fake adobe buildings stretching up the valley away from the beach, which cut between the palm trees and the blue of the sea like a scimitar.

As the DC-9 landed and taxied to the terminal, Hook did not know where he would find the strength to move when the time came. He felt not just weak but weighted, as if his body had turned to lead. He stayed seated until everyone else was out before he struggled to his feet and followed them down the steel stairway, heading for the small terminal. To the north, in the foothills of the Goleta valley, he saw not the neat ranks of lemon groves that had been there when he was young but houses, stores, shopping centers. In the other direction, a mile distant, was a stand of high-rise buildings, the university, he figured, the home of the bank-burners.

He thought of renting a car, already preparing himself for the possibility that the body would be Chris's and he would want to stay on and find out the truth of what had happened, but it was a good ten miles to the city and he did not want to risk driving that distance feeling the way he did. As it was, he practically had to drag himself into a cab at the front of the terminal. The driver, a young man with long hair and a beard, did not open the door for him or take his bag. And they were a good distance from the terminal before he even bothered to ask Hook's destination.

"The sheriff's office," Hook said.

The young man laughed. "Gonna turn yourself in, huh?"

Hook made no response.

"Just a little joke."

Hook said nothing, hoping the youth would shut up.

But he did not. To the tune of "Till Somebody Loves You," he sang out: "You're nobody, till somebody busts you." Laughing again, he searched for Hook's reaction in the rearview mirror. Finding none, he wagged his head. "Boy, you ain't much of a talker, are you?"

Hook told him to shut up and drive.

The downtown was pretty much as Hook remembered it, only bigger and busier. The streets were still lined with palm and hibiscus trees; the buildings were still all peach and white and buff adobe, with dark wood trim and tile roofs. Hook recognized the library, and then suddenly they were at the courthouse, styled by the natives as "the most beautiful public building in America," a great white Moorish castle set on grounds as lushly green as mortician's grass and covered with palm trees and other tropical flora.

The driver, surly now, had pulled over to the curb. "The sheriff's office is over on the other side there," he said, pointing. "The street's one-way—I can't go no closer. You owe me five-eighty."

Hook fumbled in his wallet. It would be a half-block walk, and he was not sure he could make it. His bowels felt loose again; his limbs were quivering. He handed the driver a bill.

"That's a five, man. I said five-eighty."

Hook barely heard him. He took out another dollar and gave it to him, and the youth wagged his head again, amused, unbelieving.

"Man, you're really with it. Now how about my tip?"

Ignoring him, Hook picked up his overnight case and walked away, vaguely aware that the young man was shouting at him, calling him a cheap sonofabitch and a motherfucker. But Hook did not stop. He was halfway to the entrance, a massive stone archway leading into the castle-like structure, and he had to concentrate all his energies on making it there. When he did finally, he was momentarily confused by a stone wall dead ahead, and then he saw the small sign stating that the coroner's and sheriff's offices were to the right. He went up a few stairs into a huge hall-like room with cool white walls and a wood counter behind which two uniformed officers sat at desks doing paper work while a pretty young woman worked at a switchboard off in a corner. There were other desks and tables, all empty. It was after five.

One of the officers, a deputy, got up and came to the counter.

Hook groped for his voice. "My name's David Hook. You have a body . . ."

The word was electric, a charge transforming the deputy from a weary clerk into a grave and efficient servitor. "You'll want Sergeant Rider," he said, reaching for a phone, dialing.

Hook nodded. "That's right—Sergeant Rider."

"It's after five—he could be gone by now. If he is, one of us can handle it." The deputy turned away then, speaking quietly into the phone, probably giving the sergeant the option of being gone.

"The father," Hook heard. "Here to identify the Hook boy."

The Hook boy. So they at least were not in doubt as to whose body they had. It was settled in their minds, the identification just a formality to be gotten out of the way.

The deputy hung up. "He'll be right down, sir." He moved to open the gate that led behind the counter. "Why don't you come back here and sit down?"

Hook thanked him but said he would rather stand. He was afraid that if he got off his feet he would need help getting up again.

"You've come pretty far, huh?"

Hook knew the deputy was only trying to help him, put him at ease, but he was in no condition to handle small talk, so he just turned away from the man. He wanted to light a cigarette but could not trust his hands to get the job done.

Hook did not know how long it took the sergeant to appear. It could have been ten minutes or only one; he had no idea. All he knew was that a burly authoritative man suddenly had appeared from a hallway beyond the deputies' desks, and now he was talking with the deputy who had spoken to Hook. The man was only five feet eight or nine, but he was massively built, a weight-lifter type carrying an extra hundred pounds of fat on his belly and broad diva's chest and loglike arms, which did not hang at his sides so much as stick out, as if ready, eager, for any threat anyone might be fool enough to direct at him. He was Hook's age or older, balding, crewcut, with small hard laugh-squinted eyes. In one hand he carried a large manila envelope, sealed.

"Naw, I'll take him," Hook heard him tell the deputy. "When you make the fancy money we do, what's a few hours overtime, huh? You're glad to do it."

The deputy grinned, sharing his cynicism. Then the man came around the counter. He thrust his hand out at Hook, who took it.

"Sergeant Rider, Mr. Hook. Sorry to put you through this, but we've got to have an I.D. on the body, of course. Afterwards, I can release it to you."

Hook could not speak. *It*. The word, the gender, struck him like a fist in the stomach.

The sergeant led him out the door and down a stairway to the basement garage, which contained four or five sheriff's police cars and a couple of unmarked cars. The sergeant led him to one of these. Inside, Rider told him that the county did not have a morgue.

"We just use local mortuaries," he said. "The one we're headed for is just a couple blocks up. We'll be there in a minute."

They were out of the garage now, heading north on the one-way street that ran past the courthouse.

"Another thing's a little different out here," the sergeant went on. "At least, different in our county. The sheriff's also the coroner. So, in effect, I'm acting as coroner right now." He looked at Hook. "In case you were wondering."

Hook nodded assent, a numb understanding. But he still could not speak. He had the feeling that the air was thinning, its oxygen content growing less by the second. He could barely breathe. His mouth was dry. The sergeant turned off on a side street and two blocks farther pulled into a parking lot behind the mortuary, a sprawling pale-pink building with meticulously kept grounds and a wrought-iron sign identifying the place as *Bowman Brothers*. Hook managed to get out of the car by pulling himself up, but he felt so unsteady on his feet that for a few moments he just stood there holding on to the door while Rider strode on ahead of him toward the building. Then, seeing that Hook was not with him, he stopped and turned.

"You okay?" he asked.

Hook threw the car door closed and started after him, on legs he could not feel.

"We better go around the front," Rider said. "You never know what you'll run into in these back rooms."

The reception room was large and plush, presided over by a

blue-haired lady with a voice as soft as the carpet under their feet. Mr. Bowman would be right with them, she said. He was just down the hall, in one of the "slumber" rooms. She had used the word, actually used it, without the slightest trace of a smile. And when the mortician appeared, Hook was not surprised to see that the man looked exactly like the woman, only male, with his face congealed in the same decorous mask of professional sympathy. One of the sergeant's beefy hands lightly prodded Hook, indicating for him to move on, and he followed the mortician down a corridor and through a six-foot-wide door into a small antiseptic room divided by a plastic curtain. Without ceremony, the mortician went to the corner of the curtain and drew it open—on the body. It was long and thin, stretching the full length of the wheeled table under a clean white sheet. The mortician, ready, looked at the sergeant, who nodded for him to go ahead. The mortician drew back the sheet.

It was Chris.

So that execution which had begun on the farm with Chief Janson, and had been temporarily called back by the word *suicide*, was consummated now. Looking at his son, seeing even under the discoloration and swelling the beauty of the boy's spirit manifest in every line and contour of his face, Hook felt his own death, the end of that life he had worked so patiently to rebuild out of the ashes of his wife's passing. Now it was gone. He would never rebuild. He would never really live again.

He longed to touch the body, to throw himself on it. But he knew the repugnance he would feel at its stillness, its death.

"It is my son," he said.

Sergeant Rider moved forward efficiently, turning him from the death table, motioning for the mortician to cover the body, which he did.

"I'm very sorry—he was a fine-looking boy," Rider said. And then it was right down to business again. "I forgot to ask you before—I'll need some identification."

Hook took out his wallet and tried to hand it to the sergeant, but he would not take it.

"Just some I.D.," he said. "Driver's license will do."

Hook fumbled through his wallet till he found it. His hands

were like baseball gloves. The sergeant checked the card, and gave it back.

"Fine. Now I'll just need your signature here, for the boy's effects." He gave Hook a ball pen and held a form up against the wall while Hook signed it. Then he gave Hook the sealed manila envelope.

"The body was posted this afternoon," he said. "I don't have the full report yet, but on the phone the doc told me the cause of death was a broken neck and general trauma. The boy fell about a hundred feet onto the beach. Alcohol in the blood was point-o-four. Which would figure out at about one-o at the time of death. If he wasn't drunk, he was damn close to it. Anyway, we're done with the body. As of now it's yours. Why don't you settle shipping arrangements with Bowman right now? I'll wait in the reception room."

Hook looked at the sergeant. "I have to make a phone call too," he said.

"Sure. No problem. Take your time."

After selecting a casket and paying Mr. Bowman to hold the body through another day, when he planned to fly back to Illinois with it, Hook called home from the mortician's private office. Aunt Marian answered, accepting the collect call in the smallest voice he had ever heard from her. He told her the body was Chris's, and there was a long interval then, over a minute, when no one was able to speak on the other end and he could hear them only in the background, especially Jennifer, crying the word *no!* over and over, and Aunt Marian trying to comfort her but at times breaking down herself. Hook strained to hear Bobby's voice among them, but he could not and he wanted to shout into the phone for Aunt Marian and Arnie to look after the boy above all else. Then Arnie came on, and Hook spoke with him for a few moments and then told him that he wanted to talk to Bobby and Jennifer. In turn, Hook told them that they all still had each other and that they needed each other now more than ever and that *he* needed them too. Finally he told Aunt Marian that he planned to fly home with the body the next day and that he would call again before leaving and tell them when he would arrive, and he asked that Arnie make arrangements with the Rohmer Funeral Home in Banner Hill.

When he hung up, he was drenched in sweat, but he no longer felt so weak, probably because there was nothing left to fear or dread now. He had touched bottom. He had lost all there was to lose.

Mr. Bowman, waiting outside his office, walked with him to the reception room, where they found Sergeant Rider leafing through a magazine. As they came in, he tossed it onto a table and, sighing, grunting, heaved himself to his feet. It had been a long day, his expression said—but a day like any other. Not waiting for him, Hook plunged on outside, into the growing darkness, and somehow made it to the car. Sagging into the front seat, he sat there waiting for the sergeant, finally alone with the knowledge, the certitude that he would never again see Chris alive. Not ever. He would grow old, and he would die. The sun would become a dead star and the earth a cinder circling it. And still he would not see his son alive again. *Never.* At the thought, he heard some dumb animal sound torn out of his body.

The door opened and Rider struggled in behind the wheel. "Get everything taken care of?" he asked.

For a time, Hook could not speak. "We have a lot to talk about," he said finally.

"That's what I'm here for. Wouldn't you rather wait, though? Get some rest? Nothing's gonna change. It'll all be here in the morning."

"I'd like to talk *now*, Sergeant."

Rider started the car, backed around, and headed out of the parking lot. "Okay. But not here. Let's get comfortable. I got a thirst—you mind?"

"No."

"I figured not. You've had a few today yourself, I'd imagine."

Hook decided not to wait on the sergeant's comfort. "The police chief in Banner Hill, he said you called it a suicide."

"That's right."

"I know this is what you'd expect a father to say. Any father. But in this case, it's true, Sergeant. My boy didn't kill himself. I don't care what your facts are. I don't care if you were there and saw it happen. You are wrong. My son did not kill himself."

Rider kept his eyes on the road. "You're right, Mr. Hook. That's what I'd expect a father to say."

Turning, Hook searched the man's beefy countenance for a trace of irony or ridicule. There was none. Past him, out the car window, Hook saw the courthouse again, only this time its facade, for they were moving south on the next street over. The building was floodlit in the darkness, a blazing white temple of tourism as much as justice.

At the next street, Rider turned off and parked, and they got out. Hook followed the sergeant along the walk, lined with hibiscus trees, to a pedestrian causeway—a *paseo*, to the natives, as Hook remembered. On each side were typical picturesque Santa Barbara shops selling antiques, gifts, Persian rugs, securities. They were all closed. At the end, where the paseo turned left, was a sidewalk café with empty umbrella tables surrounding a raised fishpond. Rider led him back into the restaurant itself, which looked as if it had once been the lobby of some small hotel for rich widows, and indeed there were a number of them, or at least their kind, sitting at the tables now, chattering and picking at their food. The sergeant went into a small alcove off the bar and took a corner booth, heaving his bulk into it with a luxurious grunt. Hook sat down across from him. The waitress, like the bartender, gave Rider a big smile and some kidding; he was evidently a favorite there. He ordered a manhattan, a double. Hook ordered coffee.

"All right," Hook told him. "I'm listening."

Rider took out his cigarettes and offered one to Hook, who rejected it. The sergeant lit one himself, taking his time. Hook watched him with a cold, growing anger.

"We'll be served in a minute," Rider explained. "Just as soon not have the girl overhear anything, okay?"

"You could stop talking when she's here," Hook suggested.

"You're a farmer, I believe your police chief said."

Hook nodded, waiting, trying to control himself. "I raise cattle."

"Your boy didn't like it, huh?"

"He was waiting to be drafted. He wanted to see the country."

The waitress came with their order and Rider asked her how her back was. It was better, she said, but not as good as it would be if she would only change jobs, get something where she could lie on her back all day. The sergeant laughed with her. Then she left.

"She's a friend," he explained. "I didn't want to just clam up when she got here. You know how it is."

"She's gone now," Hook said.

Rider took a quick drink, grimly set it down. "So she is. And now you want me to talk. Okay. Here's the story as we have it so far. We think it's the truth—there's no reason for it not to be the truth—but we're not about to call the case closed as yet. On the other hand, there are two witnesses, in substantial agreement, so there doesn't appear to be any need for an inquest. Not yet, anyway."

He took another drink and grimaced, as if he were trying to remember something, and failing. Hook waited for him to continue.

"Yesterday around noon your boy was hitchhiking down here on 101. You go through any time of day you'll see a dozen of them trying to thumb a ride—hippies mostly, but some of them straight, like your kid. I figure he probably got a ride up from L.A. in the morning. Anyway, around noon this girl—this woman —picked him up. She's about twenty-five, divorced, goes by her maiden name, Madera. Elizabeth Madera. A very beautiful girl. Comes from a very old Santa Barbara family." The sergeant's voice heaped scorn on the phrase. "And here that means something special. It's kind of like a hunting license."

"Meaning?"

"Meaning some of 'em swing pretty high, wide, and handsome —and without having to pay dues. In some societies this girl might be labeled a whore. Here, she's aristocracy."

Hook was getting impatient. "Where'd she take him?"

Rider took another drink. "Home. To a beach house she shares with an older woman, a widow name of Dorothy Rubin. Actually it's the Rubin woman's place. Miss Madera just 'stays there'— whatever that means. Anyway, she took him home. He was out there thumbing, probably hoping to get a lift to Big Sur or San Francisco. Instead he gets a ride about three miles up the coast to the beach house. Now you don't have to be a genius to figure what Miss Madera had in mind—or why he accepted. Sex, Mr. Hook."

"Go on."

The sergeant scowled down at his drink. "You're not going to like any of this—probably won't believe it even. But this is the way it was. All I'm telling you is what we have from the statements the two women gave."

"Go on, Sergeant."

"According to Miss Madera, she fixed your boy a big lunch. He ate it. They drank some wine. And then they went to bed." Rider's eyes fell away from Hook's, and he drained the last of his manhattan. "Nothing happened," he went on. "According to her, your son was impotent. He couldn't get it up."

"I know the word," Hook said.

"So your son became depressed. He started drinking vodka instead of wine and late in the afternoon he either passed out or just fell asleep, and didn't wake up till around eight in the evening. Mrs. Rubin was home by then—she works for a public relations firm in town. She wanted to kick your boy out, she says, but Miss Madera wouldn't do it. She—Madera—tried to be nice to him, she says, and talk with him, but he started drinking again. He called himself a fake and a fag, and said he always had been a fag and had never even admitted it to himself, but he knew it now and he couldn't live with the idea. She couldn't reason with him, couldn't even talk with him, so she went to bed. Around eleven. Mrs. Rubin was also getting ready for bed. She says she's used to Miss Madera picking up strays—that the girl's just got too big a heart for her own good. Mrs. Rubin didn't like it that your son was there and drinking, but it didn't bother her too much either. His whole generation are crybabies, she says. So when he kept talking about having nothing to live for, it didn't really faze her."

Hook broke in, unable to keep from repeating the phrase. *"Nothing to live for?"*

Rider nodded. "That's what he kept saying, that he had nothing to live for. But Mrs. Rubin says it didn't bother her because he was drunk. 'Just a drunk kid feeling sorry for himself'—I think that was how she put it. Anyway, she went into the bathroom to do whatever it is women do before they go to bed. And when she came out, he wasn't where she'd left him in the living room. He was gone. She went out onto the wood deck that runs across the sea side of the house. And then she saw him. He had gone down the steps from the deck and had walked right out to the edge of the cliff above the beach. As she watched him, he drew back his arms—" The sergeant drew back his own arms, demonstrating. "And he jumped. Without saying a word."

The sergeant settled back, studying Hook for a reaction, which Hook was sure showed in his eyes. From the beginning of the policeman's tale, the first mention of the sex and impotence, Hook's anger had been growing, until now it was all cold rage.

"Just like that, huh?" he said. "*And he jumped. Without saying a word.*"

The sergeant shrugged helplessly. It was not his story, the gesture said. He was only recounting what he had been told. "You don't believe it," he said matter-of-factly.

"Because it isn't true, Sergeant."

Rider tipped up his empty glass, taking an ice cube in his mouth. Reflectively sucking on it, he asked if Hook could produce any rebuttal testimony, any girls Chris had known and had sex with.

"As far as I know, he was a virgin."

"That don't help."

"So I have to prove his innocence," Hook observed. "But this Madera woman doesn't have to prove his guilt."

The sergeant shook his head. "She proved nothing. All she did was give us a *possible* motive for an act that was *witnessed* by another person. Alone, either of their statements might be suspect, but together they amount to something. And wishing it was otherwise won't change a thing. You've got to have facts. Relevant facts."

"Suppose I flew out his brother and sister and some of his friends from high school, and you talked to them? Suppose you found out that very few young men ever had more to live for than my son?"

"Kids change, Mr. Hook." The sergeant signaled for another drink, and asked Hook if he would like something besides coffee. Would he like to eat?

Hook ignored the questions. "He was a track star, Sergeant. A miler. He was an honor student. He was elected president of his senior class without even wanting the job, or even running for it. He was loved by—" But suddenly Hook could not continue. To say another word would have been to cry out, to rage.

The sergeant mumbled something about what a damn shame it all was, and that Chris had indeed been a fine-looking boy.

The waitress served the sergeant's drink and exchanged Hook's cup of cold coffee for a steaming hot one. And there was no banter this time.

When she left, Rider apparently had decided it was time for straight talk and unpulled punches. "He may have been all that, Mr. Hook, but I'm afraid it doesn't cut any ice. There's still Mrs. Rubin's statement. She saw him jump. *Saw him*." The sergeant punctuated his words by tossing off a good part of his drink.

"Why should she lie?" Hook asked him, and saw in the sergeant's eyes that it was just the question the man had been waiting for, a trump card in a game he did not particularly care to win.

"That's exactly the point, Mr. Hook. What reason would she have to lie about your boy? *None*. She didn't even know him."

"Why don't we ask her? Why don't we go there now?"

Rider shook his head. "Maybe tomorrow. I asked both of them today if someone came to identify the body, would they mind talking with them. No dice. And it's understandable, I guess. They're both overwrought, especially the Rubin woman."

"I feel for them."

Rider met Hook's eyes for a moment longer and then looked down at his drink. In his jaw a muscle tightened, relaxed, tightened again. He was not enjoying himself.

"Isn't it a fundamental right to face one's accuser?" Hook asked him.

"They're not accusing you of anything. Or your son."

33

"Just of killing himself."

The sergeant wearily shook his head. "Again—one of them claims to have *witnessed* the act—that's all."

"And the other neatly supplies the motive."

Rider put his face in his hands and rubbed it, mauled it, like an infant waking. He sighed. "Mr. Hook, please try to understand this. The death happened a few minutes after midnight *on this very day*. So there's still a heckuva lot of investigating to be done, questions that will undoubtedly come up—and be answered. In our book right now the cause of death is listed as *undetermined*. And that's just what it is. It *appears* to be a suicide at this point, and that's about all we can say. If new facts come up, and those facts indicate something besides suicide—don't worry, an inquest will be held. And if anybody seems to be guilty of anything, they will be indicted. It's that simple. We're not in the business of covering things up. Or protecting anybody. And I mean *anybody*."

Hook nodded understanding, concurrence. But nothing had changed as far as he was concerned. "I still want to talk to them."

"Maybe tomorrow," Rider repeated. "I'll try again tomorrow."

"Tonight, Sergeant."

Rider shook his head again. "No chance."

Hook lit a cigarette. He wanted to be rid of the sergeant now. He had heard all he needed or cared to hear—from him. Rider asked him if he had had anything to eat all day. Had he checked into a motel yet? Did he want to collapse?

"I'll be all right, Sergeant. I can take care of myself."

Rider looked at his watch. "It's seven. Can I drop you anywhere? Come on, let me drive you to a motel. You need rest. You gotta be worn out."

"I'll be all right," Hook repeated. "Thank you for your trouble."

The sergeant looked exasperated. "I just can't leave you here like this," he protested. "At least let me drive you to a motel. Get you checked in."

"I think I'll stay here, Sergeant. Have a few drinks, eat something, then take a cab to a motel. I'll be fine. Don't worry about me." Hook said it calmly, easily, and he saw in the sergeant's eyes, in the sudden resignation there, that his words had done the job.

Shrugging agreement, Rider squeezed out of the booth and stood up, taking the bar check with him.

"Okay then. Suit yourself," he said. "You give me a call in the morning, though, all right? I'll pick you up and we'll go out to the scene—whether the ladies feel like talking or not." And suddenly his hand was on Hook's shoulder, in a brief impulsive contact that seemed to surprise him as much as it did Hook. "You take it easy, now," he said.

And then he was gone.

Alone, Hook sat facing the bare wall in the alcove. He knew that within an hour he would be there, at the place where his son had died, and he knew it would be an act of madness to some degree, an act without any of his usual caution or circumspection. So he wondered about his sanity at the moment. His eldest son was lying on a table under a sheet a half-dozen blocks away, and yet here he was, not weeping, not lying on some lonely motel bed staring at the ceiling and longing that the ache in his heart presaged some final fatal bursting, not in the expectation that he would then be with his wife and son again in some mystic nether dimension but rather that he would simply be free once and for all time, free of life, no longer an inmate of this crowded planetary madhouse where nature somehow had accomplished the crowning monstrosity of developing a race of mortal gods, of thinking animals, beings designed for no other purpose, it seemed, than to suffer.

That should have been his reaction, Hook felt. Instead, here he was, not at all the bitter philosophic mourner of his expectations but suddenly all cold blood and colder rage—and suddenly hungry too, he realized, as the waitress came to his table to warm his coffee. He ordered a T-bone steak dinner and a vodka on ice.

When the waitress served his drink she asked him if he would like to switch to the other side of the table, so that he would not be facing the wall. He told her no, that he would stay where he was.

The cab driver who answered his call turned out not to be the one who had driven him in from the airport, and for that Hook was grateful. This one was old and taciturn, a Mexican-American with wine on his breath, and when Hook told him where he wanted to go, all the man did was grunt before throwing the battered Ford into gear and driving off. The telephone book listed Dorothy Rubin's address as 2010 Cliff Drive, a road Hook remembered from the old days, when Mrs. Cunningham had treated him to a champagne picnic on a lonely stretch of beach west of the city. They had stayed there well past nightfall, making love part of the time but mostly just sitting together huddled between blankets and wordlessly communing with the driftwood fire he had built. That night she had gone down on him for the first time and he remembered it afterwards not only as one of the most intensely pleasurable experiences of his life but also liberating, even shattering, for until then his innocence was such that he had thought of the act only in relation to whores and perverts. Back at the hotel she had continued his education by having him join her in the bathtub, where they spent almost an hour drinking more champagne and soaping the sea salt off each other's body, and where a Mexican-American waiter bringing in a late-night supper saw them together through the open bathroom door. His expression, a comic mask of studied indifference in which his black eyes kept drifting rebelliously to the open door, set them laughing like the half-drunk lovers they were, once he had left the suite.

Now, watching the old man as he wheeled the car through the December night, Hook reflected that in this age of cataclysmic change, things really had not changed all that much, not even in twenty-five years. The Mexican-Americans, like the blacks, were still serving the white man, only now the whites had been taught to feel guilt at that servitude.

He could not see much outside the cab. There were more houses than he remembered, more lights, and then suddenly they were past the lights, driving through darkness up a steep curve in the road until they came to a level again, and he was able to see lights out at sea. Trees, hills, a few houses kept moving between him and the ocean, blocking his view of it. After a while the driver slowed the cab and began checking the rural mailboxes along the road. Finally he turned in at a narrow blacktop lane where three mailboxes rested on an ornate wrought-iron frame.

"Man, I hope you got friends waiting for you up there," he said.

In the darkness ahead a few dim lights burned forlornly. Hook asked him what he meant, wondering if the man had heard about the accident and was referring to it.

"It very dark is all."

Hook asked the man to come back for him in an hour.

"That depend."

Ahead, the headlights picked the name Rubin out of the darkness—a small reflector-type sign on the carport of the first of three houses spread along the cliff.

"On what?" Hook asked. "Your tip?"

Braking, the driver gave an affirmative shrug.

Hook looked at the meter. It read $3.05. He took out a five-dollar bill and gave it to him. "Will that do it?"

The old man was unimpressed, but he allowed that he would come back in an hour.

"At ten?"

The man nodded, bored by the discussion. Hook got out. The cab backed around and drove off, leaving him alone in the driveway facing the rear of the house. And suddenly Hook felt a tremor of panic, for it struck him that he had not prepared for this moment at all, had let his mind wander throughout the drive from downtown, as if there were no question that once he confronted the women they would both automatically break down and confess to him that truth which Sergeant Rider with all the powers and sanctions of his office had not been able to elicit in hours of questioning. Then just as suddenly Hook knew the way he would go, and figured he must have known all along in some secret circuit of his being, and that had been the reason for his aplomb in the cab. He would have to play the innocent, of course, the hick, the stolid bereft peasant come to view the site of his son's passing, not unlike a typical Santa Barbara tourist making the rounds before glumly picking up his mementoes—in this case the broken body of his son—and going home to wherever it was he came from.

He pressed a button next to the back door. Inside, chimes sounded.

As he waited, Hook surveyed the scene, what he could see of it in the soft yellow light of the twin lantern-type lamps bracketing the driveway. Inside the carport were two sports cars: a maroon Jaguar XK–E and a white Triumph convertible. Behind them, parked in the driveway, was a Volkswagen sedan whose pastel color he could not be sure of in the yellow light, though he could make out the California license plate: 847AOF. Like the other two cars, it had a *Douglas for Congress* sticker on the bumper. The car was important. It meant that the two women were not alone. Beyond it, on the other side of the driveway, a scraggly lawn led to a row of eucalyptus trees that to Hook's Midwestern eyes looked like battlefield casualties, blasted and torn, their bark hanging in tatters about the bare bones of their trunks. Through the trees he could see the lights of the other two houses, which, like Mrs. Rubin's, were low and sprawling and of the same glassy modern design, all probably the work of the same architect.

Now a light came on over the door and someone looked out at him from behind the drapes in a floor-to-ceiling window to his right. Finally the door opened a crack, still chained.

"Yes?" It was a woman.

"I'm the father of Christopher Hook."

Her face went pale, a cold puffy face sticking out of a fake leopard housecoat. Her hair was wound up in rollers.

"What do you want? What are you doing here?"

Somehow Hook got it out. "My son died here today."

"We told Sergeant Rider all——"

"Who is it?" It was a man's voice.

The woman turned away from the door. "It's the father, for Christ sake!"

"Let me talk to him." Now the man appeared in the opening, a young man, small, blond, androgynous, wearing an old-fashioned tweed suit with a vest, a button-down shirt and paisley tie. His face was ashen.

"What did you want, sir?"

"I'm not here to hurt anybody," Hook reassured him. "I just want to see what happened. *Where* it happened."

The face relaxed. "Yes. Of course—come in."

He closed the door to unchain it, but for a time it remained the way it was, closed. Hook could hear the woman protesting. "I just don't want him in here, that's all! He's got no business here! I told the sergeant!"

He heard the young man trying to quiet her and then their voices became almost inaudible as they moved away from the door, but he did catch the young man's final words: *"Think! Dorothy! Use your head!"* Then after a few moments Hook heard the chain being slipped out of its rail, and the door opened. The young man smiled apologetically.

"Come in, Mr. Hook. And please forgive us. It's been a hard day for Mrs. Rubin too—I mean besides yourself. Please accept our sympathy."

It was an oddly formal little speech, like a child's rote recitation in Sunday school. Entering, Hook said nothing, and the young man closed the door behind him. He was smaller than Hook had judged from outside, almost a half-foot shorter than Hook's own six-one. He could have been twenty-four or thirty; Hook could not be sure.

"My name's Ferguson," he said. "Richard Ferguson. Mrs. Rubin and I work for the same company. I thought I'd stop by tonight and see if I could help. It's been a real trauma—a real shock for both of them."

So he was not expected to know the word *trauma*. It was a good sign. "Both?" Hook asked.

"Miss Madera. She lives here with Mrs. Rubin. She was here when the—when the accident occurred."

Hook nodded comprehension, then turned, looking for the women, but neither of them was in evidence. The house was a split-level. He and Ferguson were on the upper level now; to his right was a kitchenette and dining bar, to his left a hallway, probably leading to a bedroom and bath. In front was a balustrade overlooking a handsomely furnished living room with a stone fireplace, beamed ceiling, and a front glass wall looking out on a broad redwood deck and, beyond, in darkness, the cliffs and the ocean. A wood fire hissed in the fireplace.

He followed Ferguson down the carpeted stairway to the living room. The young man headed for the bar across the room.

"Would you like a drink, Mr. Hook?"

"No thank you. I had a couple on the plane. I flew in this afternoon." It sounded stupid. It would do.

Ferguson poured a few fingers of Black Label scotch into a glass and sipped at it.

"I admire your strength," he told Hook. "I mean, how you can come here tonight. I don't think that I——"

"I'd like to talk with the women."

"Of course. Mrs. Rubin will be right back out. But she is upset. She can't talk long. You do understand, I hope. I mean, the poor woman—" At Hook's glance, he fell abruptly silent.

"I'd like to talk with Miss Madera too."

"Oh, she's not here. She's not in yet."

"There are three cars in back."

In Ferguson's alert eyes Hook saw that his words had been a mistake. The young man was on guard now, warned.

"I mean she's outside," he said. "Walking. She's a great walker, Liz is."

"Maybe we could find her."

"I wouldn't know where to look in the dark. She walks on the beach. She could be anywhere."

"She wasn't a witness anyway. She didn't see anything." It was the woman again, Mrs. Rubin, coming down from the upper level. She was dressed as before, but with the addition of a scarf over her hair and rollers.

"But you did," Hook said.

"Yes, I did."

"Sergeant Rider told me about it. What happened. What you saw."

"Then why are you here?"

"I don't know. Just to see where it happened, I guess. See if you could add anything."

Mrs. Rubin sat down on the davenport and, flipping open a box on the coffee table, took out a cigarette and lit it, her movements those of a man, a big man, rough, careless. Watching her, Hook wondered if that was why she had a younger woman living with her, as a mate, a lover, someone to play female to her tough ballsy male.

"There's nothing to add," she said. "I don't even want to talk about it. I'm sorry for you and your family but I'm afraid this whole thing just isn't our concern. Your boy wasn't invited here, Mr. Hook—certainly not to stay. We both tried to get him to leave. Frankly, what it all boils down to is he just happened to choose our place to kill himself. It's that simple."

"Dorothy, for Christ sake!" Ferguson remonstrated.

"Well, it's the truth, isn't it? And isn't that what this gentleman came here for—the truth?"

Hook said nothing, for fear his voice would break. He went over to the fireplace and stood there staring down at the blaze, trying to keep control of himself. Then Ferguson was at his side, holding out a drink.

"Scotch," the young man said.

As he took the drink, Hook saw something move out on the deck, beyond the glass wall. It was the young woman. She was just standing there in the darkness, looking at him. As Sergeant Rider had said, she was beautiful, strikingly beautiful, with thick long black hair parted in the middle and hanging sea-damp down around a finely shaped face dominated by large grave eyes. She made no move to come on in.

"Mrs. Rubin is very upset," Ferguson explained again. "She's not herself."

Hook turned from the window in time to see Mrs. Rubin angrily bite off a fresh outburst at a look from the little man. Evidently Hook had underestimated Ferguson's power, and it bothered him. He could not get a true reading on their relationship, who was running whom. But at the moment he was more interested in the girl, who slid open one of the glass doors leading to the deck and came in now, with a surge of cold salty air. She closed the door behind her and stood there hugging her arms, trying to get warm. She was wearing faded jeans and a black turtleneck sweater. Her feet were bare.

"This is Mr. Hook," Ferguson told her. "He's the father of the boy."

She said nothing, registered nothing.

Ferguson looked at Hook in panic. "Miss Madera."

Hook nodded, but said nothing in the face of her reaction to him, the way her eyes unblinkingly regarded him, not with hostility so much as a kind of unashamed, even arrogant, self-assertion.

"Just what can we tell you? What is it you want to know?" It was Mrs. Rubin.

Hook turned to her. "I can't believe my son would kill himself."

"Well, I saw him." She stubbed out her cigarette. "Maybe he was on dope. Maybe he thought he could fly. They do, you know, these kids. It happens."

"But didn't my son do it on purpose? Because he had 'nothing to live for'?"

Mrs. Rubin's eyes went flat with anger. She almost smiled. "So you don't want to be spared, huh? You want it right in the gut."

"I want to know what happened."

"You *know* what happened! You said you talked to Sergeant Rider already. So you already know what our statements are."

"And there's no change in them?"

"How could there be? We can't very well change what happened, can we?"

Hook looked at Miss Madera, who immediately turned away and went over to the fireplace. "Is there anything you can tell me?" he asked.

Still not looking at him, she shook her head. Hook waited a few moments to see if she would change her mind, but she continued to stand there staring down at the fire, with her back to him. Hook turned to Ferguson.

"I'd like to see where it happened," he said.

"The cliff, you mean?"

"The cliff."

Glancing nervously at Mrs. Rubin, the young man nodded. "All right. Sure. But I'll have to get a flashlight. It's in the kitchen, Dorothy?"

She was lighting another cigarette. "Top right-hand drawer."

As Ferguson hurried up the stairs to the kitchenette, Hook moved closer to the fireplace, so that Miss Madera had no choice but to meet his eyes or turn away again and admit that she could not face him.

"Did he—did my son also say it to you? That he had nothing to live for?"

Again she shook her head. "I had gone to bed."

It was the first time he had heard her voice, and it held no surprises for him, was both soft and strong, with the unmistakable timbre of old money, authority.

"That was after he had 'failed' with you." Hook threw it at her without warning, a sucker punch, and suddenly her dark eyes shone with tears. Again she turned away from him.

But Mrs. Rubin came charging to the rescue, jumping up from the davenport. "Can't you see she's had it, for Christ sake! Just because you don't have any feelings, buster—coming here like this——"

"Shut up, Dorothy." Miss Madera said it quietly, easily, and when the big woman promptly lapsed into silence Hook was again at a loss to understand the relationship the three of them had with each other.

Now Miss Madera faced him squarely. "I just can't talk about it now, Mr. Hook. I'm sorry."

She swept past him then, heading for the back of the house. At the same time, Ferguson came down the stairs from the kitchen, carrying the flashlight. Watching him walk, the almost female hips swishing toward him, Hook wondered if the young man's effeminacy might not be just skin-deep, a covering for something weasel-tough and cunning underneath. Now Ferguson flipped on the deck lights outside.

"When Mrs. Rubin went into the bathroom to get ready for bed, your boy was right there, drinking," he said, indicating a chair close to the bar. "And when she came out he was gone. She turned on the light. This door was open." He slid open the glass deck door, and Hook followed him outside, onto the deck. "So she came out here to see where he was. As you can see, with the light on you can see to the edge of the cliff. He was standing——"

"I know all that," Hook cut in, heading for the end of the deck, where he went down the stairs. Ferguson followed him across the lawn, which became scraggly and rough as they neared the cliff edge. There, Hook took the flashlight from him and played it along the cliff face and the beach below, a dark-gray strip against which the surf came rolling in white and frothy and then turned coal-black as it slipped back into the sea. The cliff itself was not sheer; even leaping outwards, pushing off, a man would have struck it on the way down.

"It's pretty frightening now, at night," Ferguson said. "But during the day it can be quite beautiful. Most days you can see the islands."

Turning, Hook played the flashlight along the top of the cliff, thrusting its faint white finger through the eucalyptus trees at the two other houses. The nearest was at least two hundred feet away, so it was understandable that no one in either house had seen or heard a thing. Hook turned off the flashlight. As he handed it back to Ferguson he saw Miss Madera standing on the deck watching them. She had changed her clothes.

Hook asked Ferguson about her. "Does she work for the same people as you and Mrs. Rubin?"

"No. Liz doesn't work."

"Who is it you work for?"

"Jack Douglas. He's running for Congress."

"What are you—his campaign manager?"

"In a way, yes."

"And Mrs. Rubin?"

"Well, you see, we both are part of Jack Douglas Associates. It's a local P.R. firm. Public relations," Ferguson explained. "And now Jack is—well he's between campaigns, actually. He came very close to winning it last year. So we're already pointing for next November."

"And where does Miss Madera fit in?"

"She doesn't."

"Just lives here, huh?"

"She's a friend of Mrs. Rubin, that's all."

Hook contemplated the bland mask of Ferguson's face. "You resent these questions?"

"Not at all. I know what you must be going through. I'd want answers too, in your place. But—" And suddenly the mask was sweating.

"But what?"

"Nothing. It's not important. I just don't know if I'd have the strength to come here like this. I mean, so soon."

"Maybe my son and I weren't close."

"That would explain it."

"Or maybe people in shock do strange things."

"But would they know they're in shock?"

"Some might."

The young man shivered visibly. "I'd better get back in," he said. "I should have worn a coat."

When they got back on the deck, Miss Madera asked Hook if he had a ride back to town and he told her that he had a cab coming.

"I'll drive you," she said.

Ferguson laughed uneasily. "He just said he had a cab coming, Liz."

"That's all right," Hook said. "I can leave money for the cab."

Now Ferguson looked alarmed. "No, I really don't think she should, Mr. Hook. Not the way she's been feeling today. If you don't want to take the cab, I can drive you. I was going to leave soon anyway."

But Liz Madera was not listening. She had started down the deck stairway. "We can go around the side," she said. "I already have my keys."

"Liz, you better not! I'm telling you!"

Hook had already taken out a five-dollar bill and now as he held it out to Ferguson, the little man, his face scarlet, could barely bring himself to look at Hook. It had been a mistake, his outburst, and they both knew it and knew the other knew it.

Taking the bill now, Ferguson tried to smile. "It's been a rough day," he said.

"Yes, it has." Leaving him there, Hook followed Miss Madera around the house to the garage.

Hook had never ridden in a Jaguar XK–E before, and he found the experience something like sealing oneself up in a bomb, albeit a bomb that held rigidly to the twisting coast road despite the fact that Miss Madera drove as if sixty miles an hour were the legal minimum. In the cramped quarters, however, it was not the car he was aware of but its driver. She had changed into a blue miniskirted dress with shiny knee-high black boots and a matching short raincoat that left her thighs exposed inches from his own hand tightly gripping his knee. And there was also the smell of her, something subtler than perfume, more natural, more animal, perhaps sea air melded with the salts of her own sweat, or simply some strangely clean and cutting body musk—Hook did not know. But he knew its effect. There had been times in the years since Kate's death when he had thought the sex urge in him was almost dead, often three and four weeks at a time when he would not even have to give the matter thought, and then suddenly it would be upon him again, like a malarial fever, and he would have to invent some excuse to go to St. Louis, where he would find release with a whore or pickup. Now he felt that same fever—on the day of his son's death, and toward this woman who probably had caused that death—and it filled him with self-contempt. He looked over at her in anger, trying to concentrate only on the matter at hand, which was to get some sort of reading on her motive for driving him back to town, but all he could see in the stark white glow of the dashboard was the woman, the dark eyes and sensuous mouth, and they told him nothing. So he decided to ask.

"Why did you want to drive me?"

She kept her eyes on the road. "I don't know."

"Wasn't it to talk, Miss Madera? Don't we have a lot to talk about?"

She shook her head, not in denial so much as puzzlement, doubt. "I couldn't just leave it the way it was, that's all. I mean Dorothy and Richard letting you come in, showing you where it happened, and saying so long, that's it, tough luck." Her eyes filled with tears again. "I am so sorry, Mr. Hook. I am so sorry."

Hook looked away from her tears. "I still want you to tell me about it."

But she preferred to change the subject, remarking that he did not have a bag. He told her that he had left it in Sergeant Rider's car.

"Can you get along?" she asked.

"No problem."

She had turned onto the oceanfront drive by now and they were growling past the city marina, with its hundreds of yachts rocking expensively in the light swells of the harbor. Ahead, on the city side of the drive, were the tourist motels, each with its own discreet sign of identification, no flashing neon stars or arrows to dragoon one in off the street, for of course this was Santa Barbara, Hook remembered, and not apple-pie America. Across from the motels and restaurants was the long scimitar of sand he had seen from the air, and in between, lining both sides of the road, twin rows of date palms with their shabby skirts of dead fronds, which he had found ugly even as a youngster in the Navy. "Like French ticklers on a hairy cock," a fellow Midwestern swabbie had described the trees then, and as far as Hook could see the simile was still every bit as accurate as it was gross.

"You won't talk about it?" he asked her.

She did not answer.

"All right, then. Any motel will do."

But she did not turn in as they passed the first few blocks of motels.

"I could use a drink," she said. "In fact, I need a drink. Will you have one with me?"

Hook looked at her. "In silence?"

She shook her head. "Any way you want."

"All right," he said. "Sure."

She turned in at a place that looked at first glance like some kind of rustic wood fort, with its walls canted inwards, pyramid style, as if it had been designed against that revolutionary day when the unwanted would want in. But going inside, Hook saw that the "wood" walls were actually poured concrete and the rusticity strictly modern. The place was sumptuous, dark, candle-lit—and almost abandoned. A young woman in a muumuu-type dress led them past a few couples drinking around a hexagonal table in the center of which a gas fire blazed around fake wood.

A half-dozen people were at the bar; a few couples sat drinking alone at tables; and one large noisy group was having dinner at three tables pulled together across the room.

The hostess showed them to a small table against the back wall and took their order, a vodka on ice for Hook and a daiquiri for Miss Madera. She got out a cigarette and lit it with the table candle, ignoring the match he was about to light, so he used it on a cigarette of his own. For a few moments longer the two of them just sat there, she studying him with a cool open gaze, barren of any slightest hint of fear or defensiveness or hostility, so Hook saw no reason not to go to the heart of the matter.

"In the car," he said. "When you said you were sorry——"

"Yes."

"I meant to ask you *why*. Was it your fault, Miss Madera? His death?"

She did not even blink. "In a way, yes. If I hadn't picked him up, the whole thing might not have happened."

"But that's all? There's no other way you were at fault?"

"I wish I could say there was. I have a feeling it would help you."

"You mean I want someone to blame. Someone to put it all on."

She regarded him coolly, without pity now. "It's only natural, isn't it? It must be a hard thing to accept, that your child would kill himself. You'd want to believe anything but that."

"Yes, you would."

"And you won't accept it, will you? I can see that. You never will accept it."

Again he agreed with her. "That's right. I never will."

As the waitress served their drinks now, Miss Madera looked down at the table. When they were alone again she stirred her daiquiri, sipped at it, and set it down, still not looking at him.

"All right then," she said. "Blame me. I did pick him up. I don't deny that. If I hadn't, he wouldn't have died *where* he did. That at least is true."

"Tell me about it."

"You already know about it. Sergeant Rider must have told you."

"I want to hear it from you."

"I suppose he made it sound like something I do all the time, picking up hitchhikers. Picking up young men."

"But you don't."

"Never before."

"Why this once?"

"I don't know. Just *him*, I guess. Your son. The way he looked." She shook her head ruefully. Her eyes were heavy with anguish and puzzlement.

Hook took a long drink of his vodka and set the glass down. "Go on," he said.

"Well, it just happened, that's all. I didn't plan it. They're always lined up there on 101, dozens of them sometimes, and most of them are creeps, you know. Losers. Drug freaks. And there are these four stoplights right in a row, so you usually hit one of them, and that's when the hitchhikers come right up to the car, practically crawl in with you, so I usually lock the door." Again the look of pain came into her eyes. "*He* didn't do that. He just stood there, looking at me for a moment, and then he looked away as I looked back at him. But it was the *way* he did it, you know? With a touch of shyness. Or decency. Or—" Her eyes ransacked the room for help. "He was, somehow—*beautiful*, you know?"

Hook said nothing.

"I don't mean just his looks."

"I know." Hook studied her face, avid now, open, trusting him. It was a mistake on her part. "This boy who had nothing to live for," he said.

She reacted as if he had slapped her hard, going pale for a moment, then flushing with anger and resentment as she recovered her balance. "That's right," she said. "And maybe it doesn't make any sense. But I can't help that. It happened just the way we told the sergeant. It is the truth, Mr. Hook. It is the sickening, awful, horrible truth."

Hook said nothing. The vodka, flat, went down like water.

"I wish I could help you," she went on. "I wish I could change it all, make it different than it is. But I can't."

"You picked him up around noon yesterday."

49

"Yes. I guess maybe I thought he was hungry. Anyway, I was lonely. I wanted to talk with someone."

"And you took him to your place then."

Stabbing out her cigarette, she nodded. "I made him a big lunch. French toast and bacon and scrambled eggs. I think he ate a half-dozen by himself."

"So he wasn't feeling too bad then."

"I guess not."

"Did you drink then?"

"We opened a bottle of Chablis. I like white wine. He said he did too."

"And all of this time the two of you talked?"

"Yes."

"What about?"

She lifted her glass and took a drink. Hook had the feeling that she was buying time, using it to think very hard and fast.

She put down her glass. "Mostly me, I'm afraid. I used him, your son. I admit that. You see, I'm not much of a success at life, Mr. Hook. Not at college, not at marriage, not at a career. I'm sort of a disadvantaged minority of one, you might say. The Maderas go way back, back to the glorious old days of Spanish California. Saddlemakers, we were at first. And then we sold real estate for a few generations. And now—well, now my father simply sells the name *Madera*. To rich widows, one at a time. In fact, I hear the elegant old bastard still lives around here somewhere, cleaning paintbrushes for some fat rich old lady *artiste*. But I don't worry about him, because when she passes on—and I believe that's the way her kind goes—well, there'll still be another ten thousand more just like her for him to choose from. We grow them here in Santa Barbara—widows who do watercolors and wear floppy hats and sandals, and keep two-legged lap dogs with pedigrees. Preferably Spanish."

Hook was finding it difficult to sort out what she was saying, for the alcohol had reached him all of a sudden, and he was beginning to feel his exhaustion. It seemed like a month ago that he had gotten out of bed on the farm at his usual five-thirty, and in fact it had been almost twenty hours, he estimated, for it was about eleven Pacific time now. He pushed his drink away and dragged deeply on his cigarette, determined to see the evening through.

"And that's what you talked to my son about?" he said.

She smiled sadly, almost sardonically. "Not really. I guess I'm just trying to change the subject. The other hurts. I guess I just don't have your particular kind of sang-froid."

Hook ignored her thrust. "When you talked—was he morose then? Was he depressed?"

"Not then, no. Not till—afterwards."

"You mean *after* he failed. After he couldn't make love to you."

Nodding, Miss Madera looked at him wonderingly. "You must be a glutton for punishment."

"These were the last hours of his life," he said. "I want to know about them."

"You're very tough, aren't you? Or is it just unfeeling?"

Watching her, Hook dragged again on his cigarette, exhaled. Through the smoke her eyes looked brilliant with something like outrage. "Maybe you felt more for him than I did," he said. "You think that could be it?"

"You tell me."

Hook shook his head. "I don't have to, Miss Madera. I know what I felt for my son."

"Then why aren't you with him? Why aren't you mourning?" It was an accusation.

"There'll be time enough for that." In his exhaustion Hook had to speak very slowly and carefully. "Right now I'm more interested in his life, the kind of life he lived. The kind of boy he was. I don't want anyone taking that away from him now, after he's gone."

Miss Madera was looking down at her empty glass, revolving it slowly. She did not look up at him.

"And what kind of life was that, Mr. Hook?"

But before he could say anything, the waitress came to the table again and Hook ordered another daiquiri for Miss Madera, nothing for himself.

"Was it pastoral and blissful?" she asked, all irony now. "Was it so masculine there was absolutely no chance that he——"

"It was a good life," Hook cut in. And then he went on flatly, coldly, as if he were reading the bill of fare on the restaurant's menu. "His mother died about seven years ago in a car crash. I have two other children, a boy sixteen and a girl fifteen. They were close. But each was closer to Chris. My aunt and her husband also live with us. The farm is a large one by Midwest standards, over a thousand acres. We raise Black Angus cattle. It's a good farm. And beautiful country, colder than this, and hotter too, and harder. But we like it. We've always been happy there. Chris was happy there. He was a very popular boy. I don't like the word, but it fits in his case. He was well-liked. Girls and boys and men and old ladies—they all liked him. And we— we loved him. He was generous and decent. And bright. And strong. And he was funny too, in his way. He made you smile more than laugh."

Hook had the feeling that Miss Madera was forcing herself to meet his eyes, for throughout this speech of his she sat staring rigidly at him, almost not blinking. Her expression was flat, neutral.

"That's the boy who left us a month ago," Hook went on. "That's the boy who jumped off your cliff because he had nothing to live for."

Now she looked away, across the room at the fire blazing in the center of the drinking couples, who were all laughing loudly at something. "People change," she said.

Hook shook his head in weariness and futility. "Miss Madera, don't you think a father would know whether his son was queer or not? Don't you think I ever overheard my boys talking, and knew something about their sex life?"

Hook thought he saw a wetness in her eyes again. She was pushing back her chair, preparing to get up.

"I have to go now," she said. "I really do. It's late. I'm sorry for you. I'm sorry for everything, Mr. Hook. I really am."

And now there was no doubt about her tears. They shone in the firelight. He reached out and took hold of her wrist, holding her there at the table a moment longer. Time had run out; what had to be said he would say now.

"I'm not trying to find out if your version is the truth. I know it isn't. I know you lied—that you all lied. But I have to find out why. I have to find out what really did happen."

She looked down at her wrist in his hand, and as he relaxed his grip she pulled her arm free slowly, almost voluptuously, watching him with her huge grave eyes.

"I'll find out," he told her. "I'll find the truth if I have to come here and live."

"Will that bring him back?"

"You admit you lied, then?"

"No. I'm just saying it won't bring him back. Nothing will bring him back. Ever."

Somewhere Hook found his voice. "I know that. But you want to take more than his life. And I won't let you have it."

He struggled to his feet as she got up from the table now. She repeated that she had to leave. She asked him if he wanted a ride to a motel.

"It's not far," he told her. "I can walk."

She started to say something more, and then just turned and walked away. Watching her, Hook was reminded of Hemingway's reference to Lady Brett as having the lines of a racing yacht, for that is what Liz Madera's progress across the room was like, a sleek craft moving through still water, trailing waves of attention that spread ever wider through the small crowd until she finally disappeared out the front door. For some reason it angered him that she was so attractive, and that her anguish or fear or whatever it was she was feeling made her seem even more so to him, giving weight and substance to her beauty.

He signaled for the waitress and she came almost immediately, a young girl, very mod, like the other waitresses, the busboys, the girl in the muumuu. As he gave her money for the drinks and a tip, he asked her if she knew the woman he had been drinking with, and she smiled quizzically, wrinkling her nose.

"But you were with her," she protested.

"I know her name, that's all. I want to know more about her."

The girl's amusement began to die. "Oh, I guess I've seen her, but I don't know her."

On impulse, Hook took another five-dollar bill out of his wallet. "Ask some of your friends that work here, will you? Anybody can tell me about her, I'll give them this." He showed her the bill.

Nodding, but looking frightened now, she left him and went over to one of the bartenders, an older man who appeared to be in charge of things. She said something to him and he looked across the room at Hook and then back at the girl and shook his head. Then both of them returned to work, ignoring him. Hook waited a few minutes, finishing a cigarette. Then he got up and left.

Outside, the coolness of the night struck him as fresh as rainfall, even though it smelled of the sea, that fabled odor of fish and brine that to him was not half so sweet as the bouquet of spring clover. Above the palms across the street the moon had turned the deserted beach into an extension of itself, white and cold and barren.

He had crossed State Street and was halfway up the next block, heading toward the row of motels there, when he heard footfalls behind him. Turning, he saw one of the busboys from the restaurant coming after him, running across the street against the traffic light. By the time he reached Hook, he was almost out of breath.

"Mister, you serious about that five bucks?"

"Yes. Why? You know her?"

"Liz Madera? Sure. Who don't?"

"I don't."

"She's a swinger."

"That, I know. Tell me what I don't know."

The boy was short and muscular, shivering in white chinos and a Hawaiian shirt. "Like what?"

"Whatever you can think of."

The youth grinned, not very attractively. "For one thing, you won't get anywhere with her. She's Jack Douglas's girl."

"The man who runs for Congress?"

"Among other things."

"What other things?"

"Like he's just a wheel, that's all. He'd be pretty tough competition."

"Is he married?"

"Sure. He's establishment, man. But not too establishment, if you know what I mean."

It was something, perhaps everything. And anyway Hook was too exhausted to stand there any longer, so he took the five-dollar bill out of his pocket and gave it to the youth, who thanked him.

"One more thing," Hook said. "Did you hear about the boy who was killed this morning, on the beach, north of town?"

"He jumped, didn't he? The paper said he jumped."

"A *witness* said he did, a Dorothy Rubin. You know anything about her?"

"Never heard of her. Why?"

"Just checking. That's it, then. Thank you."

"Sure man. Take it easy now." Immediately the kid was off and running again, this time toward a green light.

Hook checked into the first motel he came to, and as soon as he was in his room he began to feel ill as well as exhausted. He went into the bathroom to get a drink of water and suddenly found himself on his knees, vomiting his steak dinner into the toilet. Afterwards, dousing cold water on his face at the sink, he stared into the fluorescent-lit mirror at an older version of himself. Normally he thought of himself as a fairly young-looking forty-five, weatherbeaten and lined perhaps, but still lean and hard, still basically young. But the image in the mirror was that of an old man, a survivor of some ultimate calamity. Hook turned from it. He would have liked to take a shower before going to bed, but he did not have the strength and in fact managed only to get off his coat and shoes and trousers before collapsing into the too-soft bed. He did not expect to sleep at all but it came in time. It came off and on throughout the night, like recurring spells of madness.

Once he dreamed he was on the deck of Mrs. Rubin's house, lying on his back with Liz Madera sitting astride him, naked under her shiny black raincoat and smiling sadly down at him as she guided his sex into her body and began to move against him. There was a muffled shouting in the distance, the cursing and panting of men fighting, and Hook wanted desperately to find out what was going on but he could not move except in answer to the rhythms of his rider. Near the deck railing the little girl from the Los Angeles airport bar watched him gravely.

The dream ended in exhaustion, not orgasm. But even then it was preferable to another, in which he found himself back in the identification room at the Bowman mortuary, sitting in a steel-tube chair with Chris's broken body draped in his lap. In a kind of paternal pietà, he sat there crooning and talking to the boy, rocking him, stroking his face, trying to manipulate his eyes and mouth in order to get them working again, for the idea seemed to be that the boy was merely in some sort of profound sleep and that if Hook only had time enough he would be able to wake him finally. It seemed like hours that he kept at it, even trying mouth-to-mouth resuscitation at the end. Then a harsh bell sounded and the fight was over.

It was his seven o'clock call. It was day. It was time to take Chris home.

3

When he left the cemetery and started down the hill through the darkness toward the gate to his farm, Hook found no real consolation in the knowledge that he had even more to go on now, more reason for being convinced that Elizabeth Madera and her friends had deliberately lied about Chris's death. The same day he had flown home with the body, a letter from Chris had arrived at the farm. In the three days since then Hook had read the letter so many times he could almost have recited it from memory:

December 8

Dear Dad and the rest of youse guys,

You're still in luck. The prodigal son isn't ready to return home yet, though let me tell you—if every place out west here was like L.A. I'd be home before Auntsy could say "get up." That place is really something else. I spent a week there in all, part of it staying with some hippie friends I met in New Mexico, and who knew some other friends who were staying in this house in L.A. (Out here nobody seems to buy or rent anything—they just use it. I guess it's cheaper that way.)

Anyway, the house was in Topanga Canyon—maybe you remember the canyon, Dad, from your old Navy days in L.A., although it's probably changed a good deal since those ancient times (joke). Now it's mostly all hippies. And drugs. I got out of the house early each day so I could see something of the city and not have to keep explaining to all and sundry that I'm a simple farm boy from the Midwest and prefer to start the day with breakfast instead of speed or acid. The others in the house were generally so strung out I think they'll all die of malnutrition before 25. And it's too bad too, because they're good people generally. Some will rob you blind—if you had anything to rob, which of course I don't—but otherwise they're peaceful enough, in fact one heck of a lot peacefuler (you can see I don't need college) than the kids at Banner High. But then I guess lying around on floor mattresses stoned all day isn't exactly peacefulness, is it? It's just pathetic. And I think one of the reasons for it is simply that place—L.A. It is like one great feedlot 50 miles long by 50 miles wide, only with people jammed cheek-by-jowl instead of cattle. The freeways are more violent than Vietnam. Back home you read about all the riots and the killings, like the Manson thing, and you don't understand. But here you do—at least I did, in L.A. The people are simply crazy. They've been driven mad by the way they live, and they don't know it. Time and again people picked me up (the mad hitchhiker strikes again!) and these people acted and talked like they were actually, clinically, crazy. In Banner Hill, Chief Janson would have locked them up. Here, they run things.

I say here, but actually I'm not there anymore. I'm in Santa Barbara, which is ninety miles north and about a hundred million miles more liveable. I'm not saying this is another Banner Hill (Isla Vista being so close and all) but you do get the feeling here that you might be able to live through to the end of the week without being asphixiated (sp?) by smog or slaughtered on a freeway or being offered up as human sacrifice at Sunday morning services (Church of the Latter Day Warlocks).

Also I've got a friend here, or at least I have had for the last few days—don't guess we'll be pen pals after I push on tomorrow. His name is—would you believe Isaac Newton Huston? No? Then would you believe he's shortened it to Icarus? Well, he has. It's a kind of professional name I guess. Says he's a photographer by trade, though I've yet to see him take any pictures for money. Anyway he's a nice guy, about 21, picked me up in Ventura, and is letting me crash here with him a few days. There's a lot to see

—oceans, mountains, museums, historical buildings. And girls! Some of them almost as fantastically, breathtakingly stunning as my little sister—which, as we all know, is saying one heckuva lot. Right, Jen? (Just kidding, sis—about the conceit, I mean, not the looks. Forgiven?)

The greatest thing about staying here with Isaac (I can't very well call him—or anybody else for that matter—Icarus, can I?—I mean with a straight face) is his bathroom. It's got a john that works and a real honest-to-Gawd bathtub, in which I've been soaking at least four hours a day. I won't say I was dirty, but the tub now has a ring that would pass for racing stripes on any track in the world.

(Got to go now. Will finish tomorrow morning.)

As you can see, I am a man of my word. Because it is morning now—and I am finishing this Epistle to the Illini at a table in a cheap restaurant right off Route 101 downtown—waiting for my ham and eggs—one of the few times I've parted with real cash these last few weeks. But I just couldn't cut another Chez Icarus breakfast of Seven-Up and Hostess Twinkies. I'll be on the road —thumb crook'd, teeth bared, eyes bright—in a very few minutes. So I thought I'd better have some real food for a change.

I plan to hit Monterey, Big Sur et al, and then on up to San Francisco to see if there is indeed a bridge there. Thereupon, I will cash my last travelers check and wing home to the frozen wastes of Macoupin County. I realize that will come as a blow to you, Bob, mon frere, since you won't have the chores all to yourself anymore. But them's the breaks, kid.

Seriously, I can hardly wait to see you all again, and see the farm and feel some real weather for a change. But I figure I'm here now, and I just might not pass this way again.

I miss you all. Much love.
Chris

First there was the tone of the letter, which Hook was confident Sergeant Rider and even Mrs. Rubin would have to admit was not that of a boy with "nothing to live for." But just as important, Hook thought, was the fact that the letter put Chris on the highway hitchhiking out of Santa Barbara a full day before

Elizabeth Madera claimed to have picked him up. According to the sergeant, the death occurred December 11 at one in the morning, some fifteen hours after Miss Madera supposedly picked Chris up on 101 around nine-thirty the previous morning—the *tenth*. But the letter was dated December 8 and was finished the next morning—December 9—just minutes before Chris intended to be out on the highway thumbing for a ride. Further, the letter was postmarked in Santa Barbara December 9, A.M. So the ladies' statements to Rider left an entire day unaccounted for, and Hook believed Chris had spent that day—and the next—at Mrs. Rubin's beach house with Elizabeth Madera. That meant the two of them had been together almost forty hours, which was a long time for a young man to remain at the scene of his sexual humiliation, and an even longer time for a pair of busy unsympathetic women to tolerate his presence. No, Hook figured that Chris had spent those hours just about as he himself had whiled away his time with Mrs. Cunningham a quarter-century before, and that Elizabeth Madera's initial objective—to give the boy lunch, to have someone to talk to—had grown into something more once she had gotten to know Chris. At any rate, she had asked him to stay. And his staying had led to trouble, possibly with Mrs. Rubin or young Ferguson. An accident had occurred, some stupid and unexpected calamity that, known, would have led to unwanted consequences for someone. So they had tried to cover it up. But what Hook could not begin to understand was why they had chosen to cover it up *the way* they had. Certainly they must have known that the boy had a history, a family, a background that could be checked, and that once it was, everything in that background might point in any direction except that of suicide. So why had they not done the simple, logical thing and called it an accident? The autopsy had put Chris's blood alcohol level high enough for him to have been drunk. It was conceivable that in the darkness he could have stumbled off the cliff, just as it was conceivable that seven years before a tired half-drunk salesman could have fallen asleep at the wheel of his Pontiac and crashed head-on into another car outside Alton, Illinois. One learned to live with what was conceivable. But suicide, for Chris, was *not*.

So why had the women insisted on it? Hook did not know. But he would find out.

When he reached the gate to his farm and started walking up the drive through the woods he was surprised at the shortness of his breath. Only four days had passed since Chief Janson delivered his message of death, yet in that time Hook felt as if he had aged twenty years, and not so much from grief, he believed, as from its denial, his refusal to face anything for the present except what lay ahead of him when he returned to California.

By the time he reached the top of the hill he was panting. Ahead, he saw lights burning in the kitchen and the family room of the house, lights that had not been on when he had gone out at around two o'clock. From the fireplace chimney a vine of woodsmoke, moonlit, climbed against the night sky. It meant that Aunt Marian was up, for she was the only other one in the family who shared his troglodytic passion for fire-gazing, and would start a fire in the fireplace as casually as most people, unable to sleep, would light a cigarette or raid a refrigerator. Hook walked slowly on, not eager to talk with anyone this night, not even Aunt Marian.

Entering by the back door, he took off his coat and shoes, and padded through the kitchen into the family room, which looked warm and comfortable with the fire raging in the fireplace he and Uncle Arnie had made out of fieldstones taken from a fence Hook's great-grandfather, the laconic James, had built just before the turn of the century. The room was carpeted and walnut-paneled. The furniture was stout maple, an originally expensive but repossessed suite Kate had bought secondhand on one of her occasional shopping forays into the rich bedroom suburbs west of St. Louis. On the davenport, in Arnie's bathrobe and with her gray hair braided for sleep, sat Aunt Marian, with Jennifer curled up against her shoulder. As Hook crouched before the fire, holding his hands out to it, she asked him if he had been at the cemetery.

"No. I just went for a walk. Down to the road and back."

She studied him sadly, not believing him. "Arnie's asleep," she said.

"Good. He needs it."

"Needs it, my foot. If that man never slept another wink in his life, he'd still be way ahead of everybody else."

The remark meant nothing. They both knew her husband's love of Chris. The only difference between Arnie and them was that he could sleep with a broken heart and they evidently could not.

Hook asked her if Bobby was in bed.

"He was up a while ago. Then he went back."

Standing now, Hook's knees popped like the wood in the fire. At the same time, Jennifer sat up and dropped her hands into the lap of her blue flannel pajamas. Firelight was snared in her long tousled hair and she looked to Hook not just pretty this night but beautiful, beautiful in her grief, solemn, older.

"Dad, we've been talking," she said.

"Yes, honey."

She looked at Aunt Marian, then back at Hook. "We don't think you should go back there, to California."

"Why not?"

"We need you here."

Hook got out a cigarette and took his time lighting it with a faggot, trying to move slowly and carefully over this ground, for he knew that he would be going back to Santa Barbara no matter how the two of them felt about it, but he did not want to leave a divided and unhappy family behind him.

"She's right, David," Aunt Marian put in. "Who'll take care of the farm? You think Arnie and Bobby could keep up with it? I don't."

"I'll hire the Jonas kid to help out. Full time."

"That costs money."

"I know that."

"And going out to the coast again—that could cost a fortune if you're there any time at all."

"We can manage."

"But can *we*, Daddy?" It was Jennifer again.

"I think you can."

"You don't think things are a little different now? A little special? And that we might need you here?"

Hook could not remember Jennifer ever being sardonic with

him except in fun, so there was no question in his mind how deeply she felt about his going. Yet he could not back away from the problem, either; he would be leaving again too soon for that.

"What else can I do?" he asked. "Can we leave it the way it is now—Chris a suicide?"

"It's police business," Aunt Marian said. "Why don't you just send them the letter and let them take it from there? If there's anything to find out, surely they're the ones to find it."

"I can't take that chance."

"And what about the chance something could happen to *you?*" Jennifer asked.

"Nothing will happen to me."

"Like nothing happened to Chris?"

"I'll be in no danger, honey. Believe me."

Behind them, Bobby had come into the room a short time before and had stood there listening, his face set, grim. Now he spoke:

"If Dad doesn't go, I'm going."

Jennifer whirled on him. "Will it change anything? Will it bring him back? Can you make him live again?"

Her vehemence shocked her brother into silence, and herself into tears. She fell against Aunt Marian and began to cry. Moving over to the davenport, Hook sat down next to her and gathered her into his arms, all five and one-half feet of her, a woman actually, but for the moment all child, all disconsolate little girl.

Softly Hook told her that one of the women in Santa Barbara had said the same thing. "And of course it's true," he went on. "We can't bring him back. But they took more than Chris's life, Jen. They took his character and his memory. They took the truth of him. And we've got to have it back. For him, as well as for us."

Her head moved against his chest, a nod of understanding or acceptance, he hoped, and he hugged her. Patting his knee, then pushing against it, Aunt Marian got to her feet and told Bobby they might as well have a cup of cocoa before going back to bed. They went into the kitchen.

Hook's bony legs did not make for much of a lap but they seemed to be sufficient for Jennifer, who fell asleep almost immediately. As Aunt Marian left, she had turned off the table lamp across the room, so he sat watching the fire in darkness now. The wood was white oak, from an old tree felled by a change in the course of the creek that ran through his acreage across the blacktop road. Using chainsaws, he and Chris and Bobby had worked on it through most of a Saturday afternoon early in November, right after they had finished harvesting the corn on the Strickler piece near town. It had been a clear, beautiful day, cold and crisp, and the noise of the saws had made the intervals of silence, when they turned them off to load the wood or just to rest, seem especially peaceful—and poignant now in retrospect, for by then Chris had made up his mind to take the trip West and see more of the country before facing his nineteenth birthday and the draft, and both boys had become unusually restrained and pensive, like lovers facing a breakup. Chris admitted hating the thought of missing Thanksgiving and Christmas at the farm, and the overburdened tables Aunt Marian would set on each occasion, but he was determined to go, and go he did.

White oak was slow-burning wood, and the logs Aunt Marian had lit were fairly large, so Hook knew he would have fire for hours yet, not that he needed it for warmth—the gas furnace in the basement furnished that without mess or effort on his part—but he liked having something to watch, especially if Jennifer were to sleep for hours. Aunt Marian came back in after a while and quietly told him that Bobby was in bed and that he should go now too.

"When she wakes," Hook said. "Let her sleep now."

Aunt Marian placed an afghan over her and then patted Hook on the shoulder and left, heading for her and Arnie's bedroom on the second floor of the old part of the house, where the temperature in winter rarely rose above sixty degrees, one of the reasons Arnie was such an accomplished sleeper, Hook judged. After a time, he had to shift his legs slightly, for comfort, but Jennifer did not stir. He was amazed at the womanliness of her body, an amazement that had begun two years before, when she had first started to develop. Now there was no little girl left physically, just this child-woman breathing shallowly against his chest while her tawny hair, smelling faintly of shampoo, tickled at his face. She was the only one of his children born after he had taken over the farm, so it was the only home she had ever known. In the beginning, though, she had fancied it more an empire than a home, with herself as undisputed empress. Hook remembered her at a year old, plump and cute, with the short wispy white hair of an old man and an air of absolute authority. She was walking by then, but she preferred to be carried, especially on Hook's shoulders, and her technique for bringing this about was simply to raise her arms and inform him what his orders were: *"Carrurdaddy!"* some of the time, and *"Wouldjaholdja?"* at others, though still without the slightest intonation of a plea. Hook and Kate had never worried much about this early arrogance, for it was more than counterbalanced by her brothers' capacity for meting out to her a justice of great clarity and swiftness, though in time all three of them got along with a reasonable degree of amity, probably because their mother watched over their egos as some women did their own laugh lines. Every now and then she would tell Hook that one of the children was "down" about something and that it would be a good idea if he treated that one with a little extra consideration for a few days. Hook sometimes worried that this attitude, and practice, might leave the children unprepared for the rocky, *un*smoothed life outside the family, especially at school, but the only evidence was that it had made them happier and stronger and better able to cope, probably because there had never been anything oppressive or cloying in Kate's solicitude.

But he did not want to think about her now. Nor Chris. His spirit begged for rest. And there were other practical matters requiring his attention. The farm would not run itself in his absence. He had to anticipate problems.

The Jonas boy would agree to come to work full time for a while, he figured. There just was not that much to do on his father's place, and the boy usually needed money. But Hook would have to warn him about smoking in the buildings; that could not be tolerated. He would tell Arnie to watch him. As for the farm itself, the Strickler piece was planted to wheat. He would seed clover on top of it in February and plow it down after the wheat was combined in the summer. Then it would be ready for corn again, at least three years of it. But that meant he would have to buy corn next fall to fatten his steers. The price was low now, after harvest, but he did not like to deal in futures; he did not like to spend money he had not yet made except when it was absolutely necessary, and that was often enough so that he would resist the temptation now, when it was a matter of choice. If the price of corn was too high by fall, he would simply sell the steers as feeders and let someone else do his gambling for him. There were no other pressing problems he could think of. There was plenty of silage and hay and feed; the mill was working properly; Arnie had finished tuning the big John Deere, and the honey wagons had been reconditioned, so he did not see any problems for the men in keeping up with the feedlot manure, unless the weather stayed mild and the ground soft. That also could mean some footrot among the feeders, but Arnie knew enough to watch for it. The most important thing, of course, was simply to check the herd out in the field every day, watch for the slightest sign of injury or disease, especially pneumonia in weather as wet as they had been having. All it took was the loss of a few head to drive operating costs out of sight; and of course anything serious, like a spate of blackleg, and a man could be out of business within a very short time.

Hook had gotten into farming more by accident than design. After his discharge from the Navy he had studied at the University of Illinois, graduating with a bachelor's degree in English and comparative literature in the spring of 1952, just four months after he had met Kate Larson there, in the corridor of the humanities building between classes. Carrying a handful of books, he had been struggling to get into his great drooping stormcoat when suddenly, miraculously, there was this hand holding his coat up for him so he could slip his arm into the sleeve. Turning, he found that the hand belonged to a girl who looked as if she had just stepped out of a fjord somewhere, a lovely smiling nordic Venus, with clothes. They were married that June and spent the summer in Greenwich Village exploring each other more than Manhattan, yet still managed to be insolvent by fall, and Hook took a job teaching junior English at a suburban Milwaukee high school. The three years he spent there were also the first years of his marriage, a time of candlelit love and laughter and happiness so perfect it was not even aware of its own existence, and a time of dazzling accomplishment too, for these were the years his sons were born, so it took him all that time to realize that he loathed the job of teaching. He liked the students as individuals and he enjoyed modern literature, but the two things, the students and the literature, made no vital connection in his mind. It was simply not important to him how the kids felt about books. So he was at best an indifferent teacher. Worse, he was an unhappy one, feeling anachronistic and unreal in the puerile school atmosphere, like a grownup who had accidentally stumbled into the center of a child's game. He felt diminished by it. And so he quit.

He and Kate had spent one month each summer at the farm with his widowed grandfather and Aunt Marian and Uncle Arnie, who lived with the old man and helped him run his small dairy-herd operation. That third summer, with no job ahead in the fall, and with Bobby an infant and Chris two years old, Hook had worked on a daily basis for other farmers in the area while he tried to think of what he wanted to do with the rest of his life. His fourth week there, combining wheat on a hot July day, his grandfather helped give him an answer. They had stopped working at noon—Hook, his grandfather, and Arnie—and had gone back to the house to restore their energies with one of Aunt Marian's typically huge noontime meals. Afterwards, the old man went out on the porch and sat down in his favorite rocker—and died. In his will he left the farm to Aunt Marian and to Hook's father, neither of whom knew quite what to do with it. Aunt Marian did not want to leave the farm, and yet Arnie, who lived in mortal fear of debt and responsibility, would not take out the needed mortgage to buy out Hook's father's half of the farm. So Hook stepped in, first as their tenant—their *sharecropper*, Kate ruefully called him—but by his third year there, he had been able to negotiate a loan to buy them out and have the farm in his own name.

Though farming had given him a feeling of satisfaction and accomplishment over the years, he could not pretend even to himself that there was no dark side to this bright harvest moon.

Always there was the small but persistent doubt that he had done his best, had become all the man his intelligence and education would have permitted him to become. To a degree, he felt monastic, as if he had withdrawn from the "world," the city-suburban white-collar arena where the substantive life of his time supposedly was being lived. And yet he could not think of any particular kind of work he might have done in that arena that would have been any more important or significant than that which he did. He never could have confused the fortunes and interests of a corporation with his own; he had already proven his unfitness for the education industry; and as for some sort of work in communications, the possibility of his having added to that cacophony of the forgettable did not excite him. Perhaps he might have done something in social work or government, but he did not know what. As it was, he produced enough protein to feed hundreds of people each year; he was a conscientious steward of slightly over one thousand acres of the planet's limited land surface; and he had raised children who would more likely contribute to society than tear it down or live off it. Yet the doubt lived on.

Now, though, watching the dying fire settle into the fireplace grate, Hook had more pressing problems. His left leg had gone to sleep and the other pained him. He squirmed slightly and kissed the top of his daughter's head, until she moved finally, waking. She muttered something unintelligible and then, seeing where she was, smiled sadly up at him.

"I fell asleep," she said.

"Yes, you did."

"Wasn't I heavy?"

"Yes, you were."

"Dad?"

"Yes, honey."

She told him that she was sorry about what she had said earlier and that if he felt he had to go back to California, then that was what she wanted too, whatever he wanted. He kissed her gratefully, and then they both got up, he on legs that felt like boards. Putting his arm around her, he walked her to her bedroom and tucked her in, and then went to his own room, where the luminous dials of his Big Ben clock put the time at a few minutes after four in the morning. It would soon be dawn.

In the afternoon, with Arnie and Bobby, Hook began moving the herd between the two pastures on the other side of the black-top road. It was a job they had to do throughout the year, rotating the cattle between these two fields and the main pasture every few weeks—in the warm months to permit the grazed grass to recover, and in the winter simply to distribute the animals' manure as widely as possible. Hook had automated their winter feeding system to the point where one man could handle it in a pinch. Silage from the big Harvestore silos was combined with protein supplement and power-loaded into low, wheeled feedbunks he had designed and built himself, a train of them, which he or Arnie would then tow by tractor out into the pasture, along with a "car" or two of haybales to give the animals dry roughage to protect them against bloat. Thus in winter as well as summer all the cattle except the bulls and feeders were kept out in the field, which greatly minimized the amount of work that went into their care and feeding. But at the same time it made them wilder and less tractable than feedlot cattle, so that even as simple a thing as moving them from one pasture to another could become a delicate operation. There were almost three hundred head in the main herd, slightly over half of them cows and the rest calves, and you had to be firm enough to keep them moving ahead, yet not so firm you caused a cow to turn on you or made it stampede the rest of the herd.

The main problem, of course, was simply the stupidity of the bovine animal. Just as generation after generation of Andalusian bulls were never acute enough to see that their enemy was not the bright muleta but the man holding it, so an Aberdeen Angus cow could stand for hours at a barbed wire fence staring at the greener grass on the other side and never think to wander along that fence in search of an opening. They had to be led.

Today, Arnie was doing the leading. Using the GM pickup, he was spreading a load of ear corn from the open fence gap between the two pastures on into the west pasture, making a kind of maize trail for the cattle to follow. At the same time Hook and

Bobby in the Jeep were driving back and forth along the perimeter of the field, pushing the herd toward the distant gap. Occasionally, as a cow or calf straggled behind, Bobby would leap out and chase it back into the herd. Hook had to be careful to keep the Jeep on grass as he drove, for the day was bright and sunny, almost forty degrees, and in the bare spots the ground had turned soft as mush, no footing even for a four-wheel-drive vehicle. He was pleased at how fine the cattle looked, especially the calves. Whatever runts there had been in the beginning, last spring and summer, evidently had caught up by now, for there was not one of them that appeared to be under three hundred pounds. And the males looked best of all, that fortunate ten or fifteen percent he had judged good enough to sell eventually as breeding stock, and had thus escaped the castrater's knife. Hook could think of no animal except possibly the big jungle cats that rivaled the beauty and majesty of a full-grown Black Angus bull, with its massive head and chest and the long cinched flanks under which its male sac swung as nobly as a bishop's censer. Beautiful but dumb, Hook thought, watching as the animals moved obediently toward the fence gap and its carpet of corn.

Finally they all made it through and it was time for the men to pause a few minutes and celebrate the event with a smoke, time for Hook at least, since Bobby was not allowed to indulge yet, and Arnie was almost never without a cigarette, though he did not smoke them so much as just let them dangle from his lips and burn, which caused him to hold his head back and to keep his right eye squinted, giving him the look of a man who regarded the world with unflagging cynicism, which in fact was how he did regard it. Small and sinewy, he was the possessor of an amazing constitution; in twenty years Hook had never known the man to be sick, even with a cold. Now, after closing the fence gap he came over and scooted up onto the hood of the Jeep.

"Duck soup," he said, wiping the sweat off his forehead.

"Not a hitch," Hook agreed.

"You got one very mean little bull in there, though. You see him?"

"No."

"Attacked the truck, he did. Tried to stove in the door."

Hook grinned. "You talked him out of it?"

"Hell no. I kicked him. I figure you better kick 'em while you can." For a time Arnie sat there wagging his head reflectively, and then suddenly tears were standing in his eyes. "It just ain't the same anymore, goddamn it!" he said. "Nothin'll be the same around here again! Ever!"

Hook looked at Bobby sitting next to him, but the boy had turned away.

"I just wish I was goin' out there with you, Dave!" the old man went on. "I'd show them lying bastards a thing or two!"

"Don't worry," Hook said. "We'll get the truth."

"That ain't enough! Somebody should pay!" Arnie—mild, easygoing Uncle Arnie—slammed his fist into the Jeep hood so hard he almost dented it.

"We'll see," Hook said. "It depends on what happened."

"I still say, you oughta get that girl Bobby says Chris put it to and make her testify. You can, you know. What's the word—?"

"Subpoena."

"That's it. Use it."

In the days since he had returned with the body, Hook had learned from Bobby that Chris, along with a half-dozen other boys his age, had had sexual intercourse with the daughter of a Banner Hill grocer, a man who was a deacon in the First Baptist Church, a Kiwanian, a community pillar of sorts. But Hook considered it highly unlikely that this man would permit his daughter to make a deposition declaring herself the town tramp. Bobby also had revealed that another girl Chris had dated, a girl whose family Hook knew and liked, had regularly made the boy come with her hand, though she had denied him anything more than that. Hook planned to tell Rider about both girls and if the sergeant considered the testimony important they could do something about it then, possibly get corroboration from the girls personally, without having to cause them or their families embarrassment. And then, of course, there was the letter. Hook was not worried. He would not be going back empty-handed.

"And if she denies it all," Arnie said now, "subpoena the other kids that was layin' her. They'll back up Bobby's word, believe me. Nothin' they'd be happier to do than brag about gettin' a little. It's only human."

"Maybe later on. We'll see what develops." Hook restarted the Jeep's engine.

Arnie slid off the hood and headed for the pickup, which he had driven back into the cleared pasture before closing the fence gap. Hook drove slowly back across the pasture and through the trees that separated it from the road. It was a beautiful woodland, almost parklike in its lack of undergrowth, which was kept down by the cattle as they used the trees for shade in the summer and shelter in the winter. Coming to the gate, Hook stopped the Jeep and Bobby jumped out to open it. As the boy swung it wide, the battered pickup of Ralph Metzler, whose small farm bordered Hook's, came rattling around a curve in the blacktop and braked sharply in front of the gate. Rolling down his window, Metzler told Hook that one of his calves had been killed that night. He had been at work, Metzler said—he worked nights at the glass factory in Alton—but his wife had been home, though of course she had not heard a thing, deaf as she was.

"And I tell you, it must've been something big that done it," he went on. "The calf was only a week old, but it's a Holstein and must've weighed one-twenty at least. But whatever it was, this thing, it dragged that calf right out beyond the fence. Killed it at the throat, it looked like. Ate through its belly, and tore one whole leg clean off. My dogs wasn't even scratched, so I figured they was just too scared to take it on, whatever it was, so it had to be mighty goddamn big, I'd say—a wolf or some big dogs gone wild or somethin' like that."

Arnie had pulled up behind them in time to hear most of the tale.

"What wolf?" he laughed. "There ain't no wolves around here, Ralph. You know that."

Metzler, always short-tempered, took Arnie's objection personally. "Well, what then? You tell me! A mountain lion? It sure wasn't no coon!"

"Dogs probably," Hook said. "And thanks for telling us, Ralph."

"Well, I thought you ought to know, all the cattle you got.

Whatever it is, it could cost you plenty. I wouldn'ta bothered you otherwise, I mean so soon after the funeral and all."

"That's all right. We appreciate it."

"Gonna get me some woven wire fence now," he said. "I got four more calves just like that one. On buckets. And I don't want to lose any more."

"Of course not."

Metzler drove off then, nodding to Hook and Bobby but pointedly ignoring Arnie, who he evidently felt had looked a gift horse in the mouth.

"Buckets!" Arnie scoffed. "Can you beat that? Handfeeding calves this day and age. That man's a real tycoon."

But Hook was more concerned about Metzler's dead calf than his live ones. "What about the killing? You got any ideas?"

"Like you said—dogs."

"Whose? If we can't find them, we're going to have to baby-sit the herd."

Arnie sagged dejectedly against the pickup. "I was afraid of that."

But Bobby had better news. "It was just one dog," he said. "And I know where he is."

From the beginning, the hunt for the killer dog did not seem like the real thing to Hook, probably for the same reason that Arnie had declined to go along with them.

"There ain't no dog there," he had said. "The boy's been seein' things. Why, the Olsons wouldn't let a dove roost free on their property, let alone a dog big as that critter was."

Nevertheless Hook went along with the boy, mostly just to be alone with him. Ever since Hook had returned from the coast with Chris's body he had watched Bobby going deeper into himself, as if he were drowning in the thing, and except for those few moments in the snow the day before, he seemed to have reached some dark cold depth to his liking now, a place where no one would reach him. As they drove, Hook glanced over at him occasionally, at his strong-boned face and mane of over-the-collar blond hair blowing in the wind, and especially at his eyes, which had the haunted look of a youth come home from combat in Vietnam, someone who had seen and done things beyond his power to understand or communicate. Driving past the cemetery, Hook tried again to reach him.

"I came here last night."

"I figured you did."

Hook slowed the Jeep. "You want to stop in now?"

"Why? What's in there? *He's* not in there."

Having no answer to that, Hook drove on.

A mile farther he pulled onto the shoulder and parked at the point where the blacktop joined the county road, a flat and barren intersection in which a corncrib and equipment shed stood by themselves in the center of a neatly plowed field. Until that fall the buildings had been part of the farm of Emma Danker, an old widow who had lived there alone for almost thirty years, renting out her land and raising roses and stray dogs. Helpless finally, she had been committed to a state institution by her relatives, who then had sold the farm to the neighboring Olson brothers, a sale and takeover that impressed Hook as truly Carthaginian, for the brothers had not only razed Emma's house and barn and garden and felled her trees but had plowed the ground where it all had stood, leaving just the distant corncrib and shed, in which they stored their combine and cornpicker.

Getting out of the Jeep, Hook checked the rifles he had picked up at the farm, both war surplus M1's.

"That's where I saw him last week," Bobby pointed. "Next to the shed, just lying out there in the sun. All that's happened, I forgot about it."

Hook shook his head thoughtfully. "Christ, when did they commit the old lady? October, wasn't it?"

"Why? Don't you believe I saw him there?"

"Sure. It's just hard to figure, that's all. It's been a long time. And I thought the humane society had picked up all her dogs."

"Not *him*."

"Let's hope he's still here."

The dog was one of the dozens Emma had taken in and cared for over the years. Only where most of her strays had been small mongrels, this one had been a spectacular crossbreed, German shepherd and great Dane, Hook had judged by the look and size of it.

He handed one of the rifles to Bobby. "You go around on that side. I'll move in from here. And remember—keep each other in view. And aim low. These things carry."

Bobby nodded impatiently. He was not a novice with a gun.

"When you're near enough, start throwing clods on the roof. That ought to bring him out. If he's in there."

"He's in there." The boy started across the plowed field, heading toward a point to the right of the shed.

Hook walked straight toward it, his gun still on safety. Both buildings were freshly painted a bright barn red, like the main part of the Olsons' farm lying a half-mile distant, in the direction Bobby was walking. The shed roof was covered with corrugated aluminum sheeting that shone brilliantly in the sunlight. Beyond it a swath of black woods, following the creek that would eventually run through Hook's farm, divided the gray of the plowed field from the harsh cerulean sky, in which a pair of hawks, far apart, wheeled patiently. Hook continued to move across the rough plowed ground toward the two structures until finally he was close enough to see a kind of opening, a tunneling, under one of the shed's sliding doors, and for the first time he began to believe that the dog Bobby had seen might indeed have been Emma Danker's huge beast and not just some other canine wandering through. Closer yet, Hook kicked a clod of plowed ground loose and hurled it onto the roof of the shed. Bobby did the same. But nothing happened. They waited for a few moments and then repeated the process, and this time the dog came snarling out of the tunnel, a blur of bared white teeth and shaggy black-and-tan hair, and it was obvious that the animal was not just fleeing the shed but was attacking, moving in a high blind rage toward Bobby, not even thirty yards away. At the moment Hook sighted and fired, the dog caught sight of Bobby's weapon and abruptly stopped, whirling in panic. Hook's shot missed. But Bobby's did not. It hit the animal in the hindquarters, knocking him over and spinning him around. Immediately the dog began pawing desperately at the ground with its front legs, trying to drag itself back to the tunnel under the door. This time Hook did not miss.

As they walked up to it, Hook was shocked by the size of the dog. He once had killed a deer in Wisconsin and had been surprised at how small the animal had looked in death. The dog, though, if anything looked larger, almost the size of a great Dane but heavier in the body and with the long hair and wolflike snout of a shepherd.

"Go around and look in the window," Hook told Bobby. "See if you can see anything."

It was the only way they had to check, for the doors were padlocked shut. But Hook was not worried. Even if there was no sign of the calf or any other killings, he felt they had done the right thing in destroying the dog. It had been on its own and apparently was not starving, so it had to have done some killing somewhere, which made it a threat to all the livestock in the area.

Bobby came back around the building. "It's in there, the hoof and part of the legs. Other bones too. You gonna tell the Olsons?"

"Later."

"I'll get the shovel." Bobby headed for the Jeep. Bringing it had been his idea, not Hook's. The boy had been that certain.

While he was gone, Hook dragged the dog around to the back of the shed, where they would not be seen by anybody driving past on the county road. Bobby returned with the shovel and Hook told him to dig in the plowed ground, which would be easier going than the strip of hardpan the Olsons had had to leave around the perimeter of the building. Hook lit another cigarette and smoked it halfway down while Bobby worked at the hole, rapidly, almost savagely, as if it too had a life that circumstances required their taking. Hook tried to spell him but the boy insisted on doing it all himself and finished the job in less than ten minutes. The hole was about five feet long and two feet down, deep enough so the Olsons' disks would not turn up what was left of the carcass in the spring.

Together, Hook and Bobby placed the dog into the hole, turning it so its legs were folded under it. Hook tried to take the shovel to fill in the grave, but again Bobby insisted on doing the work himself, only now he felt like talking as he labored, and his words came in spurts, between the heavy bellows of his breathing.

"All he did was what he had to do, right? As a dog?"

"That's right."

"And we did what we had to do?"

"Yes."

The boy shook his head. "You know what I think?"

"What?"

"That people who find something to believe in are just lying to themselves. Things like church. Or the flag. Or art. Or anything."

"That's kind of pessimistic."

"You look at life clear—I mean, just the way it is—and there's no purpose."

"That *we* can perceive."

"What do you mean?"

"Only that maybe we can't see the whole picture. Like him." Hook indicated the grave.

"I don't believe that. We're the highest animals. And the way we see life is the way it is." Bobby looked at Hook almost accusingly. "And there's nothing."

"Including certainty."

But Bobby was adamant. "There's *nothing*," he said.

He finished filling in the grave in silence, then walked on ahead toward the Jeep.

Hook was the last to go to bed that night. As he went around turning out the lights and locking up, he stepped out onto the porch and looked through the black-limbed maples of the lawn at the main pasture, which was frost-covered, silver in the moonlight. The same clearness of sky that had made the day warmer now deepened the night cold, so that his breath plumed in front of him. In the summer the porch was screened and when he was finished working in the evening he would sit out in his favorite wicker chair reading until the light failed or talking with the children or Arnie or Aunt Marian, who sat in the chain-hung swing squeaking slowly back and forth, measuring the passing of the day as evenly as a clock's pendulum. Finally, as the others turned in, he would remain there alone in the darkness drinking wine or beer and eating pistachio nuts, sometimes watching the herd out in the pasture if the moon was bright enough. Often the boys would be out somewhere, and in time he would hear their car—the Jeep usually—on the blacktop and then he would see its lights shining in the tops of the trees and then finally the headlights themselves as the vehicle crested the hill and came on toward the house. A few times this past summer the boys had arrived home less than sober, and on those occasions there was almost nothing they had not found hilarious, including their father. Most of their commentary had to do with his sitting in the dark drinking wine all by himself, sallies like "Well, it's better than in the closet" or "My father, the wino" or "You sure you can make it home, Dad?"—but a good deal of it was their own exclusive humor, an idiom that went safely over, under, around, and through him, and which they seemed to find doubly funny because of it. Usually one or both of them would sit with him for a while and he would gently probe them about what was going on in their world, seeking reassurance that girls and booze and sports were still the order of the day and that the two of them were not nightly driving off to do business with some friendly neighborhood drug pusher. He still found it preposterous that the drug plague had reached even the Banner Hills of America, but it had, and he watched his children—their arms, their eyes, their attitude and stamina—for the slightest sign of the plague. With Jenny, both boys expressed repeatedly the opinion that drug users were "creeps and losers" and he believed they meant it. Nevertheless, just as Hook's own mother had anxiously watched him for any sign of sore throat or backache during the peak polio season in late summer, so he watched his children the year around for symptoms of the dread contemporary disease.

Hook remembered one of the last late-night conversations he had had with Chris on the porch. It was a summer Saturday night and the boy had driven in slightly before midnight, probably from a date with the Baptist grocer's daughter. The herd was in the main pasture and for some reason had settled in for the night just beyond the drive fence, and the sounds of their snorting and breathing, their quarreling and moving about, combined with the usual insectival racket, had made the night seem almost African, aswarm with life. Chris parked the car in the driveway loop and came up the six stairs in two long strides, all legs still, but easy and graceful, surprised for a moment at finding his father up so late, but then smiling his quick, slightly crooked smile. Even then he had begun to wear his dark blond hair down over his ears and Hook had suffered the length in silence, remembering the futile fuss his own father had made over his mid-forties' crewcut, calling him Himmler and Bristles. They talked for a few minutes about the cattle being up so close to the house and about the condition of the corn on the Strickler hundred, which Chris had stopped to check on his way to Banner Hill, and about their neighbor Joe Silas miring two tractors one after the other trying to pull his three-gang disk out of a slough, and finally having to hire a contractor with a bulldozer to pull all three pieces out, an ignominy Silas probably would never live down. Then they got around to *the* subject: college and the draft. Chris had already been accepted for admission to the University of Illinois and could have gotten in at least a semester of study before his nineteenth birthday in February, when he would have been eligible for the draft. But his number was a low one; there was no question that he would be called up. So Hook was not surprised at the decision the boy announced that night.

"I've definitely decided, Dad. I don't want to go. Not for just one semester. I'd rather start after I get out of service."

Hook was not against the decision. "Okay. I'll call them Monday. What do you want to do this fall, then? Just work?"

Chris grinned. "Not exactly."

"What then? Lie around and eat Auntsy's coffee cake?"

"That'd be all right."

Hook studied his look, his smile, in the darkness. The boy had something on his mind. "But not that either, huh?"

Chris shook his head. "No. I've been thinking I might take a trip. Go down South and out West. See some of the country."

Hook considered it. One of his worries was that as a widower he had been overprotective of the boys, had inhibited the growth of their self-reliance. "Not a bad idea," he said. "You're a little young, though."

"*Nineteen?*"

"Eighteen."

"I pass for twenty-one."

"So I've gathered."

Chris grinned guiltily.

"How would you go? In the Jeep?"

"No, hitchhike. Everybody hitchhikes these days."

"I don't."

"Come on, you know what I mean."

"Okay, you'd hitchhike."

"And I'd take my pack and sleeping bag. I'd get along."

"When would you go? And how long?"

"This fall sometime. And as long as it takes."

Hook smiled ruefully. "You'd freeze your butt off, you know. Even down South and out in California it can get pretty cold in the winter, especially at night."

"Not like here."

"Here there's a roof over your head."

Now Chris looked serious, determined. "I can do it."

Watching him, Hook lit a cigarette. "I know you can, son. I'm not doubting that. It's just that it's all still pretty new. I want time to think about it."

Chris shook his head despairingly. "You still think I'm a kid, don't you?"

Hook did not answer immediately. He had an idea what the boy was getting at. "You mean you'll go no matter what I say."

Chris met his gaze for a few moments and then he turned away, looking out through the screens at the sleeping cattle. He nodded solemnly. "I'm afraid so."

"Then I guess you'd better go with my blessing."

Chris looked surprised for a moment. Then he smiled. "That'd be better."

"I think so too."

"It's just something I have to do, Dad. I've been thinking about it all summer."

Hook tried to appear enthusiastic. "Be good for you, I guess—getting away for a while, on your own."

"There's just so much going on in the country right now," the boy said. "And I feel like, you know, like we're kind of out of it here. Like there's a flood all around us and we're sitting up here on our hill all nice and dry looking down on the poor slobs who are losing everything or trying to save something. You know what I mean?"

Hook drained the last of his can of beer. It was warm. "High and dry," he said. "Not a bad place to be during a flood."

Chris would not accept that. "Come on, Dad. You know what I mean."

Hook allowed that he did.

Chris was silent for a while then, sitting back against the parapet that surrounded the porch. Finally he said, "You could've been just about anything you wanted."

"Hardly."

"But you chose this."

"You sorry I did?"

Chris looked out into the darkness, the swarming night. "No, I love it here. I really do. Most of the kids, they can't wait to split and never come back. But I want to someday. I really do. After service and college and maybe knocking around a while. I can't see a desk job for me. I love the farm, and the cattle, and being out all the time. I guess I'm crazy. And I hope Bobby stays too."

Hook said nothing. His son casually had filled the vessel of his life to overflowing and he did not trust his voice to shape a word. He got to his feet, starting for bed, and gave Chris an equally casual clap on the shoulder, because that was the American way.

Now, in the clear and cold winter night, he wished with all his heart that he had taken the boy in his arms and kissed him as warmly and naturally as some old-time Jewish or Italian father would have. But it was too late now. This night no headlights shone through the trees or came stabbing over the crest of the hill. In fact, besides the moon and stars, the only lights he saw anywhere were on the wingtips of a jet already descending to land at St. Louis forty miles away. And suddenly he knew that tomorrow, not the day after, he would be returning to California.

4

Because of a rainstorm moving down the coast, Hook's flight was late leaving Los Angeles. And coming in over Santa Barbara all he could see were the peaks of the Santa Ynez rising above the clouds, a condition he found ironically appropriate. For as the jet began its glide path down into all that murk he knew that was what he was doing himself—proceeding blindly in the hope that something was actually down there.

For the jet, there was. After a thumping landing, Hook rented a new Ford hardtop at the airport and drove on into town, straight to the Sand and Sea, the motel where he had stayed the week before. Only this time he specified a single-bedroom at their lowest rate, for he did not know how long he would be staying and he wanted to hold his expenses to a minimum.

The clerk gave him a room on the second floor, looking down on the boomerang-shaped swimming pool and the wet bar and umbrella tables, all abandoned now to the rain and darkness. The time was six-thirty, too late to see Sergeant Rider and show him Chris's letter. Hook would have to wait for morning to do that. And he knew the sergeant would not be overjoyed at seeing him, any more than he would be surprised, for Hook had told him that he would be coming back. That next morning, on his way to pick up Chris's body, he had stopped in at the courthouse both to retrieve his suitcase and to fill the sergeant in on his conversation with the two women and Ferguson the night before. And Rider had not liked it that Hook had gone ahead on his own.

But then the sergeant's displeasure was something he was prepared to live with. That was the least of his worries.

Now, in his room, the first thing he did was call home. Aunt Marian answered and he told her where he was staying and gave her the telephone number. She got a few words out of him about the weather and the flight, and then he said he was tired and hungry and would call them again in a day or two. After he had hung up, he looked in the telephone directory for Isaac Huston's number and address, but he was not able to find it at first, not until he looked in the Yellow Pages, under photographers. *Icarus*, it read. *240½ Mission Plaza Rd 962–4342.* Hook unpacked and washed up. He planned to lie down and relax for a while—it had been a long day's journey—but he was too keyed up, too eager to get going. So he put his shirt and tie back on, then his suitcoat and damp raincoat and went out again, stopping first at a brightly lit restaurant up the street for a quick cheeseburger and salad, which he rightly thought would be both cheap and bad. He disliked eating alone in the garish, cheery openness of the place, in fact disliked eating alone anywhere at any time, but he reflected with gratitude that it was something he had had to do very seldom in his life. He bolted his food, thinking ahead to "Icarus." He could have called the youth, but he wanted to talk to him in the flesh, see him, judge him, learn all he could. If it developed that the young photographer was not at home, then Hook would wait for him. He had nothing else to do, nothing more important.

The address turned out to be in the neighborhood of the Mission, a venerable part of the city with fine old homes rising two and three stories among towering palms and cypress and sycamore. For a time Hook thought the directory had given a wrong address, for there was a 240 Mission Plaza and next a 242 but nothing in between except a driveway curving behind 240, which was a huge two-story Spanish-style home dark as a cemetery. Following the drive back around the house, Hook found the missing half—lights burning in an apartment above a large four-car garage that looked as if it had been a stable at one time. The light was dim—candlelight, it appeared—and shone through shades as colorful as stained-glass windows and covered with psychedelic designs. From inside came the sound of a wailing sitar. Hook climbed the stone stairway at the end of the structure and knocked on the door. After a moment, the music inside was turned down, and then he heard a toilet flushing, heard it from underneath, from the garage more than through the door of the apartment. Finally there was a voice, male, someone just on the other side of the door.

"Who is it?"

"My name is Hook. My son stayed here last week."

There was no response for a time then, just the sound of voices inside, hurried, soft, much as it had been at Mrs. Rubin's. Only here there was no window for the occupants to look out through; they would have to dare. And finally someone did. The door opened and a short thin young man wearing what looked like a Samurai warrior's robe stepped into the opening. He had shoulder-length red hair and chalk-white skin that only reinforced Hook's impression of him as someone in Japanese costume, a Kabuki player.

"Are you Isaac Huston?" Hook asked. "*Icarus?*"

The youth nodded uneasily. He looked both awed and frightened. "You're Chris's father?"

"Yes. He sent a letter from here."

Icarus rolled his head theatrically. "Oh wow, man, what a thing that was to happen. I'm sure sorry for you. I still can't believe it."

"Could we talk?"

"What did you want to talk about?"

"A lot of things."

The young man nodded a reluctant comprehension. "Oh. You want to come in, you mean. I'm having a few people in."

"It's up to you."

Icarus shrugged his slender shoulders. "Well sure. Why not? Come on in."

Following him, Hook stepped into the sort of room he had seen before only in magazines, a careful assemblage of the mod, the outrageous, and the simply unlivable. The wood floor was painted black, the walls red, the ceiling pink. There was a polka-dot mattress on the floor, an Eames chair, an old double car seat, a legless dining room table painted like a checkerboard, and a huge inflated clear plastic doughnut in which a young Negro male with a huge halo of Afro hair lolled sleepy-eyed. Overhead, a mobile made of mirrors of many colors and shapes turned slowly, catching the room's candlelight and bounding it off the walls, which were covered with collages and protest posters and beautifully framed photographs of nude models, mostly male, the work of Icarus, Hook assumed. On the mattress a girl in a granny dress and rimless spectacles lay on her side, insouciantly studying Hook as she toyed with the shoulder-length tresses of a lean muscular young man sitting in front of her on the floor, with his head resting back against the swell of her hip. He was wearing an Indian headband, a threadbare serape, jeans and sandals, and he watched Hook with a look of weary contempt, as if the two of them were old enemies. As Icarus introduced Hook, not one of the three said a word.

"That's George," Icarus said, indicating the Negro. "And that's Rooney and Joan."

Hook nodded at them, but still they made no response.

"He's Chris's father," Icarus kept on. "You remember the kid I brought to Harley's last week. The kid who—"

"The kid who killed himself," the one named Rooney said.

Hook stared at the young man. He could not believe he had heard him right, could not believe the self-approving smirk that crossed his face now. Finally Hook looked away from him, trying to check his anger. The heavy odor of marijuana was in the air—Hook remembered it from the days of his weekend passes in Tijuana during the war—but for him that could no more explain the youth's comment than could alcohol, and there was that too, a gallon jug of red wine sitting on the table, and glasses spread around.

"I don't believe he did it," he heard Icarus say now. "Chris was too straight a kid for that."

"That's why I'm here," Hook said. "I *know* he didn't do it. But I don't know what did happen. I was wondering if you knew anything, or if you'd gone to the police yet—told them when he was here, when he left."

85

The Negro laughed out loud, throwing his mouth wide open, which made him look like a deranged marmoset.

"Yeah, man," he said. "Why didn't you do that, huh, Icky?"

Rooney also was amused. "You don't *go* to the pigs, friend," he said to Hook. "You're *took in* by the pigs. That's the scene today, man."

Icarus asked Hook if he wanted a drink. "I've got a beer and wine," he added. "That's all."

"Maybe he'd like a smoke," the girl suggested.

Rooney, who was rolling a cigarette from a glassine pouch, shook his head doubtfully. "I don't know, man. You already cost us a pretty fair-size roach. We thought you was pig, see? So Joannie here, she splits in there and flushes the thing down the hole. So you owe us."

"I won't be staying," Hook said to Icarus. "I just wanted to ask you about the morning Chris left here. Was it Tuesday, the ninth?"

Icarus picked up his drink, a glass of red wine. Sinking into the car seat, he revolved the glass under his nose, as if it were a brandy snifter containing a fine old cognac.

"Jesus, I can't remember," he said. "I can't be sure. That was over a week ago."

"Do you remember when you read about it in the paper? Was it the next afternoon after he left here?"

"No. A couple days later, I think. Why?"

But again Rooney intervened. He had just crawled over to the legless table to refill his wine glass and to light his marijuana cigarette on a taper burning there. Standing now, he clucked his tongue at Hook.

"Man, this is really sad, you know? This is a real sick scene, you coming out here."

Hook said nothing.

"You don't want to know why it's sick, man?"

"No."

"Well then, I'll just have to tell you, won't I? You know what it seems like to me, you coming out here, all this way? It's the ego trip of the century, man—if you'll excuse the pun. But that's what it is, all right. You just made the ego trip to end all ego trips."

"Oh lay off, Joe." It was the girl.

After passing the cigarette to the Negro, he turned to the girl. "Why, huh? Tell me why I should. He's just like all his generation. Just like my old man, for Christ sake. They're so fucking perfect, you know—such paragons of perfection it wouldn't ever dawn on them they might've screwed up someplace. Like say in raising a kid. That would never dawn on them. No, it's got to be something else—somebody else's fault. Ain't that right, man? Huh? Ain't that right, Mr. Hook or Kook or whatever the fuck your name is? You're not here for your kid, are you? You're here for yourself. For your own precious fucking good name. And that, mister—that I call that an ego trip. One big fucking ego trip."

Hook asked him if he was finished.

The youth shrugged. "Yeah, I guess so." Then he winked at the Negro. "But if I get any more opinions on the subject, I'll let you know, okay?"

The girl spoke up again. "Sometimes you're all mouth, Joe. You know that?"

"Up yours, baby."

He sat down again and leaned his head back against her hip, and her hand fled into his hair.

"Getting back," Hook said to Icarus. "You don't remember when the paper said the woman picked him up? It was Wednesday morning, according to her. And the death occurred that same night, slightly after midnight—early Thursday morning. And it was in the paper that afternoon, Thursday afternoon."

Icarus looked uncomprehending. "So?"

"So you said it was a *couple* of days later you read about it. A *couple* of days after he left here."

The young man shrugged. "Well, you know how time is. I mean, like, it depends on what you're doing—how it goes."

"Like right now," Rooney drawled. "It's kind of dragging, man."

But Hook persisted. "Tell me this. When you read about it—was it the first story, or a follow-up?"

Icarus was not in doubt about that. "It was the first one. The original story."

"And you read it a couple of days after Chris left?"

Icarus nodded thoughtfully, apparently beginning to understand. "Yeah, that is kind of weird, isn't it? I never thought about it before."

Hook felt an immense sense of relief, for he had been afraid that after mailing his letter home Chris might have returned to Icarus's apartment for something he had forgotten, and then might have stayed on another day, which would have put him on Route 101 on Wednesday, the day Elizabeth Madera claimed to have picked him up. And that would have strengthened the rest of her story, the larger lies.

Now Hook moved toward the door. He had gotten something, and figured he would not get much more with Icarus's friends there. "Thanks very much," he said. "I'm sorry I barged in on you."

"Wait. Hold on." Icarus had scrambled to his feet. "There's something I want to give you first." He swept into a small adjoining room, a photographer's darkroom, it appeared. Then immediately he came out again, holding up a large matted black-and-white photograph, which he handed to Hook now.

It was a portrait of Chris.

The boy was sitting at the legless table over coffee and a roll, smiling in the brilliant morning light.

"I took it the day before he left," Icarus said. "It's good, isn't it? The quality of light. It's got a kind of Vermeer feel to it, don't you think?"

Hook could not speak. He thought he had gotten over this part of it, the stabbing sense of loss, the pain, yet here it was again. His eyes, abruptly filling, saw only light, starbursts of burning candles and turning mirrors. He mumbled his thanks and opened the door and somehow stumbled down the stone stairs to the driveway.

He was halfway to the street when Icarus came running up behind him.

"Hey, you all right, Mr. Hook? You okay?"

"It came as a surprise, that's all."

"Well, gee, I'm sorry. I——"

"It's all right. I'm grateful," Hook told him. "I appreciate having it. It means a lot to me."

"I've still got the neg," Icarus said. "I can make more."

"Fine." As Hook went toward his car, the young man walked along with him.

"I'm sorry about in there," he said. "Rooney, I mean. It's just his way. He's really hung up on this generation thing."

"So I gathered."

"Me, I'm glad you came out here. I mean I'm glad to get to see you—the way Chris talked about you and the farm and all. I know it isn't like Joe said in there, an ego trip."

Hook said nothing. They had reached the street.

"And for what it's worth—I think you're right. Chris couldn't have killed himself. He just didn't have it in him."

"How do you know that?"

"Well, he was, you know—he really had got it all together."

"Will you tell that to the police?"

Icarus smiled uneasily. "Oh, I don't know, man. I mean, what difference would it make what I say?"

"It might help."

"No, I don't think so."

"Why not?"

"I just don't. I mean, well, I don't like to be hassled. And you know what they're like, the police."

"There'd be no problem. Just a statement."

The young man looked away from Hook's eyes. "Let me think about it first, okay? I'd just like to think about it first."

Hook had no choice. "Sure. It's up to you."

At his car now, Hook stood with the door open and got in a few more questions before leaving. Did Icarus know the city very well? Yes, he had been born and raised in Santa Barbara. Did he have much to do with the rich, the well-off? As far as he was concerned, that covered almost everyone in the city, but yes, he sometimes was hired to photograph their weddings and parties and such, and now and then he was even invited as a guest— as "a conversation piece," he added ruefully.

"Then maybe you could help me," Hook said. "I want to know more about Mrs. Rubin and Elizabeth Madera. And Jack Douglas."

Icarus laughed. "Wow, man, you keep going higher and higher."

"I've heard he's Miss Madera's boy friend."

"Her latest would be more like it. But then he's never been much of a homebody either, I guess. How come you ask about him, though. He wasn't there, was he? At the scene?"

Hook slipped in behind the wheel. "Who knows?"

The youth let his breath out in a long low whistle. "Jesus," was all he said.

Through the window Hook gave him a card from the motel. "I'm staying here," he told him. "And I'll be waiting to hear from you." Then he thanked him for the photograph again and drove off, not looking at it once during the two-mile downhill drive back to the beach.

By nine the next morning Hook was in the lobby of the sheriff's office, waiting to find out if Sergeant Rider would see him. And this time, unlike the week before, he was not alone on his side of the high wooden counter. In the row of chairs behind him three young male hippies sprawled contentedly, wallowing in the disdain of a grizzled Mexican laborer and a mink-stoled old lady, both of whom preferred to stand rather than sit next to them. Behind the counter, the desk deputy had gotten Rider on the phone and now told him that a Mr. Hook was there and wanted to see him if possible. Then the deputy listened, nodding.

"Right, Sarge. Right." He hung up. "I'm afraid he can't see you now, Mr. Hook. He's going out on a call, says for you to leave your number and he'll get in touch."

The deputy shoved a pad at him and Hook wrote his name on it and the motel number, hurrying, because he was not about to give up on Rider yet. Thanking the deputy, he walked quickly out of the building and across the bright green lawn to the driveway that led up from the basement garage to the street. If Rider had told the truth about having to leave on a call, then this was the way he would come, and Hook figured the man would certainly be able to spare the few seconds it would take to give him Chris's letter—*now*, not tomorrow or the next day. For time was everything. Hook knew at least that much about crime, that the longer a case went unsolved the greater were the chances it never would be solved.

So he waited. He stood next to the driveway like a patient sentinel, and in the next few minutes a half-dozen cars passed him, some going into the building and others leaving it. He lit a cigarette and smoked it almost down to the filter before he saw Rider coming out finally, sitting next to the driver in a plain black Ford. As they came abreast of him, the car stopped and Rider gave him a rueful look.

"You do get around, Mr. Hook."

Hook held the letter out to him. "My son mailed this from Santa Barbara two days before he died. I think you ought to read it."

Rider took the letter. "Anything else?"

"Yes. But I'd need a few minutes to tell you."

"You free now?"

"I'm free."

Rider reached back over the seat and unlocked the rear door. "Get in, then."

Hook climbed in and was still closing the door when the driver tromped on the accelerator and turned into the street. They sped through a yellow light and then a red one, with the siren growling softly.

"We got an O.D.," Rider told Hook. "Drug overdose up in the foothills. This is Sergeant Anderson. Consider yourself honored. He'll be running the FBI in a few years, won't you, kid? Say hello to Mr. Hook."

"Morning," Anderson said. He was a tall neat young man with a crewcut and a gray flannel suit and dark check tie any corporation executive would have felt comfortable in. And he had the manner to go with it, a manner Rider obviously did not appreciate.

"Mr. Hook's come here to California to help us," Rider said.

"We need all the help we can get."

"Speak for yourself." Rider took the letter out of the envelope.

"Notice the postmark," Hook said. "And the date of the letter."

Rider nodded.

"Another thing—I believe I can get testimony from a couple of girls back home. Girls my son had sexual relations with."

"They'll sign a statement?"

"Possibly. I don't know."

"You don't know."

"That's right. I didn't ask."

Rider's expression, a weary cynicism, told Hook what he thought of this bit of information. "Well, let's see what we've got here first."

As the sergeant began to read the four pages of the letter Hook settled into the back seat and waited. Anderson had turned off the siren but they continued to move rapidly uphill past the Old Mission and into the wooded, countrylike area beyond it, their tires squealing around the curves of the narrow blacktop as it snaked in between the close-growing live oak and eucalyptus and the stone walls and log fences beyond which ranch houses sat back in the leafy shadows, hugging hillsides and lying in arroyos. It was beautiful country, a beautiful day.

And they were on their way to a death scene.

They went down into Mission Canyon and then started up again, for a mile or perhaps two before the sergeant finally finished the letter. He folded it and put it back into the envelope.

"You make a copy of it?" he asked Hook.

"Yes."

"Then I'll keep this." He slipped it into his suitcoat pocket.

"Well, what about it?" Hook asked. "What do you think?"

"Later," Rider said.

They were plunging down a steep curve through the woods now, toward a small stone bridge that crossed a creek at the bottom of a canyon. On this side of the bridge, off the road, a battered old Volkswagen minibus decorated with yellow dayglo peace symbols was parked. Across the road from it were two sheriff's patrol cars, one with its dome light flashing ineffectually in the bright morning sunshine. Beyond the bridge two other cars had pulled off the road. Their occupants, a young couple and a businessman, had gotten out to look but remained on their side of the bridge, as if they feared contamination from the minibus. One deputy was standing at the rear of it, looking away from whatever lay inside its opened doors. The other deputy was across the road, leaning on the open door of his patrol car, talking to a young woman slouched in the back seat.

Anderson pulled in behind them and parked. Ignoring the girl, both he and Rider went across the road and checked the Volkswagen bus inside, with the help of the deputy there. Then they came back across the road and began talking with the other deputy and the girl, who looked like a 1935 Okie with her ravaged young face and bamboo limbs sticking out of a bulky feedsack dress.

After a while Hook wandered across the road toward the minibus, but stopped short of it when he saw the body lying inside on the floor. It reminded him of Greenwich Village drunks two decades before, scrawny bearded little men lying under newspapers in alleys and street gutters and stairwells.

"You a reporter?" the deputy asked.

"No. I'm with Sergeant Rider."

The deputy was about thirty, all spit and polish except for a scraggly mustache. He shook his head in disgust. "Christ, you should smell it in there. And they call *us* pigs."

"Bad, huh?"

"Foul is more like it. Just plain foul." The deputy pulled a pink ticket out of his pocket. "Look at this. I got half a parking ticket wrote up on them. I mean when I pulled up this morning and seen the vehicle parked there—well, I just got out my pad and started writing—you know, make, model, license—'cause you can't park here, see? Not overnight. Then I walk over to the vehicle to lay the ticket on them and what do I find? The chick is sitting in the driver's seat stark naked and plucking on this guitar, real slow-like, about one twang every thirty seconds. And the kid's just laying there on the floor, already stiff as a board. Probably O.D.'d early last night. And you know what she says to me? She says 'I tried to love him back to life.' Can you beat that, huh? *I tried to love him back to life.* That's what she said. Can you picture it? This stinking godawful wreck parked out here at night in the boonies, and inside is this spaced-out chick going down on a stiff, trying to 'love him back to life.' I tell you, man, I'm thinking of having a vasectomy. I don't want no kids. Not this kind anyway. And I'm beginning to think they're the only kind anymore."

As the deputy finished his tirade, a pale-blue ambulance arrived, followed by a press car carrying two men who got out and headed for the minibus as if it were a factory gate they entered every day of their lives. The deputy met them with a laugh.

"You'd do better with gas masks," he said.

Hook walked back to Rider's car. He lit a cigarette and waited there, leaning back against the front fender while the professionals went about their business of tidying up the mess of a lost life. The photographer got his pictures and the reporter his story and the ambulance men their body. And the girl, smiling dreamily in the back seat of the patrol car, did not even bother to go over and see it off or say a word of goodbye. Watching them, Hook realized that beyond his grief as Chris's father and beyond his rage at the suicide lie, was another, smaller hell, and it was simply that his son had died here, in this land of sunshine and desperation. For it struck him that to die in California was to fall not on foreign soil so much as in a foreign time, an alien and brutal and loveless future that he despised as well as feared.

Rider brought the girl over to his car now and helped her into the back seat as if she were old and infirm.

"Not much I can do here anymore," he said to Hook. "The kid's going to stay and wrap up. So you can get in front. And do me a favor. Keep an eye on her. Christ knows what she's got inside her. They had enough drugs in that heap to turn on the whole county."

As Rider wheeled the car around and drove off, the girl smiled sweetly at Hook. "Are you fuzz too?" she asked.

"No."

"But I suppose you think Jimmy's dead the same as they do."

"Isn't he dead?"

"Of course not. There are things you don't know. Things nobody knows."

Hook felt awkward talking to her, but he did not want to ignore her. "About Jimmy?" he asked.

"About everything. Things you can't imagine. Not without stuff."

Rider shook his head in disgust. "Smack, she means. Heroin."

"That's not all," she protested. "I mean what's inside, too. Your karma. But what would you know about that? About anything?"

"Is Jimmy still alive?" Hook asked her.

"Everything, everywhere, is always alive. At all times. It can't die. There is no death. Things just change form, that's all." She looked out the window now with childish surprise and pleasure. "Hey, I like it around here. It's very pretty. It's not like where I'm from."

"Where's that?" Hook asked.

"What?"

"Where are you from?"

But suddenly her eyes had widened in panic. "My bag!" she cried. "Where's my bag?"

"Don't worry," Rider said. "We've got it. All of it."

"Give it to me."

"Can't do that, miss. It's evidence now."

She pressed her fists against her face and huddled down in the corner of the seat. "Give it to me. Please give it to me," she begged. "Jimmy, help me. Please, Jimmy."

Rider shook his head. "Sweet little job I've got, huh?"

Hook did not answer. He had decided it was time to get down to business, *his* business. "About the letter," he said.

"What about it?"

"What're you going to do?"

"What do you think I ought to do?"

"Well, does it sound to you like the letter of a boy about to kill himself?"

"No, it doesn't."

"And the postmark?"

"Yeah, I noticed. It leaves a day unaccounted for."

"All right, then."

"All right, then, what?"

"Then aren't you going to confront the women with it? Question them again?"

"You think it'd do any good?"

"Well, I sure as hell think it's your duty to find out." It had slipped out in anger.

Rider grinned coldly. "Thank you," he said. "Thank you for pointing out my duty. Then I guess it's also my duty to tell you this Icarus character your boy stayed with is a flaming fairy. With a record. And that don't help your case one little bit."

The first part did not surprise Hook; the second did. "A record? For what?"

"Contributing to the delinquency of a minor. A fifteen-year-old boy he had living with him. Picked him up on the freeway too, as I recall."

The sergeant's clear implication angered Hook. "What's a hitchhiker supposed to do, ask someone who stops for him if he's queer or not?"

"As a matter of fact, that might not be a bad idea." Rider lit a cigarette. "I'm just telling you. The fact that your boy stayed with him a couple of days—well, it could be construed as only confirming what the Madera woman says about him."

"What about the girls back home? The ones I told you about."

Rider shrugged. "If we could get statements from them—fine. That'd be on the other side of the ledger. But I've still got to look at both sides."

"That's all I'm asking."

"You don't have to ask, Mr. Hook. We do it anyway."

"I'm sure you do."

They had come to the courthouse now and Rider pulled up to the curb and stopped before driving on into the building garage. Hook was being dismissed. He got out one of his motel cards and handed it to Rider.

"That's where I'm staying," he said. "If anything develops——"

"Yeah, I'll get in touch," the sergeant cut in.

Getting out, Hook looked back at the girl, who was still huddled down in the corner of the seat. She appeared to be shivering now. He said goodbye to her.

"He's not dead," she said. "Remember. He's not dead."

That afternoon Hook stopped in at the offices of the local newspaper to read the coverage of Chris's death. The first story had appeared on Thursday, December 11, on the front page of the local news section. *Transient Dies in Fall at Hope Ranch Beach,* was the headline. The subhead clarified: *Illinois Youth's Death a Suicide, Witness Says*. The story contained nothing new, closely followed the "facts" in the case as Rider had given them to Hook. If there was anything surprising in the story, it was its matter-of-factness, its total lack of sensationalism. Reading it, one would have thought that Chris had been simply *the* transient suicide of the day, a participant in a routine event. But then Hook reminded himself of what he had already witnessed himself that morning, and that this was the country of Charles Manson and the Zodiac killer. Also, Rider had told him that there had been a number of unsolved beach killings in the area over the past few years. So what was one more violent death, and of an unknown transient? It was pretty goddamn little. And on the next day it was even less. The second story appeared on the third page of the local news section and mentioned that the body had been identified by the victim's father, David K. Hook, a farmer from Banner Hill, Illinois. The story, barely two column inches long, was the last.

Leaving the building, Hook walked back past City Hall and turned right on De la Guerra Street, heading for his car in the next block. When he reached it and got in, he checked his watch. The time was four-twenty, which meant that he would probably be sitting right where he was for the next forty to sixty minutes watching the front of a handsome beige-colored building farther up the block and across the street. It was the kind of place, the kind of setting, a January freeway commuter in Chicago or New York City might envision in some soaring moment of fantasy, an urban white-collar worker's own true dream of heaven. Like the other half-dozen structures with which it shared the block, the building was individual in its design and shape, yet similar in its fake adobe construction and orange tile roof and superb state of repair. There was a fence in front of it, a low concrete pediment with a graceful iron grillwork above, and it opened into a red-brick courtyard with orange and lemon trees and a fountain that actually founted—all surrounded on three sides by the U-shaped, two-story building. Each story had its own wide veranda bordered by a wrought-iron railing that repeated the design of the front fence. There was no sign on the building, in fact no signs anywhere except on the doors to the various office suites, and for the most part these were no more than an inch high, discreet gold-leaf letters on black backgrounds. They could not be seen from the street. To know which office was whose, you had to go through the gate and look for yourself—which Hook had done before breakfast that morning. On the door he was watching now, the first on the second floor of the west wing, the sign read: *jack douglas associates / public relations counseling.*

Hook did not know precisely who or what he expected to see. All he knew was that the lady who claimed to have watched his son take his life was probably in the building now and would be leaving within the next hour, perhaps with young Ferguson or maybe even with her employer.

So Hook waited, and watched. A few persons entered the building, a few came out of it, but none by way of the door to Douglas's suite of offices. Hook smoked one cigarette after another and in time darkness began to fall as gradually as winter rain, until finally after five o'clock the light was almost gone. Yet he was able to make out the faces of the people who began to trickle out of the building then, pretty young secretaries at first, then a number of older ones, and finally the men, the few professionals who had not already departed for home or bar.

At ten after five a young blonde secretary came out of Douglas's office and fled happily down the stairs. Hook's eyes wanted to follow her long-legged stride up the street but she had not locked the door behind her, in fact had left it slightly ajar, so Hook knew someone else would soon be coming out after her. And now that person came—Dorothy Rubin, moving with the ponderous assurance of a man, a powerful man. She locked the door behind her and checked it, and then started down the stairs, shunning the banister all the way. And even though she was carrying a large handbag and her dyed hair was bouffant and carefully set and her coat fur-collared and feminine, she still managed to cut a decidedly masculine figure, even an ominous figure, as she crossed the courtyard and disappeared into a corridor that led to the parking lot behind the building. Hook started his car and waited, hoping that she would turn in the direction he was parked, for otherwise he knew he would probably lose her in the five o'clock traffic.

But he was in luck. The small white Triumph convertible came out from behind the building and turned west, moving quickly into the traffic flow. Hook followed just as quickly, squealing his tires as he pulled out. She turned left at the next corner and drove toward the oceanfront. Past 101 she turned onto Cliff Drive and went on for another mile or so, finally pulling into a shopping center near the city limit. Hook followed her in and parked, but stayed in his car as she got out and went into a supermarket. While he waited for her to come out again he could not shake a feeling of vague embarrassment, for he was not sure what he was doing except acting like some kind of silly amateur private eye—first sitting in his car watching an office door for almost an hour and now following a woman home from work, stopping where she stopped—to buy groceries! What did he expect, that she would lead him to some sort of hideout where the guilty parties would all loudly discuss their guilt, so he could move in and make a citizen's arrest? No, the truth was he did not know what to expect, and in fact had no real plan of action, for he was still counting on Sergeant Rider. He believed that once the burly law officer confronted the women with Chris's letter and Icarus's testimony their lying statements would undergo a rapid transformation. And if that did not happen—well, he would cross that bridge when he came to it. Meanwhile he would have to settle for playing this game of private eye. He would stay close to his pair of liars and learn what he could.

The shopping center was jammed. In the parking lot the light standards were draped with Christmas lights and decorations, and Muzak carols were booming out from some place or other. And Hook felt almost at home, for this was the garish and vulgar twentieth-century America he had come to know and loathe—in Alton and other Saint Louis suburbs—with none of those expensive little touches with which downtown Santa Barbara groped for an elegant if imaginary past.

After ten or fifteen minutes she came out carrying a bag of groceries and a six-pack of Schweppes quinine water, which she sat down while she unlocked her car door. Hook, who was parked in the row facing hers but about three cars down, continued to sit behind the wheel watching her, even though all she had to do was look his way and she would have seen him. But her attention had locked elsewhere—on a longhaired willowy girl hanging out of the open door of a pickup and smiling, laughing, at someone inside it. Despite the cold, the girl was wearing only jeans and a tank top with no bra underneath, and none needed, and what Hook saw in Mrs. Rubin's face could have been lust, but if it was, then it was the most hate-filled lust he had seen in all his life. Now, conscious of what she was doing, Mrs. Rubin looked casually around herself, about to slip back into the Triumph—and then she saw him.

For a moment she appeared not to recognize him, glared at him only as a man who had seen her naked and ugly. And then it hit her, like a snowball in the face, a moment of shock, then fear, a fear she quickly covered. And finally it was hatred again. Bedrock.

She got into her car and drove off, wildly, almost running down an old woman and a teenage clerk wheeling a shopping cart full of groceries across the parking lot. Hook decided not to follow her. He had seen enough of Dorothy Rubin for one day.

That night, as he drove past it in the dark, the old hotel looked even more beautiful than he remembered it from the forties—like the courthouse a vast white Moorish castle, but low and sprawled out along the seafront, all minarets and arches and balconies set among its anarchy of wings and alcoves. The giant eucalyptus trees in front were more gigantic now, the sweeping lawn still smooth as a golf green, the lights burning inside still somehow as soft and moneyed as before. And of course the cars parked in front, along the drive, were big and shiny, though that was hardly a distinction anymore, in an age when the average chain motel could boast a parking lot every bit as gleaming. But here there was a beach beyond the parked cars, a beach where some of the oldest and dirtiest money in the nation took the winter sun, and where he and Mrs. Cunningham had walked and swam and talked and made love.

But as Hook drove slowly past now, it was not any talk he had had with her that he remembered but one with Kate a few months before her death, on an autumn night outside when he had set logs on top of burning leaves and the two of them had sat together toasting marshmallows and talking and watching the fire until long after the children and Aunt Marian and Arnie had gone to bed. And somehow the subject of Mrs. Cunningham had come up, a subject Hook had told Kate all about even before their marriage, not as a confession but as simply a part of his life that he had not wanted to withhold from her. And if she had been a touch jealous then, in the beginning, that touch had disappeared over the years, for on this night she expressed her gratitude that there had been a Mrs. Cunningham.

Hook asked her why.

"Because I'm so happy. So lucky."

"And you think she's responsible?"

"I don't know. But maybe if it hadn't been for her, maybe you would have been different when we met. And maybe we wouldn't have gotten together. Maybe I wouldn't have what I have now."

"And what's that?"

"You. The children."

"And we make you happy?"

"You make me happy."

He was sitting back against a log, with her between his legs, lying back against him. And when he said nothing now she turned and looked up at him.

"Aren't you?"

"What?"

"Happy."

He shrugged. "I'm contented. I'm in love. I've got a hard-on."

"You didn't say you're happy."

"Maybe I'm not a happy type."

"What does that mean?"

"Just that."

"That I don't make you happy."

He hugged her to him. "Don't be an ass. I love you. I love the kids. And I guess I like my work. But happy? Happiness is Eden, Kate. It's childhood."

"I'm not a child."

"I'm just saying how it is for me."

"And how is it?"

"I feel lucky, like a gambler with his winnings piled high in front of him. But the game goes on, and the house odds are four to one against him."

She shivered between his legs. "God, you make a person feel so good."

"I'm sorry, baby."

"It's the Swede in you—your dour Swedish half."

"You believe His eye is on the sparrow. Well, my eye is on Him. I keep looking back over my shoulder."

"You want too much."

"I didn't say I was unhappy."

"Just not happy."

Again he hugged her to him. He kissed her hair, her ear, her neck. "Can you promise me it'll stay this way, Kate? Can you say we'll live forever?" He took her silence as answer enough. "Then how can I be happy? The word is too small. Too shallow."

Finally she turned between his legs and kissed him on the mouth, long enough to make him ready for her despite the late hour and the day ahead of him.

"Maybe you're right," she said. "But I'm stupid, honey. I'm happy. And I'm glad I'm happy."

"I'm glad you are too."

"And I wish you were."

"Maybe I am. Maybe more than you. Could be it's just the word, a semantic thing."

"Then say it. Say you're happy."

"I'd rather show it."

"Here?"

"Bed will do."

"Say it."

"I love you, Kate."

"Bastard." But she had kissed him again, and as truly as ever.

5

At ten-fifteen the next morning Hook sat drinking coffee in the sidewalk café of El Paseo, the carefully contrived "Street in Spain" that after the Old Mission was probably Santa Barbara's main tourist attraction. Covering the better part of a block, the "street" was a picturesque warren of small curio and art shops lining a narrow pedestrian walk that meandered free as a mountain brook, leading into and out of the irregular central courtyard where Hook sat now, sipping scalding coffee at a small metal table next to a wall festooned with bougainvillea. But despite its being contrived, Hook found that he liked the place, enjoyed sitting out in the open in the cool lemony sunshine taking in the exotic plants and trees, the gnarled vines scaling the surrounding white adobe walls, none of which seemed in plumb, not truly straight or level or perpendicular, but life-shaped, human-scaled. There were hippies at a few of the tables, a scattering of businessmen reading the *Wall Street Journal,* and the inevitable representation of powdery old widows taking a morning breather in the grim rounds of their shopping. Hook hoped the coffee would relax him. He was feeling tight as strung catgut.

Sergeant Rider had called him at the motel around nine-thirty. How would he like to have a little confab with Miss Madera in Rider's office at eleven?

"Fine," Hook had said. "I'd like that fine."

"We lucked out," Rider explained. "The lady was on her way

to the tennis club. But she graciously consented to push her date back till noon. Just for me. How about that?"

"Does she know I'll be there?"

"I forgot to mention that."

"Good."

"I got to thinking the chemistry might be a little better with you here. If she's lying, I think the lies will come harder. Anyway, it should be interesting."

Yes, it would be that. Finishing his coffee, Hook left the court-yard café and went down one of the narrow shop-lined paseos to De la Guerra and walked to his car, again parked in the next block, across from the building where Jack Douglas and his associates worked the ground of public opinion. Getting in, Hook again settled back to watch the same front door on the second floor of the building's west wing. He had no idea whether Elizabeth Madera would stop by on her way to the meeting with Rider, or even that it would be particularly significant if she did. Mrs. Rubin after all *did* work there, and she was just as involved in the case as Miss Madera. And Douglas, simply as their respective employer and lover, would naturally be interested in any new developments in the case, especially in view of his political aspirations. So it was only to be expected that she would contact them, though most likely by phone. But even if she were to come in person—what would it mean? Nothing. And he knew it. But he also knew that he would remain right where he was until he had to leave, just before eleven. He would try to arrive after she did, for fear she might see him outside the courthouse and be able to prepare herself psychologically for what lay ahead. And he wanted her defenses down. He wanted to see her true face as the letter hit her, as she read the last written words of this young man she claimed had nothing to live for, this deviate of her dream world.

Hook lit a cigarette and continued to wait. A young hippie couple with a baby sauntered past, barefoot and happy, the girl in a maxi-dress and the boy in ragged jeans and a deerskin jacket, with an Indian headband holding down his long hair. He was carrying the baby on his back, papoose-style. To Hook's surprise the little family got into a brand new four-thousand-dollar Volkswagen camper bus parked up the street and drove off. It was a funny incident, a good sight gag, but Hook did not smile. He felt there was something sad about a generation for whom life increasingly was limited to play-acting and costumery. "I don't like who and what I am, so I will be different. I will be an Indian. Ergo, I shall dress as an Indian dresses." The only problem with this new tribe was that their daddies all had to be dentists or stockbrokers or plumbers—someone solvent enough to make payments on a camper bus.

As he stubbed out his cigarette a maroon Jaguar shot past his car, braked sharply up ahead, and plunged into the driveway just beyond Douglas's building. Hook settled lower in his car seat, watching the corridor that led to the parking lot. And immediately she came into view, striding rapidly, almost running across the red bricks of the courtyard to the stairway, her long hair flowing out behind her like black fire in the sunlight. She was wearing a white turtleneck sweater and tan suede jacket and brown slacks, and could have passed for one of the girls who pushed the high-priced cars on television. All she lacked was a cougar on a leash. Then abruptly she was gone, already inside the door at the top of the stairs.

Hook lit another cigarette and settled back, waiting. He was smoking too much, he knew, but it did not worry him now. Suddenly none of the old problems mattered, had fallen away much as they did during the hours of an Illinois tornado watch. After five or six minutes she came out again, followed not by Mrs. Rubin but by a man in his mid- or late thirties wearing baggy gray slacks and a tweed sport coat that looked lived in, even slept in. He was shorter than Hook but well built and handsome in a casual, shaggy-haired sort of way. Yet there was nothing casual about him at the moment. He was trying to finish saying something to Miss Madera, but she obviously did not want to stop and hear him out. So he took her by the arm and held her there while he tried to speak his piece. She submitted for a few seconds, nodding impatiently, and then angrily pulled her arm free and went on down the stairs. He leaned over the railing and said something more, but she kept on moving and in a moment disappeared into the corridor leading to the parking lot. The man went back into the office then and slammed the door shut behind him. Hook started the engine of his car and waited.

He arrived at Rider's third-floor office a few minutes after Miss Madera, and she reacted as he had expected she would, coolly, without the slightest hint of surprise or fear. Rider said a few vague words to the effect that he believed the two of them already knew each other, and then he got right down to business. A couple of new "things" had turned up in the case, he said, and Mr. Hook had flown here from Illinois to discuss them in person. And he, Rider, had thought it would be a good idea if she knew about them also.

"Why not Mrs. Rubin too?" she asked. "After all, she was the one who witnessed the act. Not me."

"That's true," Rider admitted. "But this new information concerns your statement more than hers."

"Oh? In what way?"

Not answering her for the moment, Rider began to search for something in the litter of papers on his desk. Hook, who was still standing just inside the door of the cramped cell-like office, sidled past both of them to reach a place where there was room enough to sit—on the corner of a table loaded down with bound reports. Miss Madera, in the chair next to Rider's desk, did not look at him as he moved past her.

"I'd appreciate it," she said, "if I could be out of here before noon."

"No problem. No problem at all." Now Rider gave up ransacking his desk and began to go through his coat pockets, one of which produced the envelope and letter. "Ah, here we are. This is the main thing, Miss Madera. A letter the boy sent from Santa Barbara just before his death. It arrived back in Illinois about the same time Mr. Hook did, with his body."

Rider held the letter out to her—for a good six seconds before she finally reached out and took it.

"Go ahead," he said. "Read it."

She unfolded the four crowded pages and began reading, rapidly, with cool dark eyes purged of any expression at all.

Rider gave Hook a cryptic look, then leaned back in his swivel chair and began to maul his face. Surveying the clutter of his desk, Hook noticed the man's choice of paperweights: a pair of hand grenades. On the wall hung a number of framed photographs: Rider receiving a citation of some kind; Rider standing with three other men, one of whom was no less than the nation's only film star turned governor; and a photo of a half-dozen bedraggled combat soldiers standing in bright sunshine next to the burned-out shell of a Second World War German tank. Hook recognized Rider in the center of the group, holding up a can of Blue Ribbon beer. And he looked even more bull-like then, with no belly and a full head of hair. Hook did not miss the fact that among all the photographs there was not one family picture.

But his attention kept straying to Miss Madera as she read, as she turned the pages one after another. And she had come to the last one now, to the last paragraph, by now graven in Hook's mind:

Seriously, I can hardly wait to see you all again, and see the farm and feel some real weather for a change. But I figure I'm here now, and I just might not pass this way again.

I miss you all. Much love.

Then there was his signature.

And she had come to it now, had reached the end of the letter. For a moment Hook thought there was nothing, just the same cool dark control, but as she looked up he saw that her eyes had filmed over. She was swift with explanation, however.

"It's so terrible. So sad." She looked boldly at Hook now, eyes level, honest, grave. "As I told you last week, Mr. Hook, I am very sorry for you. For your loss. I can understand your grief."

Rider had taken out a pack of cigarettes and now he offered one to her. She declined it. The sergeant took one himself and lit it. "That's all, Miss Madera?" he said. "That's your only reaction to the letter—sympathy?"

"Not at all."

"What else?"

"I don't enjoy saying this in front of Mr. Hook. But I obviously don't have much choice in the matter, do I? The letter just doesn't

107

sound like the boy I picked up, that's all. Not like the boy I talked with. It sounds too normal. Too healthy. It sounds like someone else entirely. A stranger."

Rider glanced over at Hook, who could feel the hope draining out of him like blood from a cadaver now, and being replaced by the clear cold fluid of hatred. He had to admire the way she sat there, a girl alone in a small room with two big men, one a detective and the other the father of her victim, and yet there was not a ripple on the still surface of her composure. She was as totally in control as a girl on a *Vogue* cover, not a touch of gaucheness or doubt or weakness anywhere, not from her thick careless hair to the expensive but acceptably worn suede jacket to the tooled-leather moccasins that said she wore not some fag designer's careful ensembles but what she damned well pleased.

Rider was nodding thoughtfully to her, in apparent agreement. "Well now, that was exactly our problem with the letter," he told her. "I mean it's hard to read a letter like this and try to square it with—what was it you said he kept repeating out at the house?—that he had *nothing to live for?* Wasn't that it?"

She agreed. "Yes. It doesn't sound like the same person."

Smiling ruefully, the sergeant pretended to think long and hard about that. "But, you see, the problem is—it *is* the same person. Christopher Hook *did* write the letter. The handwriting is his. And the boy did stay with this photographer Icarus for a few days. And Icarus says Christopher seemed to him to be very happy and easygoing. In fact—" Rider casually reached over and picked up the mounted photograph, which had been lying face-down on the corner of his desk. Now he held it out in front of her. "In fact, he took this picture the day before Chris left."

It had come almost too suddenly for Hook as well as for Miss Madera. But he did not miss her eyes just before she closed them now and turned away. They had been open wounds, sockets of pain. And her tanned face had gone white, whether in anger or shock Hook did not know.

The sergeant returned the photograph to the top of his desk. "I'm sorry," he said. "I didn't mean to upset you."

But she was already in control again. "No. Of course not." She flipped it at him, dry, subtle, not an obvious sarcasm.

"So you see our problem," Rider said.

"I'm afraid not."

The sergeant tapped the letter with his index finger. "Well, this boy and the one in your statement—they just don't seem to be the same person."

"I don't see that it's a problem at all. He had to be pretending either in the letter or to us, to Mrs. Rubin and me." She paused for a moment, looking at Hook and then back at the sergeant before she slammed the lid shut on them now. "And you did find his body, didn't you? I'd say he wasn't pretending there. I'd say that was real."

Rider sat there looking at her and nodding stupidly, as if he did not know what to say next. But Hook did.

"This is real too, Miss Madera. I can get a deposition from every boy and girl in his graduating class that this letter represents the Christopher Hook they knew. And that he was straight. That he was *not* an invert."

She met his eyes for a moment, then looked down at her lap and shook her head wearily, almost hopelessly. "I just don't know what I can say to you. To either of you. I only know what happened. But I've already told you that. And frankly I don't even know why I'm here alone, why these new 'developments' of yours don't involve Mrs. Rubin the same as me. After all, she was the eyewitness. And she reported what he said too. It isn't just *my* statement that he talked about having nothing to live for."

The sergeant was nodding along with her, seemingly only too eager to agree with her. "That's very true. You're right about that. But that part, the tone of the letter, is just one of our problems. There's another one, Miss Madera. And it concerns just you, not Mrs. Rubin." He picked up the letter and the envelope again. "It's the date of the letter. See? December eighth. And the boy finished writing it the next day, on the ninth. Which as you can see is the date of the postmark. Tuesday, December nine, A.M."

Miss Madera smiled in bewilderment. "So?"

"In your statement, you said you picked him up on Wednesday."

"And I did. Wednesday morning." She was not smiling now.

"Wednesday morning," Rider repeated. "You're still sure about that?"

"I am positive."

The sergeant shrugged wearily and crushed out his cigarette. "Well, we just wanted to be sure. Because as you can see, everything else points to Tuesday morning as the time the boy left town. The letter. And this Icarus he stayed with—he says it was Tuesday too. So you can see our problem."

Her eyes coolly searched the sergeant's face for every nuance of meaning. Then she shook her head. "No, Sergeant, I can't see that it's a problem. At least, not *my* problem. I picked him up Wednesday morning. If he started to leave Tuesday morning and changed his mind, or if someone else local picked him up and he stayed on in town another day—well, I just can't see that it's my problem. Yours, maybe. And Mr. Hook's. But not mine."

"So you want to leave your statement as it is."

"The facts haven't changed, so neither will my statement."

Rider gave her a rueful, little-boy grin. "Well, I guess that was our mistake," he allowed. "We thought the facts had changed."

"So I gather."

"But you picked him up Wednesday morning, around ten. And he killed himself that night—or Thursday morning actually, a little after midnight."

In answer she nodded gravely, looking down at her hands in her lap.

The sergeant pushed back his chair and looked over at Hook. "Well, that about covers it, then. You satisfied, Mr. Hook?"

"Miss Madera knows when I'll be satisfied," he said.

She did not look up at him. "You'll be staying on here, then?"

"For a while, yes."

Grunting like a hog, Rider heaved himself to his feet. "Oh, I'm not so sure about that," he mused. "I think maybe we can talk Mr. Hook into letting us do our job without his help. After all, he's got a lot of cattle to take care of back there in Illinois. Isn't that right, Mr. Hook?"

Hook did not answer. He was watching Miss Madera, who had gotten to her feet now too. She asked the sergeant if that was all, and he said yes, he thought it was.

"Then I'll be leaving," she said. "I hope I've helped you."

Rider said that she had, and thanked her for coming in. She left without glancing at Hook.

As the door closed behind her, the sergeant shook his head approvingly. "One very snazzy young lady there," he said.

"One very competent liar."

Rider made a face. "Maybe so, maybe not."

"You know she's lying as well as I do."

"I know I'd like to handle the case alone. Without your help."

Hook ignored the request. "You know where she's headed now?"

The sergeant was gathering up a few papers, apparently getting ready to leave. "I got a pretty good idea."

"She stopped there on the way here."

"And why shouldn't she? Her lady friend works there. And so does the man she sleeps with."

"He came outside with her as she left. Gave her last-minute instructions. He seemed kind of desperate."

Rider had his papers all in a folder now. "I've got to leave. You sure you don't want to say goodbye? For good, I mean?"

"Did you check him out—find out where he was at the time of Chris's death?" His last time in Rider's office, a week ago, Hook had informed the sergeant what the busboy had told him about Douglas, and that it would be a good idea to find out if the man had an alibi. Rider had not liked the idea then, and he did not like it now.

"Look, will you forget about him? I told you last week that was a dead issue, and it still is. The man is clean. In another year he'll probably be our congressman, for Christ sake. And if you think I'm gonna blow him out of the water simply because he likes to step out a little, then you got another think coming."

Rider's vehemence surprised Hook. The sergeant's face had reddened and he had folded his arms tightly across his chest, as if to keep himself from doing anything violent.

But Hook kept his voice level, unexcited. "Did you check him out or not?"

"I said he was clean, didn't I? So yes, we checked him out."

"He has an alibi, then?"

Rider tried for irony. "Well, he was playing cards with three other men at the time. If you think that's good enough, then yes, he has an alibi."

"It depends on who the men were."

For a long time the sergeant just stood there staring at Hook. Then he grinned crookedly and shook his head in mock despair. "I'll be seeing you," he said.

After eating lunch at a drive-in, Hook had gone back to his motel to wash up and consider what his next moves should be, but he had not been able to relax there and before he knew it he was back in his rented Galaxie again, only this time heading out of the city, on Cliff Drive, toward Mrs. Rubin's beach house. He knew it was probably a stupid thing to be doing, that he could even wind up being arrested for trespassing, but he felt it was worth the risk because he might be able to learn a few things this way he could never learn with the two occupants of the house on the scene. And anyway there were the neighbors to be checked out. The fact that they had told Sergeant Rider they had seen nothing and heard nothing the night of Chris's death did not eliminate them in Hook's mind as sources of possibly valuable information. For one thing, there was now another day to ask them about—Tuesday. Maybe they had seen the tall blond young man at the house on that day, a good forty-eight hours before he fell to his death. And there were other things a neighbor might know about Elizabeth Madera and her friends, things Hook wanted to know too. As to why any of these neighbors would open up to him, a stranger, he felt that simple human nature favored his cause, that they would help him either out of sympathy for his loss or because of antipathy to Miss Madera, whom an older and plainer female neighbor would surely find very difficult to like.

But once he arrived at the beach house Hook found that his great expectations were only that. The sun was so bright it was almost impossible to see anything through the house's windows, which reflected the brilliance of the day like mirrors. He walked through the row of shaggy eucalyptus trees to the house next door and found no one at home there except a short stout Mexican maid who promptly claimed an almost total ignorance of anything, anybody, anytime. The owners of the house had a *muy* big boat and they went fishing much of the time, and were fishing now, down off the coast of Baja, she guessed, although of course she was not sure about that either. Yes, she had heard about the terrible thing that poor boy had done next door, but she had not been here at the time, in fact came in only twice a week now, on Tuesdays and Fridays, so all she knew about the tragedy was what she had read in the newspaper. Had she seen the boy over there on Tuesday, the day before his death? Oh no, she almost never even looked over there, because she had so much work to do right here—the house was a large one and her employers wanted it kept so clean you could eat off the floors if you wanted. No, she did not know either of the women who lived next door. She had seen them at a distance a few times, but that was all. And now, if the gentleman would please excuse her, she still had much work to do.

Hook thanked her for her time and walked on to the last of the three houses, where he found no one at home except two snarling German shepherds that would have eaten him alive except for the chain-link fence that enclosed them and against which they kept leaping in their frenzy to get at him. Hook walked back to his car then, which he had parked on the shoulder of the narrow blacktop lane that led in from Cliff Drive. Altogether the lane and the three houses made a very handsome cul-de-sac, neatly hidden from the road by a thick growth of live oaks.

Before getting back in his car, Hook debated whether to stay there a while longer. He did not know what more he could do, but then neither did he know what he could accomplish back in town. He had been on the coast almost two days now and he was afraid he was still running around with all the purpose and direction of a freshly decapitated chicken. He felt a first faint touch of despair and knew he had to fight it, had to stay in control. More precisely, he had to slow down, think, plan. And part of that slowing down, he decided, was to stay right where he was and poke around a little more, give things a chance to come to him instead of his rushing blindly in what he hoped was their direction. If nothing else, he could walk along the beach and think.

So, leaving his car now, he headed back down the row of euca-lyptus to the cliff and wandered along it to a point where the live oaks and Cliff Drive itself came almost to the cliff edge, pushed there by a steeper cliff behind. Under one of the trees he sat back against a boulder and lit a cigarette. The day was not only bright but so clear that the channel islands looked just a few miles out instead of the thirty or forty he knew them to be. To his right, on a headland jutting into the Pacific, a stand of high-rise build-ings identified the Isla Vista campus; and to his left, down the coast, a half-dozen oil-drilling platforms looked like tiny tran-sistors set in the sun-dazzled sweep of the sea. So in effect he found himself positioned neatly between the Scylla and Charyb-dis of the new American crisis—on the one side the hard rock of the bank-burners, a generation in violent revolt against every-thing symbolized by the whirlpool that had formed on his other side three years before, the black filth that had come gushing up out of the sea like the blood of a rectal carcinoma, a system in terminal disease. And the irony of it was that Hook's physical position, midway between the two, was a fair approximation of his philosophic position as well. He had long feared and hated the power of big business in America, yet he himself as a small businessman, an entrepreneur, feared even more the prospect of a society regimented by social activists dedicated to the proposi-tion that all men should be free to do everything *their* way. So Hook sat on the fence, and squirmed.

Despite the rock and the whirlpool, he found it a beautiful place, this place where his son had died. Ten days ago the boy had been here, he reflected, had viewed this same sea and those same islands. His eyes saw. His ears heard. His heart beat. He lived, and knew he lived. And now he lived no more. He was like rock, like sand, like a broken branch. He was a thing, a buried thing. And Hook did not understand. He had never understood life, the raw pink babies he had held, flesh of his flesh, blood of his blood. And he did not understand the death of that life now. Stars and stones and life and death, all was mystery to him.

6

When he returned to the beach house to get his car, Hook saw the familiar maroon Jaguar come up the blacktop lane and turn into the driveway. Elizabeth Madera was behind the wheel. Next to her was the man she had talked with earlier at Jack Douglas's office. At first, as they struggled out of the low-slung car, neither noticed him; they were both looking in the direction of his parked Galaxie. Then Miss Madera turned and saw him. And in the seaside quiet her voice carried clear and cold.

"It's him."

Douglas—and Hook did not doubt that was who the man was —turned easily, loosely, even smiling slightly as Hook approached them.

"Mr. Hook—I'm Jack Douglas." He put out his hand.

Hook took hold of it, a strong hand but soft as calfskin. "How do you do?"

"Fine, thank you. Liz here was telling me about your meeting at the sheriff's this morning. I want you to know you have my sympathy. I'm a father myself. I think I can understand a little of what you're going through."

The words came too easily, too glibly, yet Hook could not fault the man's expression, which had no trace of cheeriness or false goodwill. His face was strong and squarish, with small even teeth that looked almost phosphorescent against his dark tan. And Hook saw that his hair, which had appeared shaggy from the half-block distance of Hook's parked car that morning, was simply fashionably long and razor-cut. But the sport coat and trousers looked just as rumpled as they had earlier, rumpled and expensive.

Hook thanked him for his expression of sympathy.

"Were you waiting here for Liz?" Douglas asked. "Was there something else you wanted to see her about?"

"I'm not sure. I just got in the car and came out here."

Douglas's eyes flicked from Hook to the cliff edge and then back again. "Well, I think we can understand that. And I'm sure you're welcome here. In fact, why don't you come in and have a drink? I know I could use one. I've had one hell of a busy day so far."

Hook looked at Liz Madera. "If it's all right with you," he said.

Douglas smiled. "Of course it's all right with Liz. Come on, let's go in."

Hook followed them into the house, which was warm and stuffy, evidently having been closed up tight all day. It was also messy. Dirty dishes were piled in the sink; filled ashtrays and used cocktail glasses sat abandoned on the coffee table, on the hearth, on the railing of the deck outside. If not a party, then there had been a conference here the night before, a wet one. Hook would have given much to know who had attended and what they had talked about.

Liz Madera threw her jacket over a chair. Then pushing up the sleeves of her white turtleneck, she slid open the glass doors to the sundeck. Meanwhile Douglas, making no pretense of not being right at home, had gone behind the room's small bar and was getting out glasses and ice.

"Scotch all right?" he asked.

Hook said it would be fine.

"You, Liz?"

She shook her head. "Nothing."

As Douglas prepared the drinks he explained to Hook that the owner of the house, Mrs. Rubin, worked for him—actually was an "associate" of his—and her car had broken down—was already in the shop, in fact—so he had brought Miss Madera home in order to take her car back to town with him so Mrs. Rubin would have a means of getting home after work. Throughout this short tale, Hook watched Douglas carefully. His movements were swift and easy; he was consummately at ease. And despite Hook's belief that the man was somehow tied in with Chris's death, he found him difficult to dislike. He obviously had a talent for making others feel important and liked, so he in turn of course was automatically even better liked. In short, he was a natural politician. Like a Hemingway whore, he had found his profession.

As Douglas handed him his drink, Hook decided it was time to get down to business. "That's your relationship with Miss Madera?" he asked. "You're just her landlord's boss?"

Leaning back against the bar, Douglas regarded him thoughtfully. "No, we're pretty good friends in our own right," he said finally. "I guess that's a fair statement, isn't it, Liz?"

Hook looked over at her. She was standing in the open doorway gazing out at the sea. She did not turn or answer. Apparently handling him was to be Douglas's job alone.

"That's what I heard," Hook said.

Douglas grinned quizzically. "Anything wrong with that?"

"Not with *that*, no."

Douglas lit a cigarette. His expression said it all, that here he was, this bright decent fellow, this important and busy man, trying to be nice to some hick farmer from the Midwest, in fact bending over backwards to be nice to him, and where was it getting him?

"Mr. Hook," he said. "I'm the kind of man who likes to put his cards on the table. And I wish you'd do the same. Just what is it you're trying to say?"

"Not say—*ask*. I guess I want to ask if it doesn't bother you that Miss Madera picks up young hitchhikers and brings them here."

From the doorway Liz Madera finally spoke. "See what I mean?"

"I'm beginning to," Douglas laughed.

So Hook was laughable now, a comic figure. It took some doing, but he choked that down too and found it amazing what a man could do without, what he would throw into the pot when the stakes were high enough.

"Trouble is, I can understand," Douglas said, serious again, even solemn. "In your shoes, I think I'd be doing just what you are. I've got a son too, twelve years old. And frankly, I wouldn't be able to buy it either, what you're being asked to buy. I'd want to do some digging myself." He had picked up the bottle of scotch again, and now he refilled his glass. Seeing that Hook's was still almost full, he set the bottle back down. And he was frowning now, an actor conveying troubled reflection. "On the other hand, Mr. Hook, you ought to try to understand the position of Liz and Mrs. Rubin. They've told the police the truth as they saw it. The fact that you can't see it the same way—well, that just doesn't give you a license to go trampling all over their private lives. Now you can stay out here on the coast till doomsday trying to find your own version of the truth—I'm sure the ladies won't mind that at all. They've got nothing to hide. But at the same time you've got to respect their privacy. Like today. You just can't come out here nosing around while no one's here."

Hook had sat down in an easy chair in front of the fireplace. Normally, he would never have sat while a host and hostess remained on their feet, but he had felt he was being *acted* to, was being manipulated, and he had decided that was a game two could play. His position, slouched down, legs thrown out, somehow gave him a psychological advantage over Douglas, made him seem the cool casual arbiter, judge to Douglas's sweating advocate.

Now that advocate smiled hopefully. "Am I getting through to you?"

Hook did not answer.

"In other words, Mr. Hook—there are laws. And they can be invoked."

"I'm sure they can."

Douglas glanced over at Liz in the doorway as though he hoped for some support from that quarter. But there was only silence. Looking back at Hook, he shook his head in regret. "Believe me—we do sympathize with you. If there was anything in the world that girl there could do to bring your son back——"

Now she spoke. "Oh for Christ sake, Jack! Stop it!"

Hook cut in. "Stop what, Miss Madera?"

"Stop playing your game, that's what!"

118

"Are we playing games?" Hook asked.

"Of course not," Douglas said. "She's just upset, that's all. And you can't really blame her, considering the day she's had so far."

"It's not only her I'm interested in," Hook said. "And not just Mrs. Rubin either. There's also you."

Douglas regarded him thoughtfully. "You do push, don't you?"

"You could get me out of your hair if you wanted to."

"But you're not in my hair. I have no complaints."

"You will have."

Douglas had held the thoughtful look. Now he inclined it towards amusement. "All right. For argument's sake, what would get you, as you put it, *out of our hair.*"

"*Your* hair."

"*My* hair then."

"Give me the names of the men you were playing cards with the night my son died."

"You're serious, aren't you?"

"I'm serious."

Douglas looked over at Liz and shook his head incredulously. "I'm beginning to see why you were so shook this morning. I'm afraid we're dealing with a—" He turned back to Hook. "What would you call yourself, Mr. Hook? A monomaniac? Does that sound unfair?"

"It sounds beside the point."

"Ah, the point. And what is that?"

"That if you *were* playing cards that night—if you really weren't here—then you've got nothing to fear. There's no reason not to give me the names."

Douglas had dispensed with his smile now, his incredulity, his act. He stood at the bar studying Hook openly, slowly tolling the bell of his empty glass back and forth.

"You're right," he said finally. "You're absolutely right." He set down the glass and took out a ball pen and a business card. He wrote quickly, then held the card out to Hook, without moving towards him.

And Hook was perfectly willing to surrender his position for the prize. He got up and took the card.

"Will that do?" Douglas said.

Hook read the names: Rich Ferguson, Bo Parnelli, Dr. Herb Hammer.

"I've met Ferguson," he said. "These other two work for you too?"

"Not Dr. Hammer. But he is an old friend. I have this weird habit of playing cards with people I know."

Hook had what he wanted now. But to get it he was afraid he had gone too far, had put Douglas too much on guard. Placing the card in his pocket, he tried to undo some of the damage.

"Thanks for indulging me," he said. "I guess all this is just to put my mind at ease. So I'll know I did all I could. When I reach a dead end—and I imagine I will—I'll be out of your hair."

It was a hangdog, humble-pie performance. But Hook could not tell if Douglas had bought it. The man did smile, though, sympathetically. "As I said before—I can understand. I really can."

"I appreciate that." Hook finished his drink and set the glass on the bar.

Douglas was checking his watch. "Well, I've got to be going. Busy afternoon ahead of me. Come on, I'll walk you to your car."

Hook looked over at Liz Madera. "If Miss Madera wouldn't mind, I'd like to stay and talk with her a few minutes." At her look of alarm, he added: "About what my son said, that's all. During his last hours. If it really was suicide, I'd appreciate having more to go on, so I'll have some idea where it all went wrong. I have another son, you see. Two years younger."

Douglas looked at Liz Madera and shrugged. "I don't see why not."

"You *believe* him?" she said.

"Why not?"

"You don't *know* him. He doesn't believe it was suicide. He never will."

"What can it hurt, Liz? Just tell him what you know. I'd say he's got a right, wouldn't you?"

Liz gave in then, turning angrily away from both of them. Douglas shook Hook's hand and said he was glad he had met him despite their problems, and that he hoped he had been of some help. Then he suggested that Liz walk with him to the car, and they went out onto the front deck and down the stairs and headed back toward the driveway. Hook lit a cigarette and went out onto the deck himself, into the sunshine. Hitching one leg up onto the railing, he sat there smoking and waiting, and finally he heard the car's engine explode into sound.

When she returned, Liz Madera did not waste words. No matter what he or Jack Douglas might have thought, she was not in a mood to be grilled by anyone about anything, and was going for a walk on the beach, and if he wanted to go along with her that was his goddamn business, it was a free beach. She swept into the house then and came back out in a few minutes barefoot and wearing old chinos and a black sleeveless sweatshirt. As he followed her down the stairs she suggested that he leave his socks and shoes behind unless he wanted to get them wet, and while he was at it he might want to take off his tie and suit coat as well—not very many people on the beach these days were dressed for business, she threw back at him. So by the time he was properly stripped down Hook had to move quickly to catch up with her as she walked past the other two houses to a footpath that zigzagged down the sloping face of the cliff, which at that point was actually more a steep hill than a cliff. The path, moving through the chaparral, was liberally salted with horse manure, and Miss Madera explained that the Hope Ranch horsey set used the path to go down to the beach. They rode their mounts in the surf "just like on the tube," she said. The horses loved it. Salt water was great for sore hooves. But then of course as a farmer he undoubtedly already knew that. Or didn't he have horses?

"No," he said. "Just cattle."

"Just business, huh?"

"That's right. Just business."

Turning with the path, she looked back at him. "I've got to hand it to you, though—conning Jack the way you did. Not very many people con Jack Douglas."

"And how did I do that?"

"Oh, you don't have to pretend with me. That bit about your

reaching dead end—you know, accepting the idea that it was a suicide. I call that conning somebody."

Hook said nothing. They were almost down to the beach now, and he was watching both the path and her figure a few feet in front of him, her long dark hair burning in the sunlight and the clean curve of her back and her buttocks moving under the rough washed-out pants, and once again he hated her beauty, that it had cost him so dearly and still he could not ignore it.

They reached the bottom of the cliff. To their right the beach curved in a long sickle toward Isla Vista five or six miles away. But Liz Madera headed in the other direction, in which there was only about a mile of beach visible, a tan strip wide as a four-lane highway curving under the cliffs toward a distant spit, in front of which the surf foamed against a reef of black rock. All along the beach, at high-tide mark, great twining heaps of kelp lay strung out like the ocean's entrails, rotting in the sun.

As they walked along, Miss Madera commented on the way Hook had gone after Douglas. "It interests me," she said. "Just how do you have it figured? That I'm his mistress, and that he found out your son was staying with me overnight, and promptly came out here in a blind rage and threw him off the cliff?"

"Something like that," he admitted. "I figure it might have been an accident."

She looked over at him pityingly. "I'm afraid you don't know Jack Douglas very well. Now, if I could deliver ten thousand votes at election time and someone came along and threatened to take *that* away from him—well, then maybe he just might lose his cool. Unfortunately, I have just one vote, Mr. Hook. And one body—which, believe me, he will share with total unconcern." Picking up a shell, she smiled ruefully. "For instance, I remember a party in Montecito this past summer. It was—well, like most of the parties you go to around here, everybody smashed and vulgar and desperate, holding onto hearth and home with one hand while they sneak in a few extramarital feels with the other —you know, groping each other in the corners, a little soul kissing, so they can all feel at least a little bit wild and free and modern. But still safe, of course. So I usually do some unforgettable little thing to show everyone my uniqueness of spirit. I have to let them know I'm not one of them, you see. And that night—that night what I did was try to lay the host. In the back seat of his Rolls-Royce, in the garage. Well, Jack found out what was going on and got some of his cronies together and they all crawled into the garage and peeked in at us through the whole sad performance—sad because the host was too drunk to get anything up, including me. Finally, Jack turned on the garage lights —just as I'm about to fall asleep. Big laugh, of course. Lots of fun all around. Good clean civilized fun." She looked over at Hook now. "All of which I imagine sounds pretty disgusting to you."

Hook stared straight ahead, trying to keep her from seeing that it not only disgusted him but made him deeply, unreasonably, angry. "Yes," he admitted. "It does."

"They don't do things like that in Banner Hill," she ventured.

Hook did not miss it that she remembered the town's name. "I guess it goes on," he said. "Though not in a Rolls-Royce."

"But of course you'd never be a part of it—never a voyeur on his knees."

"No, I'm afraid not."

"All I'm saying is Jack's not the jealous type. Nor the faithful type. What he is, is the political type. But then it's all academic anyway, as you'll find out when you check the names he gave you. He wasn't at the beach house that night. You're taking a blind alley."

"Maybe so. But it's all I've got so far."

"Not all. There's still my word. And Dorothy's."

"Yes, there's still that."

"Only that's not much, is it?" She tossed him a smile meant to be sardonic, light, but he could see the pain in it.

"I wish it were."

Her reaction to that was to walk away from him, out into the surf as it slid up the pitch of the beach and then ran out again, trailing intricate lines of force. She went deep enough so that the water rose above her ankles, soaking the bottom of her chinos. And for a hundred yards or so she went on this way, walking alone in the water as if she felt it constituted a barrier against him and any further conversation. Then they came to the reef, whose jagged black rocks appeared to be moving landward, like sculptured surf, waves forever about to fall and crash. And the reef forced her to come back onto the beach, which was narrow at that point under the cliff and strewn with boulders and rock formations. On one of the rocks, which sloped up smoothly from the sand, she lay back in the sun and covered her eyes with her forearm. Hook lit a cigarette and leaned back against another boulder. For a while neither of them said a word. Hook stood there smoking and trying not to look at her, but that proved impossible. Her hair was spread out on the rock like some luxuriant wild sea growth and her mouth was parted, her teeth bared—against the sun probably, against the brightness—but it looked like the beginning of a smile, the smile of a woman making love, and he wondered if she was trying to seduce him, or just tease him, mock him. And he began to wonder if he understood her at all, if that honest suffering human thing he sometimes thought he saw in her eyes reflected anything inside or was just a screen, a mirror reflecting only himself, what he wanted to see in her. From the beginning he had thought of her as somehow a victim too, like Chris, a part of the tragedy. But now the possibility that she could be more, even its perpetrator, began to slip and crawl over the surface of his mind like a worm seeking entrance.

"This whole thing," she said suddenly. "I know how it is for you. You've made that abundantly clear to all of us. But do you ever wonder how it is for me?"

"I'd like to know that very much," he said.

"Why? You'd only despise me all the more."

"I don't despise you."

"Maybe you should. But then it doesn't matter anyway. So I'll tell you how it is for me—your son's death. It's an *irritant*, Mr. Hook." And she continued to lie there with her eyes covered and her mouth parted, almost as if she were waiting for him to do something, strike her, maim her, kill her.

"How do you like that?" she asked. "Not so hot, I imagine."

All Hook could do was repeat the word. "An irritant?"

"Yes, that's what I said. An irritant. But let me be more specific. It's like—well, like there was a fire in a hospital—a hospital in which I was already dying. There I am, near death. The priest has mumbled the proper words over me, and I am ready. And then there is this—" She looked out from under her arm at him for a moment, squinting. "—There is this tall intense man from the other side of the moon and he keeps shaking me and asking me about the fire—*his* fire—and I want to *feel*—I want to help him. But I can't, you see. I am dying."

Hook decided to go along with her. His rage would keep. "Of what are you dying?"

"Of life, Mr. Hook. I'm dying of life."

"You're dying a spiritual death."

"Yes, that's all. Just a spiritual death."

"I can't see why. I'd think if anyone would have been able to find love in this world, it would be you."

"Love? Or sex?"

"I said love. I meant love."

Again she moved her arm and looked up at him. And suddenly tears came into her eyes, began to run down her face. She sat up then, not bothering to hide the tears or even wipe them away.

Hook asked her why she was crying.

"Why?" She shook her head thoughtfully. "I don't know. I was thinking of him. Your son. And I *envied* him. Just the thought of it, having someone care for me as you must have for him, to come all this way, to do what you're doing."

"Is it so unusual?"

Smiling unhappily, even bitterly, she nodded. "Oh yes. In my world it would be quite unusual. My own dear father, for instance—Don Felipe Ricardo de la Madera, as he bills himself. For him, the action wouldn't have been at the sheriff's office at all but at the cemetery. It would have been a marvelous and beautiful service, and no one there would have looked more elegant and sexy than he, with his curly gray hair teased just so. I can see him at the graveside, Mr. Hook—his eyes wandering discreetly one way and then the other—looking for *cunt*, of course. He did it at my wedding, so why shouldn't he do it at my funeral? And he was successful too—with one of my bridesmaids, a nice little kid not even eighteen yet—even younger than I was—but she was old enough for Daddy. I heard later they almost arrested him over that one, but I was gone on my honeymoon at the time and didn't know about all the publicity. He filled me in later, though, one night when he was drunk. Bragged about it. I had the feeling he was trying to make me jealous."

She had stopped crying now and was just sitting there on the slab staring out at the sea and smiling coldly.

"There are some men like that, I suppose," Hook said. "They're not worth dying over."

She laughed with quiet scorn. "Don't worry, it's not him I'm dying over, and not even our friend Mr. Douglas, who's sort of the last of the line, my father's line, at least in my life anyway. No, it isn't any man I'm dying over, Mr. Hook. It's as I said—I'm dying of life. I'm twenty-six. I've been married and divorced, and I've caused other divorces. I wake up with strangers, and I've been through analysis and drugs and travel, and I've tried to find it in religion and books. But it wasn't there. Not for me." Looking up again, she smiled disparagingly, pretending she had not drilled into bare nerve. "Anyway, it's not important, is it? I'm just one among millions in this country right now. In fact, I'm not sure I know anybody who isn't dying inside or at least living as if they were. It's our contemporary Black Death. Do you have it in Illinois? Has it reached your bucolic friends and neighbors?"

"I don't think so," he said. "Not the way you describe it."

"Why is it so virulent here then? Is it affluence? Is it our fabled Santa Barbara money?"

She was playing with the subject now—playing with him too—but he went along anyway. "I would imagine that's part of it." He believed it was.

She studied him in silence. "But to you it isn't serious, is it?" she said finally. "It isn't real. I can see it in your eyes. She isn't dying, you're thinking. She's just trying to evade the issue, trying to put me off. Isn't that right? Isn't that what you're thinking?"

Hook dropped his cigarette into the sand and buried it with his foot. Reluctantly, he nodded. "Yes, it is."

She smiled. "The man who cannot tell a lie. You're a sort of latter-day George Washington, aren't you?"

"Miss Madera—"

"*Miss Madera*," she cut in. "It sounds so formal, so stilted. But then I can't very well ask you to call me Liz, can I?"

126

"No, you can't."

"All right, then—Miss Madera, what?"

So this was it then, the time to make his pitch, his one last try at reaching her, and he knew just by the way she was looking up at him, all brightness and irony, that the words would not come easily or well—and that he would fail. Nevertheless he tried.

"I realize we've already gone over this before, that first night. But time has passed since then. He's buried now. You've 'died' a little more. You've had time to think. So please—all I want is to hear it once again, here, alone, just the two of us. I want you to look at me and tell me that Chris was a homosexual, and that he said he had nothing to live for, and that he took his own life."

Even before he was finished she had begun to shake her head in a kind of wonderment, disbelief. "You are so pitiful, you know that?" she said now. "So pitifully square. Don't you think I could look you in the eye—and lie, and lie, and lie?"

"That's what I'm trying to find out."

Her look of amused incredulity withered and in its place there was only pain and anger now. She got up and strode swiftly on ahead of him, through the rocks and around the tip of the headland, a cliff jutting out into the sea like an overturned ocean liner. Following her, Hook saw ahead of them another great sweep of beach running all the way to Arroyo Burro, where in the light of a driftwood fire Mrs. Cunningham had introduced him to the pleasures of fellatio so many years before. Far in the distance he saw a few surfers braving the fifty-degree water. He came abreast of Liz, and together they walked along in silence, moving past the last of the rocks. And then Hook saw that one was not a rock at all but a dead sea lion lying in the sand, its body moving slightly as the last few feet of surf would wash in around it and recede, as if the sea were trying to reclaim it. The creature's eyes were open, a pair of milky gray orbs that appeared to see both everything and nothing.

"The beach patrol will pick him up," Liz said, as they moved around it. "It's not unusual. You see one every now and then. I think when they feel they're dying they come to land to die—to die like an animal, not a fish."

Hook asked her if that was fact or theory.

"My kind of fact," she replied.

It was obvious to Hook that he was not going to get anything from her, not if he stayed with her throughout the afternoon. So it made him feel ridiculous to still be walking along with her, like some overly friendly stray dog. His pride begged him to turn and walk away, but he could not. He told himself there was still the possibility that something might be learned.

And suddenly she sounded as if she were about to give him everything.

"Mr. Hook, let me ask you this. And this is just theoretical. If I could tell you what you wanted to hear—that Chris wasn't queer, and he didn't say he had nothing to live for, that he didn't take his own life—could you just accept it and go home? Could you let it go at that?"

Hook tried to keep his voice even. "Maybe. But I'd want to know what did happen."

"What if I said it was just an accident?"

"I'd want to know why you call it a suicide."

"And if I said that was a stupid accident too?"

"I'd want to know how. In what way."

"And if I couldn't tell you?"

Hook looked at her. Her gaze was level, calm, fixed on the distant surfers. "Why couldn't you?" he asked.

"Perhaps I was stoned at the time. Unconscious."

He took her by the arm and spun her roughly around, making her face him. "And were you?" he asked. "Is this what did happen?"

But if he was excited, she was not. Casually, even contemptuously, she stared down at his hand on her arm until he finally relaxed his grip. "I said it was theoretical, and it is," she said. "I just wondered what you'd do, that's all. If you'd be able to accept it and go home. Or would you still want vengeance? Blood?"

Hook could barely speak. "All I want is the truth."

She laughed at him. "*The truth!* Well, I can't tell you the truth. You ought to know that by now. I don't even know what it looks like. Or sounds like. It's a foreign language here. *Nous ne le parlons pas.*"

Hook was almost shaking with rage. His fists hung like mallets at his sides. "If you were a man," he said, "I think I'd beat you to death."

"Now you're making sense."

Hook heard the remark, but in his anger it did not register. "My son is dead," he got out. "You make him a suicide, and when I try to talk to you about it you get fashionable and cute. You play-act. You talk about dying and truth as if they were private little concepts all your own. But they're not, Miss Madera. There's real truth, and real death. And if you don't know it now, someday you will."

There was something honest back in her eyes now—pain or perhaps simply fear, a woman's fear of a man—but she did not give in to it. Her mouth, her beautiful lips and teeth, held their shape of scorn. "*Real truth*," she laughed. "*Real death*. How right that sounds coming from you. You don't ever doubt, do you? You *know*. In your world everything is neatly black and white, isn't it? No grays. No maybes. No either-ors."

Hook had had enough of her. He told her he was sorry for having wasted her time as well as his own, and that she could do what she wanted now, he was going on by himself, alone. But as he started to move away from her she came after him and took him by the arm.

"You better not," she said. "Let's turn around and go back. I don't like their looks."

Hook had not even noticed them until now—three young male hippies sprawled out in the sand between some rocks about fifty yards up the beach. They had an almost empty gallon jug of red wine, and as Hook observed them now one dragged deeply on a cigarette and passed it to the next. All three were watching him and Liz.

"Come on," she said. "You don't know. There are some real freaks around here. And those three are probably stoned."

Giving in to the pressure of her hand, Hook turned with her and headed back, but he was not mollified. He was not going to waste another word on her, he decided, even if she walked at his side all the way back to the beach house.

But they had gone only a short distance when Hook heard a kind of cry behind them, an animal sound, like the yelp of a kicked dog, and as he turned to look, one of the hippies came charging around him and Liz and blocked their way, followed immediately by the other two, who were breathless and heaving from their short sprint in the sand. Like the first one, they were long-haired and bearded and dressed like eccentric tramps. But there all similarity ended. Where they were small-boned and thin, even emaciated, he looked as strong and aggressive as a two-year-old bull. And he looked crazed.

"What is this, huh!" he cried, his voice again the yelp of a dog. "Huh! What is this! You come all the way up the beach—you see us—and then you turn around? What is that, huh? You think we gonna stomp ya or rape ya or somethin'? Is that it, huh? Everyone with long hair, they Charlie Manson, is that it, huh? Is that how come you turned? Huh? Speak up! Come on! Speak up!"

Hook was already so angry he did not trust his voice. All the rage he had felt against Liz had now refocused on the hippie.

"No, that's not it at all," Liz tried to explain. "We'd just come so far, that's all. It was time to go back."

Grinning, the hippie looked at his friends. "I say this bitch lies. What you cats say?"

They were uneasy. "Aw, lay off, Arn," one said. "Come on, let 'em go. What's it matter anyway?"

But to Arn it mattered. "No, I wanta hear an apology first." He looked at Hook. "Huh? What ya say, big man? Let's have an apology, huh? Just say you sorry you shit on us, and we let you go."

Hook stood there staring at the burly youth.

"Yes, we're sorry!" Liz begged. "We apologize. Now please let us pass."

The hippie was still watching Hook. "I'm waiting, big man."

Hook had not fought another man, had not hit one, since college. But then in all the intervening years he had never before been asked to apologize for walking his own way. So now, as the hippie's voice kept rasping at him—"What about it, big man? Huh? What about it?"—Hook found himself dropping his head slightly, as if he were about to say something, but instead he swung steeply from his side and punched the youth in the face as hard as he could.

The hippie staggered backwards and sat down in the sand, reaching for his pain. Then he fell back and rolled over onto his belly, still holding his face.

"Jesus," one of his friends gasped, and leaned over him. "You okay, Arn? You okay?"

Arn rolled over again and Hook could see between the youth's splayed fingers his left eye and cheek coming up like a pink balloon.

Hook took Liz by the arm and roughly propelled her forward. "Come on. We can go now."

They walked rapidly, Hook keeping his eyes fixed straight ahead, but Liz turned every few steps to look back and see if they were being followed. They were not.

After they passed the dead sea lion and made it around the point, Liz said, "I begin to understand your son now."

Hook asked her what she meant.

"What he did. Why he did it."

Hook felt a sudden weakness. "Go on," he said.

"I didn't want to hurt you before. I wanted to leave you with something. But that back there—what you did—it proves what Chris said about you. That you don't bend. That in your mind you are always right. That's what he said about you, that you are very fair and very strong and always, always, right. And he was freezing to death in your cold shadow, Mr. Hook. That's why he left home, he said. Why he had to get away from you."

Hook looked at her as they walked, but she was staring straight ahead and her look was unreadable. "That's not true," he said.

"In order to breathe—that's why Chris had to get away from you. That's what he told me."

He took her roughly by the shoulders and again told her that what she said was not true. But she just stood there, draped there in his hands coolly looking up at him.

"And all across the country," she said, "all he found was more coldness and misery and unhappiness. So he was dying too, Mr. Hook. Just like me. Only he hurried up the process a little, that's all."

"His letter," Hook said. "You read his letter."

"We all play roles. Especially with our parents. They expect it. They don't like their little ones to change."

"You lie. You're a lying bitch."

"Why don't you knock me down, then? Isn't it my turn now?"

For a few moments longer Hook stood there holding onto her, hating the cold assurance in her half-closed eyes. Then he let go of her, shoved her away from him like some foul drunk. She walked on for a short distance, and then set out running and kept on until she was well ahead of him, and walked for a hundred yards or so and then ran on again, growing smaller and smaller as she headed for the beach house.

7

At six that evening Hook telephoned home and spoke with Aunt
Marian and Jennifer and Bobby, telling them that things were
going along all right but not very rapidly and that the family
should not expect him back home very soon. They all said they
were doing fine and told him not to worry about them, but their
voices belonged to strangers, a family he had not heard before.

After hanging up, he then tried to call Icarus, twice, five minutes apart. But each time no one answered. On a vagrant impulse then he looked up Jack Douglas's home address in the
phone book and found a Douglas, John D. at 300 Sutton Lane
in Montecito. He wondered if he ought to drive by and have a
look, though he had no idea what he could learn by doing so.
But it was still early in the evening and there was not much else
to do, so he decided to go ahead.

On the way he stopped at a drive-in and choked down a pair
of doughy hamburgers, canners-and-cutters beef if ever he tasted
it. But then he knew his palate was somewhat spoiled by the
corn-fattened prime Black Angus beef he enjoyed daily at home.
While other beef-raisers often fattened cheap dairy steers for
their own use, Hook had always figured that if his beef was fine
enough for the hotels and restaurants of Chicago and New York,
then it was also fine enough for the Hooks. And anyway he
doubted that he could have endured the sight of a dairy steer
on his farm; he was a snob in that at least.

Montecito was to Santa Barbara as Beverly Hills was to Hollywood—adjacent, separate, unequal. In Santa Barbara people lived and worked; in Montecito they only lived. It was a bedroom community, and to Hook's eyes it looked as if each bedroom had its own dressing room and bath. It also had trees, great drooping sycamore and eucalyptus and live oak crowding the narrow serpentine streets so tightly Hook wondered how drunks ever managed to negotiate the maze at night, as he was trying to do now, sober, driving slowly, watching for street signs. What houses there were sat far back from the road, looking as dimly lit as forest cabins through the trees, and in front of each there was usually a rustic stone wall or iron-bar fence, the kind Carl Sandburg said would be penetrated only by death and rain and tomorrow.

By the time Hook found Sutton Lane he was convinced that he was driving the only non-foreign, non-sports car on the western seaboard, and he was happy for the difference, because most of the natives apparently thought of the streets as strictly one-way, *their* way, and swerved their low-slung Jags and Porsches and Triumphs out of Hook's lane at the very last second, as if "chicken" and not polo or tennis were the favored local sport. But then Hook reminded himself that they knew the roads and did not expect to find a jealously preserved historic fig tree growing in the center of the pavement just over the next hill or beyond the next bend.

The house at 300 Sutton Lane was newer than most in the area, modern and glassy, though it too had the required stone wall along the road. In the back, above a picket of small Mediterranean cypress, the superstructure of a swimming-pool slide was visible. A late-model station wagon was parked in the attached three-car garage, which also had a basket and board above the door. And as Hook watched now, as he was about to drive on, a boy came dribbling a ball out of the darkness of the garage and hooked a shot up at the hoop. If he was the son Douglas had mentioned, the twelve-year-old, then he was small for his age. His hair, long and bowl-cut in the style of the Kennedy young, flopped like a pennant as he moved and jumped under the basket. Hook depressed the accelerator and drove on, not anxious to have the boy see him and run inside and report to his mother that a strange man had stopped his car to watch him—Hook already had enough problems without adding that.

So he started back toward Santa Barbara wondering why he had bothered to drive out to the house in the first place. What had he learned? Did it look like the house of a murderer? No—no more than the "murderer" himself looked like a murderer. And Hook was beginning to face it now, that ever since meeting Douglas that morning and talking with him he had been losing his gut conviction that the man was somehow involved in Chris's death. The fact that Douglas had gone out to the beach house with Liz Madera, had even allowed himself to be seen alone with her, knowing that Hook was in town and what he was after—it just did not smell of guilt. But even more to the point, Douglas simply did not seem like the violent and jealous type, in fact seemed more like its antithesis, cool and calm and sure in his sense of his own worth, the kind of man not likely to be shaken by a mistress's infidelity, especially in a milieu in which infidelity was the rule, almost the one true badge of belonging. And there was also the matter of *how* Liz Madera had reacted to Hook's indictment of Douglas—with amusement more than anything else. The lady did not protest nearly half enough. So the simple fact was that Jack Douglas had not turned out to be the man Hook had imagined during the trip home with Chris's body and through the long days of the funeral and the longer days afterward. No, that man had existed only in Hook's mind, had been born and fleshed there, and Hook mourned his passing now, because he feared his death also meant the death of Hook's hopes for swift redress and, yes, vengeance—for Liz Madera had been right about that too, that poison in his blood. He felt it now, could admit its existence, live with it. Still, more than anything else he wanted the truth. But right now that truth did not seem to involve Jack Douglas.

So where did that leave him?

It left him with Dorothy Rubin.

And twenty minutes later, in El Cielito, the restaurant where Sergeant Rider had taken him that first night in Santa Barbara, Mrs. Rubin was still with him. She was the one who claimed to have seen Chris jump; she was supposedly the last one to have heard him say he had nothing to live for; and probably most important, she was the only one obviously filled with hatred, possibly sick with it, sick enough to commit murder. So as he took a stool at the end of the bar and ordered a vodka and tonic, Hook tried to conceive of what possible circumstances, what intricate mechanism of character and cause and effect could have resulted in Chris's "suicide." But there was nothing to go on, no raw material for even hypotheses. Was the woman a lesbian? Did she have a lover? Or lovers? Was she broke? Or rich? Was she a widow? A divorcée? He had no idea, in fact knew next to nothing about her. And that was a lack he was determined to end as soon as possible, and even tried to make a beginning now, by pumping the bartender. But the man was so busy Hook could not get anywhere with him, and contented himself with the drink and a cigarette, then another drink, and left before nine o'clock.

He drove past Icarus's place, past the driveway leading back to the apartment, but all he could see was darkness, no psychodelic lights burning this night. So he went back to his motel then, stopping off at the Galleon bar in the basement for another few drinks before turning in. Besides himself and the bartender, there were only two couples sitting at tables, a fat man at the bar and two girls alone, apparently waiting for their dates. The room was flooded with a ghastly green light from the swimming pool, whose depths a floor-to-ceiling window exposed. The pool was being used by a thirtyish married couple and their two children, all of whom stayed protectively in the heated water, which had to be a good thirty degrees warmer than the December night air.

Sitting at the bar, and staying with vodka, Hook tried to make conversation with the bartender, a heavy man about his own age, with slicked-down black hair and a pencil-line mustache and an air of aggrieved embarrassment, as if he were appearing on stage in a very bad play. Hook told him that he was from out of town and was thinking of opening a business in Santa Barbara but wanted some good public relations counseling before he did anything definite. Did the bartender know anything about local public relations firms, like say Jack Douglas Associates? No, the man didn't know a thing, in fact wasn't even sure what they meant by public relations. What the hell was it anyway? Pretty much what the words said, Hook explained. Maybe the bartender knew Douglas as a politician; he had run for Congress last year. But no, the man couldn't help him there either. There were so goddamn many names and propositions on the ballots these days that a body just couldn't keep it all straight anymore, so he didn't even bother to vote. Had he ever heard of Mrs. Dorothy Rubin? No, never.

And that was that. The man had glasses to wash and moved down the bar to wash them. For a time Hook sat there looking down at the drink in his hand and tried not to think about anything at all, but he was just stalling and he knew it. The time had come finally, the time to face it, to think about it, deal with it. All through the late afternoon and evening, in fact ever since she had hit him with it on the beach, he had tried to pretend it was not there and simply had gone on about his business as if everything were still the same. But it was not the same.

What bothered him most was *the way* she had said it, off-hand, almost as an afterthought, a result of his having struck the hippie. He had the feeling that if he had not done that, she would not have said any of it, ever. So it had if not the ring of truth at least the trappings of it. And he knew the first part of what she said was at least possible. Though he had always been a good father to Chris, even a loving father, he could see that in the boy's eyes he might at times have seemed "unbending" and "always, always right." But it had never been Hook's practice to insist on his own way of doing things; he had never been bullheaded or dictatorial. What he was, simply, was *right*. And most of the time. But he could not see anything unusual or harmful in that, anything Chris would have resented. After all, Hook *was* Chris's father; he had twenty-five years more experience of life than the boy had had, so naturally he had known more, been "right" more. And anyway, as far as Hook was able to judge, what boys seemed to resent in a father was not competence, not decency and strength, but ineptness and weakness. He had seen enough examples of that around Banner Hill, the contempt many of the young showed openly for lazy, boozing fathers, transplanted hillbillies who were basically coon hunters and whittlers by nature and not farmers or businessmen. And Hook in fact resented this attitude, for it was his experience that these shiftless whittlers were usually a lot longer on humanity than some of their more successful neighbors. But now Hook wondered if this general indictment might not include himself as well, that in his "strength and rightness" he had been less warm, less human in Chris's eyes than he would have wanted to be. What was it she had said? "He was freezing to death in your cold shadow." And so had left home. No, that Hook could not believe. To believe it would be the same as accepting someone's word that the sun rose in the west despite his observations to the contrary. All his senses, all his experience with the boy, all his memories of their life together told him otherwise. Yet she had an answer for that too, that the young had to "play roles" with their parents. So this son he remembered, this bright and happy and loving Christopher David Hook, was not real at all but just an actor. The real one had fled his home and father "in order to breathe," had found nothing but more coldness and misery and unhappiness wherever he had gone, and so had killed himself.

But it was not true. Hook knew it was not true. Only now he had to prove it more than ever, for he had to prove it to himself. Elizabeth Madera had sown in him not some small seed of doubt but a nascent cancer, and he knew that if he was to go on living he would have to cut it out of himself, all of it.

Lighting a cigarette now, he studied the massive rusted old ship anchor hanging above the mirror behind the bar, and then as his gaze drifted downwards he found himself looking into the eyes of one of the two girls at the other end of the bar. She smiled warmly, in open invitation. Beyond her, Hook saw the other girl on the phone near the door, and he knew suddenly that it was not a date she was making but an appointment. They were professionals. Looking back at the first girl—by way of the mirror still, for the fat man was sitting between them—Hook returned a fraction of her smile. Then he told the bartender to give her another drink—this even though he was not sure what his motives were yet, whether he just wanted to talk with her and get her whore's lowdown on Santa Barbara high life or whether he actually wanted her, wanted sex.

Whichever it was, he apparently was about to find out very soon, for when the bartender served her drink, a bloody mary, she smiled again and got up, bringing the drink and her purse down the bar with her. Hook stood as she joined him. She thanked him for the drink and said her name was Rita. He suggested that they move to a table, and followed her to one next to the pool window. Pulling the chair out for her, seeing her close up, he estimated her age at around nineteen or twenty. She was totally Latin, dark, sexy, unfashionably voluptuous, the kind of girl he would have once described to Kate as "fat by thirty," a private joke between them. During the first summer of their marriage a girl across the hall from their Greenwich Village apartment had called on Hook to open a stuck window for her while Kate was away at work, and when he related the incident to her later, trying to minimize it, he described the girl as the type that would be fat by thirty, which as Kate later discovered meant someone who was very attractive and sexy *now*, at twenty.

Across the room the second girl hung up the phone and, putting on her coat, waved to Rita and left. Rita gestured out the window at the family frolicking in the distant shallow end of the pool. "They look creepy, don't they? They never go under. You just see their bodies. Never their heads."

Hook agreed that they looked odd. "My name's David Hook," he added.

She was pleased to meet him, she said. Then she leaned toward him confidentially, smiling in happy embarrassment. "Would you believe I skinny-dipped in there one night? Well, I did. Me and this other girl. Some guy took over the whole bar for a party, and Jules there, the bartender, he hired us to put on a little show. Just swim around, you know."

"I wish I'd been here," Hook said.

It was not much, but it pleased her. She smiled hesitantly at him, almost timidly. "At the bar," she said, "before you saw me, I watched you. You looked so kind of—oh, not sad, I guess—but tense, you know? I mean, like—well, like you're not exactly having a ball, you know?"

"I wasn't."

"Would you like to?"

He doubted that she was intentionally making a pun on the word ball, but there was no doubting her meaning. He looked at her, this girl who would be fat by thirty. She was dark and attractive, as Liz Madera was dark and attractive. But she was not beautiful like Liz. She was Liz Madera unlit by mind, unshaped by spirit.

"Yes," Hook said. "I think I'd like that."

She leaned toward him. "Forty?"

He nodded.

"That's regular. Normal."

Hook did not know the nomenclature here, but he assumed it was the same as in St. Louis. "Half-and-half?" he said, feeling, as always, diminished by the utterance, irredeemably degraded.

She smiled happily. "That's normal."

Later, in the crepuscular light of his room, Hook lay on his back in bed watching her perform the first "half" of her task, the way her lush black hair, loosened, draped over his belly much as Liz Madera's had on the rock at the beach. And his eye traced the long and lovely line of her back and waist and hips, finally her buttocks, beautiful as no other thing to him, his favorite pounds of flesh, as they were to Voltaire, he reflected, recalling the great Frenchman's hilarious letters to his niece and how in them he was forever "pressing" kisses on her "ravishing round bottom." And Hook figured he would press a few himself this night, for the girl did reach him physically; he felt as big as a corner post. But he was cold in his heart. He was a voyeur to his own act.

Yet this same coldness gave him a high fine endurance, so that when he mounted her finally he deliberately stayed with her until she began to come alive under him and he could feel her whore's surprise at it, at being reached, and wanting it then, wanting to come, and finally he was able to stay with her all the way, not letting himself go until he could feel her going over first, and then raging after her, driving like some wild desperate kid trying to break an ultimate tape. Why he had waited, pacing himself, he was not sure. He felt no love for the girl, and certainly it was not something she had expected. Yet for some reason he had felt that his pleasure was dependent on hers, hers a condition of his. And hers evidently had been keen enough, for afterwards she offered to stay the night if he would let her, and said she would do him again if he wanted it later, and that it would be a "freebie." Hook had expected to be alone, had wanted to be alone to think, but the girl was so warm and decent, not at all the embittered hustler yet, that he did not want to put her down. And anyway it had been so long since he had slept with another human being through all the hours of a night that he said yes finally, yes he would like her to stay.

Later, after cigarettes, and after a number of unsuccessful attempts at conversation—did he like movies? did he go to many of them? she dug them herself, much more than TV, because they told it like it really was—she lapsed into silence and finally fell asleep. He looked at her lovely breasts and abundant hair, at her Latin darkness, and wondered if he would have taken her at all if she had been blonde, if she had not borne at least a physical resemblance to Elizabeth Madera.

8

Slightly before noon the next day Hook parked his car in the middle of a block lined on both sides with small rundown clapboard houses in a largely Mexican part of the city. Next to him, Icarus looked gloomily across the street.

"It's the yellow one," he said. "Or at least it was yellow once. And we'd better lock up. These Chicano kids will steal you blind."

Getting out, Hook locked his side of the car and followed Icarus across the street and up onto the rickety front porch of the house. After Rita had left him around nine, he had called the young photographer again and this time got him, though Icarus had sounded barely conscious on the phone, hung over with sleep or wine or drugs. Hook had told him his problem, his need for more background information on Mrs. Rubin and Douglas and Liz Madera and their crowd, and Icarus had said he knew just the man, just the source. So here they were.

As Icarus knocked, Hook hoped that the man inside would answer the door quickly and get them in off the street, for he could not overcome his aversion at being seen in public with his flamboyant young friend, who today was setting off his mane of long orange hair with an ensemble that included a maroon velvet Edwardian waistcoat, red jeans, black shirt, and red-and-white polka-dot ascot. But the man inside was much too slow. Three subteen boys came walking by and they were not polite.

"Jesus, Tino! Wouldja dig that?"

"*El Pavonito!*"

"*El Pavonito*, sheeyit! *El Queerito*, ya mean!"

Then laughter.

But to Icarus it was nothing, water to the duck's back of his aplomb. His weary heavy-lidded eyes remained just that. Finally the door opened—on a gray-skinned skeleton of a man sitting in a wheelchair, like a cadaver prepared for Egyptian burial.

"Come in, gentlemen," he said. "Welcome to San Simeon."

He slowly backwheeled away from the door, across the small living room's linoleum carpet to a position next to a stout center-leg table burdened with bottles of wine and pills and liquid medicine, boxes of Kleenex and matches and cigarettes, a thermometer, books, glasses, and among other items a bowl of soggy half-eaten breakfast cereal. The table was evidently the man's life support system and he did not stray far from it.

Icarus was introducing them. "Mr. Hook—Ray Oliver, the best reporter this town ever had."

"I appreciate your seeing me," Hook said.

Oliver grinned like a wolf. "Oh, I got time. A little time."

On the drive over, Icarus had explained to Hook that the man was dying of lung cancer, had already had one lung removed and was just pottering around now waiting for the other to go. He also had arteriosclerosis, and thus pain as well as the expectation of imminent death, but he would not stay in a hospital. He was broke and refused to die in debt as a matter of principle, he said, one last nose-thumb at a society he did not particularly cherish.

Hook said, "I'm the father of the boy who——"

"Yeah, I know," Oliver cut in. "Ike told me on the phone." He looked at Icarus now and shook his head ruefully. "You know what you look like, kid? Gainsborough's long-lost painting *Lavender Boy*. Or *Lavender Lad* I guess I should say, to keep the alliteration." He laughed softly and began to cough.

Icarus smiled. "What's a *pavonito*, Ray? You speak Spanish."

"*Pavonito?* A peacock, I think. Little peacock."

Icarus looked at Hook and shrugged.

Oliver turned his sunken eyes on Hook. "I'd like to help you," he said, speaking slowly, spending each breath as if it were a diamond. "I ain't particularly in love with Mr. Douglas and his crowd either, mostly because they steal things. They steal your work and your years, and then finally they steal your life. But *legally*, Mr. Hook. Never violently. So I think you're barking up a wrong tree. But sit down anyway. Sit down."

While Hook took an easy chair whose bottom sank almost to the floor, Icarus stretched out sideways on the davenport, like an Empire *grande dame* posing for David.

Hook said, "I'm not barking up any tree, Mr. Oliver. I don't believe my boy committed suicide, that's all. And I want to know more about these people who say he did. Icarus here—Ike—says you know more about this town and its people than anybody."

Oliver made a face. "I doubt that. Did he also tell you I'm croaking?"

"Yes."

"So you probably figure a dying man will tell you the truth, the whole truth, and so on."

"I figured you'd tell me the truth, yes."

Now Oliver lost his look of the gallows wit. "I have one pleasure, Mr. Hook," he said, nodding at the table. "Drugs. Sweet morphine and its derivatives, its stepchildren and cousins. You see, I pretend I'm on the other side of the generation gap. I swing. Only thing is it costs money, and as you can see the medicos didn't exactly leave me prosperous. I used to have a little house up on the Riviera—the local one, that long foothill back of us here. But it went too. The high cost of dying, you know."

Hook took a twenty-dollar bill out of his wallet and gave it to him. Oliver put it in his shirt pocket.

"Okay," he said. "Where do you want to start?"

In the next hour Hook learned both a great deal and nothing—many facts and fancies about the people he was interested in, and yet nothing that had any apparent bearing on Chris's death or why it had been labeled a suicide. Most disappointing of all was Oliver's scant knowledge of Mrs. Rubin. About all he knew of her was that she had come to town six or seven years ago, that her husband had been a real estate agent for one of the local companies and had died of a heart attack in the YMCA swimming pool three or four years back. If they had any children, Oliver did not know about it. As he recalled, she began working for

Douglas even before her husband had died. And to the local press she was known as a real barracuda. If there was no pickup on a Douglas news release they were as likely to hear from her as from anyone else in the outfit, and it was always gloves off and right for the crotch. But that was all he knew about her—as an employee of Jack Douglas. If she was a lesbian or a lush or if she liked balling young hippies, he had never heard anything about it. Nor did she swing at any level of local society, of which there were three, Oliver stated. At the top were a few old-line Spanish families and descendants of the Spanish land-grant Anglos. Then came the national rich, people who had once used Santa Barbara as a winter playground and then finally moved here to stay— and there was one hell of a lot of Ford and Mellon and du Pont money behind those high brick walls in Montecito, he said. And then at the bottom was the local rich, the new rich, the dagos and micks who had made it big catering to the whims of the other two groups with one hand while stealing them blind with the other. This last was the largest group by far. They ran the city, boosted it, pillaged it, and lived for the day they might move up a notch and be invited to a real honest-to-God upper-class dinner party instead of the usual sodden cocktail bashes they threw as religiously as their parents had gone to mass.

Jack Douglas was in this level, though probably near the top of it, Oliver said, since his father had been a businessman here before him, a pharmacist turned wholesale druggist, though the man never did make it very big, and finally sold out after the Second World War, a few years before he died. He had three daughters and just the one son, Jack, so what money Douglas had now was strictly through marriage to Doc Halverson's daughter Jill. The Halversons had always been filthy with Union Pacific money, Oliver said, and Jill evidently had gotten a piece of it, which was a damn good thing for Douglas, because he ran that P.R. thing of his like a political campaign office pure and simple. It was a sure bet Uncle Sam was not getting rich off the outfit's profits. Douglas had studied at USC, got his degree in journalism sometime in the mid-fifties. For four or five years he had worked as a reporter for the L.A. *Times*. Then he had come back up here and opened his own shop. Oliver figured Douglas had contracted the political virus in the mid and late sixties working on the Kennedy and Salinger campaigns, and especially Bobby Kennedy's campaign in sixty-eight.

"I think it got to him all of a sudden," Oliver said. "All that hair and teeth. All that glamour. All those joyful black and brown faces shining up at Kennedy, believing in him. *La Raza.* The great dark unwashed. And suddenly that was him up there, you know? Jack Douglas—a man of the people. A man with a cause. After all, Kennedy's politics were new to Kennedy, so why couldn't they be new to Douglas as well? Anyway, the light of the Lord did strike him and he was blinded. And, lo, he did change his spots. Until then his life had been strictly cunt and golf and fishing. Now it's politics and cunt and golf and fishing."

Hook studied the dying man's face, his sad eyes and wolfish smile. "You don't much like him," he said.

Oliver shrugged broadly, burlesquing his innocence. "How can a person not like him? He's charming and good-looking and a liberal to boot. Which is more than can be said for most of the cavemen in this burg. The only thing is—as they say—I wouldn't care to share a foxhole with him. But then I'm not about to, am I?"

Moving on to Liz Madera, Oliver's cynicism lost none of its ripsaw edge. Though they could be bought and sold *ad infinitum* by Douglas and his peers, Liz Madera and her father belonged in that small point at the top of the social pyramid, according to Oliver. The Maderas had made their mark in the area long before Colonel Frémont and his battalion raised Old Glory over the Presidio in 1846. Her grandfather and great-grandfather had been in real estate and ranching, fairly wealthy men both of them, but not anywhere near wealthy enough to build the kind of estate that could have survived the prodigality of Phil Madera, Liz's old man. His tastes ran to polo and yachting and jaguar hunting and an occasional rape—this last probably the most expensive in the long run. So he had been forced to marry rich women, four or five of them at last count, as Oliver remembered —that many because none had lacked either the grounds or the means for quick divorce. His first wife, Liz's mother, had shot herself when the girl was around nine or ten; in fact, Liz was the one who had found her body. Ironically, the cause of it all—Daddy—did not even learn about the suicide until weeks after the funeral. He had been cruising along the Mexican coast in his yacht, with one dead radio and two live ballerinas. Since then he had become pretty much persona non grata in Santa Barbara society. But when he needed a wife—income, that is—there always seemed to be one available, though they had tended to become successively less affluent and attractive. Oliver had not heard much about him in recent years. Then, grinning, he added, "Maybe he's dying of cancer."

Hook asked him about Liz then, but did not learn very much. The old reporter knew very little about the young man she had married—he was from L.A. or San Francisco, he thought. And it had been a very short marriage, as he remembered. She was back in action not long after the honeymoon. And though a lot of people probably considered her something of a tramp, a chip off the old block, Oliver did not. "Phil Madera was—is—a hedonist pure and simple. But with the girl, I think the whole thing is a kind of death-wish. That's the way it is with most broads like her. They run after pleasure, weeping all the way."

Hook tried to pin him down on specifics. Had he ever heard anything about her and Mrs. Rubin, a possible lesbian relationship? No, nothing like that. Did he ever hear if it was her practice to pick up hitchhikers and take them home? Oh Christ no, he didn't know any of these people that well, in that kind of detail. He just knew about them in general, their background and so forth, that was all. Ignoring the objection, Hook asked him if he had heard anything about Liz having any current lovers other than Douglas.

"No, I don't know any of that," Oliver repeated. "I can't help you there. About all I know is what I've told you—she's beautiful and damned, just like in Hollywood." Now he smiled and shook his head reflectively. "Jesus, though, I remember about ten years ago. You know, every summer we have our big Fiesta celebration here, and the main part of it is the parade. The rich folks put on fancy costumes and ride their horses and carriages past the poor folks who cheer and throw flowers at them. At least that's the way it's been in the past, though I got a feeling the Brown Berets are going to start throwing grenades one of these years. Anyway, this one parade about ten years ago—I'm standing on the sidewalk in the shade, half-boozed of course, wanting to either throw up or laugh at all these jackass honky dentists and plumbers and bond vendors trying to make like Spanish grandees—you know, the sombreros down over their eyes and their asses spilling over the saddles. And then all of a sudden here comes Madera and his daughter on a pair of matched black Arabian stallions—and all Arabian horses got to be stallions, right?—it's a law. Anyway, here they come, and I'm telling you they weren't no Kiwanis clown and his Girl Scout daughter. The costumes *belonged* on these two, and the horses belonged under them. They were Spain in the eighteen-hundreds—the Duke de la Madera and his beautiful daughter Doña Elizabeth. She wasn't Fiesta queen that day or ever—because of him, I guess. But by Jesus, I bet she left behind her five thousand men and boys incurably in love. I know I was. I didn't speak to my wife for a month afterwards."

Hook smiled at the story, enjoying its blend of the cynical and the romantic. He liked Oliver and worried that he might be overtaxing him. But they were not finished yet. There were still Douglas's two "associates" to ask about. So instead of getting up to leave, Hook took out his pack of cigarettes.

"Mind if I smoke?" he asked.

"Hell, I haven't quit myself." The old reporter took his own pack off the table and lit up. "I don't believe all that scare talk," he scoffed. "What proof they got?"

Hook looked away from his doomed grin. "What about Richard Ferguson and this 'Bo' Parnelli?" he asked. "You know anything about them?"

That afternoon Hook learned more about Ferguson and Parnelli—in person. After he drove Icarus home, he had lunch alone at a small sidewalk café on State Street. He expected his next stop—questioning Douglas's dentist friend—to be equally routine, one more motion to go through before checking Douglas off his list. If the future congressman had had to establish a false alibi—if he had had to ask someone to lie for him, commit perjury for him—he would have stopped with Parnelli and Ferguson. There would have been no reason to involve a third person and every reason not to. So Hook expected no surprises at the office of Herbert Hammer, D.D.S.

But he was wrong.

Hammer's office was on upper State Street, in a large Spanish-style house converted into a series of suites where the various doctors performed their various specialties, of which dentistry did not appear to be the least, judging by Hammer's elegantly furnished waiting room. And his attractive receptionist only strengthened this suspicion, for her voice had all the softness and assurance of very old folding money. Arriving at slightly before three, Hook gave her his name and explained that he did not require any dental work, that all he wanted to do was talk with the doctor for a few moments about a matter concerning a mutual friend, and that he would wait for the doctor to fit him in at his convenience.

And wait he did. He read *Time* and *Esquire* and then turned to the women's magazines, while an interminable parade of Hammer's patients came in one at a time and sat for a while and then were called into the inner sanctum and emerged twenty or thirty minutes later, made another appointment with the receptionist, and left.

At four-thirty, as he was finishing *McCall's*, Hook looked up and saw the small dapper figure of Richard Ferguson enter the room. Smiling, Ferguson came over to him, said hello and that he was happy to see him again and wondered if Hook could spare a few minutes outside, "where they could talk." The room by then was full of harassed mothers and restless schoolchildren, most of whom had stopped what they were doing in order to hear exactly what Ferguson had to say.

"Of course," Hook said. He put down the magazine and followed him out into the hall. And on the way he did some fast thinking, trying to figure out what Ferguson's unexpected appearance might mean. One thing it meant, of course, was that Hook had not been sitting in Hammer's office for almost two hours by accident. The dentist had known who he was and had not wanted to talk with him, had called Douglas's office and told them to deal with him, told them that he was *their* problem, not his. And yet that did not make sense either. If Hammer had substantiated Douglas's alibi with the police, why not do it again now, with Hook?

In the corridor, Ferguson led him toward a big muscular balding man standing just inside the front door, waiting for them. Hook knew immediately, from what the reporter Oliver had said about him, that this was the redoubtable "Bo" Parnelli, ex-Santa Barbara High School and USC football star and now great good friend, drinking buddy, associate, and "gopher" of Jack Douglas.

As Ferguson introduced them, Parnelli tried to crush Hook's hand.

"Been looking forward to meeting you, Mr. Hook," he said.

His smile flicked on and off, like a muscle flexed, though it did manage to communicate a substantial satisfaction with himself. He was about thirty-five, Oliver had said, a fanatic jockstrap, a surfer, skin-diver, golfer extraordinaire, with some of his finest muscles between his ears. In contrast to Ferguson's vested tan tweed suit and paisley tie, he was wearing a mod green, gold, and olive sport coat-slacks ensemble.

"What is it you wanted to talk about?" Hook asked them.

Parnelli's attitude was palsy, confidential. "Well, to be honest, Mr. Hook, it just isn't the kind of thing we can handle here with a few words. We just want to talk with you, that's all. About a lot of things, you know? Get to know you. Let you get to know us."

Hook looked at Ferguson and the little man's eyes drifted away. He appeared uneasy, embarrassed. Apparently this get-together was not his idea, not his show.

"That couldn't hurt anything, could it?" Parnelli pressed.

"I guess not."

"Well, fine, then. Real great. What say we all go down to El Paseo and have a few drinkies? On me."

"And get to know each other," Hook said, deadpan.

"Right on. That's the idea."

Hook did not want to appear eager. "I've been waiting here quite a while to talk with Dr. Hammer."

"Well, that's the problem," Ferguson slipped in. "He called up just a while ago, said you were here. And I'm afraid he doesn't want to talk with you."

"Oh?"

"He's a very busy man," Ferguson explained.

Hook smiled wryly. "That doesn't leave me much choice, then, does it?"

Parnelli already had his car keys out, and now he gave them to Ferguson. "You take my car, Rich. I'll drive with Mr. Hook." He turned to Hook. "If that's all right with you?"

"Of course."

On the way, Parnelli sounded at first like a one-man chamber of commerce. What did Hook think of their little burg here, their paradise by the sea? It was one hell of a lot sunnier than where Hook came from, he was willing to bet on that. In fact, it was one fantastic town if you ever really stopped and thought about it. Everything a man could possibly want was right here. The sea. The mountains. Great people. Good schools. Clean beaches. Cleaner than ever, in fact. Then the chamber got down to business.

"But let me tell you, it ain't like this in very many places anymore. Poverty, unemployment, pollution, racism—that's the story in most places today. And you know what it's going to take to fix it all—to make it all like this? Men like Jack Douglas. Men like him in government, that's what it's going to take."

Finished, he slipped Hook a glance freighted with import, making sure his meaning had not been missed. It was like being reminded that one had just been run over by a truck. And it brought to mind something else Oliver had said about Parnelli, that he was not sure why Douglas kept him around, whether it was just for laughs or for his "name," his by now strictly local celebrity, or whether Parnelli actually earned his keep—a possibility Oliver seriously doubted, because the man was outrageously accident- and lawsuit-prone, was forever totaling sports cars and settling barroom disputes with his fists, especially any involving the reputation of his boss, to whom he was ferociously dedicated. "He's a violent sonofabitch," Oliver had said.

"You been in El Paseo yet?" he asked now.

"Yesterday. At that sidewalk café they have in the courtyard."

"Naw—I mean inside. The restaurant. The bar."

"No. Not yet."

"You'll like it. Especially this time of year. No tourists."

Throughout their short drive together, not one word was mentioned about Chris's death or why Hook was here in this "paradise by the sea." But it would come, Hook knew. He would wait for it, and it would come.

As Parnelli had predicted, Hook found that he did like the bar at El Paseo. Parnelli had chosen a table in the farthest corner, next to a small fireplace in which gas flames licked at a pair of metal logs. Hook had taken the short end of the L-shaped seat, so that in effect he sat alone, facing both Parnelli and Ferguson on his right. But it gave him a fine view of the rest of the bar and the empty restaurant, which was darkening rapidly as night fell, for like the courtyard café it sat in the open air, only canopied now, in December, a great long room surrounded on three sides by what looked like the exterior of an old Spanish fort with a wood veranda fronting the second story all the way around. Hook could imagine a mantillaed Ava Gardner leaning sexily against one of the vine-covered veranda posts while Tyrone Power in a Zorro outfit tossed up a rose from below; the place had that kind of authenticity. All this Hook saw through the three graceful arches that separated the restaurant from the bar, which itself was roofed over, with a dark wood ceiling resting on great hewn beams. Inside the arches was a row of black leather booths, then small tables, then the long bar behind which a grayhaired bartender in a red jacket presided with magisterial authority. Above him, on the back wall, hung a mural-size painting depicting Indians or Mexicans migrating somewhere en masse—out of Santa Barbara? Hook wondered.

There were only ten or twelve other patrons in the bar, most of whom had been the recipients of a clout on the back and some shout of greeting by Parnelli on his way back to the corner table. Now though he was settled in, the drinks had been served—a martini for him, scotch for Hook and Ferguson—and it was time to get down to business.

"Well now, Mr. Hook," Parnelli said. "Where were we?"

"I believe we were trying to save the country."

"Right," Parnelli agreed. "And believe me, it needs it. It needs saving like it never has before."

"And you're afraid I might get in the way of that."

Parnelli looked at him like a teacher whose slowest pupil had come up with a correct answer. Smiling, he looked at Ferguson. "Now I like that, I really do. See, Rich, everybody isn't like you after all. I'm not the only one who likes to come right to the point. He puts his cards right on the table, same as me." He turned back to Hook. "You see, Rich and me, we got this little difference of opinion. I'm a man who believes in saying what has to be said and doing what has to be done. But Rich here, he's a little more cautious than I am—maybe because he's a hell of a lot smarter, who knows? Got a master's in poli sci at Stanford, Rich has, and believe me he can write position papers and articles and speeches that are goddamn works of art. But he's got this cautious streak, haven't you, kid? So when the Doc called this afternoon, well, we had this little difference of opinion about what to do. Jack's down in L.A. on business, so it was up to us, see? And I said let's talk with the man. Right? What can it hurt?" He grinned now at Hook as if it were the two of them, partners, ranged against laughable little Ferguson.

Hook nodded. He understood—but not everything. "The dentist," he said, "how did he know who I was, or what I wanted? I only gave him my name."

Parnelli's grin, his eyes, suddenly went flat. He turned hopefully to Ferguson.

"Jack must have told him you'd be dropping in," the young man said. "Jack gave you his name yesterday, didn't he?"

"Along with yours."

Parnelli had recovered now. "Right. And now we're getting to the heart of the matter, Mr. Hook. You see, that's the point of this whole thing—if you'd come to the two of us we could've saved you lots of time. The night your son died we were playing poker—the two of us, Doc Hammer, and Jack. I lost forty bucks, for Christ sake. We didn't break up till after one o'clock."

Ferguson was nodding solemnly. "That's the truth, Mr. Hook."

Hook lit a cigarette, dragged on it, blew the smoke down toward the fireplace. "It's funny," he observed. "You'd think the dentist could have taken off a few seconds to tell me that."

Parnelli shrugged. "Like Rich said, he's a very busy guy."

Hook nodded reluctantly, pretending to understand, to agree. As he drained his glass, Parnelli signaled the waitress for another round, and Hook could see in the man's expression, in the sudden lack of tautness in his beefy face, that he thought his team had it won now; they were out in front by ten points and there were only seconds left to play.

"Believe me, Mr. Hook," he said, "we all feel for you. We really do. I mean we know what a goddamn personal tragedy this thing must be for you. All we're trying to do is make sure you don't turn it into a national tragedy as well."

Hook knew he had heard him correctly, yet he could not help repeating the word. "*National?*"

Parnelli nodded grimly. "That's right—national. That's what I think it would be to ruin the career of a man like Jack Douglas—a national tragedy."

For a moment Hook thought the man was putting him on, but Ferguson's look of cold, angry embarrassment convinced him otherwise.

"What Bo means," Ferguson said, "is that this country right now desperately needs the kind of politician Jack is—someone who's really concerned for the people, someone who'll really work to help them."

"That about says it," Parnelli agreed.

The waitress served their second round of drinks just then, so Hook had time to compose himself, to resist competing urges to either laugh in their faces or dump the table over on them, which strongly appealed to him as a clownish act befitting such a pair of clowns, or more accurately, a clown and his keeper.

When the girl left, Hook said that he was not out to ruin anybody's career unless that person had had something to do with his son's death.

Parnelli shook his head at Hook's innocence. "But that's just it, Mr. Hook. These days you can ruin a man politically with nothing more than gossip. It don't even have to get in the papers. All it takes is for the wrong people to hear about it—the power people, the money people—and that's it." His index finger sliced across his thick neck. "Your man is dead. He's had it. And all it takes is a rumor. A guy like Jack, on the way up, why he's a sitting duck for someone like you."

Hook smiled coldly. "Someone like me?"

"Someone in your position. You know—someone with your problem."

"Yes, my problem," Hook nodded. "I take it you think I ought to just forget about it and go home."

Shrugging, making a face of rueful regret, Parnelli saw no other course open to him. "Look, you may have a legitimate beef," he admitted. "Who knows? Maybe your kid didn't jump. But the point is, whether he did or didn't—it's got nothing to do with Jack Douglas. He wasn't even there. He was with us, playing cards, just down the street here. Now maybe Mrs. Rubin was seeing things that night. Maybe she was—what's the word?— *hallucinating*. Hell, she's around fifty. Maybe she's having a rough menopause—who knows? I sure as hell don't. So all I'm saying is during this crusade of yours, Mr. Hook, try not to hurt the innocent, okay? The helpless. And by that I don't just mean Jack Douglas. I mean all those people he's going to help give a better life to. I know that sounds corny, but I can't help it. That's how I feel."

Hook was looking down at his drink now, choosing not to meet Parnelli's flat burning gaze, much as he did not like to stare into the eyes of a dead animal, like the sea lion on the beach or the dog he and Bobby had slain, for it was in the eyes that death spoke directly to you, there that it had its sting and victory, its last and final word, which of course was why those midwives to death, the doctors and clergy and morticians, were so quick to close the eyes of the newly deceased, to foster myths of rest and sleep and slumber that would never survive the open stare of the dead. And oddly, Hook saw something kindred to this in Parnelli's eyes, a kind of death, a denial of humanness—the innocence of an animal, or an absolute corruption. He knew he would not get anywhere arguing with the man or even trying to discuss the matter with him, especially with Ferguson there to protect him and watch over him. No, Hook figured his only hope was the hour and the booze, that if he sat back and acknowledged the error of his ways, if he rolled over for the man—well, there was supposed to be truth in wine, was there not? So why should there not also be truth in martinis? Parnelli was a big man, well over two hundred pounds and very little of it fat, so chances were he would be able to drink a great deal without becoming falling-down drunk. Yet his temperament suggested to Hook that he would get high quickly and easily, on just a few drinks, that he had the kind of fragile ego that would enjoy the support of alcohol. For himself Hook was not worried. He had always been able to hold his liquor well, and since Chris's death the stuff had seemed only to affect his body, to make it dull and heavy while his mind burned colder, clearer than ever.

So Hook sat back and drank, and let himself look troubled and full of doubt, and even admitted that he might have let himself get carried away by his grief. All he had wanted, he said, was to find out the truth. It certainly had not been his intention to destroy anybody's political career, especially that of a liberal, because he himself had always been a liberal and believed that the more of them there were in Congress, the better. And he said that he had to admit Douglas did not seem like the kind of man who would harm anybody, that when Hook had met him out at the beach house yesterday the man had been straightforward and open with him, had not acted like a man with anything to hide.

"Of course not!" Parnelli boomed, happy now, smiling. "Because he didn't have anything to hide."

"I guess I must have figured I owed it to my son," Hook said. "I had to look at every angle." The past tense was not unintentional, and Parnelli went after it like a week-old calf for mother's milk.

"Christ, nobody blames you, Mr. Hook—and hey, what is your first name anyway? I can't keep calling you mister."

"Dave."

"Dave! Good name. Well listen, nobody blames you, Dave. We'd probably done the same goddamn thing in your shoes, right, Richie?"

Ferguson nodded, but Hook could see that the young man was

not a believer yet by any means, that he was coolly studying Hook's every glance and word and inflection for the slightest note of falsity. And Hook did not underestimate him. The dying Oliver had said that Ferguson did indeed have a master's degree in political science from Stanford. He was about thirty, the reporter estimated, a bachelor for whom politics was sex and religion and art all rolled into one. After college he had worked for HEW in Washington, D.C., then in Sacramento, where he had met Douglas, had recognized him as a possible comer, and promptly signed on board. And he would just as promptly jump ship, Oliver figured, once he was convinced Douglas was not going anywhere. He would move on to another candidate and work just as diligently for him, for his real career was himself, his future as a power behind the scenes, and the bigger the scene and the greater the power the better he would like it. He was shrewd, tireless, well-informed, and supplied Douglas not only with words and political expertise but with substance as well, that amazingly flexible socioeconomic political philosophy the new young politicians all favored, because their campaigns and positions and votes had to be able to respond efficiently to the changing sands of sophisticated computerized voter profiles, and thus could not be based on anything so unwieldy as a belief or conviction. Ferguson was, Oliver said, a tiny political Edgar Bergen with a large Charlie McCarthy sitting on his lap. So Hook knew that he had to play to him as much as to Parnelli now. What the big man would swallow whole, the little one might reject altogether.

Third and fourth rounds of drinks were served, with Ferguson passing each time, and the conversation got around to football, how Parnelli had been an all-state halfback in high school but that USC had turned him into a linebacker, which he realized now had actually been a real compliment to his abilities, because it was back about then that defense began to come into its own and to be recognized as every bit as important as offense, but he sure as hell had pissed and moaned at the time. Hook, in turn, explained that though he had never played the game himself in college it was still his favorite sport, and he and his sons—*son*, he corrected—were especially high on pro ball, in fact were great fans of the Chicago Bears despite the fact that they lived only forty miles from St. Louis. Parnelli was no Bear fan by a long shot, he said, but he had to admit the best ball, the roughest ball, was played in the Central Division—the "Icebox Division," he called it.

"Anyway," he said, "they sure make those fucking Rams look lousy year after year."

Hook noted the adjective. "The Rams do lose the big ones," he agreed.

"The Rams are shit!" Parnelli snorted, scowling down at his drink, shaking his head. "They drafted me—I suppose you've heard that."

No, Hook had not. He neglected to add that until two days ago neither had he heard of "Bo" Parnelli.

"Yeah, they drafted me. Let me work my balls off at summer camp, and then what do they do? They cut me—too late for any other team to pick me up. And then after a year's layoff nobody's interested in you anymore. You've had it."

Hook nodded sympathetically. "It's like show business. Making it or not making it is just a matter of luck. Look at the pro record of the Heisman Trophy winners. Nothing."

Parnelli looked at him in loving gratitude, even raised his glass in a toast. "Here's to you, man. By Christ, you know football. You know what it's all about. The breaks—that's what it's all about."

He was already slurring his words, and when he signaled for another round now, Ferguson delicately suggested that maybe they ought to stop drinking and have dinner instead. "Remember, Jack's going to want to go out at seven tomorrow," he added.

Parnelli ignored the suggestion about having dinner, but the other excited him, and he turned to Hook. "Hey, that's right. Hey, you ever go spearfishin', Dave?"

"Never. The water's kind of cold this time of year, isn't it?"

"Not *skin* divin'," Parnelli laughed. "With a wet suit."

"No. Never have."

"Well, come on out with us tomorrow. Jack's got this boat, the *Skipjack*, a forty-foot sportfisher. We usually go out once or twice a week. Out to the islands. It's great. You'd have a great time."

Hefting his fourth drink, Hook gave the matter thought. "I don't know about going into the water, but I could watch, I guess. Just the two of you?"

"Oh, maybe Liz Madera too—she comes along sometimes. But so what? Join us anyway."

Hook had no idea what he might be letting himself in for, but the look of alarm spreading on Ferguson's face gave him all the confirmation he needed.

"Sure," he said. "I'd like to go."

Pretending to be amused now, Ferguson looked wonderingly at Parnelli. "Bo, what *are* you talking about? Mr. Hook can't go out with Jack and Liz. For Christ sake, you forgotten what he's doing here? You think he's here on a pleasure trip? Don't you remember why we're sitting here with him now, what we came here to talk about?"

As Parnelli looked down at his little partner a muscle tightened in the slab of his jaw. Very softly he said, "Who are you to tell me? Ain't you been listening? Ain't you heard one word this man has said? He's all right. He's okay. You take my word for it, hear?"

"Look, Bo, for heaven's sake. You——"

"Will you shut up!"

"Bo, come on. You've had enough. You——"

"Shut up, I said." Parnelli uttered it with a quiet deadly menace, and Ferguson evidently heard in it the same thing Hook did —the physical man's final effort at non-physical communication —for he said nothing more.

Parnelli sat there watching him, waiting. Then, the victor, he turned to Hook. "Seven in the morning, at the harbor. I'll meet you where the breakwater starts."

Hook nodded. "I'll be there."

Later, when Parnelli had gone to the men's room to relieve himself, Ferguson hurriedly explained to Hook that he should not take Parnelli's invitation seriously.

"I'm sure you can see it's impossible," he told Hook. "And I can guarantee you that's how Jack Douglas will feel about it. So if I were you I just wouldn't show up. But don't say anything to Bo about it now. He's got a pretty short fuse. Two drinks and he thinks he's back on the gridiron."

Hook was afraid that if he did not agree with Ferguson, by morning Douglas would call the thing off, and he did not want that to happen.

"I guess you're right," he said. "I'll forget about it."

The little man was on his feet then, shaking Hook's hand, thanking him for joining him and Parnelli and talking over "this little problem" of theirs. He apologized that he had to leave so suddenly but he still had some work to do at the office and it was now or never. Then he hurried to the bar, signed the check, and scurried out of the restaurant, heading for the men's room, Hook surmised, though he could not be sure, because it was located outside, off the corridor leading to the restaurant.

Sitting there alone at the corner table, Hook bet himself another scotch that he would not see either of them again that night, and he won. When the drink was served he ordered dinner, abalone steak amandine, and it proved to be quite different from the fare at the Banner Hill bowling alley grill.

Back at his motel room, Hook could not relax. Somehow he felt both tense and logy at the same time. He was used to long days of physical labor and he could feel its lack now more in his mind than in his body, a ragged nervous edge he normally did not have. So he decided to go out and walk, to do his thinking on his feet, and there was much to think about this night, much to try to sort out in his mind.

He put on a sweater and his raincoat and left the motel, crossing Cabrillo Boulevard to the beach and moving laboriously through the soft sand toward the shoreline, where the sand would be hard enough for easier walking. The beach was deep at this point, a good hundred yards from the street to the water. When he reached the shore he turned east, heading under the wharf on which were a restaurant and fish markets and facilities for the boats that serviced the oil rigs and the islands. Beyond the wharf it was open beach for miles, like a road at midnight, a long gray strip of pavement curving away from him into darkness. The night, like the last two days, had the fierce clarity of mountain air, with stars almost as brilliant as the distant row of streetlights diminishing down the palm-lined drive, and Hook found it all difficult to accept as December, as Christmas, yet the holiday was only a week away now. Even if he was not finished here by then he would have to fly home, he knew, be there for the holidays, for Bobby and Jennifer would need him then, just as he would need them, on this their first Christmas without Chris.

So he felt the pressure of time, that it was slipping away from him, yet he did not feel totally frustrated. It had been a long day and he had learned a great deal. The only problem was he did not know what value to put upon the things he had learned. He had started the day fairly well convinced that he would have to begin concentrating on Mrs. Rubin, that the combination of Jack Douglas's straightforward manner and his alibi supported not only by his employees but by a responsible third party just did not add up to his being involved. But that had been before the third party, the eminent dentist, had panicked. And Hook still could not figure out why he had. What Parnelli and Ferguson had done after the dentist's call, that Hook could understand. It made sense that they would be disturbed by Hook's crusade even if their employer and candidate had had nothing to do with Chris's death, for a politician *was* vulnerable to rumor. On the other hand, if Douglas was involved, they probably had even more reason to rise to his defense, for in all likelihood then they too might have been involved in the crime or accident, whichever it was, as accessories if nothing else. And in fact, of all the things Hook had learned today the one that stood out most vividly in his mind was Parnelli's low threshold of violence, both as Oliver had reported it to Hook and as the onetime football hero himself had almost demonstrated it on Ferguson in the bar. No great leap of the imagination was required to relate that defect to Chris's death—Chris's *violent* death.

Yet Hook felt that despite everything that had happened, everything he had learned today, he still was not any closer to knowing what actually had occurred at the beach house that night and early morning. About all he could do was try to imagine what had happened, take his small cast of characters and move them this way and that, much as the Pentagon's think-tankers sat around dreaming up "scenarios" of apocalypse. When he considered just Chris and the two women alone he could only imagine Chris's death as having been an accident, that the boy might have smoked marijuana on top of the alcohol he had drunk and which had shown in his blood level, and thus stoned, happy, flying, had walked off the cliff in darkness. To Hook, any other interpretation involving just Chris and the women would not wash. For the boy was an inch taller than Hook's own six feet one and he weighed one hundred and seventy pounds, all of it hard as bone. He could have picked up the ladies, one in each hand, and dropped *them* over the cliff. So if it was true that just the three of them had been there, Hook felt he had to rule out violence as a possibility. And yet that interpretation still left the problem of Chris's "suicide," why the women had lied about that.

On the other hand, when Hook considered the possibility that the boy's death might *not* have been an accident, then a man or men automatically came into the picture—but who, how, or why Hook could not be sure.

Perhaps tomorrow on the boat he might find some answers, and if not then maybe the next day or the day after that. Ultimately he was not worried, for if he continued to get nowhere he would simply go out to the beach house alone some night and drag the enigmatic Mrs. Rubin to the cliff edge and there discuss the matter with her. She might press charges against him afterward, but that prospect did not worry him half so much as the fear of never finding out, never *knowing* what had happened to his son.

As he continued down the beach it occurred to him that the same stars shining on him now, all except those low in the west, were shining on the farm as well, giving to the snow cover there a cold blue light that would be luminous in the darkness, and against which the cattle as they moved and stirred would appear as flattened silhouettes, black holes torn in the canvas of the night. In his mind Hook could hear them, hear the ice crackling as they moved, see their breath rising in the brittle air, and it made him feel very far from home.

9

Hook awoke at five in the morning and by six had already had breakfast, so he decided to walk to the yacht harbor, which was only a half-mile up the road from his motel. Rain had fallen during the night and the air was fresh and salt-free, clear except for a few ragged storm clouds prowling around the peaks of the Santa Ynez. By the time he reached the harbor the sun still was not visible above the mountains running down the coast, but the light that preceded its rising—a dark mauve nimbus—had already given way to blue, the blue of day, another drearily beautiful Santa Barbara day.

Though Hook had driven by the yacht harbor many times already, for some reason he still thought of it as he had seen it on television during the oil blowout three years before—the ranks of stark white boats floating in a black sea. But what he saw now was a handsome calendar of color, a sea that was blue instead of black and a long yellow stone breaker curving out around hundreds of boats of tan and green and white, many of which were veritable ships, oceangoing yachts he could not have bought with all his land and cattle combined. Fronting the harbor was a large yellow building holding a U.S. Naval Reserve facility. Then came a number of small shops catering to the needs of tourists and yachtsmen, and which did not appear to be open as he walked past them now and stopped finally where the breakwater began, the place where Parnelli had said he would meet him. But it was deserted. Carefully Hook scanned the neat rows of boats, looking for a human shape somewhere among them, some sign of Douglas or Parnelli, though he did not really expect to find any. They would be here, he figured, only if Ferguson had convinced Douglas that he, Hook, had not taken Parnelli's invitation seriously. Or maybe they would be here now at six-thirty but not at seven, not at the time he was expected to show.

As he stood there studying the harbor, a scruffy old man loaded down with fishing gear came limping past, heading down the gangway toward the piers. Hook asked him if he knew where the *Skipjack*, a fishing boat, was tied up.

The old man laughed. "Fishing boat! You mean fun and games boat, don'tcha?"

"Whatever."

"Sure. A big sport rig, that's what she is. Flybridge and all."

"You know where it's docked?"

"Straight ahead. Middle of the third dock, right side."

"Much obliged."

The old man nodded, and Hook followed him down the gangway onto the pier, which had a series of four docks leading out from it on both sides. The old man turned at the second one and dumped his gear into the stern of an ungainly little boat that looked homemade but much used. Hook went on to the third dock and turned right. And then he saw it, the *Skipjack*, smaller than some of its neighbors but still one very impressive-looking craft, new and white and expensive, with a flybridge as high as some of the sailing masts around it. Walking alongside the boat, Hook suddenly found himself face to face with Bo Parnelli, who had just straightened up from doing some chore in the stern.

Hook tried for a casual smile. "Good morning."

Parnelli said nothing, just stood there glaring at him for a few moments and then stepped down into the cabin, where Hook could see Douglas getting up from a small booth table. Like his colleague, he was wearing a blue windbreaker and white slacks and white sneakers, and this surprised Hook, for though he had figured Parnelli for an *arriviste* type that would religiously wear the proper costume for the proper activity, he had not thought of Douglas as that unsure of himself.

Douglas came up out of the cabin now, alone, working on a

wry, questioning smile, a look of pained amusement. "Well—Mr. Hook. What can I do for you?"

Hook pretended to be pleasantly bewildered. "Oh, didn't Bo tell you? He invited me to come along with you today."

"Yeah, I heard that, all right. But I also heard that Rich Ferguson canceled the invitation. And he seemed to think you understood. That you agreed."

"Well I guess I got to thinking about it later and it didn't seem like the right thing to do—I mean, just to ignore Parnelli that way. So here I am."

"So here you are."

Hook glanced down at his raincoat, which he was wearing over slacks, a white shirt and a sweater. "Not exactly the right outfit, I guess. But it's the best I could do."

"The problem isn't your attire."

"Oh? What is the problem, then?"

Douglas was still trying to look amused. "Well, let's just say it's a social thing, Mr. Hook. And I don't think you'd fit in too well."

"Maybe Bo forgot to tell you. I checked with him and Ferguson about your card game that night. They back you up, and I believe them. So I don't see there's any problem between us anymore."

It was like going through a ritual. Hook was lying and they both knew he was lying, yet somehow just the words themselves, their mystic power, counted as truth. To deny them, Douglas in a sense would be denying the credibility of his own words, his own alibi.

"Miss Madera's also aboard," he said.

Hook smiled. "There are two of you to protect her."

Douglas said nothing for a time. Then finally he nodded, gave Hook an ironic "Welcome aboard," and went back inside.

Hook climbed aboard and followed him down the few steps into the cabin, which contained the galley and table and a pair of built-in settees that looked as if they folded out into double bunks. All the appointments were brushed aluminum and teak, highly lacquered, warm, beautiful. Liz Madera, in her uniform of black sweatshirt and chinos, was standing at the galley range, watching over frypans of bacon and eggs. Hook said good morning to her but she barely glanced at him. Beyond her, through the hatch leading to the front cabin, which was shaped to the bow of the boat, Parnelli was crouched over a spear gun, working on it with a screwdriver. By his look of black Sicilian resentment Hook got the feeling he had caused the man to be chewed out by his employer, who had slid back into the booth table now, behind a steaming cup of coffee.

"Come on," he said. "Sit down. You're just in time for breakfast."

Hook sat across from him. "Just coffee'll be fine. I've already eaten."

"Hear that, Liz? Just coffee for our guest."

"Ever been out on the ocean before?" Douglas asked.

"On a Navy destroyer. Never a boat like this, though."

"Good, then. Be a new experience for you."

Liz served his coffee now, black. He looked up to thank her but her eyes did not stray his way.

"Were you an officer, Hook?"

"Just a seaman," he said, noting that he was simply Hook now, no longer Mister Hook.

"The Korean War?"

"Second World War. The end of it, anyway."

"Really? You don't look that old."

"I'm forty-five."

"Must lead a clean life."

"That could be."

"Although from what Bo tells me, you don't mind lifting a few."

"No, I don't mind that at all."

"As a matter of fact, I think you kind of drank him under the table."

"I didn't notice."

Liz brought a platter of fried eggs and bacon and set out plates and silverware.

"It's ready, Bo," she said, sitting down next to Douglas, who served her first, then himself.

"Bacon and eggs on the bounding main," he said. "One of the great ideas of Western man."

Parnelli came to the table and roughly filled his plate, as if he were scraping garbage into a sink. "I think I'll stand," he said, spurning the seat next to Hook.

Douglas had reverted to the subject of last night. "Yeah, Bo says you two had quite a talk. Right, Bo?"

"Whatever you say."

Douglas winked at Hook. "I think Bo got up on the wrong side of the bed this morning, so maybe it's a good thing you're coming with us after all. Give us someone to talk to besides ourselves."

"Oh, I think I'll just sit back and watch," Hook said. "I don't want to get in the way."

"Nonsense." Douglas downed the last of his coffee. "Bo also tells me you're something of a liberal. Is that so? Are we Democrats fortunate enough to have you in our camp?"

Hook shrugged. "I'm not very political."

"You mean you don't know where you stand?"

"No, I don't mean that."

"Then where do you stand?"

Hook met his mocking gaze and decided that a little truth might be in order. "Am I a liberal? No, not really. Not anymore. I used to be, but now I don't find much sense on either side of the aisle."

Douglas said he was awfully sorry to hear that. "Always hate to lose one from the fold," he added.

"It isn't the philosophy I'm against."

"Oh? What, then?"

"Its proponents."

"You don't mean we've let you down somehow?"

"Well, since you put it in the first person, let's take your case. This morning you left your hundred-thousand-dollar house, you drove here in your eight-thousand-dollar car, and now you're about to set out in your umpteen-thousand-dollar yacht. And I'd be willing to bet that after a couple of terms in Congress you'll be hurting even less."

Douglas shook his head sorrowfully. "Now I call that a cynical comment," he said, holding up his coffee cup for Liz to refill.

Hook agreed. "Yes, I think it is too."

"But fair?"

"Yes, fair."

"Because politicians are cynical, right?"

"Right."

"Give us a for-instance."

"For instance, the oil depletion allowance. Or tax loopholes for the rich. They both seem to go on and on no matter who's in power."

"And why is that, Mr. Hook? Why do they go on?"

Hook smiled. "Of course, you have no idea."

"That's why I'm asking."

"Then I guess it's my duty to tell you."

"Please."

"Greed, Mr. Douglas. Simple greed. You champions of the poor seldom choose to share their poverty."

Douglas made a face, as though he were scandalized at hearing such an idea. "Sounds terribly pessimistic," he said.

"Could be I'm a pessimist."

"Does that come from being close to the earth?"

Hook looked at Liz next to him and for a change she did not lower her gaze, yet he had no idea what he saw in her beautiful brooding eyes, whether it was sympathy or scorn or merely pain, the anguish of the "dying."

"No, I don't think so," he said. "For instance, my son Chris lived almost his whole life on the farm. But he wasn't a pessimist, was he, Miss Madera?" He waited but she did not respond. "No, I think Chris believed that in time we'd make it all come out right in this country. But then, that's natural in the young, isn't it, that kind of optimism? They know, they feel, their own strength and health and spirit, and they impute it to the rest of us. But it just isn't there, is it?" He looked from Douglas to Parnelli and then back again. "Time takes it away from us, so that finally the question we ask isn't what we can do for other people but what we can take away from them, right?"

Douglas, finished eating, had given Liz a cigarette and taken one himself. Now he lit them, pointedly excluding Hook. "So that's how it is with you, huh?" he said.

"That's how it is."

"And of course what's true for you is automatically true for the rest of us."

"Not if you say it isn't."

Douglas grinned. "Well, this may come as a big shock to you, friend, but it just so happens I don't feel obliged to justify myself to you. I'm sorry about that, but that's the way it is. Tell me about you, though—what is it you're after? What's your particular greed?"

Hook did not answer immediately. Finally he said, "My family. Their good name."

"Bull *shit!*" It was Parnelli. And as he said it he contemptuously tossed his empty plastic plate across the galley into the sink, where it slowly clattered silent, like a spun coin.

Douglas laughed. "I'm afraid Bo isn't moved by such old-fashioned sentiments."

"Not many people are."

Douglas said nothing then for a time, just sat leaning back in the corner of the booth, blowing smoke rings and smiling to himself. Finally he shook his head approvingly. "Well now isn't this just peachy-keen. We're all being so modern and civilized, kind of like an ex-married couple having a pleasant little tête-à-tête together. Or a dog and cat eating out of the same bowl." He grinned at Hook, in a burlesque of admiration. "Boy, you really took old Bo in, didn't you? I guess he thought you were just some poor dumb shitkicker farmer. Ain't that right, Bo?" He winked up at the big man, who was glumly leaning back against a bulkhead, his arms crossed, his face clotted with resentment. Bo said nothing.

Douglas turned back to Hook. "But that really isn't the case at all, is it, Mr. Hook? No siree. Had a friend of mine in St. Louis do a little checking on you, and what do I find out? For one thing, Phi Beta Kappa, University of Illinois, nineteen fifty-two. Then spent a couple of years teaching comparative literature in high school. Then turned to the land, worked like a sonofabitch, and now has over a thousand acres all bought and paid for, plus some three hundred head of registered Black Angus cattle. So, no, you're not some poor dumb shitkicker, are you, Mr. Hook?"

Hook did not respond.

"'Course you're not. And that's why I think you'll give some serious thought to what I'm about to say. Which is this—I'm not some dumb pushover either. And I've put way too much time and effort and money into a political career to just sit helplessly by now and watch you blow it all to hell. So here's what I've decided I've got to do. Unless you lay off and go home I'm going to have to make charges to the police and the press that you're part of a smear conspiracy against me, that somehow you're in league with the Republicans and Sergeant Rider and whoever the hell else I can throw in the pot. Now I don't want to do it, because of course it ain't going to *help* my cause any. It certainly won't win me any new support or votes. But it sure as hell beats sitting back waiting for your wild fancies to spread. Then it'll be too late. To come out anywhere near clean in politics you've got to be the one that throws first mud. And that's just what I plan to do—*if you force me*. Also, if I lose next year, I'll have established a case against you, so I can sue your ass for every penny you own."

Hook had lit his own cigarette, and now he dragged on it, thinking. "That's clear enough," he said.

Douglas was not smiling anymore, not playing his game of irony. "I figured it would be. Now, you still want to go along with us?"

Hook met his gaze, and shrugged. "I don't see why not. As I said earlier—I believe what Parnelli told me. I believe you weren't involved. So we have no quarrel."

Douglas's darkly tanned face went pale with anger. "So be it," he said. "Let's cast off, then."

For the next hour Hook was made to play the role of the leper. After piling the few dishes in the sink, Liz announced that she was going to nap on the way out to the islands and promptly went into the bow cabin and closed the hatch behind her. Parnelli, after checking over the scuba tanks and gear, climbed up into the cockpit and joined Douglas, who was piloting the craft. But when Hook tried to follow, Douglas told him to stay below, that there were only two seats in the cockpit and that the sea was too rough for him to stand up. So he slid the hatch closed and climbed back down, thinking he would stay out on the deck and enjoy the sea and air, but there proved to be too much of both, a cold steady spray that sent him retreating into the main cabin, where he stretched out in one of the bunks. Despite the yacht's considerable size, Hook found the going rough, and he wondered if he would become seasick.

By the time they were drawing near the islands, the day had changed. A cold wind had blown in from the northwest and the fog seemed to come rolling up out of the sea like snow falling from winter clouds. As it moved in upon the mainland, the mountains there soon looked like a giant stone wall against which a heavy snow had drifted, burying the coastline and the city far beneath it. Pulling the collar of his raincoat up around his neck, Hook went out onto the stern deck, and almost immediately Parnelli came clambering down the ladder from the cockpit and gathered up his scuba gear and went on into the cabin, all without glancing at Hook. As the husky Italian started to get out of his clothes, Hook climbed up on the cockpit ladder and asked Douglas if he and Parnelli were still going spearfishing.

Douglas cut the engine to idle and the boat pitched forward, leveling. "Why not?" he asked.

"It's not a very good day, is it?"

"The fish like this kind of day." Douglas punched a button and Hook heard the anchor drop into the water.

"You're going down too?"

Now Douglas spun around in his pilot's seat. "Not today. Somehow things just don't seem normal for me today."

He got up, and Hook climbed back down the ladder ahead of him. In the cabin Parnelli was pulling the armor-like wet suit on over thermal long underwear. Seeing Hook, he snapped on a sneer.

"Hey, you wanta go fishing, shitkicker?"

Hook said nothing.

"Come on. You wanta go down with me? *With* me, remember —not *on* me."

Liz came out of the low cabin now, yawning, zipping on a windbreaker with a hood. But Parnelli ignored her. He was still after Hook.

"What's the matter? This look a little bit scary to you? You don't think you'd dig it down there with all them little fishies? Shit, you'd have nothing to worry about, pal. Old Bo'd take good care of you, get you back home nice and safe with that family you're so concerned about."

"I'll pass," Hook said.

"You sure? I mean we've got the gear, man. I'll give you a few minutes' expert instruction in the drink and down we go. Christ, maybe you'll spear a whale your first shot. Now wouldn't that be something to tell the old folks at home?"

Douglas had moved past Hook into the galley, where he got out a fifth of Cutty Sark and poured some of it into two glasses, one of which he gave to Parnelli now. "I think you're wasting your time, Bo," he said. "I don't think Mr. Hook would feel at home down there in the briny deep. And as we all know, he doesn't like to go anywhere he doesn't feel at home."

"I thought scuba divers were cautious," Hook said. "I didn't know they went down in weather like this."

Douglas grinned. "Well, let's just say Bo's the incautious type. When he's down there, there's just one more shark in the water."

"One more idiot." It was Liz.

Looking at her, Douglas made a face. "Jesus, listen to it, Bo. It walks and talks. It's alive after all."

"You're very funny," she said. "Also very stupid. What're you trying to do—impress him?"

Parnelli laughed. "You found us out, Liz. That's our lifelong ambition—to impress an Illinois shitkicker."

"Why aren't we turning back, then?" she asked Douglas. "You can barely see the island, for God's sake."

The boat had swung around on its anchor, so that now the island was lying out over the stern, low and gray and peaked in the center, like a submarine passing in the mist. Douglas had made his fist into a telescope and now he was comically squinting through it, at the island.

"I can see it," he said. "I can see that island plain as day. And when you can see a mile in the fog, that ain't much of a fog."

"Hell no," Parnelli said. "I'll just get us a couple of nice big red snappers for lunch. And maybe a shark for our guest here. Unless of course he'd prefer to go down and get it himself. You sure you don't want to change your mind?"

"I'm sure."

Parnelli downed the last of his whiskey, put on his flippers and face mask and followed Douglas out onto the stern, walking like a man in deep mud. Douglas tied a line to a small plastic raft and tossed it overboard, then he helped Parnelli into his scuba tanks and positioned a ladder out over the side, down into the water. Parnelli got his breathing apparatus into place, checked it, then moved laboriously down the ladder into the water, where Douglas handed him a spear gun. As he moved off through the swelling waves and then slipped under them, like some grotesque twin-tailed fish sounding, Douglas turned to Hook with a grin.

"A tiger," he said. "The man's afraid of nothing. Absolutely nothing."

In the cabin doorway, Liz angrily pulled her jacket hood up over her head. "Except you, you sonofabitch."

Douglas pretended to be shocked. "Now, what do you mean by that?"

"You know what I mean. You could've told him not to go down."

"And why should I?"

"You're a diver. You know better than I do."

"Christ, we've been down on days a lot worse than this."

"Exactly," she said. "*We've* been down. You didn't go alone."

Douglas smiled, not very prettily. "How would you know that, sweetheart? You think I've never gone diving without you along? Why, many's the time Jill and I come out here together. Just the two of us." He winked at Hook. "Jill's my wife. We have this understanding."

"Gentlemen's agreement is more like it," Liz said.

"Touché." Douglas toasted her with his empty glass, and then went back into the cabin and poured himself some more.

Liz looked at Hook and shivered. "It's awfully cold," she said. "You want a drink? I'm going to have one."

He said yes, and she went back into the cabin.

Douglas shrugged in mock innocence as she moved past him.

"Forgive me for being such a poor host, Mr. Hook. I just don't know what came over me."

Hook smiled wearily. "Do we have to play this game all day?"

"And what game is that?"

"Your sarcasm. Why bother? I'll concede your hostility. You don't have to keep insisting on it."

"Big of you," Douglas said. "You are a generous person."

Liz came out with their drinks, water glasses a third full of scotch, and Hook tossed off part of his. In the cold it felt like brandy hitting his stomach, a feast of warmth.

"Thanks," he said. "That helps."

Douglas was grinning at them. "You know, you two make a splendid-looking couple."

"You're in rare form today," Liz said.

Douglas nodded sagely. "Yes, I think deep down, Liz kind of goes for you, Hook. Electra finds her father."

"You bastard," Liz said. "You low bastard."

She went back inside the cabin, but Douglas followed her to the doorway.

"Well, it's true, isn't it? Come on, admit it." He turned to Hook, shaking his head in mock sorrow. "My poor Liz goes through life from one hate affair to the next. I'm the current one, that's all. But what she's really looking for, I think, is Daddy, the daddy she never had. Not some slick Spanish cocksman but an All-American square like you. Someone she could cling to and be sheltered by —like a goddamn oak tree, you know?" He laughed now. "And come to think of it, you fill the bill just right. Straight, upstanding, rigid. Why, you got everything but acorns."

Hook was looking out at the water, where the small raft was bobbing like a cork. "You forgotten about your tiger?" he asked.

"Oh, he'll be up soon. Don't worry about him. What's the matter—I touch a nerve?" Looking sad, Douglas turned back to Liz in the cabin. "I'm sorry if I ruined your play, sweetheart. Sorry about that."

She walked over and slid the cabin hatch shut, and Douglas laughed. Hook wondered if the man was drunk, made drunk by a few ounces of scotch. It was hard to believe. But this Douglas was not the same man Hook had talked with at the beach house two days before.

And now he seemed to know just what Hook was thinking. "What's the matter? You figure I've flipped?"

Hook shook his head. "No. I get the feeling you know just what you're doing. All the time."

"Well, you're wrong. Today I just don't give a shit. I can't figure her out, and I can't figure you out either. So I say to myself, what the hell. Anything goes. So don't sweat it, friend. Don't try to draw any conclusions from anything I say or do today. I didn't want you to come along, but you came anyway. So I'm taking my revenge—by not being myself. Makes sense, doesn't it?"

"A perverse kind of sense."

"That's me—perverse. Polymorphous perverse. Just call me Polly." Now he looked past Hook, out at the water. "Hey, there's our tiger—and he's got a beauty."

Parnelli was leaning into the raft, trying to work a huge orange fish off the spear shaft. Succeeding, he stuffed the fish into a gunny sack, loaded and cocked the spear gun and held it up in a gesture of triumph before slipping back into the water. Hook watched him disappear with a feeling of icy dread; he could not comprehend such a casual risking of one's life. To him it was like playing Russian roulette alone, without even the possible gain of a moral victory over an opponent. And he said as much now.

"All for a fish. The man's a fool."

"Not just a fish—a *good* fish," Douglas said. "You ever eaten red snapper?"

Hook ignored the question. "I hope he's not down there on my account."

"That would bother you?"

"Why shouldn't it bother him?" It was Liz, who had come out of the cabin again when Parnelli had surfaced.

"Ah yes. I was forgetting all about Mr. Hook's finer sensibilities." Bowing in mock contrition, Douglas headed for the cabin again. "I seem to have spilled my glass."

After he had gone inside, Liz looked bleakly at Hook. "You shouldn't have come. You've really got him all shook up."

"Why is that?"

"You know why. He's scared to death of you. You keep on and you'll destroy him. I hope you know that."

"Funny thing," Hook said. "I was all ready to give up on him —until his dentist friend panicked. And until Ferguson and Bo had their little go at me. They were very nervous, Miss Madera."

"And why shouldn't they be? You could be undoing years of their work in just a few days."

"You think that was the reason, huh?"

"I *know* that was the reason."

Hook told her not to worry about Douglas's career, that she could call him off any time she wanted. "All you have to do is tell me the truth," he added. "Tell me what did happen that night."

Her eyes wandered out over the water, grave, even grieving. "You'll never let go, will you?"

"I'm afraid not."

"Beautiful! You're just beautiful together." Douglas was coming out of the cabin, this time with the bottle. "A truly winning couple. Electra and Agamemnon." He made a comic face, all amazement and discovery. "Hey, I got just the idea, Liz! Why don't we buy the gentleman off? Why don't you take him down into the bow cabin and close the hatch and—"

"I think you've had about enough of that stuff," Hook said, nodding at the bottle in his hand.

Douglas laughed again. "My God! What a guest! The man who came to breakfast!"

Liz, turning away from him, had gone over to the other side of the deck. But Hook still faced the candidate. And now he told him that he had reached some conclusions about him.

"You probably do belong in Congress," he said. "Because I think you're a self-serving bastard at heart. But I'll be goddamned if I'll worry about whether you get there." Then he walked away from him, not giving the man time to articulate the anger that had struck his face like a fist.

Hook went back into the cabin and stretched out in one of the bunks. Through the door he could see Liz sunk down on the deck now, huddling in her windbreaker as if it were a womb. Across from her, Douglas stood scowling out at the water, occasionally taking a pull at the bottle. After a few minutes he called out to Parnelli, who apparently had surfaced again, and then he leaned out over the side of the boat and discussed something with him for a few moments. Then he came to the cabin door.

"Hate to disturb you, friend. But I've got to be up in the cockpit for a few minutes. Will you watch him?"

Going back onto the deck, Hook saw Parnelli taking another red snapper off a spear. After he had gotten it into the gunny sack in the raft, he towed the raft over to the boat. Then he removed his breather and pushed his face mask up onto his head.

"Here, give me a hand!" he shouted, and held the sack of fish up towards Hook, who swung it into the stern, amazed at the snappers' eyes, which looked like ping-pong balls freshly burst out of their heads.

"Now the raft!" Parnelli commanded, and Hook hauled it up onto the deck.

That left only Parnelli himself, and he was already holding his large rubber-gloved hand up for Hook to take hold of and help pull him up the ladder. And Hook reached for the hand—too late seeing the smile that cut as viciously as a razor across Parnelli's face. For one desperate moment Hook tried to turn and grasp something with his free hand and hold on, but there was nothing, only air, and immediately he felt himself being yanked powerfully out of the boat, down over Parnelli's crouched, side-turning figure on the ladder, and then striking the water, plunging into it back-first, flailing in the boiling darkness. He tried not to panic, screamed at himself in his mind that he must not panic, but the sea was not his home, was a great deep maw of death snapping shut over his mind and he could not control himself. He fought it for his life, this sea, fought it as if it were a school of attacking sharks. He was still fully dressed—in shoes, raincoat, trousers, everything—and the sudden sopping weight of it all only added to his terror. Trying to surface, he bumped against something solid and realized it was the bottom of the boat, a coffin lid holding him there underwater. And he felt death's own true messenger, shock, steal like morphine into his body. His limbs became stone, his mind a small light receding rapidly into the distance. They *were* murderers, then. They had killed his son, and now they were killing him. Then suddenly he broke through the surface of the water and felt his lungs balloon with air. And he heard a voice—Parnelli's.

"Hey, shitkicker! Any sharks out there?"

The big Italian was standing in the stern, laughing, holding on to a struggling Liz with both hands, evidently to keep her from throwing out a line. And Hook realized that it was not his murder they were trying to effect but only his humiliation, and with that realization the faint light in his head began to burn brighter and he knew that he would be able to go on swimming for hours, even with arms and legs of stone. And he swam, he treaded water, he watched the yacht moving closer and closer until Parnelli, still holding on to Liz, finally picked up the raft and tossed it out to him. Hook managed to pull himself up onto it and then took hold of the line connecting it to the boat and laboriously pulled himself in to the ladder. A happy, laughing Parnelli reached a hand out to help him up but Hook ignored him and somehow made it to the top on his own and rolled over the gunwale and collapsed on the deck. He could not stand. He could not speak.

Parnelli kept asking him what was wrong. "Shark got your tongue?" he piped. "Shark got your tongue? Jesus, Hook, you'll never make a frogman this way. You just never will."

From the cockpit Douglas leaned out and said he hoped Hook was not mad. "Bo's just got this kinky sense of humor. And we've got to indulge him every now and then. Keeps him happy."

Still Hook could not speak. He was gasping for breath; his heart battered at his chest; his arms and legs shook like freshly killed meat.

Shaking his head and laughing still, Parnelli climbed up into the cockpit with Douglas and the boat got underway. Liz came over to him, knelt beside him.

"You all right?" she shouted above the roar.

He nodded weakly and she took him by the arm and helped him across the pitching deck down into the cabin and into a bunk. She got some dry pants and a sweatshirt and socks for him —Douglas's, he assumed—but she did not say another word, nor would she look directly at him. As she was about to leave, he reached out and took hold of her arm and only then did she meet his eyes. Her own had filled with tears.

"Thank you," he got out. "Thank you, Liz."

She started to say something, but gave it up. Pulling away from him, she went on into the bow cabin and closed the hatch behind her. As Hook slowly struggled into the dry clothes, he thought he heard her crying once, but he could not be sure over the sound of the engine.

That evening Hook sat awake in the dark of his room watching television with the sound turned off. On the Formica-topped dresser next to him the fifth of Red Label scotch he had had delivered that afternoon stood only a third full, yet he still felt sober, clear and cold and deadly sober under the surface numbness of his body, the lethargy the alcohol had bought him. But he had felt numb even before he had begun drinking, when he had first come back from the yacht harbor in the early afternoon, and it was the numbness of shock, he knew, the walking sleep of those who had passed through the shadowed valley and for whom the shadow somehow grew colder and darker the further they moved on from it. And then anger had set in, a black bull of rage that had battered at him throughout the afternoon—rage that he had almost been killed *as a prank*, rage that he was all but helpless to do anything about it, and finally rage that he could not understand what had happened, could not even begin to comprehend the psychology of it all, *why they had done what they had done*.

If it had been Parnelli alone, he could have understood the incident to a degree, much as one understood the casual brutalities of animals and children. But Parnelli had not been alone, in fact had not even been the thing's creator. No, that honor belonged only to Douglas, for it was he who had called Parnelli in from the raft and leaned down to talk with him; it was he who had suggested Hook take his place at the ladder. In other words, it was Douglas who had almost killed him—Douglas who had performed the act of a madman. Yet Douglas was not a madman, and Hook knew it. So he could not deal with the incident in his mind, could not put a ring of understanding through its nose and hold it captive but had to go on being battered by it through the endless afternoon. For a time he thought of calling Sergeant Rider and telling him what had happened, but he could not think how to put it into words without sounding like a raving idiot. "They pulled me overboard, and I almost drowned before they rescued me." Oh really? And what else was new? In his frustration Hook smashed his suitcase.

Finally he decided his only choice was to get drunk, to control through oblivion what he could not control any other way. Only the oblivion had never come, just this numbness that let him sit hour after hour watching motion pictures forming soundlessly in the dark. He had the television tuned to one of Los Angeles's non-network channels and all evening there had been nothing but reruns of old series, *Ben Casey* and *The Fugitive* and *The Invaders*, a short history of a pathetic people's pathetic myths, the TV seasons with which they had measured out their lives, happily surrendering the treasures of community—family, church, club, bar—for the narcotic of endless spectatorship. And it infected Hook with despair, almost an illness of despair, for he realized that he had come to despise so many things about his own country and its people, that they had settled for so little.

Often in the winter, when his work was caught up, he would walk in the woods on his farm and there were times when he would come to the top of a hill and rest for a while, stand there in silence looking down through the barren trees at the snow-covered ground, and he would find it difficult to believe that it was all only winter, only a temporary death, and that within a few short months those same trees and brush, that same earth, would burgeon again with life. Somehow it seemed too great a miracle, too fine a gift for his kind, and that the only seasons men truly merited were those of their own making—seasons like the kind he sat watching now, in a plastic electronic box in a motel room in a tourist city by the sea.

So he watched television and he drank, and the hours went by. And he had no idea what time it was when he heard the knocking on his door. He got up from the chair slowly, carrying not just the weight of the alcohol but an aching stiffness that had already set in from his swim that morning. When he opened the door he could not make out who it was for a time because the streetlights behind her made her appear as just a silhouette, a girl leaning back against the balcony railing in the rain, with long dark hair plastered down over her shoulders like a nun's hood. And then he recognized her raincoat, the shiny black one she had worn on that first night, when they had had drinks together in the bar a few blocks down the street.

She looked at him now, cocking her head to one side and smiling the smile of the stoned. But her eyes were clear, clear and cold, their light the light of diamonds.

"Aren't you going to invite me in?" she asked.

In answer, he left the door open and went back into the room. She followed.

10

After she had come in, Liz stood there in the television-lit darkness leaning back against the closed door. Hook turned on the lamp next to his bed and watched her as she surveyed the small room, which had no more than the rate called for, just the single bed, an orange plastic chair, a dresser that also served as a desk and bedside table, and the color television, which he turned off now.

"I wasn't sure you were in," she said. "But I thought I'd knock anyway."

"What'd you want to see me about?"

"What did I want to see you about?" She smiled mockingly. "Ah yes, I suppose one does need a reason to come calling on Mister David Hook."

"People generally have one."

"And could that be because calling on you isn't all that pleasant? I mean you don't exactly welcome one with a smile, do you?"

Hook did not answer.

Moving over to the dresser, she picked up his pack of cigarettes, took one and lit it. As she opened her raincoat, he saw that she was wearing a tan knit pantsuit, and he wondered where she had been, what sad party she had abandoned.

"Do you think I'm here as Jack's emissary?" she asked. "You figure he finally convinced me to—how was it he put it this morning—to buy you off, with my body?"

"I don't figure anything. You tell me."

"You've been drinking too, I see." She snapped her finger against the mouth of the bottle of scotch. Then she turned and came back, smiling, looking up at him with sardonic, bloodshot eyes.

"I just wanted to see you, that's all," she said. "I was worried. I mean after your swim and all. You Hooks do keep falling off of things."

He struck her with the flat of his hand, so quickly even he had not known it was coming, and she fell backwards spinning, dropping face down onto the bed. She did not make a sound, just lay there supporting herself on her arms, with her head hanging and her hair draped over the bedspread. Hook wanted to say something to her, apologize or explain, but the words would not come. And finally she sat up, slowly, and was a different woman now, this one small and grave and vulnerable.

"I'm sorry," she said. "I didn't mean to say that. I'm smashed, you see. And scared. I'm so scared."

"Of what?"

She did not answer.

"What are you scared of?"

Her eyes darkened in bewilderment. "Did I say I was scared?"

"Just now."

"Then I guess I am."

"Of what?" he repeated.

"The truth?" she asked.

"You tell me."

"Yes, the truth."

"What truth?"

"Just the truth. I guess the truth that brought me here." She smiled dreamily and dropped her head, as if she were about to fall asleep.

Hook tried to bring her back. "Where were you, Liz?"

"Where?"

"Yes, where?"

She scowled in a burlesque of concentration. "Let's see, where was I? Oh yes. I was at the country club, at a party for a friend of Jack's."

"And?"

"And I just got up and left. I had to come. Here."

"To tell me the truth?"

She nodded, and Hook found that he could barely breathe. Suddenly the air in the room was like that before a spring storm on the farm, dry yellow airless air, with the grass and leaves whispering with the knowledge of what was on the way.

"Go on," he said. "I'm listening."

"Just like that?"

"Just like that."

She closed her eyes as though she were in pain and her breasts swelled as she sucked in the deep breath of the sufferer. But her voice when it came was almost matter-of-fact. "What I told you on the beach the other day, it was a lie. Chris didn't leave home because of you. He loved you. And he *didn't* kill himself. His death was an accident. I picked him up on that Tuesday, as you figured, and we had two days together. Just two days."

As she said this last, her voice trickled away and she gazed absently across the room, as if she had come to the end already, had no more truth to tell.

Hook thought otherwise. "What did you do?"

"When?"

"The two days."

"Oh we talked, that's all. We just talked."

"And sex? You didn't make love?"

Her eyes suddenly filmed with tears and she shook her head. "No, we didn't make love. But it wasn't his fault. He wanted me. He tried. I put him off. I didn't want to spoil it, what we had together. And it would have, for me. I don't think I've ever had sex with someone I didn't despise in one way or another. And I guess it's rubbed off on the act itself. In my mind anyway."

She raised her hands like a little girl and smeared twin ribbons of tears running down her face.

"It wasn't impotence, then," Hook said. "He didn't fail."

But she did not seem to have heard him. So he repeated the question, almost angrily now, hoping to bring her out of her alcoholic daze.

"No," she said finally. "That was a lie too."

With that, Hook sat down in the chair facing the bed, facing her. "Tell me about the second night," he said. "The night it happened."

For a long while Liz said nothing, just sat there staring down at her hands and frowning, as if she were trying to get it all straight in her mind. Hook waited. Finally it came.

"I began drinking that afternoon. And I mean drinking a lot, for me anyway. Later I switched to pot and then I tried to keep the high going with wine that night. I locked myself in my room and I got stoned. Why, I don't know—maybe because I wasn't eighteen anymore. Because I wasn't—*unused*. Because I couldn't have him, at least not the way I wanted him."

Her voice broke and Hook felt it in his own body, like a bone breaking. And this angered him. He wanted to keep his emotional distance from her so he could judge what she was saying, try to separate the truth from the half-truths and the half-truths from the outright lies. But so far everything she said sounded just the same, was uttered with the same perfect pitch of anguish and conviction. Yet he would not let himself believe her, not yet anyway.

"Go on," he said.

"Where was I?"

"Locked in your room. Stoned."

Closing her eyes, she nodded. "Yes. So he was alone. I left him alone. And I guess he drank more wine than he should have. He must have gone walking. He must have walked off the cliff in the darkness."

Hook thought of the cliff, its almost sloping face at the top, with the tough-rooted chaparral clinging densely to it, and he could only wonder how a lean strong nineteen-year-old boy could have plunged helplessly down it, even drunk. But he did not protest. Instead he sat waiting for her to go on, to explain the inexplicable. Finally he brought it up himself.

"And the suicide?"

"What?"

"His death, Liz. Why'd you call it suicide?"

She shook her head in bewilderment. "I don't know. I really don't. I was in shock after it happened. And Dorothy told me not to worry, that she'd handle everything. And the next thing

I knew I was sitting there and the police were asking if there was anything I wanted to add to what Dorothy had told them, and I said no, there was nothing, Dorothy had told it all just as it happened. Only I didn't know what she'd said till later. And then it was too late."

"Why would she invent such a story?"

"You'll have to ask her."

"I'm asking you."

"Well, I'm afraid I don't know the lady. I've lived with her for six months, but I still don't know her. I guess she owns some stock in Jack's company. She's very loyal to him. Very dedicated. Like the others. You'd think he was Jesus Christ. Which kind of makes me his Judas, I guess. His female Judas. I'm destroying all their careful work. They hate me. Especially her."

"Mrs. Rubin."

Liz nodded. Her eyes went heavy and distant again and suddenly she stretched out on the bed. Hook resisted an impulse to pull her back up and slap her awake, alert.

"Is she a lesbian?" he asked.

"Who?"

"Mrs. Rubin."

"I don't think so. Never made a pass at me, anyway."

"Was she jealous of Chris?"

"Could be."

"Of the way you reacted to him?"

Eyes closed, she nodded dreamily. "Hated him, right off. Maybe because he had so much. And she had so little. So she—she—"

Hook waited, then finished it himself. "So she transformed him."

"Yes."

"Made him into a failure, a fag, a suicide."

Liz nodded again, apparently almost asleep.

"And Douglas? He wasn't there?"

She did not respond, so Hook repeated the question. This time it reached her like a bucket of cold water. Her eyes opened and she struggled to a sitting position on the bed again.

"Jack? No, he wasn't there. Just the two of us, Dorothy and me. And Chris."

Hook neither believed nor disbelieved. Her voice, her wounded eyes, her manner all said it was true—just as they had that first night, when she had told him an altogether different story. So he could not be sure. All he could do was go along and try to get it all: the truth, or simply another, newer lie.

"Then that just leaves the one question," he said. "The big question. Why you haven't told this to the police."

"What would it change? I didn't see it happen. Dorothy claims she did. So it would only be my word against hers. And anyway, Jack doesn't want me to. He's afraid it would ruin him politically. Dorothy's his employee. I'm his mistress. He says the thing would be bound to rub off on him. Hurt him."

"And you wouldn't want that."

She shook her head. "It wouldn't be fair to him. It wasn't his doing. He wasn't even there."

"And his career is worth more than Chris's name."

She looked at him with stricken eyes. "Jack Douglas is alive, Mr. Hook. Chris is dead."

Hook looked away from her tears. Getting up, he went over to the window and gazed out at the rain pocking into the dark pool below. What could he say? Chris is dead, Mr. Hook. Yes, you are right. My son is dead.

Behind him, she got up and poured herself a drink from the bottle on the dresser. Then she went into the bathroom, where he heard her adding water to the scotch. When she came out she sat down in the chair he had vacated. And she asked him if he would turn off the light.

"I just want to sit here in the dark for a few minutes," she added.

Hook flipped off the wall switch, which controlled the bedside lamp. This did not put them in total darkness, however, for a light was still burning in the bathroom, and it lay softly along the side of her face, making her look even more beautiful. But Hook did not believe vanity was behind her request. All she wanted, he figured, was to sit there and not have to meet his eyes.

"You say you cared for him," he said.

"Yes."

"And yet you can leave it the way it is? Leave him a suicide?"

"I think he'd understand. I don't think he'd want me to hurt innocent people. Even for the sake of your pride."

"My pride."

"That's what it comes down to, doesn't it? No one can hurt Chris anymore. So it's you we're hurting. Your pride."

Hook tried hard not to lose his self-control. "You said you came here tonight for the truth," he got out finally. "To tell me the truth."

"I did."

"Chris had his truth too. He had a life. A real life. And you've taken it from him. You've taken it from me."

"I can't help that."

"But you *can*."

"No."

"You've got to tell the police."

"I can't."

"You've got to." Hook tried to keep his voice level, but it was his rage that spoke now, again and again. "You've got to! You hear me? *You've got to!*"

And suddenly the glass dropped from her hand and thumped on the carpet, spilling, and she was out of her chair and into the bathroom and he could hear it coming out of her, like the mess stuck in his own body, a sour filth of pain and anguish. He did not go in until she was finished, and then he found her crumpled on the floor next to the toilet bowl shaking her head and shuddering. There was vomit on her suit, on the bowl rim, on the floor.

"Oh God, I'm sorry," she said. "I'm so sorry."

"It's all right."

She started to get up and almost fell before he caught her, and he realized she was much drunker than he had thought. He helped her out of her pantsuit and then a mini-slip that was soiled too, and which was all she was wearing besides her underpants. He wet a towel and cleaned off her face and hoped she would take the towel from him to clean the front of her, but she just hung there in the grip of his arm, with her head resting on his shoulder, and he found himself washing her between breasts that were as beautiful as the rest of her. He walked her into the bedroom and helped her into his bed, pulling the sheet and covers up over her. Then he went back into the bathroom and cleaned up there.

When he was finished he came out and she watched him with grave unreadable eyes until finally he turned off the bathroom light and set himself up with a pillow in the armchair across from the bed. He lit a cigarette and smoked it down and listened for a change in her breathing to signal that she was sleeping. But it did not come. Instead there was her voice.

"David—"

"Yes?"

"Thank you. I'm very sorry."

"Forget it. It happens."

"Not to me. Never like this."

"You feeling better?"

"Yes. Do you mind that I called you David?"

"No."

"Could I tell you something, a kind of story?"

In the light from the street he could see her body under the covers, her hair spread like the wings of a black swan on the white pillow, and he could feel his heart begin to strike hard at him. "Of course," he said.

"It's a stupid little story. I wouldn't bother you with it if I weren't stoned."

"Go ahead."

"It happened when I was—oh I don't know, eight or nine. I was playing after school at a girl friend's house and her parents asked me to stay to dinner and go on to church with them that night. I called my mother and she said it would be all right, so I went. And it turned out to be one of those fundamentalist churches, with a visiting evangelist. And I don't know why, but it seemed all evening long that this man, this preacher, was speaking directly to me. He convinced me that I was a sinner and that I had to be saved. I longed to go down that aisle and give myself to Jesus. That was how he put it—give yourself to Jesus. And I wanted to. I wanted so much to be saved. But I was scared. I thought I'd better tell my mother and father about it first. So when I got home that night, that's what I did. I told them I wanted to be saved." She paused for a few moments then, and when she went on there was something new in her voice, a hardness he had not heard before. "And they laughed. They were both very attractive people, with beautiful teeth, and when they laughed they showed their teeth. I've never forgotten their teeth that night. My mother died four or five years later, by her own hand. But that night she was happy. She laughed, right along with my father. And since then—well, I haven't thought much about being saved. Being damned seemed much better, so much safer."

Even in the darkness, in the light from the streets, he could see the pain in her eyes as she looked over at him.

"Until what happened to Chris," she said. "And then today, when I saw you in the water and I thought you were drowning —I knew it was over for me. I knew I couldn't go on living the life of the damned anymore. I had to change. Or die."

Hook did not know what to say. "That's fine," he tried. "I'm glad to hear that."

"Would you come here? Would you sit next to me?"

For a time Hook did not move. And then finally he got up and made it across the few feet, the light-years, separating them. As he sat down on the edge of the bed she took hold of his hand.

"You could help me," she said.

"How?"

"By not hating me."

"I don't hate you, Liz."

"I'd give my life for him. I'd take his place. I would."

Hook looked down at her eyes in the darkness, at the tears shattering them. And he nodded. "I believe you."

"Could you do more?"

"What?"

"Could you hold me? Please. Just tonight. Hold me."

She was crying now and her nails were digging into his hand. But his other hand was free, was separate from him, a being moving with a will of its own under her shoulder and bringing her up to him, and then it was her lips and teeth and the saline taste of tears, and he felt himself falling, locked in a dream of falling, as if he were plunging from his own life.

When he woke, with the first light of morning, he remembered the night as a sequence of dreams, all flesh and mouths and darkness, and crying too, for he remembered her crying once, coming long after he had come and almost perishing with it, sobbing, clutching him as if he were saving her from drowning. And he remembered the sleep and the waking, the feel of her hands trembling in dreams on his body and her voice softly crying no over and over, and then plea or please—he could not be sure which it was.

Now though it was morning, and he found himself lying on his side with one arm draped across her body and his face just inches from hers. And he was shocked at how young she looked in sleep, with her eyes closed and her mouth slightly parted, her face cleansed of its customary expression of fashionable hardness and cynicism. Just to look at her gave him a feeling of pleasure and self-satisfaction that was almost as palpable as the feel of her flesh against his under the covers. He looked down at her breasts and wanted to hold them again and kiss them. He wanted to take her in his arms again and penetrate her, fill her, possess her.

But along with desire, he felt guilt, for this after all was the woman who had cost his son his life. This warm and supple body, this sleeping beauty, had reached halfway across a continent and torn the heart out of his family, not intentionally perhaps, but in the end that hardly mattered. The fact remained that if it had not been for her, his Chris would still be alive. His family would still be whole.

And he wondered about what she had told him last night, which parts of it were true and which were not. That Chris had not taken his own life—that of course he believed, had known all along. But as for the boy's death simply being an accident not involving Douglas or anybody else, that he could not accept, not yet anyway. He had been so convinced Douglas was involved, especially after yesterday's incident at sea, that now he found himself unable or at least unwilling to let go of the idea. And then there was the problem of the cliff, the difficulty he had believing that Chris even drunk would not have been able to arrest his fall, dig into the chaparral, and crawl back up. It was possible of course. He had to accept that. And further he had to remember that Liz herself had been drunk last night, in no state really to do anything except stick with old lies or blurt the truth. And she had not stuck with the old.

Beyond these thoughts, however, beyond his guilt and pleasure, was simply practicality. Liz Madera was all he had going for him and he knew it. Until she agreed to tell Sergeant Rider what she had told him, he had nothing real, nothing that would change anything; Chris would remain a suicide. So for now he would have to be practical. He would go on just as he was. He would stay with her and try to keep alive whatever it was they had begun last night, even though he had no firm idea what that was, whether it amounted to no more than a night of lovemaking between a pair of semi-drunks or whether she had known what she was doing and saying and would feel the same way now, this morning, sober.

He did not think she would. He believed she would wake as the old Liz Madera, the one on the beach, the one who looked at you with beautifully suffering eyes—while she ripped out your entrails and spilled them at your feet. He believed she would deny everything she had told him. He believed she would dress hurriedly and leave in a cold rage of disgust, with herself as much as with him. So as the minutes passed and the room slowly brightened, he found himself lying there watching her as if she were some exotic wild animal of unknown disposition, tranquilized now, but destined soon to wake, soon to reveal its true nature.

Weary of waiting finally, he got out of bed. In the bathroom he closed the door behind him and stood at the mirror looking at the wreck of himself. His head was pounding and he was so thirsty he drank three full glasses of water. A few minutes on the toilet made him feel better. Then he took a long hot shower that left his skin so numb he barely felt it as he switched on cold at the end. After toweling off, he shaved and brushed his teeth. Then he put on his robe and went back into the bedroom.

She was awake. As he lit a cigarette, she lay in bed watching him. He asked her how she was.

"Alive, I guess."

"No more than that?"

"No more."

"You remember much about last night?"

"Enough."

"Does it surprise you?"

"It does you, I take it."

"I guess so."

"You regret it?"

"No," he said. "Do you?"

"Yes."

"Why?"

"I've messed up your life enough as it is."

"Sex messes up a life?" he asked.

"In this case, yes. Suddenly everything's out of whack. I don't know which side is which."

Hook dragged on his cigarette, thinking, wondering whether to plunge ahead. He decided to. "You could clear it up. You could see Sergeant Rider with me. Today."

She shook her head. "No. That hasn't changed. I still can't do that."

"Because of Douglas."

She shrugged, made a face that said her reasons were her own.

"Because you love him so much," Hook kept on.

"You should know who I love by now. Nobody. Least of all myself."

"And Chris? Did you love him?"

For a time she did not answer. "Only in a sick, sisterly sort of way," she said finally.

"Sisterly? Then what you said last night was true? You didn't have sex with him?"

She looked at him quizzically. "You're still worried about that. Why? Would this be repugnant to you then? Would it be like incest?"

"You could say that," he admitted.

"Well, don't worry. It wasn't like this." Sitting up, she drew her knees up under the covers and rested her face against them. Hook went over to the bed and sat next to her. He reached out, barely touching her, but it was as if he had hit her with a cattle prod. Immediately she was out of bed on the other side, pulling the sheet with her, wrapping it around herself. Going to the window, she opened the drapes a few inches and a slab of sunlight divided the room.

"I'd better be going," she said.

"Where?"

"Does it matter?"

"It does to me."

She looked at him with sudden anger. "What did you think, that I'd stay on here? That we'd go on playing games?"

"I'd like you to stay," he said.

"So you can work on me? Sort of help me along, give me handy little shoves—all the way to the courthouse?"

"That wouldn't be my only reason."

"What else?"

"You know what else."

"No I don't. Tell me."

She stood there waiting, meeting his eyes, but he could not give the half-truth even half a life. So she let him go then, let her eyes drop him and move on to her clothes, which she gathered up, including the soiled things he had rinsed out the night before. She went into the bathroom and closed the door.

While she was gone Hook dressed slowly, putting on the one pair of slacks he had left after his ocean swim, then a white shirt and tie, and his old gray herringbone sport coat. All the while he tried to think what he could do to keep her with him, but there was nothing except to try again to persuade her. And if that failed, he did not know what else there was except to tag along after her, make a nuisance of himself, keep pounding at her until he made her see that she could not leave the thing where it was.

When she came out finally she was wearing the tan pantsuit again. She had combed out her hair and put on a touch of eyeliner, and she looked beautiful, austere, Iberian.

"Thanks for cleaning this," she said. "I thought I'd have to go home in just my raincoat."

"You hungry?" he asked.

"I'll eat at home."

"Why not with me? Certainly that couldn't spoil your plans for the day."

"I have no plans."

"Good, then."

"Except to be by myself. And away from you."

Hook nodded, as if in agreement. "All right. Fine. But a few minutes for breakfast won't hurt anything. Please, Liz."

For five or six seconds she stood there looking at him, as if he were a pane of glass. Then she shrugged.

As they got into his car, Liz suggested they go to Moby Dick's, so Hook drove down the beach and turned onto the wharf and they clattered slowly out over the planks past the Harbor Restaurant and the fish shops and workboat facilities to the small café situated near the end of the structure. Inside, Hook ordered a breakfast steak and scrambled eggs, with hashed brown potatoes and toast and orange juice—so much that he got a smile of embarrassment out of Liz, who settled for coffee and toast.

"I must be a weakening influence," she said.

Hook grinned. "Could be that. Then too, I haven't eaten since yesterday morning."

"Then that's it. I'm not guilty."

They both had left their sunglasses on because it was bright where they were sitting, at a corner table next to the window. The day outside was brilliant and clear, the sea alternately dazzling or deep blue depending on the slant of the waves. A quarter-mile in was the beach and the palm-lined drive, then the city rising toward the foothills, and finally the mountains in the distance, so clear Hook could make out trees along their crest, a serration of conifers, like the spine of a stegosaurus. Closer, just a few feet beyond the window, seagulls as fat as geese sailed back and forth, looking to become even fatter. But it was across the harbor that Hook's attention focused, on the yacht basin with its forest of masts and flybridges, one of them on the *Skipjack*.

195

After the waitress served them, Hook asked Liz about the incident yesterday.

"I haven't been able to understand it," he said. "What Douglas did. What he had Parnelli do. It doesn't make sense. He could have killed me."

Liz sipped at her coffee. "If you knew Jack better, you wouldn't be so puzzled," she said.

"You mean he often tries to kill people?"

"I mean he's not what he seems, that's all. He always *appears* to be in control, to be cool and stable. But he's not. Actually he's very unstable."

"In what way?"

"He's unpredictable, moody, impulsive. Like after he lost last year's election, he went around cheering everybody else up. He took it like it was nothing. But a few weeks later he killed a neighbor's dog that barked at him when he was riding a bike. He kicked it to death."

Hook thought of himself in the water yesterday and a feeling of panic brushed lightly past him, like a cruising shark. "I thought that was Parnelli's bag," he said.

Liz shook her head. "He's hotheaded all right. A brawler. But Jack's worse. He's sick. He needs barbiturates to sleep and amphetamine to get through the day. He was in the hospital twice last year for bleeding ulcers. He's a mess."

"And that's the man you want to send to Congress."

Behind her sunglasses Liz's eyes remained level, calm. "I believe in the same things he does. Politically, I mean. And his votes would be out in the open. It wouldn't be like putting him in charge of the FBI or something like that."

"That you wouldn't do."

She looked down at her cup of coffee. "I wish you wouldn't patronize me."

Hook said nothing.

She smiled and shook her head. "Although I can imagine what you're going through, trying to be calm and reasonable and patient. And all the while your body must be begging you to grab me by the scruff of the neck and drag me down to the courthouse and wring it out of me."

"But that wouldn't work, would it?"

"No. And neither will this."

"This?"

"Waiting me out. Being nice."

"Then you've got no reason to be alone today," he concluded. "No reason to leave me."

"You think not?"

"It follows."

"Not for me."

She said nothing for a while then, just sat there watching him eat, and he could see her pain even through the dark glasses.

"If there was only some way I could make you understand," she said finally. "I don't want it this way, believe me. I'd like nothing better than to be able to tell the truth, shout it for the whole world to hear. For Chris's sake the same as yours. But I can't."

"Because of Douglas's career."

"I never said that."

Hook had taken off his sunglasses, and now she did the same, as if to prove she was not ashamed either, had nothing to hide. "Maybe last night I didn't hear you right," he said.

"I said because of innocent people. Because I didn't want to hurt them."

"What innocent people?"

"His wife. His kids. And for that matter, Jack himself—what we were talking about just now, his instability. I don't know how he'd react, what he'd do."

"Would he kill?"

Liz studied him resentfully, knowing what he had tossed at her. "I wouldn't know," she said finally.

"You know him."

"I don't know anyone, Mr. Hook. And I don't know anyone who knows anyone. I live in a world of strangers, remember?"

"Did you know Chris?"

She did not answer. Her eyes fell away from his, fastened on the tangle of her hands. For a while Hook sat there watching her and then he reached over and covered her hands with his own.

"Stay with me today," he said.

She looked up at him. "Why?"

"Because I want you to."

"I repeat. Why?"

"I don't know."

"Don't you?"

For long seconds Hook met her pained, ironic gaze. "I'm not sure," he said finally. "Why don't we find out?"

And somehow he managed it. He got around her. So instead of driving her back to the motel to pick up her car, they drove on out of the city to the beach house, where she changed into a yellow turtleneck sweater and brown corduroy slacks stuffed into boots of brushed leather. She was going into the mountains, she said. She felt a need for physical exertion and solitude, so she was going to hike up to one of her favorite canyons to her own "special secret place," and he could come along if he wanted but she doubted that he would enjoy himself; it was a steep trail and his shoes, loafers, were not exactly made for rough country.

"Another thing," she said. "You'll have to get rid of that tie. I won't go hiking with someone wearing a tie."

Hook took it off and they drove back through the city, heading for the foothills. But as they were driving past the Old Mission she asked him if he would like to stop and go through it.

"Have you ever seen it inside?" she asked.

"No. Never."

"Then let's stop."

As they parked and walked to the entrance, Liz told him a little about the place, how it had been founded ten years after the Declaration of Independence was signed, and how the early fathers had gone about rescuing the local Chumash Indians from their heathen ways, with such success that now there were no Chumash left.

"But it is beautiful, isn't it?" she concluded.

"Yes."

And it was. Situated on a hill about midway between the mountains and the sea, the Mission with its twin bell towers and rough adobe facade was one of the most photographed, most "toured" buildings in all the country. Twenty-five years before,

Hook had almost gone through it with Mrs. Cunningham—"We can confess in the chapel," she had said, "and drive some poor celibate wild." But somehow the appointed day had slipped past them, in bed and on the beach, and they had never made it.

Inside, in the musty gift shop, Hook paid the receptionist a dollar and he and Liz started through the five or six rooms that once had been the living quarters of the missionaries and their guests. He found the place oppressive, the thick dank walls and airless rooms with their doll-like crucifixes and old chalices and psalters. And his reaction must have shown on his face.

"I imagine all this violates your wasp soul," Liz said, smiling.

"Not at all," he lied.

There were about a dozen other visitors going through the rooms with them. One, a frail old woman wearing a black coat with a ratty fox pelt draped around her neck, kept glancing at them, especially at Liz. In a room displaying old cookware the woman touched Liz on the arm.

"Don't I know you from somewhere?" she asked. "Were you at my husband's funeral?"

Liz looked at her in bewilderment. "No, I don't think so."

"What's your name, dear?"

Liz told her, and the old woman shook her head and wandered off, muttering that it was odd, she could have sworn they knew each other. A few minutes later, in the church, a long dark narrow room painted and gilded like a Babylonian brothel, the old woman struck again.

"Perhaps it was in the hospital, when he died. Are you a nurse?"

Liz said no, she was not a nurse. Then abruptly she headed out of the church into the walled cemetery next to it, and they moved along quickly now, with Liz setting the pace. The circular walkway passed in front of vaults and mausoleums and a few small slabs, the only ones left to mark the graves of some four thousand Indians the chapel brochure estimated had been buried there.

As they walked along, Liz kept glancing behind them. "I think we got away from her," she said. "At least I hope so."

"I imagine you hear that more often from men."

"What?"

"The don't-I-know-you routine."

She looked at him in confusion. "No, not really. I guess I'm forbidding."

Hook could not determine if she was being ironic, so he said nothing.

As they came to the end of the cemetery walk, Liz drew Hook's attention to a metal plaque on the wall at the exit. It read:

Juana Maria

Indian woman abandoned
on San Nicolas Island
eighteen years
found and brought by
Capt. George Nidever
in 1853
Santa Barbara Daughters
of the American Revolution
1928

As they walked on to the car, Liz told him the story of the Indian woman, one of a ragtag tribe barely eking out a living on the small and bleak San Nicolas Island, the outermost of the Channel archipelago. In 1835 the captain of an American schooner offered to carry the tribe to the mainland, and they accepted, gathered all their possessions, and boarded the schooner. But as they set sail, the Indian girl discovered that her younger brother was missing, and despite every effort to prevent her, she leaped overboard and swam back to the island to take care of him. The ship continued on its way, and no other came for eighteen years, until a Captain Nidever visited the island in 1853. His crew found the Indian girl dressed in cormorant feathers and living alone in a crude hut. At the Santa Barbara Mission, where she was taken, and later buried, it was learned that her brother had been killed by wild dogs soon after the first schooner had set sail.

"So all those years she lived alone," Liz said. "And she kept her sanity. She survived."

They were in the car now, heading back up into the mountains on Foothill Road. "You sound envious," Hook observed.

She was staring out the windshield as if she saw not beautiful trees in sunlight but a stretch of forever empty sea. "When I think what it would take to survive something like that," she said, "what should I be but envious?"

"Because you don't have courage?"

"Not that kind. Remember on the beach—all that drivel about me dying of life. Well, I imagine Juana Maria or whatever her real name was would have been very happy to 'die' the way I do. With the same comforts."

Hook told her she was not being fair to herself.

"You think not? You think when I see a picture of a starving Pakistani child or a napalmed Vietnamese I shouldn't feel absurd? I shouldn't feel that my hangups are a little ridiculous? Even pathetic?"

Inside, Hook could only agree with her. But he figured that what she wanted was argument. So he gave it to her. "I think life is pretty much the pursuit of happiness—for starving children, the same as you. Only they're still stuck down at the bottom of the ladder, without even the necessities of life. But once they got them, I think you'd find them moving on to 'hangups.' Even pathetic ones."

As they drove, Liz gave him directions and after a time he realized they were taking the same route he had traveled with Sergeant Rider three mornings before. They turned onto Mountain Drive and when they came to the curve that plunged steeply through the trees down to the canyon below—the creek and the stone bridge, the barren spot where the minibus had been parked —Hook was not surprised to hear Liz announce that this was it, *her* canyon.

He pulled in under the trees on the right of the road, where the squadcars had been parked the other morning, and for some reason he decided not to say anything about having been there before or about the dead youth, about Rider and the girl. It had all been in the newspaper. He figured she must have read it. But apparently it had not registered, was not the kind of story that could seize the attention of a native Californian.

After locking the car, Hook followed Liz across the small stone bridge to a dirt path that cut up the canyon. As beautiful as it had seemed the other morning from the road, Hook found it even more so as they walked deeper into it. For the first quarter-mile it was almost level, a worn dirt path winding through the shade of the dense-growing trees, live oak mostly, but also sycamore and alder. And the undergrowth, nourished by the creek waters, was almost Midwestern in its lushness: fern and wild blackberry, nightshade and poison oak. Soon the path doubled back on itself and they began to climb steeply, moving up and away from the canyon floor, the creek bed, which in a short time was a good two hundred feet below them, an almost sheer drop from the narrow path. But it was not a creek as Hook knew them, was more like a gradual waterfall, a steep rocky grade rising as the path rose, so that a few hundred yards farther on they came to the creek again and crossed it, without having walked downhill. And Hook found himself wondering how it all had been formed: slowly by rainfall over the ages, the water chipping and sliding the earth out from under the rocks, or all at once in the same cataclysm that had formed the coast and the mountains themselves, buckling them up out of the earth with such violence that huge pieces had come tumbling down into the sea, carving out such canyons as this and leaving behind a trail of rock, the great white boulders over which the creek waters now bubbled and crashed and pooled, as clear as light.

"In summer," Liz told him, "hippies swim nude in the pools. Pot smoke drifts down the canyon. And their canteens are filled with dago red."

"That part sounds all right," Hook allowed.

"But not the skinny-dipping? Or the pot?"

"Not the pot anyway. Not for me."

"The skinny-dipping, though."

"I'll watch."

"You may have to. This place I told you about, it has its own little pool. *My* pool. And I've brought grass. It's part of the ritual. I warned you not to come."

Hook watched her as she walked ahead of him, her black hair moving against the yellow sweater, the corduroys stretched tight over her splendid buttocks, and he found it difficult to believe that it all had been his last night, that he had embraced it and kissed it and filled it with his semen. It—she—seemed irremediably remote now, as much a stranger as on the first moment he had seen her, through the glass door on the beach-house deck.

As they kept on, the path kept crossing the creek. Occasionally they would reach a spot from which they could see all the way back down the canyon and out over the foothills and the city to the ocean, and even to the islands, a distance of at least fifty miles, Hook estimated. But they did not pause very long to look at anything. Liz doggedly kept on, heading for her "place." And finally they seemed to have reached it. Ahead of him she left the path, moving through the brush and trees up over a hillock next to the creek and then down again, to a barrier of rocks, some as huge as railroad cars. He followed her into a narrow corridor between two of the rocks and then came out into the open, onto the almost level top of a boulder in which the creek pooled at one end before spilling over, falling some twenty feet to the rocky bed below. Part of the rock's surface lay in sunshine and part in shade, shielded by the boulders towering behind it. This was it then, Liz's "special place," a beautifully isolated sundeck with its own private pool, water as cold as it was clear, Hook discovered, scooping some up to drink. Liz spread out her suede jacket and lay down in the sun.

"You like it?" she asked.

"Yes. It's great."

"Trouble is, it's not really mine. Others know about it too."

"Who?"

"A lot of people, I suppose. Like one time last summer I was lying here in the buff, and in comes this young couple. Just kids they were, seventeen or eighteen."

"Did they stay?"

She smiled. "They stayed."

"You enjoy playing the scarlet woman," Hook said.

"Not really. If I smiled it was because they were nice, that's all. We got along."

Hook had already sat down and now he took off his jacket. It was warm in the canyon, warm and quiet. All he could hear was a single jay squalling somewhere below. "Did you come here with Chris?" he asked.

"No."

"Where did you go with him?"

"We stayed around the beach house, like I said."

"And you talked."

"Yes."

"About what?"

"Me, mostly. Chris was a good listener. Or rather, he was a good confessor. He made me want to talk, to get it all out. Maybe I was trying to scare him off, I don't know. Only he didn't scare."

Hook asked her if the boy had talked about himself at all.

"A little."

"Can you tell me what he said, how he was?"

Her smile faded. "One thing I remember was about you," she said. "I had told him about my mother, how I went into her bedroom one morning and found her dead. She'd taken a whole bottle of sleeping pills. I was eleven then. So he reciprocated. He told me about his mother, and the accident, and how you took it afterwards. He said you never let it show very much in front of anyone, but one of his strongest memories was lying in bed at night and hearing you get up and go outside, and then he'd watch you through the window as you headed down the road, toward the cemetery, he said. And he said he cried for you. Many times."

For the moment Hook could not speak. He closed his eyes against the sun.

"You loved your wife very much," Liz said.

"Yes."

"How about me? Did you feel any love for me last night?"

The question surprised him and he looked down at her. But her expression had not changed, was still solemn, bare of irony. "I don't know," he said. "I wanted you. I guess I've wanted to make love to you since I first saw you. But that isn't an answer, is it?"

She disagreed. "Yes, it is."

Hook tried to explain. "It's just that the idea of love, romantic love, is dead for me, Liz. It's meaningless. Especially now, after Chris. I have no feelings left."

"Except the one," she said. "The rage. The vengeance."

Hook did not respond. He took out his cigarettes and offered her one, but she declined. Instead she brought out her own pack of Trues and shook out a single cigarette, which was not a True. It was home-rolled and fat, with pinched ends.

"Why don't we share this," she said. "A joint, Mister David Hook. A lovely high-class joint." She lit it and dragged deeply, held it, finally exhaled. "I'm not trying to shock you or impress you," she went on. "It's just that I like it, better than booze. And especially here. You want a drag?"

"No." Hook was not afraid of marijuana, in fact tended to believe the reports that said it was no more harmful than alcohol. But he thought of it as essentially part of the youth cult, and if there was anything he despised it was seeing some middle-aged jerk frantically trying on the dress and jargon and vices of the young. Hook had his own, he figured; let them have theirs. And anyway he wanted to remain clear-headed now. He wanted to know what he was doing. So he lit his own cigarette, settled for his own vice. And he watched her lying beside him in the sun, smoking, her eyes closed, a band of sweat beginning to gleam in her hairline and above her mouth. She was braless still, the nipples of her breasts thrusting lightly into the yellow wool of her sweater. And Hook could feel it beginning in him, like the first true pang of morning hunger, an almost specific pain, a need.

"After today," she said suddenly, "after all this has failed, what then? What will you do?"

"What do you think I should do?"

"Go home."

"No, I don't think so."

"What, then?"

Hook thought for a moment, and decided on the truth. "I'll see Sergeant Rider again. I'll tell him what you told me. I'll offer to take a polygraph test, prove it that way if I can. Then maybe he'll call you and Mrs. Rubin in again. If you won't agree to a polygraph—who knows? Maybe he'll think it's time they held an inquest and got the two of you on the stand, under oath."

She was exhaling again, slowly, reluctantly giving up the smoke. "I'll lie," she said.

"That's perjury."

"I know." She looked at him. "You sure you don't want to smoke?"

"I'm sure."

She smiled happily. "The trees are growing taller. The world is slowing down. Just a little. But enough."

"Perjury's a serious offense," he told her. "I wouldn't want you to go to jail."

"Why not?"

"Why would I?"

"Well, after all, you did make love to me—without feeling any love. And I'd say that bespeaks a certain indifference, wouldn't you? A certain coldness."

She was smiling but her eyes were closed and there was nothing in her face to tell him what she was actually feeling. Apparently he had hurt and angered her.

"Why do you care about that? I thought that's how it was with you. Or worse—that you only made love with men you despised."

She sat up, dragged on the cigarette again and dropped the butt over the edge of the boulder into the creek below. Then she looked at him, level, grave.

"I lied," she said. "On the boat yesterday Jack was right. I wanted you. And before that too—I guess I first felt it on the beach the other day, which was why I struck out at you, why I lied about Chris. I had to hurt you—because I wanted you. I don't mean sexually. I mean I wanted something from you—your strength maybe, I don't know. I suppose I just didn't want to stand alone anymore. I wanted to hide in you, David. And I guess I still do. Which isn't much, I'll admit—" Now she smiled, a smile that did not reach her eyes. "But it's more than I've felt for anyone, for a long time. So that's why it hurts some, David Hook. That's why it hurts that you made love to me for hours, and felt nothing."

Hook wondered if she was playing with him, ridiculing him with a subtlety beyond his powers of detection. "I didn't say I felt nothing," he offered.

"Then precisely what did you feel?"

"Now who's patronizing whom?"

"I'm not. I really mean it. What did you feel?"

But Hook could not answer her, not honestly. He felt so many things toward her, desire and hatred and tenderness and more he could not even articulate to himself.

"Pleasure," he tried. "Gratitude, for——"

"For telling you the truth—yes, I know." She smiled then, with beautiful, slashing irony. "Zap! A left to the gut, a right to the jaw. Down goes the bad girl."

Hook tried to explain but she hushed him up. "No more talk, all right? This is my secret place. My place of ritual. And now it's my time for my sacred bath. You may sit there and watch. Or you may join me if you want. Love is not a requirement."

Hook did not join her at first. He sat and watched as she pulled off her boots and slipped out of her clothes. And somehow he found her even more desirable now than she had seemed last night, more beautiful here in the wild and the sunshine, in the spangled shade of the sycamores rising beyond the rocks. Her long black hair shone like a net of prisms in the golden light as she moved into the pool, her body hunched against the coldness of the water. And then she went all the way in, sliding down with her teeth bared in a smiling gasp as the mountain water seized her flesh. For a few moments Hook felt almost weak with desire for her, and then the weakness was gone and there was only the desire, his blood rising high in him. And he remembered a summer night the year before Kate had died, a night they had gone to a movie in St. Louis and later had had drinks and dinner on the River Queen paddle-wheeler restaurant and then had driven home in a fine high madness of wine and lust and happiness, with her kissing and fondling and teasing him nearly out of his mind all the way home and both of them half undressed by the time they reached the farm drive, the hill, where he had killed the lights and parked and they had tumbled outside naked and made love in the grass and afterwards had walked by the road and through the woods hand in hand in the night light, a sated and guiltless Adam and Eve. Hook felt there was nothing finer than that, nothing better than love and sex in the woods, in the out-of-doors. Only two of those conditions would apply now, he told himself, but even that was a combination he knew he was not strong enough to pass up. And as he began to undress, as he met her level gaze with its subtle burden of pride and pain and tenderness, he was not so confident that love also did not apply.

Naked, he slipped into the pool, which was not just a depression in the boulder but part of the juncture where it touched the canyon soil, so that while most of the pool was rock, one side was earth, was soft, with grass and weeds growing along the edge. Hook barely noticed the cold of the water. For him there was just her eyes, their gravity and sadness before she closed them, as he took her in his arms and her mouth opened on his and she wrapped her legs around his trunk and lowered herself onto him. As they kissed, as he filled her, she uttered his name softly over and over. And he lifted her up out of the water onto the grassy area and there thought he would die of love for her, was not sure the crash and roar he heard was the creek plunging past or simply his own breathing, his blood beating in his ears.

Afterwards he lay there holding her, in her still, his lips brushing lightly over her closed eyes, her mouth, her cheeks. She had her arms around him and he could feel her hands lightly tracing the ridge of muscle along his spine.

And it was then she said it:

"Your back is just like his was."

It was as if a snake had slid between their bodies. For a time neither of them breathed. There was no sound. The creek had stopped running. The distant jay fell silent. Immediately soft, he pulled out of her and knelt above her, looking down as she opened her eyes for the millisecond it took to see the cold rage of knowing in his own eyes and to turn from it.

"You liar," he got out. "You pitiful liar."

And then abruptly he had her by the hair and had pulled her down to the pool's edge.

"The truth," he said. "All of it. Now."

11

The threat of being drowned like a kitten had not frightened Liz at all. He had held her by the hair in the pool for what seemed like minutes, with just her face above water, her arrogant eyes unblinkingly meeting his and her mouth parted, teeth bared, as if he were still in her, still giving her pleasure. So he had let go of her finally, had stumbled up onto the dry rock surface and had begun to punch his way back into his clothes. And it was only then, only out of danger, that she had given him anything, in fact gave him all of it.

"It was Jack and Parnelli," she said. "They did it."

Driving her back into town, Hook considered that statement and what had followed, and for him it was not simply a more recent version of how Chris had died but the truth itself, the immutable rock of fact. But because this truth was so close to what he had suspected all along, he warned himself to be wary of it now, to hold it in his mind the way he would hold soil from available land, lightly, letting it sift through his fingers.

As in her earlier version the night before, she admitted that she had picked Chris up on Tuesday morning. Only where in that version she and Chris had gone to the beach house and spent the next day and a half in endless talk and sustained sexual continence, now she confessed that there had been very little talk in the beginning and even less continence, for she had had him in bed before noon on that first day and they had left it only sporadically during the next thirty hours, only to eat and drink and bathe, and twice to walk on the beach. And, as in the earlier version, Mrs. Rubin had been furious with her for letting Chris stay at the beach house, but now Liz added that the lady had done something about her fury, had called Douglas long-distance Wednesday afternoon in Los Angeles, where he had gone on business with Parnelli and Ferguson, and reported to him that some "hippie kid" was sleeping with *his* mistress and drinking *his* booze and even lounging around the house in *his* pajamas. Douglas, supposedly not a jealous type, nevertheless had come back to Santa Barbara that same night with his two assistants in tow, stopping along the way only long enough to get comfortably high before they finally arrived around eleven o'clock. Douglas and Parnelli were not really angry, Liz insisted, just good and smashed, like college kids out for a high old time, some innocent roughhouse at the expense of this unknown hippie kid. With Ferguson standing idly by and Mrs. Rubin urging them on, the two of them had overpowered Chris, stripped him of Douglas's pajamas and tossed him out of the beach house naked. Liz had tried to help the boy but Parnelli had stopped her dead with a playful yank of her hair that sent her sprawling across the floor. Then while he and Douglas symbolically wiped their hands clean and went to the bar to celebrate with more drinks, Mrs. Rubin gathered up Chris's clothes and backpack and threw it all out the door after him.

But the boy had not left. Fifteen or twenty minutes later Parnelli spied him sitting out in the front in the dark near the cliff edge, dressed by then, and apparently waiting for the men to leave. Liz said Parnelli had seemed genuinely elated at the discovery, this chance for more physical contact. Douglas had wearily followed, as if he were heading out to finish some irksome chore.

"And this time we're going to kick hell out of him," Parnelli had said. But Chris had kicked back.

He evidently had gone for the big athlete's groin, and Parnelli, twisting to avoid the blow, had his legs kicked out from under him. That left Douglas alone against Chris for a few moments, but then Parnelli was back on his feet and finally it was impossible to see what was happening. The three of them kept working closer to the cliff edge—Liz could remember screaming at them from the deck to watch out, to stop their fighting—and then suddenly there were only the two of them standing there, Douglas and Parnelli. She still did not know precisely how it had happened, which of them had actually thrown Chris over or whether it was both of them who had done it or simply something that had happened without anyone knowing how, but she did recall their shock and panic immediately afterwards. "It had to have been an accident," Liz said. "They both just came unglued. It was Ferguson and Dorothy who kept Jack from calling the police. And I think Parnelli wanted to too—he was crying like a baby. As I was. I broke down completely. I don't remember running down the cliff at all, but I got down there somehow. I remember touching his body, trying to turn him over. But he was so limp, like foam rubber. Dorothy and Ferguson finally got me back up to the top and I found Jack and Bo already gone—Ferguson and Dorothy had already done their job on them, I guess, convinced them to get out of there and go home and shut up and let them, Rich and Dorothy, handle everything. And they did. They gave me a couple of sleeping pills to calm me down, and then I guess Ferguson helped Dorothy clean up and told her what she was supposed to tell the police, and then he left too."

From that point on, the story was essentially the same as in Liz's earlier version. Instead of telling the police that the thing was an unfortunate accident, as Ferguson had instructed her to do, Mrs. Rubin concocted the suicide fable, for what twisted personal needs Liz could only guess at, and the rest of them had finally had to go along with her, for the same reasons Liz had already explained to Hook.

So that was that. He had it finally. The truth.

Throughout the drive back to town, Hook was almost oblivious of Liz sitting next to him in the car. Most of the time she kept her face averted, looking out the window at the dry sundrenched day as the car plunged down out of the foothills, squealing around curve after curve, with Hook holding his foot on the brake most of the time. In the fifteen or twenty minutes it took to reach the downtown, she said nothing, did not even ask where they were going, probably because she already knew.

After he had pulled into the lot behind the tan U-shaped building and parked, Hook could not rid himself of an intense feeling of unreality, as if somehow he had stepped out of this moment in time and space and had become his own spectator, an indifferent deity observing this spare unstylish man squint uncomfortably in the sunshine as he looked first at the archway that led to the building's front courtyard, and then, stooping, glanced back into the car, at the young woman still sitting inside it.

"You coming?" he asked her.

"No."

He shut the car door then and walked through the archway and across the red-brick courtyard to the stairs that led to the second-floor portico and the offices of Jack Douglas Associates. Lemons hung like gaudy Christmas trinkets on the trees and he had to duck under the bougainvillea that climbed one side of the staircase, small red blossoms that evoked in his mind images of bare-breasted Gauguinesque women forever waiting on a white man's whim. So the sense of unreality persisted. It was as if he were walking into battle, through a formal garden.

Just inside the door a receptionist smiled up at him from a stack of newspapers out of which she was apparently scissoring articles. He remembered her from last week, the long-legged girl he had watched skip down the stairs at five o'clock.

"May I help you?" she asked.

"My name is Hook. David Hook. I want to see Mr. Douglas."

"Do you have an appointment?"

"I won't need one."

"He's in a client conference now, sir. Mr. Parnelli and Mr. Ferguson too. Perhaps if you left a number where——"

"How long will the conference last?"

She had stopped smiling now. "I have no idea."

"Is Mrs. Rubin here?"

The girl reached for her phone. "I'll ask if she can see you."

Hook looked beyond her at the half-dozen office doors facing the reception room, which had a warm old moneyed ambience, gleaming dark wood walls and sturdy pre-World War II

Grand Rapids furniture upholstered in red leather and resting on gray wool carpeting that gave like wet loam underfoot. The first door, closed, and beyond which he could hear men's voices, apparently was to the conference room. The one farthest back would be to Douglas's office, he figured, knowing the hallowed tradition that placed the top man as far as possible from his clients. Through the second door he saw a glass case jammed with football trophies, undoubtedly Parnelli's, so he headed for the next door in line. The receptionist was calling after him, asking him if he would please wait by her desk. But she was too late. Hook was already standing at Mrs. Rubin's door, watching her as she absently stabbed a console button on her phone and picked it up, dragging on a cigarette and hurriedly exhaling as she croaked an irritable "yes?"—and at that moment saw him.

Her expression—her reaction—would have been no different if he had been a naked savage. The phone spilled out of her hand and clattered on the glass desktop. Behind him the receptionist was trying to speak around him.

"He just came on in," the girl said. "I couldn't stop him."

But Mrs. Rubin was back in control now, carefully replacing the phone on its cradle, then leaning back in her high-backed executive chair and clasping her hands across her torso, which was stuffed into a dress of peach-colored jersey.

"That's all right, Carol. I'll talk to him. But maybe you could get us some coffee first. Would you like a cup of coffee, Mr. Hook?"

"No thank you."

Dorothy Rubin nodded to the girl, who then returned to her desk in the reception room. Hook moved on into the small office and sat down in a chair facing Mrs. Rubin's desk, which was cluttered with a number of open catalog-type volumes titled *Standard Rate and Data*. Behind her, burlap window drapes were drawn against the sun. A number of handsome Navaho blankets hung on the walls, above long glass shelves crowded with potted cacti and other desert flora.

"I'm here to see Douglas," he said. "When will they be finished?"

"I have no idea."

Hook lit a cigarette, dropped the dead match into an ashtray on her desk.

"Liz has been with me since last night," he said. "She told me."

"Told you what?"

"The truth."

"Did she, now? And of course you recognized it as truth the moment you heard it."

"I did."

"Good for you."

"You want to hear it?"

"Not particularly."

Hook gazed at her until she looked away. She angrily stubbed out her cigarette and immediately set about lighting another.

"I'll wait for Douglas, then," he said.

She blew out a pall of smoke. "All right, try me. What is this great new truth you've discovered?"

"My son didn't kill himself. Douglas and Parnelli threw him off the cliff."

Dorothy Rubin pillaged her face for a smile, a sneer, but there was nothing, just the pale shocked look of someone who had been slapped hard.

"Liz told you that?"

"Liz told me that."

"I don't believe you."

"We can ask her. She's down in the car now. You want me to have her come up?"

"No. Why bother? Maybe she did say it. It doesn't matter. These days she's liable to say anything, she's so spaced out all the time. If it isn't booze or sex, it's drugs. The girl's psycho."

Hook asked Mrs. Rubin if that was what she would tell the police and she dragged deeply on her cigarette, took her time exhaling, all the while fixing him with the look of a dubious loan officer. "There'll be no police," she said finally. "I'd say your coming here proves that, wouldn't you? I mean if Liz was willing to tell the police this fantastic story of hers, that's where you'd be, right? Swearing out a complaint or whatever it is one does. But you're not there, are you? You're here. And I think your time is about up."

"She'll tell them," Hook said. "You all will."

"You're entitled to your opinion, I'm sure. But as I said, your time is up. I have work to do."

"I'll wait for Douglas."

"I'm afraid not. You're leaving now, Mr. Hook. If you don't, I'll call the police."

"Go ahead."

She reached for the phone but did not pick it up, just left her hand lying on it as if she were testing its surface temperature. Then she withdrew her hand and Hook could see the control running out of her.

"You son of a bitch," she said. "You fucking maniac."

"Why?" Hook asked her. "Why am I that?"

"Because you are, that's all. Because you won't let go. You won't ever let go."

"Wouldn't you, Mrs. Rubin? In my place?"

"Anyone would! Anyone sane!"

"If he'd been your son?"

Her eyes suddenly reddened, and for a moment Hook thought she was about to break. But he was wrong.

"Well, this isn't getting us anywhere, is it?" she said. "If you insist on waiting for Jack, I suggest you do it in the reception room. I have work to do."

She began to shuffle papers, pretending that the matter was settled and that he would automatically obey her and get up and leave. But he did not. Almost mesmerized by her gross proximity, he kept thinking how easy it would be to reach across the desk and take her plump throat in his hands and squeeze. And he thought of the lie, *her* lie, how painstaking she had been in showing Sergeant Rider exactly how Chris had taken his life. He knew it was all there in front of him, the answer to every question he still had. The problem was how to get it out of her.

"What you said about Liz," he tried. "The sex thing. Is it true? She pick up a lot of hitchhikers? Bring them home?"

"Any age, any color, it doesn't matter to her. As long as it's warm. As long as it moves."

"You must put up with a lot."

"You could say that, yes."

"So my son wasn't all that unusual."

She looked wary for a moment. Then came a cold smile of triumph. "Except he failed, remember? He couldn't get it up. He couldn't satisfy the slut. So if you'll excuse me."

"The night it happened," he kept on. "After Liz had locked herself in her room, you were alone with him for quite a while, weren't you?"

Her look of triumph faded. She pushed back her chair and got up. "I want you to leave now, Mr. Hook. I insist."

Hook got to his feet slowly, not letting his eyes leave hers. "I keep wondering," he said. "I keep asking myself what he could have done to make you hate him so."

She was trembling now. "Get out. *Now.*"

Hook looked down at the stout cylinder of her body, at the heavy arms and shoulders, the broad Slavic face under the grotesque beehive hairdo, and all the jewelry and makeup and perfume, and suddenly it was there, came to him like the high keen stench of putrefying flesh in a summer woods. And he saw in her eyes that he was right.

"Did he turn you down, Mrs. Rubin? Did he laugh?"

Her face was melting wax now, character running.

"No, of course not," he went on. "Chris wouldn't have laughed. That wasn't in him. It must have just been his look, the way he looked at you. He was probably embarrassed for you. It probably never even occurred to him that someone like you—"

But she had come around the desk now and had begun to swing at him, wildly. Hook caught her hands at the wrist and held her there in front of him, like a caught game fish.

"You bastard!" she cried. "You filth! Get out! Out! Out!"

Immediately Hook heard the door to the conference room opening and Douglas came into the office. Seeing Hook, his initial look of puzzlement switched to rueful comprehension. He threw out his hand at Mrs. Rubin, like a symphony conductor *pianissimo.*

"Shut up, Dorothy. For God's sake, will you shut up."

"Get him out of here!"

Hook let go of her and she stumbled back behind the desk and collapsed into her chair.

"You heard the lady," Douglas said to Hook.

But Hook had sat down again. He was not going anywhere, not empty-handed. "Any place will do," he said. "You're the one I'm here to see."

"Well, I'm afraid I'm in conference. You'll have to come back some other time."

Behind him, Parnelli came in now, garish in an electric blue suit. From the desk, Dorothy Rubin spoke through a handkerchief pressed to her face.

"He thinks he knows something. Liz told him."

Hook watched Parnelli's eyes drift toward Mrs. Rubin, vague and uncomprehending at first, and then a light came into them and a muscle bunched in his jaw as he turned to Hook, understanding now, knowing. And immediately he performed like the born athlete, the man in whom there was no visible trace of intellection between stimulus and action—in this case an open hand coming at Hook's chest as abruptly as one of his Angus bulls unexpectedly tossing its head his way. And the blow had that same kind of impact, shocking in its power, yet obviously only a small part of something vastly larger. And as Hook found himself banging back against the wall, in that instant it struck him that this was only part of the force his eighteen-year-old son had had to fight against on the cliff edge, and with that thought Hook let it all out of him, let himself come pushing off the wall like some maniac fighter off the ropes as he swung at the big Italian's face, and hit, felt it give, break, tear, felt pain run like a hayfork tine through his fist and up his forearm.

Parnelli went down like a man trying to find a movie seat in the dark, feeling behind and beneath him as he backed into the racked shelves of potted cacti and brought them crashing to the floor. Sitting down against the wall, his face grew a luxuriant mustache of blood. Ferguson had come to the door now too and stood staring down at Parnelli as if the man had been blown to bits. Douglas calmly put his hand on Ferguson's shoulder and motioned for him to return to their clients.

"Get them out of here. Now. I don't care what you tell them. And have Carol and Joan take an hour off too. Lock up. I don't want anyone here. Go!"

Ferguson went. And Douglas casually closed the office door,

as if he were about to discuss a minor business matter in private. Though he was looking down at Parnelli, he spoke to Hook.

"So you think you know the whole story?"

"All I need to know."

"For what?"

"To nail you. All of you."

Parnelli was beginning to pull himself to his feet. His eyes had cleared and he was staring at Hook in a leaden trance of rage. Watching him, seeing what was to come, Hook felt his mouth go dry. But Douglas stepped in between them and picked up a tomahawk-head paperweight from Mrs. Rubin's desk.

"Back off," he told Parnelli. "I mean it, Bo. You touch him and I'll use this."

Parnelli did not seem to understand. In bewilderment he looked from Hook to Douglas to the paperweight, all the while holding his coat sleeve up to his nose to blot the blood streaming from it.

"No more muscle," Douglas said.

"Just let him get away with it?" Bo asked.

"That's right."

"But you heard him! You heard what he said."

Douglas looked at Hook. "I heard. But I don't know what it means yet. I don't know what he plans to do. What he *can* do."

The door opened again and Ferguson came back in. Beyond him Hook could see the receptionist's abandoned desk, the locked front door, the darkened room. And it vaguely crossed his mind that he could be in danger, here alone with four persons who would probably wind up in prison because of him. Yet he felt not fear so much as excitement, the heightened sensibility of the hunter finally come upon his quarry.

"I can do enough," he told him. "And I will. I promise you that. But it'd be easier if you did it yourselves. If you went to the police now, voluntarily."

Mrs. Rubin told him not to hold his breath.

"I'll give you tomorrow," he went on. "I'll give you all day tomorrow to make up your minds and go to the police. If you don't, then I'll do it for you—say by ten the next morning. That means you've got forty hours. If you haven't turned yourselves in by then, I will start with Sergeant Rider. I will tell him the whole thing. I'll take a polygraph if he'll let me. I'll hound him into holding an inquest. And I'll take the story to the newspapers, in Los Angeles as well as here. And to the bars, every bar in this city. I'll tell the same story in each of them. A week from now I figure this town will know the truth about my son's death. And about you. All of you."

Douglas made no response for a time, just stood there searching the faces of his colleagues. Then, grinning cryptically, he replaced the tomahawk head on the desk and turned to Hook. "I've got this sudden urge to have a drink," he said. "You join me?"

Hook did not answer, for Parnelli had moved in between Douglas and the door, and his stance was that of a linebacker about to blitz.

"He ain't going anywhere," he said. "And neither are you, Jack, not without me."

"Get out of the way, Bo." Douglas said it wearily, like a parent.

"Look, man, I'm in this too, remember!"

"Nobody said you weren't."

"And I'm telling you—I ain't gonna let him get away with it. I ain't gonna let him railroad us."

Douglas nodded indulgently. "What should we do, then? Do we kill him here? Throw him out the window? Call it suicide? What?"

"All I'm saying is I won't do time, Jack! Not because some goddamn drunk kid fell off a cliff! That ain't my idea of a crime!"

"So what do you propose?"

"I don't know! You tell me. Maybe the three of us—maybe we could do business."

Douglas looked quizzically at Hook. "What about it?" he asked. "You for sale?"

Hook did not answer.

Douglas turned back to Parnelli. "Get out of the way, Bo."

"I'm telling you, I won't buy this! I'm not gonna roll over and—"

But Douglas had begun to move past him, at the same time reaching out to lay his hand on the big man's shoulder in a gesture more of camaraderie and reassurance than command. Hook followed, expecting Parnelli to knock him to the floor at any moment. Instead all he got was the man's hot breath, an effluvium of gin and olives.

"Later, shitkicker," Parnelli said. "Later you gonna pay."

Hook did not break his stride. In the reception room, as Douglas unlocked the front door, Hook glanced back into the small office and saw Dorothy Rubin at her desk, still holding the handkerchief pressed to her nose and mouth. Above it, her eyes followed him like lasers.

When they reached the parking lot, Hook found his car empty, Liz gone. Douglas asked him if he would drive.

"I'm kind of shaky," he added. "Can't imagine why."

In the car, he suggested they drive down to Cabrillo, the beach drive. "There's a bar there," he said. "Top floor of a motel. It's a nice big room. Maybe we can get a table way off in a corner. So no one will hear me cry."

He was smiling ironically as he said this, as if the two of them were about to engage in some casual business deal that would cost him a few dollars, which they both knew he could well afford. Hook decided to set him straight.

"This isn't a laughing matter to me, Douglas. And I can't see why it would be for you. You'll wind up in prison. Don't you know that?"

"If we confessed—yes, you're probably right. I was a police reporter once, so I know a little about these things. It would be manslaughter and conspiracy. And you don't get a wrist slap for that."

"But you still find it funny."

Douglas shrugged. "It's just my way. The gallows humorist. You must've run into a few of us before. Say, a farmer making jokes at his own bankruptcy sale. That sort of thing."

Hook did not respond. When they reached the oceanfront drive, Douglas told him to turn left, and he did.

In silence they arrived at the motel, parked, and took the elevator up to the penthouse bar, which had a typical three-in-the-afternoon atmosphere, like a gathering of strangers at a wake. A pair of businessmen sat in solitude at the bar, each apparently more interested in his drink than in a small attractive Eurasian

girl sitting a few stools down, talking languorously with the bartender, a stocky freckled man who called a warm hello to Douglas as he and Hook entered. Two overdressed, overpowdered
old women were equally excited by Douglas's arrival and avidly
bent his ear at the windowside table where they sat nursing tall
frosted drinks full of shrubbery. But Douglas pushed on, to a
window table at the far side of the room, which was L-shaped and
Polynesian, all potted plants and rattan and cane furniture. Across
from their table was a huge aquarium in which a colony of lob-
sters moved fitfully, like creatures in a delirium dream.

The waitress, a collegiate-looking girl wearing a split hip-
hugging sarong and halter, came smiling to their table. Douglas
of course knew her.

"Ginny, honey," he said, "I want you to take it easy today. Just
bring us a bottle of Cutty Sark, some glasses and ice." He looked
at Hook. "That all right with you? Scotch?"

Hook said it was. The girl left.

"You like it here? The room, I mean? The view?"

Hook looked out the window through the palms at the beach,
the sea, the Channel Islands—where he had almost drowned just
yesterday morning, an age ago. "Not particularly," he said.

Douglas got out a cigarette and lit it. "They do a big night
business here. Got this brother-and-sister team. Both sing and
play a whole mess of instruments—sort of a two-man band.
Great sound. You'd like it." He paused for a few moments then,
sat there smoking and watching Hook with a vague, ironic smile.
"But then that wouldn't interest you, would it? Nothing but the
matter at hand. Nothing but nailing old Jack Douglas's ass to the
barn door."

"That's about it."

Douglas wagged his head in mock sorrow. "Hook—I'm afraid
you're a monomaniac."

"Better that than a fool."

"Which is what I am?"

"I'd say so."

"And why is that? Why am I a fool?"

But the waitress had returned to their table, with the glasses
and ice and the bottle of scotch. She started to break open the

bottle but Douglas told her not to bother, that he would do the honors, and she left in the warm glow of his politician's smile. As he uncapped the bottle and poured their drinks, he asked again why he was a fool.

"To let it come to this. If you'd stayed at Liz's that night, what would it have meant? A plea of involuntary manslaughter. Probably a suspended sentence."

"And a suspended career."

"That would have been so bad? I can't see why. I can't see any qualities in you the public is in such desperate need of."

Douglas took his first drink of the whiskey. "Not only a monomaniac, but a moralist too," he observed. "That's a tough combination to beat. And tough to take."

Hook said nothing. As he drank, with his left hand, he saw Douglas's eyes stray to his swollen right hand.

"You break it?"

"No."

"But it hurts, huh?"

"Yes. It hurts."

"You surprised you got out of there in one piece?"

"Should I be?"

Douglas grinned. "Well, I can't recall anyone else ever doing it—decking old Bo, and getting away with it."

"Thanks to your paperweight."

"You think that was it?"

"That was it."

"Anyway, don't sweat it. He'll cool off. I'll talk to him."

"I'm not afraid."

"The fearless farmer."

"That's me."

Douglas shook his head in rueful amusement. "This is really wild, you know? Here we are—you drinking with me in the forlorn hope I'll get smashed and let you talk me into going to the police so I can spill my guts—that is the phrase, isn't it? And me, I'm hoping that if we drink enough and talk enough, maybe you'll get to see me as a human being and decide not to crucify me after all."

"Neither of which is very likely." It was as much a question as a statement.

Douglas shrugged. "Well, I know I won't go to the police. I'd rather lose my reputation than my freedom any day. And I figure that's all you'll get, because the others won't break. Liz may have told you, but that's only natural. Kind of like confessing to God. She purges her conscience, without running any risks. But she'll stop with you. She won't tell anyone else. And neither will Dorothy. They'll stick with their original statements. So all you'll be able to do is spread the rumor—ruin me politically. That, you can do."

"So it will be a standoff," Hook said.

"If you won't treat us as human beings—yes."

"A standoff it is, then."

Douglas drained his glass and put it down with a comic flourish. "Well, that's that," he said, refilling the glass, then Hook's. When he was finished, his eyes drifted to the tinted window, the brilliant sweep of sea. "Guess I should've left you out there yesterday," he mused. "Christ, that was wild. The original idea was just to get you good and wet. But we almost lost you, didn't we? I wonder if it was really an accident or maybe my subconscious taking over, my heart's desire to see you dead. And me safe."

Hook said nothing, did not know what he could say in the face of such an admission. Again Douglas picked up his glass and drank, as if the scotch were iced tea on a hot day.

"Liz," he said. "How'd you break her down? You make it with her?"

Though Hook said nothing, his expression evidently was answer enough.

Douglas made a face. "Don't let it go to your head, pal. In these parts, that's no great achievement. Liz is one girl who truly believes in charity. Except when it comes to me, that is. Old Jack foots the bills, and keeps footing them. Maybe that's why I lost my cool with your boy. I mean the fact that he was *living* there, eating the food I'd paid for. The booze. The pot. *The girl.*"

"You figured she was bought and paid for," Hook said.

"It's not the way I wanted it, believe me. I'm not a rich man.

It's what *she* wanted. Maybe you haven't noticed, but Liz isn't blessed with very much of that old Puritan work ethic."

Hook wanted to backtrack, to the cliff edge. "You said you lost your cool."

For a time Douglas sat there looking down at his glass. "You want to hear about it?" he asked finally. "*My* side?"

"Just the part on the cliff, how he went over. The rest I know. Or can guess. Or don't care about."

Douglas refilled his glass, drank, set it down. "It was an accident pure and simple. All we wanted to do, Bo and me, was march him out to the road and send him on his way. But he reacted like a wild man. Kicked Bo in the nuts, knocked him down. And I couldn't handle him alone. So when Bo got up—well, we were fighting for our lives, believe me. One second he was right there, your boy. And the next he was gone. It was his momentum, I think. I figure he must have lunged at one of us, and we ducked. It's hard to know for sure. It was dark. We were drunk."

Throughout this brief account Hook had tried to make Douglas meet his eyes, but the man preferred to study his drink and cigarette, the patrons at the bar, the islands floating like giant hippos at the edge of the sea.

"So it wasn't anybody's fault," Hook said.

"I know you can't accept that. But yes—I'd say it wasn't anybody's fault. Oh, we were there, of course. We tried to make him leave. To that extent we're responsible. But then so was he, for not leaving. If he'd reacted differently——"

"If he'd let you kick him out, like a dog."

"That isn't the way it was. You weren't there."

"No. Just you and Parnelli."

"On the cliff, yes."

"And you knew what was happening every second?"

"What do you mean?"

"I mean was there any time you were out of it? Dazed, maybe? Or looking the other way?"

"Why?"

"Just tell me."

Douglas smiled in puzzlement and disbelief. "You're wondering if Bo did it alone. And I'm protecting him."

"Are you?"

"I've already told you what happened."

"He's a violent man."

"A physical man, maybe."

"No, violent."

"But not a killer, Hook. Never."

"You're sure of that."

"I'm sure."

"I have this feeling you cover for him. In your business, for instance. I think you carry him. And I wonder why."

Douglas wearily shook his head. "Could be you don't know the P.R. business."

"I'm wrong, huh?"

"Dead wrong. In fact, I think you'd be a little amazed how the average businessman reacts to a jock. The idea of rubbing shoulders and bending elbows with someone who's played in the Rose Bowl—it really turns them on."

"So he's good business."

"And a good friend. From way back. High school, even. The football teams he starred on, I was a sub. Now I star. But it works out. The relationship is the same."

"The leader. And the led."

Douglas shrugged. "I guess you could say that. Bo's very loyal, and that counts for a lot in politics. But don't get the idea you know the man. You don't. You've only seen him at his worst. And that's scared. Of you. Normally, he's a very warm guy. Very funny."

"Yes. Very funny."

Douglas made a face, as if he were giving up on Hook altogether.

"What about Mrs. Rubin?" Hook asked.

"What about her?"

"You know why she called it a suicide? Instead of just an accident?"

"I have no idea."

"And you never wondered? Never asked? Knowing what it could cost you?"

Douglas filled his glass again and took a drink. "I take it you know. Or at least have a theory."

"I *know*."

"She told you?"

"I just know."

"So tell me."

"My son turned her down."

Douglas laughed. "Dorothy? Oh come on, man! Dorothy Rubin hasn't got one erotic zone in her whole body."

"You know that for a fact."

"Well, I'll admit I haven't felt around for them. And I'm not about to. But I know the woman. I've worked with her for almost ten years."

"I imagine she's good at her work."

"As a matter of fact, she is. And I might add she's not the ogre you take her for either."

"Just a little funny," Hook said. "Like Parnelli."

Douglas ignored the sarcasm. "Like Parnelli one way at least. You've only seen the lady at her worst—scared to death. And that's not her. Normally she's just your average hard worker. More competent than most maybe. More dedicated."

"And loyal too? Like Parnelli?"

"And loyal, yes."

"That's the big thing."

"You're damn right it is. To me anyway. And let me say it cuts both ways. To people like Dorothy and Ferguson I'm not just an employer. I'm their whole goddamn career—until I fail anyway, until I'm dead politically. Why I imagine Bo sees himself as some kind of future Henry Kissinger or God knows what. And Dorothy —why do you think she'd take in Liz for me? Put up with all her shit? For the same reason she's got just about all her capital tied up in the company. Because if I make it, she does too. Her life will be bigger than it is now. Fuller. More exciting. And she'll have power. Part of my power."

Hook said nothing. Douglas took another drink, a deep drink, and when he set his glass down and looked up again it was as if a light had gone off in his eyes, and Hook was able to see into them, to a dark unused corner of the man's spirit where a different Jack Douglas lived, one normally kept out of sight, like a defective offspring. It seemed a timid creature, reflective, fey.

"Christ, Hook," he said, "you know I almost had it made. I mean all the way. To you, I suppose, I'm just a local P.R. man. An amateur politician. But not to the boys that count, believe me. Not to the makers and shakers. Not to the check-signers. To them I'm one very important piece of property—the next congressman from this district. And not just any congressman either. I'm the one with the magic scepter, Hook. All the way. The right looks, the right family, the right kind of image on the tube—and that's the whole ballgame these days—I guess even you got to know that. So they have—or *had*, I guess it is now—they had great plans for me. They were all ready with the money. One or two terms in the House, and then they light the fuse and we have liftoff. Governor maybe . . . senator . . . who knows?" He had been smiling as he went through this, with eyes distant and reflective, as if he were talking about someone else, in some other time. But now, looking at Hook, the smile faded and he came splashing down into the present. "And now here I sit drinking scotch with some Illinois farmer they don't know from Adam, and yet who's gonna change all their plans, not to mention mine."

Hook told him he was not the only one who had made plans. "Mine, for instance, was to work with my sons. Make our farm grow. Turn it over to them someday."

Douglas nodded ruefully. "Of course. That's life. The best-laid plans and all that."

"And all that." As Hook muttered this, he began to feel the alcohol. He decided to slow down.

"But there is one difference," Douglas was saying. "One crucial little difference. Your plans went awry *by accident*. Mine —well, mine are being bent out of shape pretty much on purpose, wouldn't you say? Deliberately. By one man. With malice aforethought."

"Not malice," Hook amended. "Justice. All I want is justice. And my son's good name back. That's all I want."

And suddenly Douglas had broken. Tears had formed in his eyes and his hands were shaking. Finally he got them together, as if he were clasping them in prayer. "If I got down on my knees,

227

Hook," he got out. "If I begged. Oh Jesus. Jesus Christ. Please, man. Please."

Hook was more surprised than moved. "Let's get it over with. Let's go see Rider. Now."

Douglas did not answer. For a time he sat there staring down at his glass. He got control of himself. He picked up the bottle of Cutty Sark and refilled his glass and drank again, set it down again. "What was it you said we had? Forty hours. Or thirty-nine now? Thirty-eight? Well, I'm going to use it, every blessed minute of it. Maybe you'll change your mind. Or better yet—maybe God will strike you dead."

"You believe in God, do you."

Douglas grinned crookedly. "I would then. I certainly would then."

"Well, I guess that about covers the subject," Hook said. "So I think I'll be leaving. You take your thirty-eight hours. Use them. You got a lot to think about."

He pushed back his chair, preparing to get up, but Douglas reached across the table and took hold of his arm. "Come on, you're not going anywhere," he said. "You got nothing better to do. Anyway, I don't *want* to be alone. I don't want to think, Hook. Not yet anyway. All I want to do is drink—which ought to fit right in with your plans. You know—truth in booze and all that. So you might as well stick. Who knows? I just might spill my guts right here in front of everybody. Wouldn't that be peachy? I can just see it in the paper. *Local politico arrested for drunk and disorderly. Tells all . . . manslaughter . . . conspiracy.* For a show like that, you might as well stick around, right?"

Hook remained in his chair.

Smiling now, Douglas filled their glasses again.

"A couple more out of this, and we can move on," he said. "We can paint this old town red. Blood red."

In the next hour Hook held to his decision to slow down and not let himself lose control. Douglas, however, kept working on the bottle of scotch as if he could not get drunk fast enough to suit him, and in time it was apparent that he was reaching his objective, for he began to slur his words and to smile in secret amusement as he talked—gossiped, actually—about the locals filling the bar now in the after-five "cocktail hour." Most of them stopped at the table to exchange words of greeting with Douglas, who had reached the point where he was introducing Hook as his millionaire mortician cousin from Peoria.

Much of the time Hook did not listen. He toyed with his drink and smoked cigarettes and watched out the window as the sun slipped into the sea, setting red fire to an armada of high cirrus clouds moving down the coast. And finally there was no light at all out there except the streetlamps along the boulevard and the drilling platforms shining like Christmas trees at sea, and then themselves, him and Douglas, reflected in the glass. And Hook began to lose his resolve, gave in to a growing feeling of anger and impatience, and drained his glass, filled it again, and drank again, keeping up with Douglas now until the fifth was almost empty. He was afraid Douglas would order more, but instead the man suddenly shoved back his chair and carefully stood up, apparently still sober enough to want to hide from his friends and once-future constituents that he was not altogether sober. On the way out, he gave the waitress a twenty-dollar bill and a pat on the bottom, for which he received in return a smile that suggested their relationship was not confined to the penthouse bar.

Downstairs, in Hook's car, Douglas proposed that they drive out to his house because he thought it "only fitting and proper" that Hook meet his family "on this, the last happy night of their lives." Hook agreed to drive him home but said he would not go in.

"I still don't share your gallows humor," he said. "None of this is a joke to me."

"You won't come in because you're chicken," Douglas explained, grinning in the glow of the Galaxie's dashboard. "You're like a bomber pilot. You'd just as soon not see your victims."

"My 'victims' will live."

Douglas was still grinning. "Sure. On crutches."

Hook dropped the conversation, aware suddenly that this drive to Montecito was nothing like his first one a few nights before. Now the narrow road curving back and forth through the eucalyptus trees held no threat for him, and the trip was going much more rapidly, like a movie montage, just bits and pieces his mind casually selected to honor with his attention. So he told himself—warned himself—that he was half drunk, that he had to slow down and concentrate, stay in control.

Nevertheless, when they came to Douglas's house, and Douglas again asked him to come in and meet his family, Hook impulsively acceded. What was there to lose? He did not care if they were all as happy and handsome as a television comedy family; it would not affect him. What shame and pain they might have to endure would not be of his making; it would be a gift of their father and husband, and no one else. So Hook got out of the car and followed Douglas up the flagstone walk to the front entrance, a pair of ornately carved doors, which Douglas had to unlock to open. Inside, he cheerily called for, first, his wife, and then his children, and finally settled for a "Hey—anybody home?"

There was no answer. An English sheepdog padded into view, regarded the two of them indifferently, then returned to the kitchen. Douglas looked at Hook with a gesture of comic despair.

"Can you beat that, huh? The breadwinner comes home from a hard day in the mines, and what does he find? Nobody. Not a goddamn soul. Makes a guy feel real important."

As Douglas went down a hall to the left, looking into the rooms opening off it, Hook surveyed what he could see of the house— the dining room, living room, and part of the kitchen—and found it a pretty close approximation of the lavish decor Hollywood once had considered comfortable middle-class. The style was basically Spanish, though without the clean uncluttered look Hook associated with that tradition. And he figured the reason was as much a matter of finances as of taste, that only a woman totally free of budgetary concerns would have so overburdened a house with oil paintings, sculptures, art objects, and just plain bric-a-brac.

Douglas came back to the foyer. "My wife must be at the club," he said. "Probably went with a friend, because her car's still here." He crossed into the living room and roughly pulled a photograph off the wall, one of at least a score, each framed as if it were a miniature old master on loan from the Louvre. He brought it over to Hook, a color snapshot of Douglas and his wife and two children posing on skis in a snowy mountain setting that contained a chalet in the background. They all looked handsome, healthy, happy. Douglas's finger rapped on the figure of the girl.

"Tammy here," he said. "She's sixteen. Probably out having an abortion somewhere. And Jack Junior—I figure he's down the street shooting up with one of his junkie friends." He grinned at Hook and tossed the picture onto a grand piano a good twenty feet away. "After all, kids got to do something, right?"

Hook said nothing. Douglas went over to a marble-topped liquor cart, picked up a bottle of scotch and headed for the front door.

"Come on. I'll show you where the real action is here in town. Heavy, I'm telling you. We'll have to beat 'em off with clubs."

On the way out Hook asked him if he was sure he wanted to drive with an open bottle in the car, and Douglas laughed happily.

"Jesus Christ! Tomorrow he crucifies me. Today he worries I might get arrested for drunk driving." He got into Hook's car and took a long pull on the bottle. "Anyway, you're doing the driving," he concluded. "I've got nothing to worry about."

The place with the "action" Douglas had promised turned out to be only a few blocks away, a darkly posh Montecito restaurant crowded with elderly people going at their food and drink as if they hoped to uncover youth and happiness at the bottom of it all, like Orphan Annie's image in a childhood cereal bowl. Around a piano bar, a half-dozen desperate-looking old women sat with a few surviving males, all trying to move and shake in rhythm with the tune being played by a handsome young black man with a rigid smile and eyes of molten hatred. As in the penthouse bar, there were people who knew Douglas and tried to have a few words with him, but he simply walked past them now, heading for a second bar at the rear of the restaurant, where he promptly picked up two hard-looking young women—whores or socialites, Hook could not tell—and shepherded them and Hook to a vacant table.

Later Hook would remember almost nothing about the girls except that neither of them, in an hour's time, and after three or four drinks, had been able to muster a genuine smile or laugh. They were like pawnbrokers, patient in the knowledge that in the end, after all the fuss and furor, this transaction like so many before it would be resolved dully in their favor.

But it was not.

Into their second hour together, Douglas had left to go to the men's room, and minutes later Hook saw him leave the restaurant altogether, lurching out the front door. Leaving money for the drinks, Hook excused himself and followed Douglas outside. He found him in his car, dozing in the front seat. Pushing him over, Hook got in.

"One more place," Douglas mumbled. "Just one more place. Near the Mission. After that, you're free."

"I'm free now."

Douglas raised his head to look at him. "As a favor. And no more booze. No girls. I promise."

"Near the Mission?"

"Near the Mission."

As Hook backed out and drove away, Douglas sagged against the car door and closed his eyes.

On the way back to Santa Barbara, this time via the freeway, Hook tried to think his way through the alcoholic mist in his mind to understand what was happening to him this night, why he was "painting the town" with this man who was nothing if not his enemy, even his quarry. There was the moth-to-flame explanation, of course. But he figured that probably described Douglas's behavior more aptly than his own, for by the time the thing had run its course he did not doubt it would be Douglas and not himself who would be burned. Or perhaps the explanation lay in the old saw about the criminal's fascination with the scene of his crime. Maybe deep down that was how he felt about what he was doing, that it was in some way a crime, and Douglas its victim, and thus his momentary fascination with the man, his inability to just drive away from him and let him sweat out his predicament. But Hook discounted that possibility too. He was not a sadist.

Whatever the reason, he went along. They drove past the floodlit courthouse and uphill toward the Mission, through the neighborhood where Icarus lived, and then west past State Street into a less affluent area with neat rows of old clapboard and stucco houses lining the dark street. Hook saw no bars anywhere.

"There," Douglas said. "On the corner."

It was an old three-story stucco house crumbling behind a scraggly row of pine trees. Hook parked and looked out. On every floor lights were burning. From one came the sound of Jesus rock, insistent and blaring. Douglas got out, on the street side, and came around the car. He leaned down and looked in at Hook.

"You just gonna leave me here?"

"Where?"

"Here, man. My home. My ancestral home."

"I think it's occupied."

Douglas shrugged. "Well, hell yes. And by hippies, no less. It's a commune, I hear. But they'll welcome us, believe me. They don't turn anyone away."

"Some other time."

But Douglas would not take no for an answer. He opened the door and pulled Hook out of the car onto the grass parkway with him. "You got to see this," he insisted. "Maybe it'll help you understand me."

Hook pulled his arm free. "Why should I want to understand you?"

"Know thy victim. It's an old Socratic principle." Douglas lurched toward the front porch.

"You're so drunk you can hardly stand," Hook told him.

"Then help me. Come on, Hook old buddy. I need your help."

Not knowing why, Hook followed him up the porch stairs and stood waiting while Douglas leaned on the out-of-order doorbell for a time and then began to pound on the door with his fist.

"Would you believe it?" he asked. "*My home.* Where I grew up, where Mom served tea and oatmeal cookies. Now it's just tea." He gave Hook a conspiratorial wink.

Hook did not respond.

"Where are the snows of yesteryear, huh?"

And Hook heard himself intone, *"Où sont les neiges d'antan?"*
—heard it and knew he was drunker than he had thought.

Grinning, Douglas shook his head. "Some kind of shitkicker you are. Parlez le français and everything."

The door opened and a young woman in a sack dress stared out at them, a girl who could have been a twin of the one whose lover had overdosed in Cold Spring Canyon. This one did not even ask them who they were or what they wanted but simply opened the door further and turned away, zombie-like, admitting them into a world of incredible filth and chaos. There was an attempt at dissident decor—battered art nouveau posters advocating Maoism and fornication and grass; a prayer rug; a mobile made of inflated condoms—but to Hook it was all negligible, overmatched by the cloacal stench that hung in the air like lines of drying fish. There was food on the floor and fecal matter and dogs and naked squalling infants importuning three youths—two boys and a girl—rooted in front of a small Sony TV as if it offered not the tepid black-and-white images Hook saw there but some resplendent riot of color and sound and significance. They did not even look up.

"He's upstairs," the girl said, and headed back toward the kitchen, where food was burning on a stove.

Hook asked Douglas who was upstairs, and Douglas shrugged. "Let's find out," he said.

As they went up the stairs Hook felt the alcohol reach some vital center in him and spill over, so that as he came to the second floor it was as if he had arrived at a different level of consciousness as well, a level at which time began to move past him like a speeding passenger train at night, a series of windows flashing past, all dark and dimly seen except for a special one every now and then which would burst brightly in his mind and remain, floodlit, a tableau.

He remembered being blocked with Douglas in a narrow corridor by a neat, cleanly dressed young couple who smilingly railed at them that Jesus had died for their sins and that only by accepting this fact and by purging their lives of alcohol and drugs and by loving their fellow man could they hope to attain the kingdom of God. Hook kept wondering if the couple lived there, and if they did, how they felt about the graffiti in the place, especially the poster that proclaimed *Jesus sucks*. Then out of nowhere a filthy bearded smiling youth appeared and began to blow pot smoke on the couple, smiling as they smiled back at him, everybody happy and loving and unreal.

And Hook remembered Douglas somberly showing him through a corner bedroom containing nothing except a water pipe and empty wine bottles and a scattering of sleeping bags and cot mattresses.

"Here's where I slept," Douglas said, indicating an area next to two windows that looked out on the backyard. "I used to put my pillow right on the windowsill and just lie there and look out and dream, you know? I would be great, of course. A great man. I never doubted that. The night was like some woman out there waiting for me, a world waiting for me."

"A beast slouching toward Santa Barbara," said the bearded youth, their unofficial host and escort by then.

"Yeats," Hook heard himself say.

The youth laughed. "Right on, Pops."

Then later there was wine, a bottle of red and a bottle of white being passed back and forth between the bearded youth and Douglas and the girl from the kitchen and two other men Hook had not seen before, one with a bald pate and silky blond hair hanging down his back. He was sitting in a rocker, holding a little girl who was sucking hard on a pacifier as she watched the miniature television set, on which a roller derby was playing now. Douglas was the only one talking, telling them all how he remembered being on the floor in this very room, in front of his family's four-foot-high Philco radio on the Sunday the Japanese bombed Pearl Harbor. "I was only seven or eight," he kept on. "And I was sitting right there playing with lead soldiers, and I think the 'Disney Parade' was on when they broke into it and made the announcement. You know what? I bawled. I really did. I cried because there was a war on, and I was too young to be in it. Can you believe that?"

Hook had looked at their faces one by one, but not in any of them did he see a thing. They were vacant, Locke's *tabula rasa*.

And finally Hook remembered being up in the attic alone with

Douglas and the bearded youth, who by then had given up his role of host in order to play one-man audience to Douglas's buffoon, most of the time patiently and smilingly hearing him out, though wincing every now and then as the older man slurred his words or doggedly kept repeating them, struggling to make himself understood. And then abruptly the youth would cut in with some hip word of amazement or just an easy laugh, a gesture of utter, unbelieving contempt.

But Douglas kept on. He had practically dragged Hook and the youth over to a built-in window cabinet, which he said once had contained his father's World War One uniform. Lovingly, Douglas recounted how as a child he had come up to the attic and regularly hauled the uniform out of its moth-balled box and tried it on in front of an antique swivel mirror—and oh Christ, the smell of it, he said, the weight, it was like a coat of mail, it really was. The cabinet also had contained three old war books, he went on, pictorial histories of "the old man's war," volumes that he had never been able to get enough of, had thumbed and studied and absorbed until they were almost falling apart in his hands, until names like Belleau Wood and Big Bertha and the Marne and Black Jack Pershing were more real to him than the names of his own family and the streets where he lived and played. And it was then he stripped himself before the bearded youth, knelt down and laid his head on the block of the young man's scorn.

"It was an odd way to learn to love your country, I guess. But that's how it happened for me. All those pictures. Those faces of the doomed. They looked out at you, and you could see they knew they were doomed, that in a day or a week they would be dead. And I kept thinking that they must have felt about themselves, about their own lives, just as I did about mine—that there was nothing else, that they were *it*, everything, the whole ball of wax. And yet they knew someone was going to tell them to advance in the next few days or hours, and they would do it. They would move ahead. And they would die. In a stupid war, maybe. Maybe they defended nothing. But they gave—they gave everything they had. And all I could think of then was that when I grew up, when I became a man, I'd want to do all I could, any way I could, to make this country worthy of their sacrifice."

Like a dropped lightbulb, the youth's laughter exploded in the dusty attic. "You are so pitiful," he said. "So full of shit."

That seemed to get through to Douglas. For a time, he just stood there looking foggily at the youth, like a drugged bull about to drop. "Why?" he asked finally. "Why is that?"

"Because you are, that's all."

"No. Explain it."

The youth, grinning, wagged his head. "Well, just being here tonight, man—you know, back to the womb and all that shit. That's weird enough. And now you come on with all this militarist, patriotic shit. You're pathetic, that's all."

"Militarist, patriotic shit?"

"That's what I said."

"Then you don't know me very well, friend. I'm Jack Douglas, for Christ sake—the Democratic candidate for Congress. A liberal, you jackass. Why listen, I been fighting against Vietnam and militarism in this country since before you were in grade school."

But the youth was still grinning. "Jack Douglas—the liberal. You just getting in deeper, man. More pathetic by the minute."

Now Douglas seemed to gain some perspective on his predicament, some understanding of his foe. He smiled too, miming the youth's contempt. "What are you? One of those sad circa nineteen-seventy neo-anarchists? You gonna burn it all down, so you can start fresh, build clean?"

"Something like that, old man."

"So we're old at thirty-seven now, huh?"

"You called it."

"The whole system stinks, right? No reason at all to work within it, change it with the tools the founding fathers gave us?"

The youth, who had brought a bottle of Chablis with him to the attic, was taking a long pull as Douglas said this last, and he wound up choking on it, coughing, as he laughed. "*Founding fathers!*" he got out. "You are unbelievable, you know that?"

"Why? Because I believe in the past? And in people? Instead of bombs and blood?"

Again the youth shook his head. "Just 'cause you're unbelievable, that's all."

Douglas advanced on him, as if he were contemplating throwing a punch at him. "No, answer me," he insisted. "Come on. Name me one good thing, one decent free society ever created by creeps like you. Who ever created anything by throwing bombs?"

The boy grinned. "I lay a bomb on you, dad, I'd be creating something—a less pathetic world, for one thing."

At that, Douglas seemed to give up on him. Turning to look at Hook, he almost fell down and had to take hold of the stairway banister for support. "What you think, old buddy?" he asked Hook. "Is he right? We pathetic?"

From his seat on the window cabinet, Hook regarded this man who was addressing him as *old buddy*, including him as *we*. Was he so drunk he had forgotten who Hook was, why they were together in the first place? It was possible, of course, for they had been drinking steadily for over six hours now.

"Huh?" he repeated now. "We pathetic, old buddy?"

Hook could not have begun to tell him, knew he would have had even less chance of getting through to him than Douglas or the bearded youth had with each other, for they at least spoke the same language, the language of politics, while Hook did not. To him, liberal and conservative and Marxist and anarchist were all out of the same garbage bag, labels on empty cans, tactics before policy, frenzy in a void. He wanted to go over to Douglas and seize him by his coat and shake him and shout in his face that his son, his Chris, even now was only a week in the ground, lying between his mother and great-grandfather, and they were just three in a long row of graves and there was row after row of similar graves and graveyard after graveyard all across the world, because Death was the one true and final government, the king of kings, the worm emperor of the universe, and the worm was right there in the attic now, in all of them, in Hook and Douglas and in the bearded youth and in the infant sucking on the pacifier downstairs. Yet in the face of that awesome knowledge these two prated about politics. To Hook, they were like rabbits gorging in the soybeans—while the owl watched.

But Douglas was still after him. "Tell him, old buddy. Tell him."

Hook got to his feet, wobbly as a toddler. "I think it's time we cut out. Time I got back to my motel."

Douglas dismissed him with a swipe of his hand and turned back to the youth, who was taking a pull on the wine bottle again. Douglas watched him for a moment and then roughly tore the bottle out of his hands. "Give me that, ya creep," he slurred. "And get outa my attic. Ya don't belong here."

The youth did nothing for a time, just stood there looking mildly incredulous as Douglas, holding onto the banister with one hand, tipped up the bottle and drank, deeply, as if it were water. Then Hook saw the new thing come into the youth's eyes, a glint like gunmetal. And abruptly he stepped in close to Douglas, as if he were going to kiss him, but instead hit him solidly in the stomach. The bottle clattered to the floor, spilling what little wine was left in it. Douglas staggered forward a few steps and then dropped to his knees at the top of the stairway and began to vomit, not much, for like Hook he had not eaten all evening long. But he could not stop, it seemed, just knelt there in the dust of his past retching violently over the meager pool of vomit he had produced.

12

At a quarter after nine the next morning Hook was wakened by the ringing of the telephone in his motel room. Hung over and still half asleep, he was not sure at first who it was on the line, just some small urgent voice going much too fast for him, so that finally he had to tell the person to slow down and start over.

"It's Icarus," the voice said. "You know—Icarus."

"Yes. Good morning."

"You all right?"

"You woke me, that's all."

Then again the voice began to speed up. He had news for Hook. Important news. "There's this kid I know. He found out Chris had stayed with me and that you're in town checking up on Chris's death and all. And, well, that's what he wants to see you about. He says he's got proof Chris didn't kill himself. He was there, he says. He was a witness. But he's afraid to come out in the open—don't ask me why. He wouldn't tell me. And I guess he wants money. A hundred dollars, he said."

"Will he meet me?"

"That's what I'm calling about."

"Where? When?"

Icarus had to explain it twice before Hook understood. There was this monastery, the youth said, Mount Calvary Monastery, halfway up the mountain slope, at the very end of Mount Calvary Road, which connected with Mountain Drive or El Cielito—Hook could check his map to make sure which it was. The road was a lonely one-lane affair all the way up, a narrow blacktop curving back and forth up the mountain, with nothing on either side but boulders and trees. This boy, the "witness," would be parked along it somewhere in a pickup truck at six o'clock that evening, when it would be good and dark. Once Hook "eyeballed" the truck, he should park and get out.

"The kid says he wants to see you first," Icarus explained. "To make sure it's you. Don't ask me why. He sure is scared of someone."

Hook did not suggest who he thought that someone might be. "And he said he'll want a hundred dollars?"

"That's right. That's what he said."

"All right. Six o'clock. Tell him I'll be there."

After he had hung up, Hook rediscovered his hangover, like a sack of feed dropped on his head. Getting up, he went into the bathroom and showered. And gradually the night before, all the long hours of drinking with Douglas, began to uncover itself in his mind like some grotesque bird struggling out of its shell. He recalled having gotten Douglas out of the hippie house and into his car and then somehow driving him home to Montecito, with what combination of raw determination and purblind luck he could only guess at, marvel at. And he remembered Douglas on his knees in the attic retching as if he were trying to bring up not vomit but a part of his own being, some foul malignancy laced into his very spirit. Hook wanted to stop the process right there, push the ungainly chick back into its shell, but it would not go, and despite his exhaustion and hangover, he knew what he had felt then, watching Douglas, in fact still felt, almost the anguish of a father, a brother. He did not want to like anything about Douglas, wanted only to think of him as a shallow egocentric monster, a man who had pushed the vices of self-love and ambition beyond the point of criminality. But after last night, Hook found it impossible to think of the man in those terms alone. Now there was also his rueful sense of humor, his self-mockery and his honesty and vulnerability, none of which Hook considered normal baggage for an ambitious and arrogant politician, especially one who could be a casual participant in manslaughter and then just as casually join the conspiracy to cover it up.

Yet that was what the man was, nothing more or less than your good old average American male, one of that race of decent likeable fellows who tended to get carried away at places like Sand Creek and My Lai. But even as Hook's mind served up the analogy, he already saw it for a fake. In the cold clear center of his mind he knew Jack Douglas would not kill another person, not in hot blood or cold, not anywhere, anytime. And as for the conspiracy afterwards, the convenient silence, Hook wondered if he himself would have done any differently if it had been his own family's happiness at stake, his own skin in jeopardy. The thought was like a knife edge at his throat. He stepped back from it.

He dressed hurriedly and walked down the street to the nearby family restaurant, where he tried to restore his body's water balance with copious quantities of orange juice and coffee, and then looked to scrambled eggs and a double serving of bacon to restore some of the thiamine the long night's drinking had leached out of him. He was not worried about his health so much as anxious to get rid of his hangover as soon as possible, for he knew it was going to be a long and difficult day of waiting, not only for the rendezvous with this new "witness" at six but also to wait out Douglas and Liz, see if they would take advantage of this last full day he had given them and go to the police, tell the truth, gain for themselves at least the advantage of voluntary confession.

During his breakfast Hook thought about Icarus's call and the new "witness." He could not help wondering whether the youth would turn out to be real or counterfeit, whether he would actually have information about Chris's death or simply be out after an easy hundred dollars, part of a con game that might even have been initiated by Icarus. It was a cynical thought, Hook knew. Yet it was one he could not discount. There were things about Icarus he liked, especially how the youth had reacted to Chris and what he had said about the boy that first night. And Hook appreciated the help the young photographer had given him, agreeing to tell Sergeant Rider what he knew and then putting Hook in touch with the reporter Oliver. But the fact remained that Icarus was not the kind of man who inspired trust. In his very weakness and bizarre inversion there was the promise of treachery, the treachery of the fox trying to survive in a world of hounds and guns. So Hook accepted it that the meeting might turn out to be a con game, with himself the victim. But he hoped it would be academic by then, that Liz or Douglas would come forward during the day and render the meeting a mere formality to be gone through, possible icing on the cake of his day.

Hook thought of calling Rider and telling him what he had found out and that he expected to have it corroborated by Douglas or Liz before the day was out, but he knew what the sergeant would say—that all he could do was wait for such corroboration. Until he had it the case would remain unchanged. So Hook decided not to call him. And for the same reason he would not call home, not until the thing was over, and he had won.

He did want to talk with Liz, however, and dialed her number when he returned to the motel. He waited a long time but there was no answer. So he got in his car then and drove out to the beach house, through a gradually lifting coastal fog. Along the way he considered what might lie ahead of him, perhaps even a gathering of the clan, all the guilty assembled to discuss what they would do on this last day of reprieve. But when he reached the turnoff and followed the narrow blacktop to the first of the three houses, he found no cars in the driveway, just the Jaguar parked in the carport. He got out and rang the back doorbell. When there was no answer he knocked, hard, thinking Liz might still be in bed, drugged on wine or marijuana or whatever her last night's pleasure might have been. But there was no response, no sound inside, nothing.

He went around to the front and looked through the deck windows. All he could see, however, was the living room in a state of casual disorder, a few empty glasses on the cocktail table, a green wine bottle on the floor with a pair of girl's panties and the yellow sweater Liz had worn the day before. Then Hook noticed that the deck door—a sliding, patio-type door—was slightly ajar. For a moment he considered entering the house and looking around, but decided to try the cliff first, see if she might be down below, on the beach.

When he reached the cliff edge he felt a sudden weakness and nausea. But he remained there, looking up and down the beach, straining to see through the fog which drifted past like tattered flags of gauze, bleached pennants of some decimated ghost army stranded up the coast. Then he saw her, almost directly below, a tiny figure huddled in a cleft of rock which the surf kept reaching for, and then pulling back from, as if it were intimidated by her presence.

Hook set out along the top of the cliff, moving past the two other beach houses to the trail that led down to the beach. When he reached the bottom she did not see him at first, so he was able to observe her face unguarded for a few moments, and what he saw was sculpted grief. She was leaning back on the rock, hugging herself against the salt wind even though she was wearing her windbreaker, with chinos and old deck shoes. As she saw him her expression changed hardly at all.

"Good morning," Hook said.

She nodded slightly. "I've been expecting you."

"I'm that predictable?"

"Well, this is your big day, isn't it? The day your victims begin to sweat. I didn't figure you'd want to miss any of it."

"I don't think of you as my victims."

She smiled with weary irony. "Oh, I know. I know. You are our victim, right?"

"I didn't come here to go over that again."

"What then? To what do I owe——"

"You just said it, Liz. This is your last day."

She had picked a pebble off the boulder, and now absently tossed it into the water. "What else is new?"

"Today you can confess freely. It will mean something. But tomorrow and after——"

"I know all that," she cut in. "The others told me about your gracious ultimatum."

Hook wanted her to face him but she continued to gaze out at the sea. So he spoke to her profile. He told her that he did not want her to go to jail, that if she confessed now she probably would receive a suspended sentence. He told her not to wait for Douglas to make the first step.

"He won't do it," Hook explained. "He doesn't have the guts. I was with him most of last night. All he did was drink himself sick and wallow in the past. He won't face this thing."

Again she smiled. "Neither will I, David. Or Mr. Hook, I guess it is now. I don't care about what might happen in the future. In fact, I don't care much about the present either. You say Jack wallowed in the past? Well, I'm kind of stuck back there too." She looked at him now, her eyes brilliant with pain and irony. "I wonder if you could guess where?"

He saw her mouth trembling, fighting to hold the smile. And then abruptly her eyes had filled with tears.

"Aren't you going to try?" she demanded. "Come on. Guess."

"His death," Hook said. "I know."

"You know what?"

"It wasn't easy for you either."

"Why?" she shot back. "Did I love him? Did I ever say I loved him?"

Hook did not know what to say, what he could say.

"After all, I just knew him a day and a half, didn't I," she kept on. "Just a few hours. Certainly not long enough to have felt his death as you did."

Hook looked back at her. "I know you felt it."

"But not as strongly as you?"

"I can't weigh my grief against yours, Liz. Mine is enough for me."

For a while she just sat there on the rock looking at him and crying, but crying like a mute, with her eyes alone. "You didn't answer me before," she got out finally. "Did I ever tell you I loved him?"

Hook shook his head. "Not in so many words. But I got the feeling—"

"I don't care what you felt," she snapped. "I just want you to listen, that's all. I want you to *know* how it was. The truth finally. You think he was so special, don't you? So beautiful. Well, maybe he was. I don't know. And you see, that's where it's at for me—the pain. *Because I don't know*, no matter what I told you before about how he and I talked and talked, and how special it all was. Because it wasn't. To me, he was just like all the others. I drove

245

down to 101 and picked him up just like a junkie making a connection. His body was the stuff, the bag of smack. And I put it to use. I used his head too, like a garbage bag, a place to dump all my exquisite sufferings." She looked back at the cliff, her eyes streaming tears. "And then suddenly it happened. He was dead. Inside I was still wet from him, and I didn't even remember his name. It was only then it began to dawn on me what had happened, that while I was crying for myself and all of us and all our ugliness, maybe something beautiful had come and gone. Just maybe. But me, I was too busy to notice."

Hook did not know what she saw in his eyes now, perhaps some slight indication of what he was feeling, for she turned from it. She scooted down off the other side of the boulder and walked aimlessly away from him, toward the cliff face at first and then turned, wandering down the beach for a short distance before she stopped and stood there with her back to him. Hook walked over to her and raised his hands to place them on her shoulders but hesitated, like the surf afraid to touch her. And then he did, and he felt her come alive under the light pressure of his hands, felt her shoulders lift toward him, her sea-smelling hair brush his face as she let her head fall back and rest against him. And then just as abruptly a stiffness shot through her and she pulled away, walked on. Hook followed.

"I'm glad he knew you," he got out. "I'm glad Chris had that, his last hours."

"Yes. He had that," she said.

They had come to the trail that climbed the cliff now and she went ahead of him, leading the way.

"Have you never loved anyone?" he asked. "Not even——"

"The men I screw? I'm afraid not. But I've already told you that."

"Jack Douglas? Never him?"

They had come to a turn in the trail, and she stopped and looked at him. "No. And not you either."

"Was I asking that?"

"Weren't you?"

She moved on without waiting for his answer, which made it easier for him, easier to confess his weakness, his sudden soaring madness, to her back than to her face. "I guess I was," he admitted, his breath coming short now, as they climbed. "I know it doesn't add up. I want to hate you for what you are, for having been a part of Chris's death. But I can't. I——"

She had stopped again, turned to face him with cool inscrutable eyes. "You what? Are you saying you love me?"

He shook his head. "Only that I don't want to walk away from you. I want you in my life."

"How much? Enough to give up this vendetta of yours? Enough to let me—and the others—go free?"

He did not answer her, just stood there looking up at her searching, beautiful eyes until she shook her head finally, almost imperceptibly, in pity, he assumed. Then she turned again and went on to the top of the cliff, moving through great pools of sunshine now as the fog thinned.

When they reached the beach-house deck she turned to him, almost formally, and he had the feeling she was going to reach out and shake his hand. Instead she smiled, a cold social smile, a smile forged in the foundries of hatred. She told him not to worry about his little speech back there on the cliff.

"You don't want me," she said. "And I don't want you. I never could. For me, it's always been the soft and easy things. The warm things. Like this coast. I don't want any part of your cold winters, Mister Hook. Your cold righteousness. And that's what it is, isn't it—a kind of God-playing. Like Jack and Bo played God with Chris's life, you are with theirs. Only you're sober, aren't you? Cold sober."

Hook was still shocked by the look of her, this new and sudden carapace of hatred she had grown. Yet he heard her words. He weighed them. Finally he repeated them.

"Cold sober. You're right, Liz." He did not add that he considered the judgment a fair one, that cold sober was not an insult but a compliment, the proper state and attitude and philosophy of a man, if he would live as a man.

That afternoon Hook could see no reason to go on waiting through the entire day and put in a call to Sergeant Rider to learn if Douglas or any of the others had contacted the police. But

Rider was not in, the switchboard operator said. Would Hook want to talk with someone else? No, he would not. He would call later.

He was downtown at the time, in a parking garage across from the courthouse. He considered walking a few doors up the street to El Cielito and taking a sidewalk table there, sitting alone and drinking slowly through the afternoon in the hope that Rider might pass by or stop in to eat. But he decided against it, mostly because he did not want to drink—just the thought of more liquor made him feel almost ill—but also because he knew he would not be able to sit alone in public for very long without feeling uncomfortable and wanting to leave. So he walked around the downtown area for a time. And again he was impressed by Santa Barbara's old-world elegance and solidity—buildings and fountains and benches and even bus stops that appeared to have been designed with a view to beauty as well as function, all of which proved to him only that Americans could build a decent city to live in—if enough of them were millionaires. But handsome as the place was, Hook found his patience fraying, found that sunshine and flowering hibiscus and picturesque curio and art shops were not strong enough distractions during these long hours of tension and waiting. So he tried a movie, in an ornate old theater with twinkling stars in its ceiling and walls simulating the perimeters of a Spanish courtyard.

In that ersatz world he ate a candy bar made of flavor substitutes and watched a Danish film that told in living color the tale of an eighteen-year-old girl's personal triumph over frigidity. For a good portion of the film she was nude, a modern Alice in Wonderland innocently moving on from the rudimentary pleasures of masturbation to the higher accomplishments of copulation and fellatio and cunnilingus and finally orgy. Hook watched the huge images moving in the darkness, the acres of technicolor flesh, and yet he did not really see any of it. His mind was elsewhere, on Douglas and Parnelli and Dorothy Rubin. For this was the first real chance he had had to sit back and think about them as other than *suspects* in Chris's death. Now they were guilty, each of them, and he knew it, and knew the world would soon know it. So for the first time he was able to think about the *degree* of their guilt. The suicide lie was of course a simple matter, Mrs. Rubin's act alone, part and parcel of her ugliness and loneliness and, perversely, her normality. She had craved love or at least sex and had tried to get it the only way she knew, as crudely as a ghetto mugger seizing cash, and rejected, had converted all that pent-up need into easy hatred and revenge. But as for Chris's death, there Hook could not find any simplicity. All he knew for sure was that Douglas and Parnelli had been on the cliff alone with the boy, fighting with him, and the thing had happened. Beyond that, he could not be sure of anything, whether Chris had indeed lunged at them and missed, gone over the edge due to his own momentum, or whether one or both of the men had thrown him over in a moment of drunken rage. Even then it was not much—only manslaughter, death caused without design or premeditation. So that was all Hook was left with—the sexual frustrations of a middle-aged woman, a senseless accident, or the casual brutality of a pair of drunks. In the way of twentieth-century guilt it was not much, in fact was almost innocence. And to the average liberal mind—to a liberal such as Hook had considered himself until recent years—it should have been innocence enough. To understand was to forgive, was it not? And Hook understood.

But he did not forgive.

If Chris's death were truly only a senseless accident, then that was how he would judge those involved—without sense or mercy. And if Douglas or Parnelli had actually done it, acting out of drunken instinct, so Hook would act out of instinct now. And all the lineaments of his soul called for redress, for justice, for vengeance. He could not possibly accept Chris's death in the cold blood of rationalism. It would have been like observing the passing of the sun with a benediction.

When he left the theater it was almost five o'clock and already growing dark. He walked to El Cielito and telephoned Rider again, and again got the same response. The sergeant was out. Was there anyone else Hook would talk to? No, but he did want to leave a message, that he would be coming in at nine the next morning to give Sergeant Rider new information regarding the alleged suicide of Christopher Hook two weeks before. The switchboard operator said she could not guarantee that Rider would be in his office then either.

"It doesn't matter," Hook told her. "I'll wait for him."

And that was that. Hanging up, he got a scotch on ice at the bar and took it over to a table in the corner. At five-thirty, after a second drink, he left.

As Icarus had told him on the telephone, the road up to Mount Calvary Monastery was narrow and twisting, a lane of asphalt climbing back and forth between limestone boulders and withered old live oaks, which his car's headlights kept picking out of the darkness like static explosions, wood forever bursting out of the ground. All the way up, Hook did not see any parked pickup truck or in fact any vehicle at all. But then he was early, he knew. It was only a quarter to six when he reached the monastery, which looked like a barracks in the darkness, a long white adobe building with an asphalt drive tightly bordering it at the front and one side, as if to keep the structure from tumbling down the mountain. If there was anyone in the building, Hook saw no evidence of them. There was not a light burning anywhere.

At the end of the drive he turned the car around and started back, moving slowly until he reached the parapet at the front, where he stopped. Far in the distance he could see the lights of the city and even those on the drilling platforms out at sea. But what commanded his attention was a single pair of headlights moving up the monastery road. He lit a cigarette and waited. Halfway up the drive, the lights stopped moving and he thought he saw something else for a moment, as if the person inside the vehicle had turned on the interior light. He could not be sure, however; the vehicle was too far away and was half obscured by the trees growing along the road.

Hook put the car in gear and started down, keeping his foot on the brake instead of the accelerator. When he rounded the last curve and saw the lights dead ahead he had to resist an urge to drive on past and settle for what he had, for there was something uniquely sinister about it now that he saw it, was part of it, this curious meeting on a lonely mountain road at night. Nevertheless, about fifty feet in front of the headlights he pulled off and parked, on the outside of the narrow road the same as the other vehicle, so any other traffic happening by would be able to pass with ease. Leaving the car's motor running and the headlights on, he got out and walked forward into the glare. As he drew closer, he could make out that the vehicle was a pickup truck, a white one. And he could hear its motor running. Then the door clicked open and a light went on inside the truck and Hook saw the round swinish face of a young man with curly black hair and dark glasses and a handlebar mustache. As the door opened further and the man got out of the truck, Hook stopped short, out of some involuntary tic of caution. For an eternal three or four seconds he stood in the roadway waiting for the youth to say something, and when he did not, Hook finally ventured his own name.

"I'm Hook. David Hook. You wanted to see me?"

Still the young man said nothing, just stood there looking heavy and stupid and as frightened as Hook himself felt.

"Well?" Hook snapped. But even as he said it, he got all the answer he needed, heard a pebble turning over somewhere behind him, shoe leather lightly touching asphalt. And he whirled.

It was Parnelli.

"Well—shitkicker."

The big Italian grinned drunkenly. And Hook saw that this night the man was not wearing electric blue or grasshopper green but black, a black sweatshirt and Levi's, black shoes. Hook knew that he should already have been running as fast and far as he could. Instead he found himself standing there as if he had taken root.

Grinning still, Parnelli reached out and took hold of Hook's shoulder, lightly for a moment, and then the hand began to bite like ice tongs into his flesh.

"Hey, relax, man," Parnelli said. "Don't sweat it. This ain't the way it looks."

"How is it then?"

"I'm drunk, that's how it is."

"I can see that."

Laughing, Parnelli turned to the younger man. "See, Joey? See what I tell you. He's all balls, our Mister Hook. All balls and no brains."

"Why's the boy here?" Hook asked. "What do you need him for?"

"Joey? Joey's my nephew. My sister Angela's kid. Kind of my gopher too. Ain't you, kid?"

The youth's face remained expressionless, all mustache and sunglasses.

"What's he doing here?" Hook persisted.

"Nothing. Just used him to get you up here, that's all. So we could be alone."

"So you could tell me you were drunk."

Parnelli laughed again. Letting go of Hook's shoulder, he turned away. "Come on. Let's walk down the road a little. We can talk."

Hook went with him, moving downhill away from the truck, into the darkness.

"We could talk at the sheriff's," Hook suggested.

"Yeah. Sure. There's always that." As they walked, Parnelli held his hands out in front of Hook. They were shaking. "Look at them. They been like this all day. And all last night. And I been drunk the whole time. How about that, huh? Can you figure that?"

Hook was only half listening to him, for he knew the man had not gone to the trouble of luring him up onto this lonely mountain road just to talk. So as they walked he watched the big athlete's every movement. And he studied the trees and night boulders along the road, wondering who might be crouched and waiting behind them. Douglas? He doubted it. But it was possible. He had learned that anything was possible.

"I never been so uptight in all my goddamn life," Parnelli was saying. "I mean it. I'm really coming unglued. Like getting in touch with that cat Icarus and setting this whole weird thing up —I mean what the fuck was I thinking about anyway, huh? Can you tell me that? I guess at first I figured I'd lean on you a little and you'd just fold up and go home." He laughed ruefully at this, shaking his head. "Then when I got to thinking about it I knew that was just a lot of horseshit. Any bastard crazy enough to come up here alone at night on a phone call from some kid he don't even know—well you ain't gonna scare him off with a little muscle, right? No, you gonna have to kill him. You gonna have to beat him to death."

Again he laughed, looking hopefully at Hook, as if he wanted him to share his amusement. And there was absolutely no raillery in his face, no slightest touch of irony. For Hook its absence was like a stair giving way underfoot. Suddenly he was in a world without balance or bottom. Till now he had thought the man was only drunk. Now he had to wonder if he was sane.

"But that wasn't any answer either," Parnelli kept on. "'Cause you see, Hook—no matter what you think—I ain't much of a Sicilian. I don't kill people. And even if I did—even if I could—I figure they'd right away know who did it, my buddies in the sheriff's office and the local fuzz. They'd have old Bo's ass in the slam before your body was cold. So what's it all about, huh? What we doing here?" Again he held up his trembling hands. "You think maybe it's these? You think I brought you here just to show you these? Does that make any sense, huh?"

Hook did not answer. They had reached the first hairpin curve in the road and Parnelli abruptly turned around and started back. Hook followed. Up ahead, the young man and the truck stood silhouetted in the glare of the car's headlights. Against the blackness of the mountain the scene looked oddly unreal to Hook, even staged, like a movie set. On it, the star was still holding forth.

"Jesus, it's never hit me like this before. The nerve thing, I mean. I never come all apart like this before in all my goddamn life. Why, this morning at the office I even leaned on poor old Dorothy, for Christ sake. Can you believe that? I was trying to talk the cunt into going to the police and change her story and tell them what happen to your boy was a accident and not suicide. And she wouldn't. So I slapped her. I shook her. I just picked her up and shook her. Ferguson kept trying to make me lay off. They both kept yelling at me that it wouldn't make any difference now—that you wouldn't quit anyway—and I guess I knew they were right but I kept right on shaking her anyway. I wound up throwing Ferguson against the goddamn door and he gashed his head. Bled like a pig. And would you believe he cried? He did all right, like a regular goddamn baby, the little creep. And Dorothy too. Both of them. And me, I'm shaking all over by then and praying Jack would get there. But he never showed. Wasn't home, either. He's been gone all day."

It was pure stream of consciousness, a mind hemorrhaging. Hook wondered if the man had any idea where he was or what he was saying or who was listening to him. As he talked he fumbled out a cigarette and lit it.

"You know, I think I even told Dorothy something about this, about me meeting you. Only not *where*, I don't think. I don't think I told her that."

He looked anxiously at Hook, as if for approval.

"Did she know why?" Hook asked. "What you had in mind?"

"What I had in mind? I just told you. Even *I* don't know that."

"How'd you know about Icarus?"

Parnelli shrugged indifference. "I guess Liz told us about him. I don't know. I just knew he knew you, that's all."

"So you got to him."

"But why, huh? Can you tell me that?" He looked eagerly at Hook, like a child expecting a gift. "What was I after, huh? You think maybe it was to beg? You think that could be it? That's what I had in back of my mind all along? Get here alone with you and go down on my knees and beg? You think that was it?"

As he spoke, his voice had fallen to a whisper and Hook knew the man was going down into himself, into his rage as helplessly as a hooked shark sounding in the sea. Hook felt his own body begin to brace itself, tightening against the coming of the rage. But all Parnelli did was reach into his pocket and pull out a roll of bills, which he unfolded.

"And then there's this," he said. "The saddest part of all, I guess. The part where you laugh. But this afternoon, when I knew finally I wasn't going to lean on you or kill you, I didn't know what to do—besides drink, that is. So I decided to come with this. There's ninety of them here—nine thousand bucks—all I got to show for fifteen years of work. It was my equity in a condominium up at Mammoth. I like to ski."

His right hand closed on Hook's arm, stopping him. With his left he offered the roll. It shook with his hand. "Take it," he said.

"Please, Mr. Hook. Maybe you don't need it, but take it anyway. Take it and go home. Leave us be. Don't ruin us. *Please*."

Seeing the man's desperation, Hook wished that he could have reached out and taken the money. For he knew that not to take it would be to step to the edge of an abyss, to walk along it. But his hands, freighted with the habits of a lifetime, would not rise. He pulled away from Parnelli and went on ahead, moving into the long shadow cast by the nephew standing in the center of the road.

"Bo?" the youth called. "What I do, Bo? *Bo?*"

Behind Hook there was no answer save the sound of footfalls finally, quick and heavy, and then came the rage, the huge hands dropping on Hook's shoulders like felled trees. And immediately he was being spun around and thrown backwards into the nephew's arms, which held him for perhaps a second, all the time Parnelli needed.

Hook was aware that he had been hit in the lower abdomen and that he had sagged in the young man's grasp, that he had been let go of, that his face had slapped against asphalt. And he was aware of the big hands gathering the front of his sport coat together and pulling him to his feet and shoving him back into the arms of the nephew again. And finally he was aware of Parnelli crying, the big man standing in front of him crying openly and shaking his head.

"I didn't want this, man! I didn't want this! Oh, Jesus, I didn't want this!"

Despite the scotch he had drunk earlier, Hook could smell Parnelli's breath, a sour muck of booze and garlic and fear.

"I didn't want this! You hear me? You hear?"

Instead of waiting for an answer, Parnelli swung, and Hook, somehow conscious still, had the feeling that the lower part of his face had been torn off. The powerful hands clutched Hook's coat again and yanked him out of the other man's grip. Then, half-spinning with him, like a hammer-thrower, Parnelli tossed him across the narrow roadway, over a boulder and down into a gully lined with chaparral that ripped at Hook's face and hands. For a few moments he lay there on the gravelly earth trying to breathe, trying to stay alive, and then he got hold of himself and started to scramble up out of the gully. But with his first movement his clutching hand came down on a rock the size of a baseball and he did not move further except to roll over and look up as Parnelli loomed above the boulder now, the gross wedge of his athlete's body limned by the headlights behind him. And there Hook waited, holding the rock out at arm's length as the man vaulted nimbly over the boulder and came at him, reaching down as if he were gathering up a pile of clothes.

Hook swung with all his strength, yet it remained very quiet there in the gully, just the sound of the rock striking Parnelli's skull and then a grunt, soft, almost a sigh. Desperately, Hook squeezed out from under the big Italian's body and got to his feet, scrambling up to the boulder just as the pig-faced young man reached it on the other side. His look of surprise was comical—Lou Costello caught in an act of mischief by Bud Abbott—but Hook had no time for comedy. As the youth turned away, Hook clambered up onto the boulder and dove onto him, pulling him down in the middle of the roadway. And there he began to punch him, not like a fighter so much as a carpenter, a raging lunatic carpenter hammering nails into concrete. The youth, who was almost as tall as Hook, and a good deal heavier, cried and begged for freedom like a child being whipped by a parent. But Hook kept on swinging, smashing his glasses along with his eyes and nose and mouth, until finally the young man broke away, crawling and scrambling for the truck. Hook followed him slowly, exhausted now, but confident, determined that he would take them both into Rider and have done with this coast of violence once and for all.

As he moved toward the truck, Hook watched the young man rummaging frantically for something under the front seat. Indifferently he saw him come up with it finally and whirl around, holding it out toward Hook as if it were an offering. For a moment Hook thought it was only a tool of some kind, a tire iron possibly, and this did not worry him, for he had seen the fear in the youth, his soul's sharp hunger for defeat. And he knew he would be able to satisfy that hunger. So he kept coming.

And the tire iron flamed, twice, followed by the sound of shots, twin explosions that set Hook's ears ringing. He had read about people being shot or stabbed and not knowing it or feeling it till long afterwards, so as he stood there facing the gun not even fifteen feet from him he wondered if there could be an unfelt hole in his body even now spitting out his life's blood. And once again his answer came from behind him, a sound very much like the one before, a shoe touching asphalt, scraping. And turning, he saw much the same sight as before—Parnelli standing in the road. Only this time it was the big Italian who looked surprised, not Hook, and he was holding his hands to his chest as if he were clutching something very dear to him, something he did not want to give up.

He went down like an old woman kneeling in church. At the edge of the blacktop, he rolled over on his back. The gunman, still holding his weapon, ran to him.

"Bo?" he cried. "Uncle Bo?"

Parnelli weakly shook his head. "You dumb guinea. You chickenshit guinea." He coughed and his mouth bloomed blood.

In his shock Hook did not even think to seize the bloodied youth or take the gun from him. Instead he stood there like a passerby, some numb witness to violence and tragedy. The young man kept shaking his head, as if he were trying to convince his uncle that the thing had not happened. Then he gave up the argument. He turned and ran, leaped into the truck and threw it into gear and started off, not even waiting to close the door. In amazement, Hook watched him try to turn around on the narrow roadway. First he swerved left, up over some rocks and into a boulder on the inside of the road. Then he put the truck into reverse and swung backwards, smashing into Hook's car and driving it off the road down into a gully, where it came to rest on its side, one headlight still burning. Again the truck surged forward, crashing into a small oak this time and losing a headlight; and then back again, tires screaming. And suddenly Hook got hold of himself, realized that in another few seconds the truck would go roaring down the monastery road toward the city— right over the spot where Parnelli was lying. Hook knew the big Italian had been shot in the chest and he was afraid that if he lifted him by the shoulders he might cause him further injury, so he took him by the ankles instead and hurriedly dragged him off the road—just as the truck came shooting past. It careened wildly around the first curve below, and Hook found himself standing and watching, like a spectator at an auto race, as the pickup continued down the mountainside, screaming around the hairpin curves one after another, smashing over rocks and through brush and then gaining the roadway again only to lose it on the next curve, until finally, almost at the end, it did not make it out of a curve but came to an abrupt and plangent stop in the trees growing there. And, oddly, as the truck's one remaining headlight went out in the crash, its horn came on, like a timorous cry for help.

Hook looked down at Parnelli. "He crashed down below."

Parnelli did not care. He was trying to see his hands in the darkness, the blood on them from his chest. "Oh Jesus," he gasped. "Oh Jesus. A priest? Do I need a priest?"

Hook looked first at his car lying on its side and then he gazed up where the monastery was. All he could see was darkness. But he knew how far up it was. It would probably take him an hour to carry Parnelli that far, and at the rate the man was losing blood, Hook doubted that he would make it alive. Also there was no way of knowing what they would find up there even if they did make it, perhaps only what he had seen earlier, only darkness and silence. But even as he was thinking this, he knew he had no choice; they were much closer to the monastery than to the houses down in the foothills. And he could not stay where he was, not just stand there and watch the man die.

"Could you take it, being carried?" Hook asked.

"I'm getting weak."

"Your nephew wiped out my car. I'll have to carry you."

But Parnelli did not hear. He was crying. "Oh Christ, I'm not ready. Oh please, God. Please." He coughed and again blood came out of him like vomit.

Hook tried to roll him onto his side, but he resisted, rolled onto his back again.

"Oh Jesus Mary," he moaned. "Mother of God."

Hook told him he was going to pick him up now and carry him to the monastery. "You're going to be all right. We'll get help there."

Parnelli struck feebly at him, resisting. "No. First, my confession. You tell it to a priest, hear?"

Hook looked down at the massive face, gray in the single beam of light coming from Hook's car. He nodded. "All right. Hurry."

Tears welled out of Parnelli's eyes. And he spoke slowly now, softly, fighting for every word. "It was me, shitkicker. Only me. When he kicked me, I blew. I picked him up and . . . It was me, no one else. You tell that to priest, hear? Tell him I'm sorry. For this too. For all my sins."

Tell him I'm sorry. Hook heard the words as though from a great distance, for he was as much on the sea cliff now as on the mountain road. He stared down at this huge dying animal and saw it alive and raging, saw it tear his son off the ground and toss him like so much garbage over the edge of a cliff, and Hook felt his body begin to shake with the effort to hold his fists at his side. Slowly he stood up.

"You hear?" Parnelli got out. "Tell him I confess all my . . . tell him . . ."

His voice died. But Hook would not have listened to it anyway, for his attention had locked on a car turning into the monastery road far below. He watched the beams of its headlights sweep the first curve and then come to the second, the wooded one where the pickup had crashed. There the car stopped. Because of the distance and the trees bordering the road, Hook could see nothing but the lights of the car. And he could still hear the pickup's horn, fainter now. He looked down at Parnelli. The man was unconscious; his mouth was open; blood gurgled softly in his throat. Hook waited, expecting the car to come on at any time, for the headlight of his own car was still burning and he knew it had to be brightly visible against the blackness of the mountainside. But the car down below stayed where it was.

Finally Hook got out his pocket knife and cut off branches of chaparral and set them afire one at a time, holding them up in the air like torches as long as he could and then dropping them onto the roadway. As he lit a third branch, he saw far in the distance the flashing emergency light of a police car or ambulance speeding through the foothills. And then he heard the vehicle's siren.

In a short time, it drew in behind the first car. Then, after a few moments, the first car started moving again, accelerating rapidly as it moved up the mountainside. When it came out of the last turn Hook stepped into the center of the roadway and went through the unnecessary motions of flagging it down—unnecessary because it turned out to be Rider's car, Rider who stopped and got out, followed by Liz Madera.

"Where is he?" the sergeant asked.

Hook led him to the side of the road, the rocky shoulder where Parnelli lay. Grunting, the burly Rider got down and felt for a pulse in front of Parnelli's ear. Liz came around on the other side of the victim, apparently not wanting to stand near Hook. Nor would she look at him.

"Is he alive?" she asked Rider.

Getting up, the sergeant shrugged helplessly. "I can't find a pulse," he said.

Liz turned and headed back for the car.

"An ambulance will be here any minute," Rider said to Hook. "You okay? You look a little beat up."

"I'm okay."

"You're lucky to be alive, you know that?"

Hook did not answer.

At nine o'clock that night, almost two hours after Bo Parnelli had been pronounced dead on arrival at St. Francis Hospital, Hook stood at a second-floor window in the courthouse looking down on the floodlit formal garden below. And he told himself that for the time being he would try to become like the palms standing there, a living thing and nothing more. He would ignore his feelings; he would have no fears or worries or regrets. He would go through the motions, do what had to be done, say what had to be said, and time would pass. And he would be home again, on his own land, with his own family, his own silence.

He had wanted none of this. He had *caused* none of it. Bo Parnelli was dead simply because he had been Bo Parnelli, because he had been vicious and stupid and finally unlucky. All Hook had done was seek the truth about his son's death, and for no more complex reason than that he could not have gone on living the rest of his life without that truth. And there was no crime in that, no guilt. Yet as he turned away from the window now his limbs felt leaden, his throat was dry, his heart sprinted in his chest.

He came to the end of the corridor, to a doorway that opened into a large bullpen area containing a half-dozen officers' desks, all but one abandoned at this late hour. Near the deputy working at the one desk, Liz Madera sat alone, in one of eight old wood chairs lined up against the wall. Across the bullpen from her was a row of three small conference rooms with glass walls facing in, so that their occupants were visible to anyone in the bullpen. In the middle room, Jack Douglas was leaning back against a table and gazing down at the floor as he listened intently to the earnest counsel of his lawyer, a very expensive-looking man who earlier had spirited his client like a rock star through the small band of reporters and photographers assembled outside, the same group that had accosted Rider and Liz and Hook at the hospital. Next door to Douglas, Richard Ferguson paced nervously while Dorothy Rubin sat glaring at Liz, though Hook could not see why she would resent the girl any more than herself, for it was she who had first heard about Parnelli's planned ambush, and later, half drunk, half hysterical, had told Liz about it.

Liz had gone to Rider with the story at slightly after four that afternoon, knowing everything except where the meeting was to take place. For the next ninety minutes, the two of them, along with a good part of the sheriff's department, had scoured the city and county for Icarus. They finally had turned him up in an Isla Vista head shop, at almost the exact time Hook was reaching the monastery and turning around, preparing to start back down the mountain.

Now Hook went on into the room and took one of the empty chairs in the row where Liz was sitting. She did not look at him, just sat there smoking and staring into space. And he understood why, could see clearly in her grave and beautiful eyes the terrible burden of the hanging judge, the whole story of his indictment and conviction and, now, sentencing. And, strangely, it disturbed him not for himself but for her, because it meant that all the lines were down between them now and she had no one to fall back on except Douglas and her hitchhikers and Mrs. Rubin, and he doubted if any of them could save even themselves, let alone her.

"Any word from Rider?" he asked.

Still she did not look at him. "I don't work here."

"I thought you might have heard."

"I haven't."

Hook lit a cigarette, dragged, waited. "What will you do?" he said finally. "Afterwards? When it's all over?"

"Will it be over? Ever?"

"Well, I think after what you did today—"

"And what was that?" she snapped. "Do you really know?"

"I know it wasn't for me, Liz. You did it for Parnelli. To keep him from doing something stupid. Something that could hurt the rest of you. That's all it was. I realize that." Hook was not trying for such obvious sarcasm, but that was how it came out and there was no calling it back.

Even then it was not enough to make her look at him. He watched her get up and walk over to an ashtray stand, where she put out her cigarette.

"How much longer?" she asked the deputy.

He pushed back his chair, stretched, yawned. "Still the same, lady. Sergeant's on his way. Be here any minute."

"They're long minutes."

The man grinned. "Naaw. They just *seem* long."

She returned to her chair. Hook decided to try again.

"You didn't answer me before. What will you do when it's over?"

She smiled bleakly. "Go directly to jail."

Because she would not look at him, Hook found himself speaking to the floor. "That's not true. After today—I mean your going to Rider and telling him everything, voluntarily—well I can't see you getting anything more than a suspended sentence."

"Or maybe a medal," she suggested. "Don't you think that might be in order too?"

"Liz, I want to help you."

"Help me? Then stay out of my life." She looked over at him now, and her eyes were cold with loathing. "Just stay out of my life."

So that was that. Hook settled back in his chair and closed his eyes.

In time Rider returned from the hospital, with a deputy and Sergeant Anderson, the young detective Hook had met the morning they found the drug overdose victim. As before, he looked relentlessly neat and fresh compared to Rider, who was tieless and red-eyed and in need of a shave.

Rider told Liz and Hook that he was sorry to have kept them waiting. "But you know these doctors," he went on. "You and me, we could die in their waiting rooms and they wouldn't bat an eye. But a felon—him they watch over like a mother hen. We ask a question, it's like asking for a quart of the kid's blood."

"He's all right, then," Hood said.

"The nephew? Oh sure. Wasn't hurt too bad. Aside from the damage you did, all he's got is a concussion and a couple broken ribs. Thought he might be able to tell us a few things, but he don't know from nothing. All 'Uncle Bo' told him was they were gonna meet someone up on the mountain, and that it might get hairy. The gun was the kid's idea. I don't think Parnelli even knew he owned one."

"That can't do much for your case," Liz said.

Rider's expression did not change. "Oh, I'd say our case is in pretty good shape. Good enough anyway to put our friend over there where he belongs." He looked across the bullpen, at Douglas.

"Even though he's not guilty," Liz said.

Rider looked back at her. "Who's not guilty?"

"You heard what Mr. Hook said—Bo's confession. His *dying* confession."

Hook had told him on the way to the hospital, and at the time Rider had not said much about it. Now he did.

"The law doesn't make a distinction. They were both involved in the fight. So they're both responsible for the boy's death."

Liz smiled in pain. "The law. The majesty of the law."

"I don't know about majesty. But it's law, all right."

Liz abandoned the subject. "When can I leave?" she asked.

"A few more minutes. You go with Sergeant Anderson here. A couple more points we want to have in your statement. Then you can cut out. You won't need bail. We'll see to the details."

Getting up, Liz followed Anderson. And for the time it took the two of them to cross the bullpen and go through a doorway at the far end, Rider and Hook both stood there and watched. Earlier, Hook had seen Anderson lead a pale and frightened Icarus through that same door, and the similarity disturbed him now.

"What about her?" he asked. "She won't have to serve time, will she?"

Rider shrugged. "That'll be up to a judge. Conspiracy's no misdemeanor."

"She came to you, Sergeant."

"That'll be in her favor." Rider regarded Hook ironically. "She kind of got to you, huh?"

"I like her, yes. I'd like to help her."

"Is that all?"

"How do you mean?"

The sergeant shrugged. "Oh, I don't know. You look like you hurt."

"Well, I do. He was a rough man."

"I don't mean that kind of hurt. I mean inside. Parnelli. You feel it was your fault? Because you kept pushing?"

"No."

"I didn't think you would."

Hook strained to keep the anger out of his voice. "Should I?"

For five or six long seconds Rider stood there looking at him, and then he shook his head. "Never for a moment, Mr. Hook. It was the wop's fault." Now the sergeant looked across the bullpen again. "And theirs. And the sexy Miss Madera's. And if anybody else should feel guilty, I guess it's me, for letting you do my job. So don't sweat it. Ever. You did what was right."

A feeling of gratitude as sharp as anger struck Hook and he looked away from the burly law officer's bloodshot eyes.

"You can go anytime you want," Rider told him. "Just don't

leave town before I see you again, okay? There'll be loose ends to tie up, details, you know."

Hook nodded, still dumb, shaken.

"Well, I got some more work to do," Rider said. "Call it divide and conquer."

Hook watched as the sergeant made his way across the bull-pen toward the small room where Douglas and his attorney were conferring. As Rider entered, Douglas straightened up and for some reason looked out through the window at Hook. Their eyes met. But all Hook could see of the man was a politician's mask, a blandly handsome face poised and ready, as if he were about to smile absently at a stranger. Then he looked away.

Hook left the courthouse.

Back at his motel, he thought of calling home and telling Marian that he would be flying in the next day. But he did not want to talk with her or the children either, not this night. And anyway it was late, after midnight in Illinois. They would all be in bed. He would call in the morning.

Because he knew he would not have an easy time sleeping, he went downstairs to the Galleon bar and had three drinks of scotch among the fishnets and harpoons before he dragged his aching body back upstairs and went to bed. In a week's time he had not had one good night's sleep in the motel and he knew this night would be no exception.

But he was wrong. It was worse. He lay awake hour after hour. And he thought. He worried. He went through the day over and over in his mind. And often during those interminable hours the memory of Douglas in the courthouse, that last brief look that passed between them, would click like a slide across Hook's mind and he would wonder what had been behind that politician's mask, what the man was truly feeling on this dark night of his life.

Hook got his answer at five o'clock in the morning, when the ringing of his bedside phone brought him gasping up out of a shallow pool of sleep, one of the few he had found all night long.

It was Liz Madera.

"Before you leave, I want you to know the full measure of your victory," she said. "I'm at the hospital again. Jack Douglas just died. He put a bullet in his brain about an hour ago."

13

After Liz's telephone call, Hook did not move from his motel bed. He thought of checking with the hospital or Rider's office, but he knew the effort would change nothing. Liz had not lied. Her message was not some sick attempt at revenge. It was fact. He knew it in the dead weight of his limbs and in the chill void of his stomach. He knew it because he had seen it in Douglas's eyes at the sheriff's office, not the mask of the politician as he had thought but only the indifferent stare of the dead, the stare of the ultimately condemned.

When he finally got out of bed, almost two hours later, his hands were shaking so uncontrollably he could not shave or brush his teeth. He tried to drink a glass of water and immediately vomited it. In his frustration and rage he smashed the plastic cup down against the sink and it came apart like glass in his hand, cutting him deeply across the palm. Dripping blood, he stumbled back into the bedroom and dialed the desk clerk and told him to make up his bill, that he was checking out. Then he made a plane reservation and finally called long-distance to Illinois. Marian answered. Briefly, even curtly, he told her that his task on the coast was finished and that he would be arriving in St. Louis at three-twenty in the afternoon. When she began to ask questions, he cut her off, saying he did not have time to talk now, that he would explain everything later, after he arrived. Then he hung up.

After he had checked out of the motel, he took a cab to the

sheriff's office and found Rider sitting alone in his small third-floor office. The sergeant's eyes were still heavy and bloodshot and there was a violet band across his forehead, as if he had been resting his head on his arms on the desktop. He glanced at Hook, then looked away and began to maul his face. "You know about Douglas," he said.

"Liz Madera called me."

"Made sure you got the good news, huh?"

"Yes."

"Thoughtful of her." Rider reached out and pushed a document across his desk toward Hook.

It was a handwritten note already interleaved between sheets of clear plastic. Hook did not trust his hands to pick it up, so he read it from where he stood. It was a broad, loose scrawl, barely legible:

> *If I knew way out*
> *some other   then maybe*
> *not this*
> *But none now is there*
> *Sorry you all gave so much*
> *for so*
> *But I never asked*
> *never*

The note was unsigned.

As Hook read it, Rider had placed his hands behind his head and leaned back in his chair. Now he spoke and his voice was a hammer, his words nails Hook felt going into him one by one.

"He was drunk. There was an almost empty bottle of scotch on his desk, in his study. That's where he did it. He was out on his own recognizance. Left here about one with his lawyer. Shot himself a little before four. Thirty-two caliber. The slug entered an inch above his right ear. He lived about an hour. You never know about head wounds. Unpredictable."

Hook said nothing.

The sergeant picked up the note and put it in a drawer and then locked the drawer. The matter evidently was closed. They could move on to those loose ends the sergeant had said he wanted to tie up. But apparently they were going to be left hanging, for the only other thing he had Hook do was sign a release freeing the department of responsibility for any damages to Hook's rented car, which they had towed in early that morning. Rider said that the nephew had insurance, so Hook would have no problems there. Beyond that, all the sergeant wanted to do, he said, was get the hell out of the office as quickly as possible. And to that end, he offered to drive Hook to the airport.

Unlike the garrulous cabbie who had brought Hook into the city two weeks before, Rider was glumly silent throughout the fifteen-minute drive. And in fact he waited until after Hook had picked up his ticket and the two of them had settled in over lukewarm coffee in the airport grill before he opened up. He had experienced some heat earlier in the day, he said, heat not from his superiors so much as from theirs, the political movers and shakers who had awakened that morning and found the lead horse in their stable dead.

"The gist of it," Rider said, "was I had leaned too hard on the poor fellow. I hadn't been politic. I should've gone out there to his fancy house and discussed the situation with him, like one gentleman to another. Or maybe I should say like servant to gentleman—I guess that'd be more accurate."

Hook knew he should try to say something, try to help Rider along, but he could not do it.

Rider went on without him. "I don't mean it was my bosses that felt this way, but the others, the power boys. Anyway, I blew my stack. I told them to shove it. I even went so far as to suggest that if any of them commit manslaughter in this county, I'd have their asses in the slam just as fast as Douglas's. Then I stormed out." He smiled ruefully. "Put on a real show, I did. Joe Rider, the retiree."

Still Hook said nothing.

"But it'll work out all right. Don't sweat it. I'm just burned, that's all. The chickenshit bastard."

Hook did not have to ask whom he meant.

"Manslaughter, conspiracy—what would the guy have got? A

couple years at most. Maybe even a suspended sentence. But he couldn't cut it, the chickenshit——"

"I can understand," Hook broke in suddenly, for some reason angry that Rider would abuse the man now.

"You can understand? *You?*"

"If a man lost everything. His *self*. His idea of himself."

Rider shook his head in scorn. "Naaw. Oh, I could buy it under certain circumstances maybe—like if you chickened out, say, in war. If you let your buddies down and got some of them killed. Something real. But not this. Whose good opinion was he so worried about, for Christ sake? A bunch of country-club drunks. Leeches."

"There was his family," Hook suggested.

Rider mauled his face. "Yeah. But I still can't buy it. It was a chickenshit act. And I ain't gonna lose a second's sleep over him ever—that I can promise. And you shouldn't either."

Hook regarded the sergeant's blood-ridden eyes, the exhaustion that showed like a week's growth of beard on his blocky face, and said nothing. He finished his coffee and waited, and finally Rider checked his watch and said he had to be on his way.

Hook's flight was not due in for another quarter-hour, which he figured would stretch into thirty minutes and more because of the heavy holiday traffic, the students flying home on this last day before Christmas. So he took the time to walk with the sergeant back to the terminal entrance, where they shook hands goodbye, Rider barely glancing at him before turning away and striding briskly across the curving blacktop drive, heading for his car. As Hook watched the burly figure move through the crowded parking lot he wondered if the man had been less his ally than his victim, another of his victims.

Hook was so deeply lost in himself that the flight home passed almost unnoticed by him, including the time spent transferring to another jet in Los Angeles. Later he would remember being served champagne with a lunch he had not been able to eat. He would remember an excessively sweet old lady sitting next to him trying vainly to draw him into conversation. And he would recall seeing land occasionally under a vast white cloud cover below. But most of all he would remember reading the newspapers over and over: the Los Angeles *Times*, which he had bought at the motel in the morning, and the Santa Barbara paper, which he had picked up at the airport. The *Times* had gone to press before Douglas had killed himself, so he did not figure at all in their story, which ran under a three-column headline on the third page:

Ex-USC Football Star Slain in Santa Barbara

> *Bo Parnelli Shot in Apparent Assault*
> *On Illinois Man Investigating*
> *Son's Alleged Suicide on Coast*

Hook was amazed by the accuracy of the story that followed, for he knew how little cooperation he had given the reporters at the hospital and outside the courthouse, and he had not seen Liz or Rider offer them anything at all. Yet the *Times* reporter had dug it up from somewhere or pieced it together, for it was all there, the details of the assault on Hook by Parnelli and his nephew, the accidental shooting of Parnelli by the nephew and the youth's subsequent confession, which "alleged that Parnelli was in some way responsible for the death of Mr. Hook's son, Christopher, 19, till now considered a suicide by the Santa Barbara Sheriff's Department." The story did not mention Liz Madera, though she was in a photo with Rider and Hook coming out of the hospital, a picture that looked brutally real and immediate compared to the one adjoining it, an antique publicity shot of Parnelli posturing violently in a USC football uniform. So, except for the fact of Parnelli's death and the reporting of it, the story was all Hook could have asked for, everything for which he had come to the coast in the first place. It was his certificate of injustice redressed, his sheepskin in revenge.

And it lessened his pain and anguish no more than the version in the Santa Barbara County *News*, which had been printed after Douglas's suicide and addressed itself almost wholly to that event, but with a restraint and decorum that would have better fitted the peaceful passing of some elder local statesman. Parnelli's death, Hook's presence at the scene, the nephew's arrest and confession—it was all reported, and that was all. None of it was connected into a meaningful whole. If any inferences were to be drawn, the reader would have to do the drawing himself; the paper obviously was not about to.

Yet as the jet plunged across the continent, Hook found himself reading the Santa Barbara news story just as avidly as the one in the Los Angeles paper. But no matter how carefully he combed them, he was unable to find anything to counteract his growing suspicion that he was bringing home not some precious hard-won prize of war but rather its opposite, a curse, a disease of war. He felt infected, a bearer of plague.

It was bright sunshine when the jet touched down in St. Louis and taxied toward the Saarinen-designed terminal building, which looked to Hook as if it had melted in the steamy Missouri summers, the way its great roof sagged in some areas and ballooned up in others, like unevenly corrugated tin. Within minutes he would be inside the building, he told himself. He would be with them. So he tried to prepare himself, tried to will the pain and exhaustion and dread out of his spirit and out of his face. He did not want them to see how it was with him, not yet anyway.

Then suddenly he was there, inside, walking with his fellow passengers toward a crowd of day-before-Christmas travelers and welcomers milling beyond the gates. When he finally picked them out, Bobby, Jenny, and Aunt Marian pressed against a railing, he thought his heart would burst with the joy of seeing them again. Jenny looked beautiful, tall and golden in a new Laplander coat, while Marian looked only herself, splendidly herself, wearing one of her silly Sunday hats and the venerable dark brown cloth coat with the squirrel collar. Both she and Jenny were smiling and crying at the same time. Bobby, however, was all stiffness, all pain and pride and jailed emotion. And perhaps because of this, he was the one Hook wanted the most to embrace and yet he knew the boy could not have accepted it any more than he himself could have given it, not there, in front of half the world. So all he did was lay his hand on the boy's shoulder and squeeze him slightly. The women, though, he hugged and kissed, especially Jenny, who would not let go of him. Bobby immediately asked him what had happened in California, but Hook told him that it was too noisy there in the terminal, he would explain it all in the car on the way home.

He did not, however, at least not in the beginning. That chore he left to the newspapers, which the three of them passed anxiously back and forth while he drove.

"Oh my God," Marian kept saying. "My dear God. I am so sorry, David."

But Jenny rushed to her father's defense. "It wasn't Dad's fault! Was it, Dad!"

Bobby answered for him. "Fault! What do you mean, fault? They only got what they deserved."

"No more of that," Hook told him.

"But they—"

"*No more.*"

Within an hour he was home again, driving up the hill on his own road through his own stark winter trees and into the open, past dun-colored pastures and the black cattle that meant so much to him and to whom he meant nothing at all. Then he circled up to the house and Arnie and the dogs came out to the car, and somehow they were the final seal on his homecoming. He was back. He was safe. He was home. Life would go on.

And it did. Christmas morning the family gathered around the tree and opened their presents, almost all of which had been bought by Aunt Marian, including an electric blanket that was marked "to Marian from David." Jenny played Christmas carols and rock numbers on a new portable stereo and after chores Hook and Bobby and Arnie settled down in front of the television and watched the Dallas Cowboys football team defeat the Vikings on a gray day in Bloomington, Minnesota. Then, with Jenny, the men tried to do justice to one of Marian's typical holiday feasts, a groaning table of roast turkey and dressing and mashed potatoes and yams and two kinds of cranberries and the same of oysters, and of course pumpkin pie and whipped cream.

Then Christmas was over, and New Year's passed too, and

gradually Hook found that sometimes entire hours would pass without his thinking about California and Liz and the others. The family knew the whole story by then of course, except for the truth of his relationship with Liz. And from the beginning Marian seemed to be the only one who understood how much his "success" out on the coast had cost him. Hook in fact was shocked at the attitude of Jenny and Bobby, though he reminded himself that they were only a few years out of childhood, and as a father and onetime teacher he needed no instruction in the callousness and even brutality of the young.

But he was unprepared for the reaction of his neighbors and the townspeople once they began hearing about it, and especially after the weekly Banner Hill *Bugle* featured the story on its front page, including a verbatim reprinting of the articles from the two California papers, which Bobby had taken to the editor without his father's permission or even knowledge. Suddenly Hook was everybody's hero, the local man who had "showed them California dudes a thing or two." Men who before had always given him a wide berth as "uppity" and unfriendly were now thrusting their hands out at him to shake and even clapping him on the back—doing it once anyway, for he did not welcome the friendship of people who could find easy pleasure in the deaths of strangers.

Near the end of January, Hook received a brief letter from Sergeant Rider informing him that the case had been closed. Liz Madera and Richard Ferguson each had been given suspended sentences of eighteen months. Ferguson had taken a job in Sacramento, and the last Rider had heard of Liz she had "joined some of her jet-set friends on a yacht cruise down to Acapulco or some other spic spa." Dorothy Rubin finally had pled guilty herself and had been sentenced to a year in prison. As for Douglas and Parnelli, the town had swept the whole mess under the rug, the sergeant wrote, and he hoped Hook would do the same, "or better yet, sweep it out of your mind."

Hook did not bother to try. Instead he settled for keeping his body so exhausted he did not have the will or energy to think. Normally the winter months were the easiest because there was no field work, but Hook had no trouble filling his days—and

Arnie's—cleaning the feedlot and bull barn and repairing equipment and buildings and fencing. In the evening he found that he could not relax enough to read or watch television, so he would go out again and work alone or with Bobby until he could feel his exhaustion like logs lashed to his back, and only then would he go to bed, to fall asleep immediately and remain asleep until his dreams would wake him finally in the middle of the night and he would lie there sweat-drenched in his great-grandfather's antique fourposter, which Kate had reclaimed from under generations of paint and varnish. He would lie there and give himself over to his mind, as if he were surrendering a criminal suspect to the law. And then the grilling would begin, the unanswerable questions and accusations coming at him like fists and boots through all the long hours till morning light, when he would rise and begin pre-breakfast chores, already dead on his feet.

As the weeks passed, his digestion became poor and he began to lose his appetite, and then weight, until finally Aunt Marian was always pestering him about it, saying he looked like a scarecrow and that if he knew what was good for him he would have a checkup. Instead it was the old woman herself who began going to the doctor, almost as faithfully as she attended church. Suddenly she had all sorts of complaints, rheumatism and kidney trouble and nervous exhaustion. She napped excessively, and often Hook would come upon her crying alone. Jenny too was different, had become moody and quiet. She developed a great passion for music and now spent whole evenings alone in her room listening to country and rock records as if they were rites in some esoteric teen religion destined to sweep the world.

But of all of them, Bobby had changed the most. There seemed almost nothing left of the boy he had been as Chris's brother. The muscular body and strong-boned face now had taken on a character to match, hard and dedicated, especially in his work on the farm, which he performed with grim efficiency. At school, he became a loner, shunning the company of friends he had known all his life. And he told Hook that he did not plan to go on to college, that all he wanted to do was raise cattle and the best place to learn the business and practice it was right there at home. Hook suggested that he could study something else, languages or history, but the boy said no, he was not interested.

So they were all different now, all changed. The plague bacillus had done its job. Death became for Hook what his family once had been, the very content of his life. It became his companion, a dour hired man forever at his side. He could not look at anyone without seeing it, like the skeleton under their flesh, the white bone naked to the truth of the cathode ray tube. He would look at Jenny and wonder how it would come to her finally. In childbirth? Some silly accident, a casual oversight by a hung-over intern? Aunt Marian he would see in a hospital bed, cadaverous and silent, with plastic tubes running into her nose and veins and her fine sharp eyes glazed with morphine as she drifted away. And Bobby. Always with Bobby it was an accident, a car chopping into a tree at night or their big new John Deere tipping on a hillside and rolling over on the boy or one of the bulls getting him against a building or fence post and crushing him so quickly Hook would barely have enough time to get there and gather him up, clutch the quicksilver of his life as long as he could.

And it was no different in town. There Hook had the feeling he was passing through some kind of modern open-air death row unknown as such to its inmates, with himself a stranger among them, some alien being privy to a secret that if known would have caused all of them to lay down their work and begin to fast and pray and weep and wait.

But they did not know. Only Hook knew. Only he had the dour companion.

He began again one night in late February, dressing silently and slipping out of the house and heading with the dogs down the drive through a cold clear moonless night to be with his other family, his family of the dead. As he walked, they kept pace beside him, Douglas and Parnelli and Liz, for she was dead now too, dead to him. And he wondered if they thought his tears were for them or simply because of the cold. Himself, he did not know.

He came to the end of the open ground and started down the hill through the trees toward the blacktop, which shone like a lane of lava in the starlight. In a few seconds he would reach it and follow it uphill to the cemetery, the altar of his cathedral, where he would be alone for a time with what was left of his son and wife, his Chris, his Kate. And he knew what he would feel there, a pain that would open him like a plow dropped in spring soil and he would want to offer his companion all he would ever possess just to see the two of them alive again for even a few seconds, to hold them and love them and lose for those moments the burden of his aloneness.

It would be futile, of course. But that would not matter. As long as he lived, it would not matter.